The Sleeper Awakes

EILIS FLYNN

Cerridwen Press

A Cerridwen Press Publication

www.cerridwenpress.com

The Sleeper Awakes

ISBN 9781419959806
ALL RIGHTS RESERVED.
The Sleeper Awakes Copyright © 2007 Eilis Flynn
Edited by Jaynie Ritchie.
Cover art by Philip Fuller.

This book printed in the U.S.A. by Jasmine-Jade Enterprises, LLC.

Electronic book publication April 2007
Trade paperback publication February 2010

Cerridwen Press is an imprint of Ellora's Cave Publishing, Inc.®

THE SLEEPER AWAKES

Dedication

❧

This is for all my friends, family, and critique partners (not that they're mutually exclusive) I've used as a sounding board over the years; for my husband MIKE, who ignored me when I said I should just go get an MBA instead; and in memory of my brother GEORGE, who would have laughed when he found out my first book was a fantasy.

Trademarks Acknowledgement

❧

The author acknowledges the trademarked status and trademark owners of the following wordmarks mentioned in this work of fiction:

AstroTurf: Textile Management Associates Inc. Corporation

BMW: Bayerische Motoren Werke Aktiengesellschaft

Indianapolis 500: Indianapolis Motor Speedway Corporation

Lamaze: Lamaze International Inc. Corporation

Mickey Mouse: Walt Disney Company

Nordstrom: Nordstrom, Inc.

Ren & Stimpy: Viacom International Inc.

Safeway: Safeway Stores, Inc.

Timex: Timex Corporation

Prologue

ഇ

Seven gates stood out in the open, some of wood and some of iron, carved and decorated, unopened and unopenable. The curious could walk between them and see through them but the gates seemed to have no purpose. They were older than memory. No one had ever seen them open but legend had it each gate held a secret. And when the gates were all opened, the legend went, peace everlasting would be theirs.

One day the first gate opened.

No one was there to see it. The gates stood on a hill overlooking the town from where the merchants could look up and see the enormous, meaningless edifices. Once in a great while, an outsider with an eye for coin would suggest using the gates for one bright idea or another but the idea would die down quickly, hushed into a nervous silence.

Some townspeople thought the gates not unlucky so much as unnerving, like entering a graveyard after the sun set. Others felt comforted, as though the gates somehow guarded their town. And it was true no natural disaster had fallen on the town since time immemorial, despite the wars. When a battle raged near, its leaders would bypass the town, almost against their will.

But the gates also discouraged the rise of commerce nearby and that was only natural. It was human nature to be unnerved by the inexplicable.

And so it was the day the first gate opened. It had rained the night before, the first hard rain before the start of the long, bitter winter. The autumn harvest was almost done and the farmer grumbled about the mud as he and his sons waded through the sodden fields.

The glint of the opened gate caught the attention of the farmer's youngest as he began to load a crate onto an awaiting wagon. At first he thought nothing of it but then he glanced up at the hill again.

He froze. The crate he hoisted dropped to the ground, glancing off his toes. Later, when he took off his boots, he would see his foot was bruised black.

But at that moment of wonder, the farmer's youngest stared up at the hill, his mouth open, until his brother's shout startled him into awareness again. He shouted back, pointing to the hill as he started back to the farmhouse. His brother stood for a moment, uncomprehending. Then he too began running to the farmhouse, slipping in the mud in his haste.

The first gate had opened.

The boy was dispatched to town, running as fast as he could, stumbling in his haste. By the time he arrived at the town elder's door, he was muddy and panting, his leggings covered with grass stains and rich black soil. His pounding at the door caused a commotion but that was nothing compared to the one his message caused. At first there was no reaction — they had all lived too long in the shadow of the gates to grasp what happened. Then the Elder, followed by the farmer's youngest, hurried out to the village commons to get a glimpse of her own.

The slippery mud outside clung to the skirts of the Elder almost instantly but it went unnoticed when she saw the gate in the distance, its arms open to the tentative sun.

The farmer's son had the far-seeing eyes of youth and so it was he once more who saw what the other did not. "There's something up there," he shouted. "Do you see it? There's something on the ground!"

Now, despite the rains, the path up to the Gates was dry. The townsfolk making the journey could see the grasses along the way look as though the torrents of the night before never touched them. More than one of the townsfolk shivered, though the cool in the air should have felt pleasing.

At last they reached the top.

The townsfolk gaped at the land around Gates Mount. No raindrops reflected off the blades of grass, no rust ate at the iron gates. They could see the town and the valley below, a mist at the edges burning off in the early sun.

Next they turned to the gates with trepidation and not a little terror in their hearts.

Three immobile forms, clearly human, were sprawled at the threshold of the open gate. The bodies were wet, yet the hill was dry; the townspeople could see the water dripping from them. The Elder walked forward and touched one. Then she gently turned it over onto its back.

She gazed at the body for a moment before motioning to the townsfolk to come forward. "Whoever they are, they are not from here," she said. "But they are human. Two women and a man. Come see."

The first one the Elder examined was the man, dressed in clothing the likes of which they had never seen. The Elder raised the sleeping stranger's hand to examine the ornaments he wore—a ring of gold and a silver bracelet with a round, flat surface. She glanced up at the sun and at the bracelet. "This must be what you saw flashing," she said to the farmer's youngest.

The Elder heard a sharp breath. It was the farmer's son, who edged forward, his eyes round. "The colors," he said in wonder. "I've never seen such bright shades. How did the dyers get such—"

"They worked more on the cloth dyeing than on the shoemaking," the cobbler said, pointing. "Only one's got shoes. And I'm not so sure they *are* shoes." He was right—the sleeping man and the first woman wore nothing on their feet but woolen stockings, while the second female had twisted footgarb wrapped around hers, brightly colored but made of some substance they could see *through*. And the stockings she wore—the Elder touched them gingerly. "So thin," she said, wondering.

The footgarb was an equal mystery. "How does anyone walk in such?" the baker said, puzzled.

"Maybe she gets carried, like the Dragnians," the farmer's youngest suggested. He was partial to the bizarre stories the traveling goodsmen told about their trips around the Circles. "Maybe they *are* Dragnians."

Most of the party nodded. They had all heard of the Dragnians, with their odd and exotic ways. But the Elder was practical. "Have any of you ever seen a Dragnian?"

"No," the butcher said. "But we've heard the tales."

The Elder glanced at the sleepers and sighed. "I have seen Dragnians. And these people are not. We're taking them back to town. Yosh, Marn," she said to the butcher and the baker, both of whom loomed over the others, "the two of you are the strongest. Pick up the man."

"Elder, you think we should?" the baker asked, alarmed. "Maybe we're supposed to keep them up here."

"Maybe we are, but they look like us and if they are like us, they might sicken after being soaked," the Elder pointed out. "And if they belong up here, I imagine we'll find out soon."

The three were carried into the Elder's household. "Wrap them warmly," she instructed her housekeeper. "In front of the fire. We'll send a messenger to Court. But not you, Boyo," the Elder added, glancing at the farmer's son. "You'd find yourself in the army quicker than a hen lays eggs. Who could—" she paused.

"There's Yellinsire," the housekeeper pointed out, referring to the cobbler who had been in the searching party that had gone up to Gates Mount. "He should be safe enough."

And so the cobbler—silver-haired, a foot twisted and crippled from his own time in battle—went on horseback, no danger of his being conscripted off gentle Ellys. Nor was the swaybacked mare in any danger of being conscripted off to the front lines herself.

By the time Yellinsire was on his way, shaking his head in surprise at it all, the sleepers were wrapped in furs in front of the great hall fireplace. The fire was roaring, and even the kitchen help took turns peeking out to see and hear, with Poro the cook the most curious.

But neither the heat of the fire nor the smell of the roasting food being prepared made the three sleepers stir. "They're not asleep, are they, Elder?" Boyo the farmer's son asked, squatting for a closer look. "They don't toss and turn, they don't mutter. But they're alive."

The woman nodded as she, too, watched. "They are strangers, dropped into the heart of the Gates," she said, as if to herself. "I will wait. Will you do the same?" she asked the townsmen who accompanied her.

"Waterfire couldn't keep us away, Elder," the baker exclaimed.

That said, they turned and began their vigil.

Behind closed eyelids, one of the sleepers dreamed of things both familiar and unfamiliar, of a man both loved and hated, of a time and a place that was out of place and out of time.

And she dreamed…

11

Chapter One

෨

She could hear and she could breathe but her eyes would not open and she could not speak.

The scents she could smell were as vivid as memory, as sharp as fresh ginger and pungent as garlic broken open new from the ground. Deeper in her memory was what she had been doing, when she still had sight and voice and motion—what was it?

"I know you think I'm too excited to do anything else, but really, I've got to get to work, all right?" Catherine Deveney said as she rose from the worn metal chair and grabbed her cane.

Where were they? The library, that was where. They were in the university's main library. It was very large and very old, with thick, heavy stone walls keeping the weather at bay. The windows were leaded and of some age themselves, that was clear the way they warped and waved, and patches of grime clung to the glass. "I'm serious, Mark. Those books aren't going to wait forever, and I don't have any more to say to you right now. You know the way out."

"I want an answer, Cathy," he shouted, slamming his fist on the rickety table that held the stack of books she was working with.

What was his name? Mark? All she could see was the shock of dark hair and just remembering him made her recall all the lies, and how tired and defeated he made her feel. His face was a blur. "I want an answer. Cathy, are you going to marry me or not?"

In rising irritation, she shushed him then snapped, "Don't call me Cathy! And do you mind? This is a library, if you'll remember!" Startled at the sound of her voice echoing in the great chamber, she looked around to see if someone had noticed.

But the library was almost empty so early in the morning. The few who were in the sunny reading room appeared not to notice the little drama of love lost.

"I told you I'd think about it," she repeated. "I'm not going to rush into anything, considering how many little affairs you rushed into when you thought I wouldn't notice or when I was in the hospital. Go home, Mark. I'll call you."

"Go home. If you've work to do here, I'll make sure you're called," the Elder said, glancing at her overgrown assistants in the great mystery.

"We're mad curious, Elder. We just want news to report to our families, one way or another."

"Can't you tell me one way or another which way you're leaning?" Mark wheedled. "I'd like to know whether I can start looking for a ring to surprise you with." He raised his left hand and wagged his ring finger in a way he must have thought was inviting.

Cat sighed. She looked around, hoping for someone to come by who could interrupt this conversation. She was weak. She wanted nothing more to do with him but she didn't seem able to tell him so. Whenever she tried, she sounded tired and uncertain. But this she was certain about. "No surprises, Mark," she warned. "Even if I said yes, I'd pick out my own ring."

"If I'm going to pay for it, I'm going to pick it out, sweetheart." Mark was trying as hard as he could to be charming. At least charming to somebody.

She knew as well as he did she would end up paying for it – and it wouldn't surprise her if it ended up on the finger of some other woman. No. She wasn't going to do this. "I have to work, Mark." She pinched the bridge of her nose. Her headaches were coming more frequently and with greater intensity these days, which was why he was getting more and more insistent. He knew his time was running out, much as hers was. "Goodbye. I'll call you tonight."

"Call me any time you decide, okay, sweetheart?"

"Goodbye, Mark," she repeated. She watched as he swaggered away. She wasn't sure she wanted to leave a message on his *answering machine to give him the bad news right away or wait until that evening.*

She was such a coward. When had she become such a weakling?

No, it would be best if she told him later. Otherwise he would be back, trying to get her to change her mind and ruining the rest of her day.

In the meantime, she waited until he walked out of the room before she returned to her task.

"Did that one woman twitch?" she heard. "The small thin one, with the wheaten curls? Elder, they *are* alive, aren't they?"

"They're alive, Yosh. I think perhaps they are asleep. Whether they'll wake up, though, only Hala knows."

Why can't I move? Cat wondered. *Why aren't they making me move? Am I in a hospital again?*

It didn't smell like one. She didn't feel any IVs, a sensation she had become used to in recent days. She tried to open her mouth, but her lips would not move, her tongue remained where it was and not even her larynx would cooperate. Help me! Please help me! she wanted to scream. As it was, she couldn't even squeak.

"Elder! That woman, her mouth did twitch!" Cat heard. She tried to move again, to no avail. She concentrated on her hands, on something, to at least give some indication she was awake.

She flexed her shoulders and stretched her arms. The books would take hours to sort, but processing them would be a welcome relief.

Or at least it would have been but for the shadow that filled the doorway. She didn't look up at first. A sensation of dread twisted at the pit of her stomach, something that told her she knew who it would be.

She took a deep breath and finally looked up. "Mark," she said. The eerie sensation of dread dissipated as quickly as it had come over her. She could do this. "What are you doing back here? I told you I'd call you when I decided. Now go away."

"*Cathy, I want to talk to you. I have to know, one way or another.*"

This was getting ridiculous. "*Stop calling me that. Why do you need to know right now? Now or tonight, what difference does it make?*"

Not answering immediately – it was that sense of drama he loved so much – he looked around. "*My God, this is a depressing place. How do you stand it? You could have done better. And you don't have much time –*" He shut his mouth.

She looked around the room. It was one of a warren of back rooms the university library system boasted. It was dark and it was small, but she always thought of it as cozy and the cracks in the ceiling and walls as picturesque. For her own sake, she avoided thinking about the numerous safety violations. "*Go away, Mark,*" she said, her voice hardening as she struggled to keep her temper in check. "*I've got work to do.*"

"*What's going on here, Cat?*" a new voice inquired.

She turned. It was one of her coworkers. Margot, that was her name.

Cat grit her teeth. "*Mark was just leaving.*"

"*I was not,*" Mark said. "*Not until I get an answer. I've got my eye on a car –*"

She rolled her eyes. She should have known. "*Then you're going to be disappointed, because here's your answer. No. And I don't want to see you again.*"

His eyes narrowed. "*You're going to regret this, Cat.*"

"*I don't think so. I may not have much time left, but I'm going to spend it with something that matters, and that's not you.*"

"*Go to hell, bitch.*"

Charming lover's words. "*Not if I see you there first, sweetheart,*" Cat replied with honeyed sarcasm. Tough words, but would she ever be able to make good on them? She and Margot watched as Mark turned on his heel and stalked out.

"I saw her face move, I know I did," she heard another voice exclaim, away from her dream. "Will they be waking soon?"

"I think so," replied another voice. Cat had heard it before, but where? She couldn't remember.

"Are you finally waking up, Cat?" Margot asked as she turned to the stack of books. "Congratulations! He's a catch — if you like scum."

Cat smiled. "I am awake, Margot." She picked up a book and handed it to her coworker. "I don't like to be pushed and he finally pushed too far."

"No kidding." Margot scribbled a notation on a form and placed the book back on the table, balancing it on top of the heap. She looked at the ceiling, appraising. "But I heard what he said, and for once he's right. This place is a dump. The plaster's about to go. I just hope I'm not here when it does."

"It just needs a little work," Cat said defensively. "And it'll get it. The budget's almost approved. It's all over but the yelling."

"How long until Yellinsire arrives at the capital, Elder? And Court can be informed?" one of the voices said. It was an old voice, rusty with age but still vigorous. Court? Cat wondered. Why would a court be involved?

"Yellin should be at the Podani anytime now. Whether Court himself will respond, I don't know. In any case, the message has been sent."

"Haven't you gotten the message yet?" Margot said. "This place isn't going to get worked on whether or not there's money in the budget. It's always going to look like this until the day we die."

"Think of better, brighter days," Cat advised in a blithe tone she didn't feel as she continued to work. "Some rich alumnus will die and leave the library system a boatload of money. A bequest could fix this place up. Who knows, maybe it'll be mine."

Margot snorted. "Morbid today, aren't you? But you know I'm right. This place is falling apart. God knows what the big earthquake we'll be getting sooner or later is going to do to this section of the library. A major disaster's the only thing that's going to force them to remodel the place."

"There's hope," Cat insisted, but her voice faded a little.

They continued to sort the books. "Why are we so depressed today?" Margot said after a while. "It's sunny, the smog's not so bad and I'm seeing the new Johnny Depp movie tonight. I should be on top of the world."

"At least you have the baby to look forward to," Cat said glumly. She stamped a book. "I just told Mark to go away, but he's going to be back tonight with those damned white roses he always gives me after we have a fight, and I'm not going to have enough strength to tell him to leave. I am so gutless."

Margot opened her mouth, then paused. "You're not weak, Cat," she said gently. "After all, you've never been good at going with the flow, have you? If you don't like something, you fight it every step of the way even if it seems inevitable. A weaker person would have just given in to that persistent jerk, but you haven't. He just hasn't gotten the message yet."

Cat sighed. "I don't have enough time to go with the flow. He wants to marry me because of my insurance policy and the money my parents left me. I have no desire to go to my deathbed knowing my grieving husband's already ordered his brand-new BMW."

Margot looked at her with something akin to pity. "You should have stayed home today," she said, stamping another book. "You're going to depress me if we keep talking like this."

"I didn't know Mark was going to drop by or else I would have stayed home."

At that point a thin, blond bespectacled man came running in, a small gold ring shining in his ear. "Was that Mark I saw? When is he going to get the message?"

"Surely Court will respond to the message. Surely this is part of the prophecies—"

"The Court has other matters to worry about," another voice broke in. "The rebels have broken through the defenses of the Winter Gardens, and that's hitting too close to the Sea Cities and the Podani, I'm thinking."

"Yosh, there's something else to consider," the older, female voice said. "Remember your readings of the Kuriti scriptures, the part of the prophecies that concerns the Gates also mentions the Wars. I think these *are* the Wars Never-Ending, considering these battles have been fought for what seems like forever, and the honorable uncle only the most recent of the battles."

"You've been breaking up with him, like, forever."

"It hasn't been that long. Just about — three years," Cat *muttered, embarrassed.*

"It's been — what, three years? Surely it's been more than that since Queen Faia died, leaving the Swan Throne empty, and still there is no victor or vanquished. Only three years and it seems as though it has been fought forever."

"The prince was not confirmed dead until two weeks ago, Marn," the older feminine voice said, sounding testy. "Since his kidnapping, up until Court received word, indications were still that the young prince was alive, being kept in the caves of the Winter Gardens."

"There was no way the rebels would have let him go," Marn protested. "The Court should have assumed he was gone and fought back right then."

"He was his only child, Marn," the woman retorted. "Can you blame him for hoping the boy was still alive? Is that the way you would have reacted if it had been *your* son?"

"Are you afraid of how he's going to react?" Margot asked. *"He's not violent, is he?"*

"No, but he can act like a spoiled child. He doesn't like losing. And I give in because I get so tired of his whining."

"Losing a child is never easy, Marn," the woman answered, her voice weary. "Especially if the child is all you have left."

There was a hushed silence. "It's been too long, Elder," Yosh said in hushed tones. "The Court should have contracted marriage again before now. Especially with the troubles."

"It takes time, Yosh," the woman reminded him. "He was grieving. Still is, I daresay. And the boy. The boy was healthy until—"

"So was she until—"

"It happens, Marn," the woman said. "All the time. Women in childbirth die."

The silence that fell was bitter.

"How do you feel today, Margot?" Cat said, changing the subject. "Any morning sickness?"

"Oh, I'm fine. I'm just hungry all the time. Are there any more cookies?"

"No. If you want something, I've got a sandwich in the fridge."

"Cat, you need to eat."

"I'm not hungry. And why don't you sit down if you're going to be processing the books," Cat suggested. "Rest your feet."

"Elder, I think you should rest," Marn said. "They may not wake up for some time yet."

"I *am* tired. I'll send in my granddaughter to watch a while," the Elder agreed. Cat heard a scraping, as if a chair was moved, and then the rustle of clothing, a scent of lavender and leather, a faint breeze as someone moved close by. "Perhaps Court will have received the message by the time I return. And you," the woman said, her voice changing, addressing someone new, "don't think I didn't see you, sitting so quietly there. Don't you have to go home?"

The answering voice was a new one, one Cat could not remember having spoken before. It was a young voice, newly changed—a boy, but not for much longer. "I'm thinking if I don't see the end of this, I'll see the end of *me*, Elder. I should run errands my mother requested of me a sennight ago, but we hadn't time then to come to town."

"Knowing your mother, I imagine she would appreciate her errands be done," the Elder said. Cat could hear the smile in her voice.

She could hear the shuffle of their feet on the floors—not heavy shoes, were those wooden floors? Cat couldn't tell but the floors seemed to tremble all of a sudden. Then she heard shouting.

"What the hell is that?" Kevin said, looking up at the small room's light fixture, which started to sway. The floor began to shake, rippling in waves.

Cat grabbed at the nearest table. "Uh-oh. This could be it," she shouted above the rumble. "Margot! Under the table!"

"Not without you!" Margot shouted back. Kevin ran forward and grabbed her arm, and together, they ducked under the table with the books piled on it. "Cat! Get under the table, quick!"

"I will! Just stay there!" She looked up and saw with horror the cracks in the ceiling were splitting apart with every shake. "Oh, dear God," she whispered. The light fixture fell before she could move, shattering as it hit the edge of the table. "Damn," she whispered. "This is it."

Cat scrambled to join Kevin and Margot under the table, just in time to watch as chunks of the ceiling joined the shards of the light fixture on the floor. "Well, the university's going to have to fix this for sure," she shouted.

"Good God," Kevin said as he looked up. "Look out!"

The chunks of ceiling hit not only the ground but, Cat realized, the table under which they were hiding. Onto the rickety table barely strong enough to withstand—"The table's going to collapse! Get out!" she screamed. She shoved Margot out as Kevin began to scramble back out.

Too late. The ceiling, the table, and the mountains of books they were cataloging all fell in a single deafening crash, with Cat still under the table.

Cat screamed as the crushing weight jammed her against the ground. She felt her leg snap as the table, and whatever was still on top of it, pinned her. She screamed as she felt her shoulder rip out of its socket. She tried to shove the table away, but she was trapped and the darkness was presenting itself, quicker than she thought it would.

She couldn't breathe. She couldn't move.

Is it done then? So soon?

Give me strength.

And with that, Catherine Deveney opened her eyes.

Chapter Two

§)

The first thing Catherine saw was the ceiling.

That confused her, because the ceiling was intact. It should have been in pieces, in large chunks, the way she remembered seeing it before the world went black.

In fact, the longer she thought about it, the more she knew this was wrong. This ceiling was white-washed with smudges of soot along the edges, but it had no cracks in it. And she could have sworn the ceiling in the library's back room didn't have big, rough-hewn beams crossing it. She tried to look around but found her sight impeded.

She sneezed. Whatever it was, it smelled — and felt — like a fur coat, but it was bigger than any fur coat she had ever seen. She was surrounded by it, covered by it, and from the way her back itched, lying on it.

Cat closed her eyes. Her head hurt more than usual, but this time it was just a headache, nothing more. The fog in her head, though, was new and so thick it seemed to have mass. She could feel it pressing against her eyelids.

She opened her eyes again. This time she succeeded in raising her head a little to look around.

The room was still unfamiliar. Larger than the cramped little space she had been in, this room also had more light from the windows — *windows!* — lining two walls.

But this room had no light fixture. The ceiling was bare.

No, that was wrong. She tried to shake her head, only to have her head flood with waves of nausea. There were sconces on the walls, she noticed after the queasiness subsided, but they weren't lit. Aside from the windows, most of the light in the room came from the roaring blaze in the enormous stone fireplace in front of her. Or did it?

Her head hurt.

Cautiously, Cat looked at herself. As she suspected, she was under a pile of furs. She stretched. She felt unbelievably stiff, as though she had not moved in ages. Her lips were dry. But most of all, her head ached.

She looked to her side. What she saw there was familiar, at least. Her coworkers at the library, Margot and Kevin, shared a pile of furs much like hers. But they appeared to be asleep and both looked as though they had been drenched. In fact, Kevin's glasses glinted with beads of water.

Cat touched her own head. Her hair was wet too. She sat up ever so slowly, her body sore but wanting to move, at odds with her head, which cautioned her to stay still. *Why* was she wet?

She mulled over what she knew of the university's library system. Some branches of the system were brand-new, thanks to generous endowments to departments and schools, while some library facilities were as old as the college itself. While she didn't recognize her current surroundings, it was conceivable she didn't know the entire complex. A water main might have burst during the earthquake, flooding the room she was working in and forcing an evacuation. If she were this wet, she shuddered to think what had happened to the books.

Earthquake. That had to be what happened. The immediate mystery was solved. A wave of exhaustion overwhelmed her and, almost against her will, her eyelids drooped.

Her eyes popped open again when she heard footsteps. A girl hurried into the room, balancing a tray with simple earthenware cups filled with a steaming liquid. She headed straight toward the low, small wooden table in the middle of the room.

Cat cleared her throat. "Hi," she whispered.

The girl's head whipped around as she skidded to a stop. For a moment, she stared at Cat. Cat stared back.

The girl—and she had to be no more than in her mid-teens—was flaxen-haired, braids around her head, ribbons intertwined in the plaits. Atop a bright, full skirt, she wore a laced waistcoat of textured wool woven in intricate patterns of swirling blues and purples, with generous sleeves so broad they could nearly fly on their own. Cat blinked at the colors; she had never seen any so bright. Some designer had gone nuts.

The braids—Cat looked again. The girl's hair wasn't blond, it was silver—but the tips of the braids were black and Cat knew instinctively the effect was natural.

She cleared her throat again. "I like your hair."

The girl's mouth dropped open, her honey-brown eyes wide. The tray in her hands began to tilt.

"Careful," Cat croaked. "You're—"

The girl didn't seem to hear. The cups slid off the tray, shattering on the floor. Cat winced.

"Grandmeren!" the girl screamed, paying no attention to the pale green liquid splattered everywhere. "One is awake! *Grandme!*" She ran out of the room.

"Not so loud," Cat moaned, the scream vibrating through her head. Then she heard more footsteps, a great many this time. These footsteps were louder, faster—and headed toward her.

She looked up warily when the footsteps halted nearby. This time the girl—not as young as Cat thought at first glance—was accompanied by others. A small older woman stood in front of two big, burly men, who in turn were standing in front of a boy about the girl's age. The boy—a young man, really—stood in front of the young silver-haired woman, who peeked around him. Their expressions all mirrored the girl's—shock, fear—and fascination.

Somewhere in the back of Cat's mind were questions. Why were these people in period dress? Why didn't she recognize the period? Where *was* she?

Her head still ached. Would it ever *stop*?

They stared at her and she stared back. After a while Cat finally broke the silence. "I think I scared the young lady," she said, her voice hoarse, gesturing to the mess of cooling liquid and broken pottery on the floor. "It's not her fault. She probably didn't think I would be awake. Say, do you have any aspirin? I've got a killer headache." She waited for a response. She hoped someone had some aspirin because if not, she was going to settle back into the cocoon of furs, close her eyes and sleep this headache away.

The older woman, her hair as silver as the girl's but clearly not premature, came forward. "I am the Elder of this our village S'nal," she said gently. "I am called Quer'Ali. The girl is my granddat, Q'Atha. What are you called?"

Cat rubbed her temples. The headache was reaching out with sharp claws and tearing off pieces of her brain for the sheer joy of it. "My name is Catherine Deveney," she muttered. "You can call me anything you like. My insurance card is in my purse. Where am I?"

The older woman's eyes widened, making her look not much older than her granddaughter — Cat assumed that's what the word meant — for a moment. "You have no ekennomen?" Quer'Ali asked.

"What?" Maybe some Seattle locals opened their homes in the aftermath of the earthquake, but somehow she didn't think this home would have been high on the list to do so. The place looked like a rest home sponsored by the Society for Creative Anachronism. "Just call me Cat. That's what I'm called. Is that what you mean?"

Behind the older woman the men glanced at each other. Cat wondered if the Medieval Classics Department at the university overdid on the holiday punch again — no matter there wasn't a holiday in sight. "You have no taboo about telling your true name to strangers then?" the older woman asked.

Cat stared at them. "No," she said finally. "My Social Security number, sure, but not my name."

Not even overdoing on the holiday punch would cause this conversation. "No taboo," she added. Then, "You do?"

The older woman looked thoughtful. "Yes, for the women." She glanced back at the others before she resumed the conversation. "Where are you from?"

The fog in Cat's head threatened to close in again, but she fought it. "Seattle. But that's not where I am. Right?"

"I have never heard of such a place. Did you come by sea or by land?" the older woman asked. She took a step closer, gesturing behind her. One of the men promptly moved a chair to where she stood and she sat down, not taking her eyes off Cat.

"One if by land and two if by sea," Cat murmured. The pain was spreading. Her face was starting to feel numb, it hurt so much. She needed…

The Elder continued to look at her. "Would you like to eat or drink?" She folded her hands in her lap, prim and waiting— for what, Cat couldn't say.

"I would appreciate something to drink. And aspirin. Something for this headache." Her eyes drifted shut as she sank back into her fur cocoon. "And how are you speaking English? I have to be dreaming."

Behind her eyelids, beyond the pain, her memory awakened. She saw an image of a dark man—his hair, black and thick, with a streak of silver running through it. Who it was, she couldn't say—only that he was familiar. Then the image vanished.

"Elder, I don't think we should deal with this until we get a message from the Court."

Startled, Cat opened her eyes. It took her a moment to recognize the voice. Yosh—that was what the others called him, she remembered. Now she could see him as well as hear him. The body matched the voice. He was a giant of a man, at least a half-foot taller than most of the others, and his tunic was splattered with something dark. From the looks of it, the splatters had to be blood.

Cat swallowed. "I take it the fax or the phone isn't going to help me any."

"The what? I don't understand," the Elder said. She edged closer, seeming to pay no attention when the chair she was sitting in was picked up once more and neatly placed under her. "What are you saying?"

Cat closed her eyes. "It's how we communicate." The pounding in her head was getting worse. It was just as well because she wasn't getting anywhere talking to these people.

"But you are speaking to me. That is not how you speak with your own kind?"

"I'm not having this conversation," Cat murmured, her eyes closed. "I'm having a dream."

"She's talking to herself now?" she heard Yosh say. "She's saying she's not here? Elder, this is past strange."

"I was up too late last night," Cat continued softly.

"This is more than strange, Yosh. This is making me afraid," another voice said, almost as deep as Yosh's.

Cat slitted open her eyes wearily. The new voice had to belong to the other man, almost as large as Yosh, with frizzed white hair crowning his red, round face. His apron was liberally dusted with flour. Two guesses what he did for a living. "Elder, I say we wait to hear from Court," he insisted.

"Marn, she's here and awake. Are you suggesting we sit here and ignore her questions?"

"Elder, we don't know these people!"

"I think your ways are different from ours," the Elder said to Cat.

Cat couldn't deny that. "That chunk of ceiling must have hit me on the head, and hard," she said aloud.

The Elder looked at her. "What ceiling?"

"In the library. Where I work," Cat added. "In Seattle."

"This Shiatta again," the Elder murmured. "But now a library. Would you like something hot to drink?" she asked, glancing at the broken cups and pooling liquid on the floor.

Cat's gaze followed. Whatever the liquid was, it smelled good. "I could use something to drink," she admitted. If her headache would allow it. She wasn't sure she could drink something and manage to keep it down.

"I promise Q'Atha will not spill any this time."

"Sure," Cat murmured. "There shouldn't be anything more to scare her, I don't think. I'm not that scary."

"She is young," the Elder said. She turned to the boy—not so young, Cat realized now—who was hovering in the background, his own cheeks pink. He may have considered himself a man, but everyone else would have said he was just barely so, his eyes wide and eager to absorb everything going on. He was dressed in much the same way the others were, in heavy wool and cotton. His boots were leather worn smooth, etched and beaded patterns edging the tops of the shafts. They looked handmade. They probably were.

Fuzzily, Cat wondered how much they would cost at Nordstrom.

"Why don't you go help Q'Atha?" the Elder suggested to the boy. Her eyes twinkled as she said this, Cat noticed. "And help her not to spill the drink this time."

He flushed. "Yes, Elder," he said, his gaze shifting to the floor before he turned and left, the slap of his boots against the floor echoing as he ran down the hall.

"A fine family," the Elder explained when she turned back to Cat. "Farmers. Do you have farmers in Shiatta?"

Cat rubbed her temples. Her headaches were changing in intensity. Before the earthquake the pain pierced her brain between her eyes, but now, they stabbed her in a broader range. Maybe she was suffering a concussion too. "Seattle. Sure. Outside of the city. But—"

"So Shiatta is a city? So the farmers work to support your city?"

Cat stared at her. No, the woman was perfectly serious. And this was not the time to get into politics. "Not exactly. Listen, if you don't have a phone, can you at least make sure my boss knows where I am?"

"Surely," the older woman said promptly. "What is a boss?"

Cat stared at her some more. "Never mind."

The boy came back, holding another wooden tray laden with thicker, perhaps sturdier earthenware cups, with the Elder's granddaughter following behind this time. "Did you hear that, Boyo?" the Elder said. "They have farms!"

The boy's eyes opened wide again. Cat would have been amused—he was so young—if she hadn't felt so out of place. "Are you a farmer?" he asked eagerly, his shyness dissipating in his interest. He knelt on the floor, carefully placing the tray between the Elder and Cat.

"Would you like something to drink?" he asked, offering the cup. "Do you raise cows? Or wheat?"

Cat blinked. Too many questions. "Yes," she began. The grayness impeding her thoughts paused, but it was still waiting. "Yes, to something to drink, no, no cows, at least I don't raise 'em. Not even a dog. Thanks."

The boy's eyes widened still as Cat took the cup from him. Impulsively she continued, trying to ignore the fact she had an audience—who, she guessed, thought she should be humored. "It's cheaper to buy milk and meat at Safeway. Bread, too."

Yosh nodded. "City folk," he said to Marn. "What is a Safeway?" he asked Cat.

"A very big market, where you can buy all kinds of food," she said between sips. The warmth of the liquid coursed through her, helping more than the layers of furs could, although it did little to lessen the pain in her head. But the taste—"What *is* this?" she asked, puzzled. She stared into the cup. All she saw was a clear pale-green liquid, without even leaves or grounds to give her a clue.

The Elder looked at her. "It is *oja*. You do not have *oja* in Shiatta?"

Cat shook her head. "Orangey with a chocolate aftertaste," she muttered. She took another sip. "There's mint in there somewhere too." She took a deep breath. Whether it was the warm liquid or her system finally overloading, she couldn't have said. In any case, her eyelids started to droop again, though her head still felt ready to explode.

"*Oja* is made from our local plants," the older woman said, her voice lower, almost soothing. "Our drink of choice. It has healing properties. It's just as well," she added. "We grow no grapes worth making wine with, nor hops for beer."

"The *oja* batch of leaves you are drinking from were picked from my family's farm," the boy offered. He still knelt in front of Cat, his big brown eyes intent.

"Your farm," she repeated, her eyes heavy. This kid was familiar—she could have sworn he was familiar somehow—was he one of the volunteers at the library, finding his way into her subconscious? "I was just at a strawberry farm last week. Is yours a strawberry farm?"

"N-no," he stammered. He flushed, and he glanced at the Elder. "Y-yes. My little sister grows them in the garden, with my grandmother," he went on, sure of his topic now. "I grow wheat with my brothers and tend the cattle, and in the winter I weave cloth, for us and the army when they come through town."

"Why does the army come through town? You've got a war here too?"

She heard a stifled gasp. "You do not know about the war?" the Elder whispered. "You appear, you and your companions, at the Gates, which were foretold to be where the Sleepers would emerge, and you don't know about the war."

"Elder, I think we should hold off doing anything about these people until the Court replies," Yosh said. "This is more than passing strange, this is downright sinister. Who's to say they're not from—"

The older woman raised her hand. The butcher shut up. "Enough," the Elder ordered. "Yosh, you have no proof. And we have heard nothing about the—honorable—uncle that he would do this."

"But Elder—"

The older woman silenced Marn with a sharp glance. "If you have proof, tell me now. Otherwise, these three shall be accorded all the hospitality we can give them."

Marn opened his mouth again, then closed it. He looked at the floor, shuffling his feet. Though her head was still throbbing, Cat stifled a smile.

"Now, Cadrine—is that your name?" the Elder asked, turning to Cat. "I'm sorry, but your name is not easy for me to say."

"Catherine. Never mind. Just call me Cat. Like—a cat."

The older woman broke out into an unexpected smile. "Cat. We have them too. Now, Cat, we are at war," she began. "Sadly, it is a war of family. The Court has been fighting his own."

"The Court is a person?" Cat asked fuzzily. The *oja* coursed through her, warming the pit of her stomach. Little by little, she felt herself relax.

The older woman nodded. "The Court is our leader, he whose family has watched over us since my grandperen's grandperen's grandperen was not even conceived."

"Who is he fighting?"

"With the late queen's uncle and all those who side with him and his."

"Why?" Cat asked, feeling adrift. She was tired again, but she wanted to hear as much as she could before it all went away again.

"Because the uncle is laying claim to the throne."

"Family can be such a pain," Cat murmured. The gray mists had worked their way well into her mind by then, and she knew she was going to let them take her away. But not until she decided. "Why would he have a claim?"

"Because the families have been intermarrying for generations," the Elder explained. "The Court is also cousin to several of the late queen's honorable aunts. It is not a strong claim, but it is yet a claim."

"Isn't it sad when cousins marry," Cat murmured. "Couldn't just talk it out, I guess?"

Perhaps the Elder was too polite to comment or did not recognize the flippancy in Cat's voice for she said, "The point of reason is past. It was already past when the young prince died."

"Prince?" Cat opened her eyes again. "Like in the tower?"

The older woman was leaning forward, hands folded in her lap. "The son of the Court," the Elder said, and here her voice trembled. "He would have been four this spring."

Would have been. Unbidden, the thought of toddlers came to Cat, chubby and trusting and innocent. She winced. "What happened?"

"He was taken and kept in a pit by the uncle, to force the Court to rescind his claim on the throne. The child died from exposure, they say," the older woman said.

Cat's stomach roiled. "Maybe you should start at the beginning, tell me about this war."

The other woman sighed and came a little closer. As though bidden, the others clustered on the floor around her, looking for all the world as if they were children being told a tale. "It is not a happy story," she began.

Cat wanted to hear the story—she couldn't believe the detail her imagination was coming up with—but the headache was threatening to destroy the neurons in her brain. She closed her eyes. Maybe that would help. "I'm listening."

Suddenly, she heard a shout in the distance. Cat's eyes popped open again as the floor trembled under her.

"What in the w—" Marn's head whipped toward the bank of windows. "No. It can't be!"

"Elder?" Yosh said. "Waterfire. This early?"

The older woman stood up. "It's too soon. It's not season yet!"

Had she heard right? *Waterfire?*

So tired but too curious not to pay attention, Cat watched, her eyelids drooping again, as the Elder and the two men hurried down the hallway. She heard voices, slamming doors, footsteps hurrying near and hurrying away. Shouting in a distance. And whispers. Many, many whispers.

As she began to doze, she heard footsteps she didn't recognize stop not far from her. Whoever it was seemed to be breathing fast, as though he or she had run a ways.

Whoever it was, she wished he would either speak or go away, because she wasn't going to be conscious for much longer.

The voice she finally heard was eerily familiar.

"How can this be?"

That voice—but it couldn't be. No.

Almost against her will, she opened her eyes and looked up.

He was a vision in black leather and cloth, a heavy black cape hanging heavy on his shoulders. His long hair was swept back, but Cat could tell it was dark as well.

Then she looked at the man's face and her world went topsy-turvy.

"Mark?"

Chapter Three

ॐ

A sword was slung at the man's hip and a shorter, more ornate blade anchored on his sternum on the intersection of the leather straps crossing his chest. A gold medallion finished the look, etched with an intricate design.

A gem of a brilliant blue flashed in the hilt of the short sword over his heart, astonishing in its clarity. It was mesmerizing. Cat forced herself to look away from it.

Nothing about this felt familiar. But his face…

"Mark?" Cat repeated.

She shoved aside her exhaustion. The contradictions pushing past her mind's demands for rest clamored for attention. She struggled upright. All of a sudden her head didn't hurt. She wasn't going to let it.

This man wasn't Mark—but he could have been. This man was just as tall and his hair the same color and texture, but there the resemblance ended. Mark had a streak of silver in his hair, which he maintained impeccably. This man had a streak through his hair, but it was a pure violet cutting a swath through the black. Moreover, the streak matched this man's eyes. She had never seen eyes that color. At least not naturally.

Now that she was awake and discerning, she could see other differences. Mark spent his life in the city, indoors. This man was tanned and weathered, his body broader, and he looked as though he would be a formidable opponent. Mark always looked as though he would have been happy as a brain without a body, disdaining the physical. This man, this almost-Mark, looked as though he had come to the conclusion his mind and body should be regarded as one, each as strong as the other.

And at the moment his mind was suspicious. His eyes narrowed. "Who are you? You don't look like anything that would come through the Gates." His voice was deeper than Mark's, and at that moment, he sounded as angry as Mark had been the last time Cat saw him. "You don't look strong enough to come through unscathed."

Angry? Why would this man be angry? At her?

Cat shrugged. "I don't know."

"You don't know? You don't know who you are?"

"I don't know anything about any *gates*."

They stared at each other before some light, quick footsteps came down the hall, and then a voice she was starting to recognize.

"Pir Strian," the Elder said. She looked anxious. Cat was startled to see the older woman, so self-assured minutes before, wring her hands.

The Elder took a step back and bowed.

What, no curtsy? Cat thought, but she held her tongue.

"Pir Strian, I had not realized you had arrived! The waterfire burst in the commons distracted us—"

The man was direct. "Waterfire season is early this year everywhere. I met your man Yellin as he was en route and decided to see these Sleepers for myself, as my brother would have bade me. So Quer'Ali..." he paused and looked at Cat. He frowned. "Are you telling me this is one of the Sleepers?"

"We believe all three are, Pir Strian," the Elder said. She gestured behind him, beyond Cat.

"Pir Strian!"

The Elder's granddaughter stood in the doorway, her face bright. "I thought I saw Lol outside! How are you? Is your jackoval with you? I have a new spice for him to try—"

"Q'Atha," the Elder interrupted, with a smile.

The girl's eyes got wide. "I beg your pardon, Pir Strian!" She bowed deep, the ends of her braids brushing the floor. "Welcome!" She righted herself with a little hop.

Cat watched as he nodded, a twinkle in his eye. "Thank you. Grace personified, little cousin. The jackoval is visiting with Poro," he added. "You may visit with him later."

"Has Grandme told you about the Sleepers, Pir Strian? Have you met Quer'Cadrine? But the other two have yet to awaken."

He turned and looked at the two slumbering forms. Then he caught Cat's eye, no trace of the warmth that had been in his expression with the Elder's granddaughter. *Fine. Be that way,* Cat thought.

"We found them at the foot of the Gates up on Gates Mount," the Elder added. "But Quer'Cadrine is the only one who has awakened thus far."

Strian stared at Cat. She stared back. He turned away first, shaking his head. "You could come from Faiora for all we know," he muttered. "You don't look as though you could solve anyone's problems, let alone ours."

"I didn't say I could," Cat retorted. She rubbed her temples. The pain had diminished but this conversation wasn't helping any. "I just woke up here. I don't *know* anything. Do you have any aspirin? My head's killing me."

"Any *what*?"

"Aspirin. Pain-killer. Boiled willow bark," Cat improvised. "Never mind. I'll suffer in silence."

He stared at her a second more. Then, shaking his head, he faced the older woman again. "How are we so sure they are not spies planted by Son-Toruai? How can you be so sure the other two are asleep and not waiting to kill you in your beds?"

The old woman's face smoothed. "Because they were found at the foot of the first Gate and not even the uncle would use the Gates in such a way," she said, her belief clear in her voice. "Despite all that has happened, even he knows his bounds."

Grimly, Strian turned back to Cat. "What do you call yourself?"

A simple question. She could handle this one. "My name is Catherine Deveney. I was working in the university library with my two friends here when there was an earthquake. I woke up here."

He gaped. "You expect me to *believe* this?"

She shrugged. "It's the truth. For all I know, I'm still unconscious."

He gave her a look before he turned back to the Elder. "Quer'Ali, this is foolishness." The muscles in his neck twitched. "Why should I believe this woman is the answer to our troubles? She doesn't look strong enough to defend herself against a child."

"If you're going to insult me, do it to my face!"

He turned, his violet eyes flashing. "Do you deny it?"

Cat shrugged. "No. But if you're going to be abusive, talk to me instead of her. *She* hasn't done anything to you."

He stared at her. "Do you know who I am?"

Out of the corner of her eye she saw the Elder wince. "No. But considering you don't know who I am either, I guess we're even."

He shook his head. "I do not believe this. Dragged out here and there is—"

"So who *are* you?"

The Elder moved toward her. "Quer'Cadrine, he is the grand prince." She knelt and spoke to Cat urgently. "He is the brother of the Court and he met our messenger by chance. He came here straightaway to see what the truth of the matter was."

"And he doesn't believe you." Cat looked at the man again. "Since he doesn't seem to be big on introductions let me introduce myself. My name is Catherine Deveney. I'm from Seattle, a place nowhere near here, I guess. And you are?"

"I am Strian of Kurit, brother to the Court, late of the Kama, Protector of Kurit. And I do not know Shiatta."

Cat sighed. "Of course you don't. If you did, we would have a point of reference and we'd be able to talk to each other intelligibly."

The Elder's eyes widened. Emboldened, Cat went on. "Why would I pretend to be—what did you say, a Sleeper? Why would Uncle Whozis have me as a spy? Aren't spies supposed to convince people to believe them? I'm not good with that."

The Elder stood again. "Pir Strian, I do not think she is artful enough to be a spy. I do not think she is here of her own accord and I think she is a Sleeper. It is all of a piece."

He rubbed his face with his hand. "I do not believe this," he told the older woman, exhaustion straining his voice. "I cannot."

"Is it the scrolls you have trouble believing, or yourself? Nothing has happened up on Gates Mount for centuries. Those Gates have stood there since before there *was* a Kurit. Kuriti children know this." The Elder's voice softened. "And I cannot think all of a sudden, any Kuriti would slap tradition in the face by planting false Sleepers."

Strian seemed unconvinced. "The Faiori have no such taboos."

"They know what would happen," the Elder shot back. "They know the curse they call upon themselves if they came near the Gates. Even Kuriti do not approach Gates Mount, let alone the Faiori. And not since—"

There was a silence. Cat sensed an almost palpable sorrow steal between them.

Pir Strian sighed. "But that, too, is of a piece. I would not put it past—" he stopped, gritting his teeth.

He started again. "Quer'Ali—Elder—I came because my brother would have asked me to once he received your message. And I know you would not send one unless you were convinced of what you had."

"So what will you tell him?"

He looked at Cat, and his expression saddened. "We have a mystery among us. Perhaps the Gates themselves are involved in our struggle. Perhaps the answer is in front of us. But I do not know for certain."

Cat stared up at him, her mouth twisting. "So you're willing to give me the benefit of the doubt? That's kind of you."

He leaned in. "It is not kindness, Quer'— What did you call her?" he asked the Elder.

"Cadrine. As close as we could pronounce the ekennomen she gave us."

"Thank you. It is not kindness, Quer'Cadrine." The expression on his face was not warm. "We need the answers to our questions. And it's as likely as anyone to be you to answer them."

Cat snorted. "If *you* want to explain anything, please do. I'm clueless here."

Strian's lip curled. "Does she know the sorry tale?"

The older woman shook her head. "We started to explain but the waterfire…"

"Then she must be told. Can you stand?" he asked Cat. "Unless you choose to remain abed."

Cat shook her head, shifting as she prepared to rise. "No, I'm getting stiff here. And I have to exercise my leg before it cramps. The table in the library," she said suddenly, remembering. Her leg twitched at the memory. "I was under a table that collapsed. I remember…I remember my shoulder and my leg hurting. My shoulder feels all right but—it was my good leg, wouldn't you know it?"

Their faces were blank. "My leg," Cat explained, glancing at the older woman. "If you carried me here, you must have noticed one of my legs is a little shorter and skinnier, a little twisted, than the other one. I have to exercise it or else I can't walk for a day or two afterward."

The Elder stared at her, mystified. "I saw nothing amiss with your leg, Quer'Cadrine. Nothing that would—"

Cat cut her off. "Don't pretend you didn't see it." She felt her face flush. She shoved away the furs covering her, suddenly too hot. "I was in a car accident when I was a little kid, okay? There was a fire, I was trapped, my leg was caught and when they rescued me, the doctors couldn't straighten my leg or take care of the burns fast enough. And my parents died in the accident, the insurance took years to clear up and by the time I could afford it, the surgery—oh, hell. I don't have time for this." She was free of the heavy furs, feeling free finally. "The scars aren't pretty but—"

She stopped, her gaze fixed on her legs.

There wasn't a mark on her. And her legs—they were the same length.

Her mouth dropped open. "How?" She looked up at the Elder and Strian then back at her legs.

Unblemished. Cat ran her fingertips across the surface of her thighs. Her legs were smooth, with none of the twisting, glaring scars part and parcel of her for years. "Hold on," she burst out, scrambling to get up. "I have to try this."

"Sleeper, do you need help?" the Elder's granddaughter cried, darting toward her.

Cat shook her head. She was sore and a little dizzy, but... "No, I should be able to do this on my own—"

Strian reached for her hand and grasped it. "Quer'Cadrine, let me help you."

Before she knew it, she was standing up with a grace she had not experienced outside of her dreams or memories in years. One minute she was looking up at him, his eyes reflecting light and dark. The next she stood, square on her feet, closer to his face. His eyes were not violet as she thought. Instead they hid shades of dark aquamarine, reflecting darkness instead of light, perhaps because he was surrounded by it.

She looked around, startled. That was true. It was almost dark beyond the windows, that point between late afternoon and early evening, before dusk settled.

She could have sworn it was day.

"Quer'Cadrine, are you aright?"

She flushed, suddenly aware she was staring at him. "I haven't been able to stand up straight in years," she whispered.

He smiled, almost uncertain, but he didn't let go and so she didn't care. His hands were still wrapped around hers, broad enough they nearly eclipsed her hands. "It's hurt every morning for as long as I can remember," she went on, "and during the really hot days, I've had to—"

"Try them then," he said. He stepped back, letting go.

She teetered for a second. No crutches, no cane—but she didn't fall. Both legs were planted firmly on the floor, and…she could. "Oh God, it's true!" The trembling sensation in her legs made her feel as though she were on a roller coaster, all movement and force and on the brink of disaster. But nothing happened.

She took a step, then halted, just letting herself—*feel*. The pain deep in her hip, the ache she had borne for years, sharp and shooting in the morning, dull and throbbing in the evening, was gone, as though it never was, except, again, in her dreams. She could *stand*! Suddenly, she remembered what it felt like when she was a child, free from the troubles of illness and horrifying, life-altering car accidents.

"I can stand without a cane," she whispered, delighted. "Do you think I can dance? I've never been able to, and I really wanted to try at least. Do you want to dance?" she asked Strian.

His expression was a mix of amusement and mystification. "Perhaps you would like to walk first, Quer'Cadrine," he suggested. "To reacquaint yourself." But he didn't step away. He waited.

Cat took a tentative step, her first without aid in decades, and faltered for just a second. Was the ground beneath her moving? No... She stumbled, feeling weak and dizzy. She flailed for a moment, afraid she was going to lose her balance yet again, but then he reached out and grabbed her hand.

The world spinning righted itself in a flash. She looked up at Strian, her heart pounding. "Thank you."

She shook her head. He looked like Mark. But he didn't.

The astonishment melted away, replaced by disbelief when she concentrated on her feet. No pain.

Heart pounding, Cat took a deep breath and walked gingerly across the room. "It doesn't hurt."

He held onto her hand. *"How?"* she whispered. Was it a dream?

She raised her head. "What's that?" Something was cooking, something like manna from a heaven she had lost faith in. Her mouth watered. "I'm hungry. For the first time in years, I'm hungry."

If this was a dream, it was the most vivid she had ever experienced. It was the most pleasant one she ever had in decades and that didn't hurt either. She could walk without a cane! Her legs were as smooth as rose petals!

If she wanted to she could even *dance*.

Tears prickled at her eyelids. Her lips started to tremble and when she took a deep breath to calm herself, much to her horror she began to cry.

Cat didn't know how long she stood there, sobbing. Eventually, she took a deep breath, but no more tears came.

Just about then she realized the room around her had fallen silent.

Oh crap. She'd burst out crying. In front of an audience. They were all looking at her, some in pity, some even in horror—

"Are you aright, Quer'Cadrine?" Strian asked. He looked wary but smiled at her anyway. Impulsively she squeezed his hand.

Cat looked away, embarrassed, as she rubbed her eyes. "I'm sorry. This room's big," she said as she looked around, trying to change the subject—if, indeed, there had been a subject before her outburst. She knew she must have looked like a child, her eyes swollen after a tantrum, but she didn't care. This had to be a dream. It was too good to be real. She could sort out the psychological implications later.

Right now she had to analyze the dream. What did each item mean? "The room's big and the ground is uneven. It's not linoleum or vinyl, is it?" She looked down. It looked like wood, felt like wood—but wax had never met this wood. She lifted her foot. "My stockings are going to be in shreds if I'm not careful. Are my Jellies around somewhere?"

"Your—? You mean your footgarb, Quer'Cadrine?" the Elder asked, her brow furrowed.

"I'll get them, Sleeper," Q'Atha volunteered. She slipped out for a second and reappeared with the shoes.

"The floor is good Kuriti wood," Pir Strian answered, still bemused. "If that's what you mean. Strong, long-lasting. Timber cut from the forests by the Winter Gardens, not far from the Faiora border. The stone of the fireplace is from the same area."

The name reminded her. She had heard it before. "So Faiora's a place."

There was a hush behind her. Cat turned around. The older woman looked uneasy but Strian—he looked as if all the blood in his body was drained. "What's wrong?" Cat asked, alarmed. "What did I say?"

"Where are you from?" he asked, his jaw set. "Why are you here? You are a Sleeper. How can you not know about Faiora? How can you not know why you are *here*?"

Whoa!

What the hell was going on?

Cat took a breath. "I told you what I know. I'm from Seattle, and I have no idea why I'm here." She wanted to step back—but she wasn't going to. She hadn't done anything wrong, damn it. And she wasn't going to let this guy—this Mark-alike—wear her down. Not like Mark. Not now.

Instead, she met his gaze. "I don't know what your problem is, *sir*, but I remember you using that word."

"Faiora," the Elder supplied almost inaudibly.

"I wasn't awake yet. There were people here, different voices, I don't remember much else—but I remember that word. But it wasn't a place," she added as she remembered something. "It was someone's name."

Strian stared at her before he nodded. "Faia. Faia was my brother's wife. The queen of the Swan Throne." He started to pace. "Dead these three years."

"I'm sorry," Cat ventured. She didn't know what else she could say.

"She died in childbirth."

"I'm sorry," she repeated, and would have left it thus, except her curiosity got the better of her. "Did the baby—?"

"Stillborn." He added, "The Court's surviving son and heir died not long ago."

She winced, thinking momentarily of Margot, her coworker. "I'm sorry."

The man in black watched her for a moment before he glanced at the Elder. "Are you hungry, Quer'Cadrine?"

Cat's nostrils twitched. She didn't expect anything like this in a dream. "Yes. I don't know what's cooking, but it smells wonderful."

"Is the food ready?" the Elder asked her granddaughter.

Q'Atha nodded, glancing at Strian before her gaze settled on the floor.

"And the jackoval says the food is worthy of the Court's cook in Podani Plains, Grandme," the girl added.

"Then the Sleeper will be accorded the best," the Elder said with a smile. "And Boyo, you will dine with us."

Startled, the farmer's son looked at her and nodded, stealing a glance at the granddaughter.

"What about my friends?" Cat asked, her gaze drawn again to her coworkers still fast asleep.

"They are as safe here as they would be up on Gates Mount," Strian said.

"Why haven't they woken up? If I did, why not them?"

"Perhaps you are here to discover why," the Elder said. "Or perhaps you are here for a purpose not their own."

The dining hall was almost as big as the great hall. This room, however, had only one window, but torches were burning bright on the stone walls — walls that, unlike the great hall, were not covered with tapestries but armor, polished to a dull gleam.

Cat admired them for a second. "If this *is* a dream I didn't think I was that imaginative."

She turned and took a deep breath. "Oh man," she whispered.

The food! Cat's mouth watered. She could smell fresh-baked bread and juicy, roasting meats, and a sharp, unidentified scent made her nose quiver.

"I don't recognize your foods," she said finally, looking at the feast. "I don't recognize most of what's on the table."

"But some things you do. What do you know?" Q'Atha asked, her curiosity getting the better of her shyness. She lifted a ceramic cover and loosened the linen that covered the food. "This is daran bread. Do you know it?"

Cat gazed at the round loaf, nut-brown and steaming from the cracks on the top. It looked better than any other bread she had ever seen. Her mouth watered some more. "I know bread. That's a start. These—" She picked up a small stylized stick on the side of one of the plates. "Do you eat with this?" She examined it. There was a small bowl at one end. "It's— This looks like a spoon." She looked up. "We have these. What else do you eat with?"

Sampling each delicacy on the table she learned the knife and spoon were the main utensils, no forks in sight. How no one had deep scars in their fingers she couldn't figure out, but she managed to avoid slicing herself as she tasted the local cuisine. She chewed on her breast of chicken—she recognized roasted chicken and it was heaven—with a gusto that made her appreciate she still had teeth to chew with.

Gradually she realized the others seemed to be waiting. For her? Quite possibly. For what?

Pir Strian, in particular, seemed to be. His gaze met hers for a moment before he glanced at his own goblet. "You look thirsty, Quer'Cadrine," he said. "Have some more lene wine." He picked up the heavy ceramic jug.

Cat chewed the heel of daran bread and shook her head. "Thank you. You're just waiting for me to finish, aren't you? Why?"

He shrugged. "We have a story to tell you and I thought you would want to finish your meal first."

She took one last sip of her wine. The wine had a sting, almost like vodka, but it was the aftertaste of cinnamon that made her eyes water. After some consideration and another

sip, she decided she liked it. "No time like the present," she said, pushing away her plate. No napkin, she noted. Her imagination was messy. She rubbed the edges of her mouth as discreetly as she could. Was she supposed to use her sleeves or her fingers? "Am I going to like this story?"

The Elder smiled wistfully. "It depends."

* * * * *

"The marriage of the Court Gilcris of Kurit and his bride, Faiao'ria of Faiora, was contracted in the grand tradition of political unions. This way two long-feuding branches of a single far-extended family could join adjacent warring countries, presenting a united front at last after a thousand years. And so it was that Gilcris, after a decade of uncertain rule, wedded Faiao'ria, his fourth cousin twice removed, whom he had known most of his life and, fortunately, of whom he was very fond.

"The household of the Court was satisfied with the alliance, mainly because the Court was happy and the reign seemed to be solid. The household of Faia was less so.

"Her allied cousins and uncle—Faia's mother had died when she was but a child and her father some years after, leaving her as sole ruler—were quiet for the first year, and even lined up to admire the son who was born a year and a day after the marriage contract was signed. The boy was, after all, heir to two countries, soon to become one united nation. He was the crown prince, the heir to the Kuriti lands and protectorates—which now included Faiora.

"Faia's uncle and cousins quickly made themselves at home, availing themselves of Kuriti amenities. In the case of the queen's uncle, Son-Toruai, taking the time to do so allowed him to postpone returning to the monastery of the warrior priests of Kama, who trained and waited for an outside threat to the Kuriti throne, as tradition required.

"It had been many years since the Podani Plains, which are the home and lands of the Court, were full of family," the Elder explained. "At first, it was a joy for the Court, and Faia, though fragile, managed to brighten the Podani. But then the question of the young prince's education arose, and the families found themselves once more in conflict."

"Harvard or Yale?" Cat asked. "Schools," she added hastily at the blank stares of the Kuriti. "Where I come from, people argue about...never mind."

The Elder continued, a flash of confusion in her eyes that made Cat feel guilty for a moment.

Like all the royal offspring of the Circle of Seas, the Kuriti Court's heirs were educated at the Island Garde, where the heirs of the Circle countries had gone for generations to be taught. The practice was instituted to enforce the peace in the Circles, first by the heirs being kept in a common place — mutual hostages, so to speak — and then, with the heirs eventually ascending to respective thrones, by familiarity diminishing the likelihood of a war — not eliminating it, but lessening it. It was not the most comfortable of decisions when it was first instituted, by all accounts, but the outcome had been good no matter how painful at the beginning.

"What was the problem?" Cat asked. She chewed on another chunk of the bread as she listened. Food had never tasted so *good!*

"Landwar," the Elder said.

Cat shrugged, unimpressed. "All war is about land. Or property of some kind." She hadn't spent half her life in a library without learning something.

"Landwar is a war within a country. Brother fighting brother, the Court fighting his queen's uncle."

Cat nodded, understanding now. "A civil war. You're in the middle of a civil war. You started to tell me about this before Pir Strian showed up. What happened?"

49

Faia's uncle, Son-Toruai, spoke up when the young prince's education was discussed. He opined that as the surviving heir of Faiora, the boy should receive some instruction in the queen's homeland, certainly until there was another child.

"Son-Toruai's reasoning was sound. No one could fault him for the sentiment or think it was odd, for his niece was with child again and wanted to have her son nearby, not across a turbulent sea. And her health, never good, was failing."

With this, the Elder stopped, glancing at Pir Strian.

"Then Faia died in childbirth and the child was stillborn. We grieved," he said, picking up the story. "Son-Toruai took advantage of the confusion to seize control, and all chaos broke loose. Even as Kurit prepared for an imperial funeral, the uncle kidnapped the young prince, taking with him one of the Three Treasures of Kurit—"

"What a nice thing to call a child," Cat murmured, her eyelids heavy. The abundance of food was catching up with her, making her feel comfortable and relaxed.

Strian glanced at her. "The Treasures of Kurit are not children. The Treasures are how the imperial family hold the right to stay in power."

"Didn't the uncle take the torc off the queen?" the farmer's son piped up. Someone hushed him, but the Elder nodded, picking up the story again.

The uncle took the Treasure of Joining, as the torc the queen had worn was called, from her body when he approached to pay his respects. By the time the funeral procession was under way and the family discovered the torc was missing, Son-Toruai had disappeared along with the young prince and the Treasure.

By the time the cremation ritual was over, the uncle claimed control of Kuriti and Faiori lands, claiming the Treasure of Kurit his niece's by marriage as his own by right of blood and his guardianship of the young prince as the rationale. To help him in his cause, he enlisted the help of Faiori mercenaries known as the Benihe merchants, best known for their nationalist pride — and resentment toward Kurit.

The countries were torn asunder in a way the Circles had not seen in generations.

The war was three years old when the news no one wanted to hear came in the form of a messenger. The unthinkable had happened — the young prince was dead.

From what Strian and the Court learned, the child had been kept in the Winter Gardens, so named because there never seemed to be a hint of summer in the Gardens themselves, always staying cool. Son-Toruai had placed the boy in an oubliette, a deep pit — for safety's sake or to assure he couldn't get out no one knew — where the boy had stayed — and stayed — and stayed. And sickened in the chill of the pit.

The child died crying for his mother.

Up to then the war was going in favor of Kurit, with territory reclaimed and more to come. But when the messenger from the warfront requested to see the Court, it was with cap in his hands and sorrow on his face.

Without a word uttered, the Court had known.

When the messenger confirmed it, the Court was inconsolable. The war stopped, even briefly on the part of the uncle, and both Kurit and Faiora mourned.

But Son-Toruai persevered. He no longer had the guardianship of the prince as his rationale, but he did have one of the Treasures of Kurit and he had no intention of giving it up. Without it the other two Treasures were simple ornamentation, useless for their intended purpose.

"Which is what?" Cat asked. "Stopping a war? How?"

Quer'Ali waved her off. "Later." With this final treachery from Son-Toruai, the Elder explained, Strian, who was himself a Kamaite, left the monastery and joined the war.

Strian bowed his head. "I left the Kama because my brother needed me."

"You don't sound happy about it."

He sighed. "Quer'Cadrine, please do not misunderstand. I was torn between my training and my bloodright. Kamaites can only intervene when Kurit is threatened from the outside, and because those of Faiora are not counted as outsiders, having been of Kurit from long ago, I could not leave Kama beforehand. But as brother to the Court and now heir—" he paused, as though that admission made him uncomfortable— "I joined my brother. And I was closest to S'nal when I intercepted the message about the Gates."

He picked up his goblet, peering into it. "But the time of the ceremony is coming soon. We can only hope the uncle will be at the Podani at the time of the ceremony."

"You keep mentioning the ceremony. What ceremony?" Cat turned to look at the Elder.

Who, Cat noted, did not meet her gaze. "What ceremony? Why would you have a ceremony if you didn't have to, especially if you have to involve the enemy? How will a ceremony change anything?"

"Because without the ceremony and the torc the uncle has stolen, we will all die, Sleeper," Strian snapped. "The waterfire season is upon us again. Without the ceremony and the torc, we will all die in the most gruesome way possible. Without stopping the war, we cannot join for the ceremony. And you, according to the Book of Gates, are here to stop the war."

Chapter Four

ഇ

Mouth open, Cat looked from grand prince to town elder, aghast. "Stop a *war*? I can barely walk. I'm having a dream here. An elaborate, intricate dream."

"This is no dream," the Elder said sharply. "All the signs are in place. You are one of our Sleepers. You are here to stop the war."

Cat shook her head. "Suppose I *am* here to do that. How? I can't even get rid of a boyfriend I don't want!"

"The Book of Gates offers no details," Strian said. He leaned back in the heavily carved wooden chair. "You just— do."

Cat sighed. "I knew this was too good to be true." Everything she had eaten seemed to lump in her stomach.

The Elder leaned in. "You are here to stop the Wars Never-Ending. Why is that so hard to understand?"

"Are you *listening* to yourself? Look at me. I'm not your savior."

The Elder stared at her, looking puzzled. "Why?"

Cat's jaw dropped. She didn't know whether to be offended or worried. But it wasn't their fault. They wouldn't know. "You need someone whose life expectancy is better than a year," she said bluntly. "I don't even have that left, according to my doctors. I'm pretty much at the end of my usefulness."

The older woman's face softened, and Cat heard the dismayed murmurs around her. She grit her teeth, and hoped she wouldn't have to say much more. She hated having to say it in the first place, but she didn't want to get sucked into dreams of heroism. They would hurt too much when she woke up. In fact, her head hurt now.

But she was lucky. Perhaps the Elder sensed her discomfort for next she said, "Then perhaps this is the way the hyagoths have arranged for you to be immortal."

Cat twisted her mouth into a reluctant smile. She had to hand it to the older woman. She wasn't going to let anything get in the way of her goal, even the impending death of the one involved. "Maybe. But I doubt it very much. In fact, I consider this to be a sign I'm getting worse. Clearly I'm delusional."

The Elder sighed. "All I can ask is for you to consider the signs. All the signs are here, the—" And then she used a word that sounded like a sneeze.

"The *what*?" Cat rubbed her forehead. "My head hurts," she muttered. "Why—"

Then she knew, and her stomach twisted. "Oh, no," she whispered. That little throbbing in the back of her eyes was back, and it was spreading, sending spasms of sharp, needling pain across both lobes. "Not again," she moaned. The headache was back and this time, instead of starting with just an uncomfortable niggling between her eyes, it arrived full bore.

Cat fell to her knees, hugging her head before she lost her balance and hurt herself. Vaguely she was aware of the burst of frenzied activity around her, the voices babbling—but once more, she understood nothing. She could hear nothing, see nothing. She could only feel the overwhelming grayness threatening to send her to her final rest.

"Just put me out of my misery," Cat moaned. Her skull felt as though it would split and her eyeballs burst from the sheer violence.

In a flash the frenzied activity faded. The world seemed to go away for a while, and she slipped into a place gray and soft and without pain.

* * * * *

When Cat opened her eyes she was bundled in the ermine pelts again. This time, however, the gaggle of patiently waiting townsfolk was gone. In their stead sat Strian and the Elder, waiting for her.

They didn't look happy, but they didn't look particularly unhappy either. "It happened again," Cat guessed, her voice raspy. "My headaches have never been this bad before. I'm not going to be much good to you at this rate."

"We had waterfire again out of area, worse than we've ever seen here," the Elder said flatly.

Cat frowned. "What does that mean?"

"It is what the ceremony is supposed to end for another hundred years." Strian's voice was tired. "The ceremony is what the Wars Never-Ending may prevent from happening. It is why you must stop the war."

Cat closed her eyes again. Her head didn't feel any better, but she couldn't blame a headache this time. "So what is waterfire?"

"Waterfire is our curse, Quer'Cadrine," the Elder said. Her voice became softer, more contemplative. "Waterfire has been the curse of Kurit and part of Faiora since before we had history to recall. But it is also our blessing for though waterfire destroys all that it touches, leaving a barren wasteland for seasons on end, when the land comes back, it does so fertile and rich."

Strian rubbed his forehead. "But where the waterfire will strike we cannot predict. And once it makes its appearance, there is no way for us to stem it. Neither water nor fire has any control over it. It destroys everything it touches—but it can be stopped with the ceremony."

Cat rubbed her neck. "You're telling me this to persuade me."

"No," the Elder said calmly. "I am telling you this because Pir Strian and I both saw you fall ill when the waterfire came upon us."

"Twice." Cat met the older woman's gaze. "A coincidence. That doesn't mean anything."

She thought she knew what was coming next when Strian responded. "We think it does. We believe you can predict waterfire. With that alone you can help us, no question."

Bingo. First a savior, now... Cat looked at him in disbelief. "I'm a *barometer*? I can't get respect in my own hallucination!"

"If it is true, you could save lives," the Elder said. She glanced away, toward the window behind Cat. Without looking Cat knew the sun that had flooded the great hall had disappeared into the dusk, leaving the undraped window gaping black. "Beyond stopping a war, you could save lives—women, children, the elderly, those caught unawares by the outbreaks of waterfire. That could be your legacy," the Elder said, her eyes barely visible in the room now illumined only with torchlight. "You could stop a war and protect our children."

Cat took a deep breath. Oh, this woman was *good*. She was being manipulated, and she knew it.

Her time was growing short. She would leave no parents, no children, no lover who would remember her for herself, and few friends. When this dream would end she had no idea but she might as well have something to remember when it did, something to make her smile after all was said and done.

She was so tired. "I wish I knew if this is what I have to do," she whispered.

It didn't help Pir Strian—this prince—reminded her so much of Mark. But unlike Mark, there was no flirting, no confidences. Nothing except a bidding for her to go on a wild-goose chase, deep into places she knew nothing about. For the good of his country and his countrymen.

For him.

In that he *was* like Mark.

"I don't know." Cat's voice drifted lower. "I don't know what to tell you."

The Elder looked at her. "You could speak to someone about this. And it would be on the way to the ceremonial grounds."

Cat looked at the older woman, who wasn't looking her in the eye. "Like a therapist?"

The Elder hesitated, with a glance at the prince. His expression did not change, but he seemed to watch carefully. "I would not have suggested this, but the Nurui—"

Strian stood. "No." His voice was sharp. "Are you mad? We cannot expose her to the Nurui. You know what they did to Q'Atha. At least your granddat knew the risks. And this woman is not nearly in the good health Q'Atha enjoys. Exposure to the Nurui could kill her."

The older woman lifted her chin. "She wants to know, my prince. The Nurui are the best hope she has in the time we have left before the mother waterfire appears."

Strian shook his head. "We cannot control the Nurui, cousin, no more than we can control waterfire," he said, emphasizing each word. "If a meeting between this Sleeper and a Nurui goes awry, we lose her and the ceremony will be lost."

"If she gets no answers, we will lose Quer'Cadrine and the ceremony will be lost still," the older woman answered. "It is of a piece."

Strian didn't answer. Instead, he turned to Cat. "Your choice, my lady. There are dangers involved in getting the answers you seek. Are you willing to risk them?"

Cat looked from one to the other. There wasn't a choice, as far as she could tell. And what did she have to lose, after all? "What the hell. Sure."

* * * * *

"They have to stay? Aren't Kevin and Margot, what did you call them, Sleepers too? Shouldn't they come along?"

Cat regarded her two coworkers still asleep, wrapped in ermine, only a stone's throw from the briskly burning fire. Now that she was awake, Cat could only marvel at the heat from the fireplace. She could feel it now, but she could not recall how it must have felt to sleep alongside it. All she could remember was the wet. "How could they be safe here?" she asked again. "Shouldn't we keep them near me? Us? Aren't we supposed to be together?"

She was perched on a low burnished-wood trunk, her legs folded under her. Instead of her own clothing she wore a tunic borrowed from the Elder, who was notably shorter. The hem fluttered far above her ankles, almost up to her knees, and the heels of her feet dangled off the back of the clogs she wore—also borrowed from the Elder. But the fabric felt light, warm, comfortable. She liked it.

The Elder shook her head. "As long as the other Sleepers are asleep, they must stay close to the Gates. The Gates are from where they derive their sustenance during their slumber, I think." She looked over her shoulder. "Don't forget to make up packets of fenneril, Q'Atha, they're good for ailments up in the mountains," she called out.

"And perhaps the other Sleepers will waken by the time Pir Strian comes back from Court giving us leave to travel," the Elder added as she gathered a shawl. She was supervising the packing for the journey. Her granddaughter and her chatelaine were rolling blankets and heavy clothing for the higher altitudes they would be traveling in.

Cat stroked the soft wool of the blanket she had wrapped around her. "Is their staying close here part of the prophecy?" The blankets were muted in color, so different from the vivid wools of the clothing they wore.

The Elder paused. "No. It simply seems wisest."

"Maybe we really aren't your Sleepers."

"But you *are* the Sleepers," Q'Atha exclaimed, her brown eyes shining. "You must be. No one else would have been found on Gates Mount."

Cat rolled her eyes. The Elder's granddaughter was hard to resist. "There has to be a logical reason why we were up there. Think about it. We don't know anything about helping you through a war or this firewater —"

"Waterfire," Q'Atha corrected, her eyes round.

"Right, sorry. Kevin and Maggs have got to wake up soon enough, and they'll tell you so. I think they have to come with me. Us."

"The others, they will not wake up," Q'Atha insisted. "The scriptures say so. Only one Sleeper will wake in Kurit's time of need, and only one Sleeper can stop the Wars.

"And that's you."

As soon as the girl said it, there was a hush in the room. The Elder took a deep breath, the housekeeper clapped her hand over her mouth and both of them glanced at Q'Atha.

Who stood there, biting her lip, looking from Elder to chatelaine.

Cat looked from grandmother to granddaughter. "I take it she said something she wasn't supposed to."

The older woman shook her head. "My granddat should not have mentioned the scriptures. They are not to be spoken of lightly."

"But they speak of the Sleepers and what they are to do, Grandmeren," Q'Atha insisted. "And the scriptures say only one will wake to save us now. Why is it wrong to say?"

"I am pleased you did your reading as you were bade, granddat. If only you knew when to discuss them."

The girl blushed, but she didn't seem to take the gentle reprimand to heart. "Yes, Grandme," she said demurely, and spoiled it all by grinning.

Cat paused. "You're not going to persuade me, and I'm not going to persuade you. Now what do we do?"

"We wait," the Elder informed her. "We wait for Pir Strian to return with an answer. We should hear soon."

Cat's heart sank. "When will that be?"

The Elder shrugged. "Two days at most. We are running out of time before Pir Strian must be at the ceremony."

"You mean I'm going to be stuck here for a couple of days? Forget him, *I'm* running out of time here!"

"Now you know how we feel, Quer'Cadrine. Between the war and the waterfire, we can only go day to day. You are our last hope."

Cat sighed. Even in her dreams she was susceptible to guilt. "Fine. But I hope it's soon."

Q'Atha shoved a bulky linen envelope into a corner of a leather satchel. "I think Quer'Cadrine needs to rest, don't you, Grandme?" she said, appealing to her grandmother. "If she's ill as she says, she should rest before the journey."

Cat glared at her. "I've rested as much as I can," she answered, her lips pulling down. "I just want to get going."

"Sleeper, can you tell us more about your land?" Q'Atha piped up. "Are your people like the Dragnians?"

Cat stared at her. "Who?"

"Q'Atha, make sure we have enough lene wine for the journey," the Elder interjected. "Or even dokka ale, in a pinch."

Cat unfolded herself and stood. "I want to take a walk. I haven't been out since I woke up." She gazed out the heavy leaded windows, where she could see children playing with a stick and a leather ball. The game was something like baseball, then something like four-square, then something she couldn't figure out at all. "C'mon. I haven't been able to walk without hurting for so long, and I want to. And I don't feel a headache coming on, so even if I am some sort of barometer," which she doubted, but she wasn't going to mention it, "it should be safe. I want to see the town. C'mon."

"Q'Atha, go with the Sleeper. Show her our village and introduce her to those who brought her and the other Sleepers down from the Gates," the Elder added with emphasis. "Take the clothing Quer'Cadrine was found in and find garments for her. We do not have time for Infa to make up more appropriate wear."

Brightening, the girl obeyed with speed. "It's such a pretty day today," she said as she grabbed Cat's hand, nearly skipping down the hallway, grabbing the bundle of Cat's clothing. "We must go now," she said in a low voice to Cat, who was surprised at the sudden speed. "Grandme is not in a good mood."

Cat felt a sudden rush of guilt. "It was me, wasn't it."

The young girl shook her head as she grabbed a gray woolen cloak off a hook and thrust it at Cat. "Take this. The wind is rising. No, Sleeper, it is not you. With Grandme, it started days ago," she confided. "She received word the crops around the countryside are failing. The waterfire season has come early and the crops are being destroyed. And the waterfire just past here was the first time it has appeared this deep in the valley this early."

Cat wrapped herself in the cloak. It felt good, warm, and the wool soft. She looked out the window. "This is comfy, but it doesn't look cool enough to really need this. And maybe your weather patterns are changing. That happens all the time where I'm from."

The girl shook her head. "The cloaks are not for the cold. We need them for the dust. And this was the first time since the last ceremony that waterfire has come this far."

"When was the last ceremony?"

Q'Atha reached for her own cloak, bright blue, matching her skirts. "The last ceremony was a hundred years ago," the Elder's granddaughter answered as she wrapped herself in the cloak. She shivered. "We have waterfire every year but Grandmeren says it is rising, faster and harder than before. Then once every hundred years, the worst of all the waterfire comes, the mother waterfire, we call it." She paused. "Without the ceremony, the crops will be destroyed all over the countryside and we will all starve...and worse. And we will have to take shelter with the Dragnians, who are very nice from everything I hear but very odd." She tucked one hand beneath the cloak. "And without the cloaks, we will be covered by the dust. You'll see." She pushed open the doors and stepped out.

Shaking her head, Cat followed. How could a *ceremony*, of all things, make a difference in weather patterns?

She shut her eyes as soon as she stepped outside. The sun was shining, clear and bright—too bright. "I can't see," she muttered. She stopped short, trying to slit her eyes open, trying to see something around her, waiting for her eyes to adjust.

Q'Atha waited alongside her. Cat realized the younger woman must have found the light glaring too—she was shielding her own eyes. "The sun seems to get brighter every year as the waterfire becomes stronger," Q'Atha informed her as their eyes grew used to the light. "But the winds are cold, even in the sunshine, and the winter snows even heavier. And so it will stay until the waterfire is vanquished again."

A gust of air obscured Cat's vision for a moment, making her eyes water. Q'Atha started to walk so Cat followed, trying to keep the girl between her and the breeze. "You've got sun, all right," she muttered. "And that wind is pretty stiff." She coughed. "And the dust—oh *man*!"

Cat stood still, letting hot tears wash out her eyes. The moisture cooled almost immediately, making her cheeks sting. If this was what the breeze was like now in late autumn, she didn't want to be around during the middle of winter.

Q'Atha paused to let Cat catch up. "Sun is a rare occurrence in Shiatta, Sleeper?"

Cat sighed as she looked around. The glare of the sun and the whistling wind was at odds with the heavy moss and the muddy puddles on the cobblestone streets. She looked at her borrowed clogs, already layered with dust, even though they were standing on a porch of sorts, an elevated platform built of stone running the length of the house and further. "Is this usual? This looks like a sidewalk, but it's higher than the street."

"A little elevation helps if waterfire bursts appear," Q'Atha explained. "Waterfire appears on the ground. For whatever reason, it will not rise above it."

Cat nodded. "Makes as much sense as anything else." She added as she continued to look around, "There's water everywhere, but there's enough dust to make me think there hasn't been any rain in weeks. I can see why you need the cloaks."

"Waterfire leaves dry heat and scorched earth, Sleeper." Q'Atha pulled the hood of her cloak forward and tipped her head, avoiding the dust-laden breezes through long experience, Cat guessed. "You have sun in Shiatta?"

Right then, another gust of wind blew strands of hair against Cat's face, bringing with it a choking blast of dust. She coughed, swiping at her mouth and nose, trying to clean the dust away. "In Seattle? Sometimes," she said, suddenly nostalgic for weather patterns she understood. "Sometimes we don't see the sun for months on end. We don't get much snow, but during our winters, we have week after week of rain," she explained as she gave up and pulled up her own hood, wiping the dust away from her mouth. "And there isn't any dust, not like this, for months, until maybe the summer."

Cat looked around again. Some of the locals were out, she noticed, wiping down dusty windows. "If the summer comes. Sometimes it's just more rain. No waterfire. Nothing like waterfire." She looked at the sky. "Sometimes we don't see the blue skies for mo— What the *hell*?"

The sky wasn't blue. Unless there was something wrong with her eyes, the sky was definitely not blue. Not powder, not robin's-egg, not azure, not cerulean. No. It was...

Cat whirled. "What is this? Why is the sky—" She looked up again. "Why is the sky *purple*? And that color... Why does it look familiar?"

"The sky is the color it is because of the waterfire," Q'Atha replied, looking surprised. "Otherwise, the sky is the blue you know—and is in Shiatta—?"

"Some of the time." Cat could feel the curious glance of the young girl, but she wasn't going to go into the usual diatribe about the rain and the lack of sun that Seattleites were prone to. Any more and she would make Seattle sound as though it were a modern-day Atlantis, post-deluge. "So when waterfire season comes around, the sky turns that color?"

"And the imperial family's eyes too," Q'Atha added. Now the young woman looked as though she were feeding a tranquilizer to a somewhat disturbed patient. "Like my cousin's eyes."

That was where she remembered that color from. "The prince." Strian's eyes were that same violet shade. "And they stay that color until the waterfire—goes away?"

Q'Atha nodded. "We are told the sky and the eyes of the family are reminders the waterfire must be vanquished, and as our protectors, it is the duty of the Court to do so."

It was on the tip of Cat's tongue to ask about the consequences—what if the waterfire wasn't vanquished? But she had a feeling the answer would not be to her liking.

"How much will the new clothes cost?" she asked, changing the subject. "I don't know how I'm going to repay you." She shook her head in wonder. "It's a dream and I'm worried about how much things cost."

"You're the Sleeper, so you should not worry about such things," Q'Atha said.

"That's not fair. I think—"

"You are going to the Great Ceremony of the Treasures. You cannot go like that. You'll see."

The wind whipped dust against Cat's legs and she could already feel the sand work its way into the clogs, settling uncomfortably between her toes. She figured she could get rid of it by walking through one of the mud puddles but it wouldn't be the cure for long, and her feet would have been covered with quickly caking, flaking mud. "I can't argue with that," she conceded.

* * * * *

Cat could have passed for a native after Q'Atha was done, save her curly, flyaway fair hair and leaf-green eyes. Her Seattle wardrobe had been exchanged for one better suited, item by item replaced in an elaborate, ongoing ritual with various vendors. By the time the sun hung low in the sky, she was clothed head to toe in garb not out of place at a Renaissance Fair or even a comic-book convention.

Her jelly sandals first had been presented to Yellinson the cobbler, the child of Yellinsire, who accepted them with an expression of wonder on his leathery face. In return Cat received a pair of boots that fit surprisingly well, soft and laced from the ankles up, and she knew from the minute she stepped into them there was indeed a difference between boots made by cold unfeeling machines and supple boots painstakingly sewn by hand.

Next Cat presented her cutoffs and the short skirt she wore over them to Infa the Seamstress, wife of Marn the Baker, and in return she received a warm woolen skirt down to her ankles, with pockets not only on the seams but in the front and the back as well. The last item of clothing she had to trade— that she was willing to trade, since she refused to consider trading her underwear—was her cotton T-shirt, a belated birthday gift from Mark, with an image of the Ren and Stimpy cartoon characters on the front. Ren was, for some reason, silhouetted in gold leaf while Stimpy was dressed as a ballerina, but the details hadn't mattered to Infa, who had had her eye on the T-shirt from the start. The T-shirt, which Cat was happily and cheerfully willing to trade—its presentation had been the start of a nasty argument between her and Mark—had netted her another item of clothing from the seamstress, this one a woolen tunic with wool from Wilis the Weaver, to be worn with the skirt.

Altogether, a glance into a polished brass mirror showed Cat just what she looked like—a Kuriti villager, but perhaps one with uncertain origins with that hair and eyes—perhaps a Dragnian, who knew?

"Now your hair, Sleeper," Q'Atha exclaimed. "Only little children wear their hair loose. I will braid your hair into patterns and weave a flower into it. You will look as exotic as anyone from the Outer Circles."

"Yes, but why would I do it?" Cat asked.

"The flower woven into your hair would say you would be willing to accept a mate," Q'Atha said, her eyes bright. "I am just old enow. Are you wedded, Sleeper?"

Cat took a deep breath. "No, I'm not." An image of Mark glancing at his watch, lips twisting when she was late for a movie, flashed into her mind, then of Strian smiling as he held her hands as she danced in delight at the unexpected strength of her legs. "And I guess I will wear my hair braided."

She paused, though she could guess the answer. "Do you have anyone in mind for yourself?"

Q'Atha smiled in response, but said nothing more.

The shopping trip around the village was beneficial in more ways than simply reclothing Cat. She met those who brought her down from the Gates and along the way, the Elder's granddaughter introduced her to every villager they encountered, so by the end of the afternoon Cat knew a good many of them.

She also ended up stuffing odds and ends into her brand-new reticule, which in itself was a gift from the local leatherworker, a shy tiny frizzy-haired man named Dar. The token gifts from the villagers — a carved figurine here, a fan pieced together from ivory and light, watered silk there — were a source of amusement, for she could not identify many. Even if she could identify them, she still had no clue as to how to use them.

The sole exception was the last meeting, one with the silversmith, who presented Cat with the one thing she would need by far but gave her a touch of wonder too.

The silverist, Ginkgar by nomen, was an elderly man, deceptively quick and graceful. He was trotting down the middle of the street when Cat and Q'Atha encountered him.

"The Sleeper!" Ginkgar exclaimed when Q'Atha named her to him. "This is a good omen. I had been feeling tired but chose this noon to run my errands, so we are chance-met. I have a token for you, Sleeper. I have been keeping it with me for the next good omen I saw."

Cat remembered to smile and bow slightly, as Q'Atha taught her to. "Thank you, but we've barely met." And unlike the others, this tiny, elderly man could not possibly have been one of the party who went up to Gates Mount, she knew even without Q'Atha telling her.

"Ginkgar's guild of silverists work with omens, Sleeper," Q'Atha explained. "Some meetings are filled with good portent, while some are not. We are fortunate this one was good."

Cat stared at the little man as he rummaged through his reticule, easily three times the size of any others she had seen carried and nearly as large as the man himself. "I guess so," she said. How he carried it she couldn't imagine, but clearly he did.

"Very, very lucky," Ginkgar assured her. "If it had been a bad omen I could not have created protectors for the rest of the day, and our villagers will need many. And I think I will create no more."

"Protectors?" Cat echoed. She wanted to take a step back, but she couldn't, because Q'Atha was right there, pushing her forward. "Like what kind of protection?"

"Like swords and knives and fighting staffs," Q'Atha said. Cat could hear the excitement in her voice and wondered why the girl would be so excited about weapons. "This is so wonderful, Miru Ginkgar. Will you be joining us on our travel to the ceremony?"

The little man looked up at the girl, a smile on his face. "Oh, no. My time is almost done. My job is to provide, not require. No, I stay here. You go, Mia Q'Atha."

The girl shook her head. "Grandmeren said I should stay."

"Elder will change her mind. Ah, here it is," he exclaimed as he stuck his hand into his reticule one more time, reaching in up to his shoulder. He drew out a slip of burgundy worked leather bound with cord. He deftly turned his wrist and a knife fell out onto his palm, hilt down. "This is the sciarra for the Sleeper. I made it weeks ago, expecting a good omen," he said proudly.

Cat stared at him. "And I'm your good omen?"

"Truly," the little man demurred. "I expected the Wars Never-Ending to end but not how. I had a good omen that day. So I wrought the sciarra and knew there would be a reason for it before too long." He bowed deeply, offering the long-handled knife in his hands. "*Aya patina*, Sleeper."

Cat stumbled forward, assisted in part by Q'Atha's insistent hand, but more uneasy than before. With the clothing, it felt like bartering—an item of clothing for another item of clothing, each exotic to the recipient. "Thank you, Silverist," she began, she knew by now the offering required an acknowledgment of guild, "but I have nothing to give." She paused. "Actually, I do."

Without thinking, she slipped her watch off and bowed just as deeply as the elderly silverist had, offering her Timex in front of her. "*Aya patima*, Silverist, and my thanks to you for your generous gift, and my sorrow for such a poor offering in return." She glanced at Q'Atha and was gratified to see the girl beaming. "Was that right?"

Predictably, what was mundane to her was exotic to the silverist. He straightened—as much as he could—and accepted the watch, his rheumy eyes wide. "My eternal thanks for such a gift for one as undeserving as I, Sleeper." He stared at the Mickey Mouse watch, tilting it to catch the sun.

"And my eternal thanks for such a gift for one as undeserving as I, Silverist," Cat returned as she accepted the knife. She had the words of the ritual down, at least. She held the sciarra in her hand, staring at it in much the same way that Ginkgar stared at the wristwatch. But she held it warily—she had never had a weapon of any kind before, let alone something made by hand or as ornate as this. "I think my gift from you will be much more useful than your gift from me. It hasn't worked since I woke up, and I just haven't bothered to take it off."

He looked up then, and he smiled mischievously. He was missing most of his teeth, but that didn't change his elfin expression. "But the sciarra would have been nothing for me, Sleeper, for I made it for you, while the omens say this magnificent item—"

"A watch, and it tells time when it works," Cat filled in.

"This *votchi*—yes, such a wonderful thing—will be of use to me and mine."

"But it doesn't work."

"Perhaps it does not function in the way you think it does," he observed. "The omens say so."

She shrugged. "It's a watch, and I think it's waterlogged. It doesn't tell time anymore."

Ginkgar had no reply. He simply beamed, reminding her somehow of Q'Atha.

There was nothing else to add, so Cat and Q'Atha bid their farewells as the silverist made his way again, his reticule bouncing against his leg, his new watch gripped in his frail hand.

Cat and Q'Atha watched him go, watching until he disappeared from view. "Sleeper, that was a magnificent sciarra he made for you," the girl said, awe in her voice. "It was a good omen!"

Cat gazed at the knife. It was long and thin and delicate, like a stiletto, except the handle was heavy though the easy balance could not be denied. The hilt looked as though it had been carved from warm wood instead of gleaming, cold silver.

Somehow, it made her feel...uneasy, though she didn't know why. And then she did know. She brought it closer, examining it. There were three images worked into the hilt. She knew, even without looking too closely, one looked like Kevin asleep, one like Margot asleep and one—

"He knew, Sleeper," Q'Atha said, stroking the hilt with a finger. "He knew."

The last figure on the knife's hilt looked like Cat herself, eyes open instead of closed like the other two, dressed the way she had been when she had first awakened in Kurit—in her T-shirt, her shorts, her jelly sandals and her watch.

"I guess he did," Cat said.

Chapter Five

ॐ

"When was the last time you ate?" Strian demanded of the silent man sitting on a fallen log in front of him, a wooden platter of bread and cheese nearby attracting flies.

The Court rubbed his temples. "I haven't been hungry, Stri."

Strian of Kurit—he who was brother to The Court, late of the Kama, Protector of Kurit and Bearer of the Treasure of Compliance—swore. A nursemaid he was not, but clearly he would have to become one.

"You have to eat something."

"I'll eat when we get to S'nal, brother," Gilcris said. He closed his eyes and leaned back against the giant fir. "I just want to sit here for a bit. I remember coming here with Faia and Temer when he was just born." He opened his eyes and looked around. "She wanted to come back when he was old enough, teach him the forest. She liked it here."

In despair, Strian took a deep breath. Years in the Kama taught him many things. He knew how to defend himself and others against attack. He knew how to track people and even objects with the most minuscule of clues. He even knew how to communicate with the personification of a prophecy—if that was, indeed, what the Sleeper was. But he did not know how to defend his brother against overwhelming sorrow.

Nor did he know how to make his brother want to live again.

Strian was tired but he knew his brother had to be exhausted. He suspected Gilcris had not eaten or slept, for certain not in a while. The wear and tear of waging a bloody war, family on family, tragedy and death, was beginning to wear on him.

But only Strian could tell. If anyone had glanced at the Court, all they would have seen was a reserve, even an understandable melancholy.

But it was more. "Gilcris, look at you! Are you strong enough to stand, let alone wield a sword? How will starving yourself help? Do you want Son-Toruai to rip that earring from you and pronounce himself Court because you are too weak to defend yourself? Don't think he wouldn't. And if he had two of the Treasures in hand instead of one, there would be no question."

In the light of day, Strian could see the gleam of his brother's earring, the clear large sapphire at its center a match for the one in his own heartsword. Between the two of them, they had two of the three gems. But that was not enough. With only two of the three, Strian and the Court still could not do what all three of the gems had been designed to do.

Much in the same way, Gilcris could not do with his heart alone what he and his Faia could have done—build a family, rebuild a nation. Merge two nations.

Strian exhaled. He remembered Faia, birdlike and filled with a passion about all things. He remembered having that kind of passion too, when he was young.

When had that enthusiasm disappeared for him?

It must have been the minute the messenger from the Podani had come running into the Patima in the Kama monastery, with a note for him. Of course, as a Kama elder, Son-Toruai had grabbed it on the pretext of not allowing the outer world to disturb his peace, but in hindsight Strian knew the honorable uncle—and the traditional nickname left a bad taste in his mouth—had been waiting for a sign, anything, that would give him a reason to bolt from the confines of the Kama.

And neither of them had known peace since.

The note from the Podani, the seal broken and ripped open, fell from Son-Toruai's fingers, and Strian would never forget the look on his face. At the time the honorable uncle's expression seemed frozen, even shocked, with something else he could not identify. But he had no time to think of it for Toruai grabbed his arm and said, "My niece is dead and we are needed. We must go to the Podani *now*."

The ride alongside Toruai, down the treacherous trails of the Kama mountains and across the valleys of Kenai, had passed by in a blur. Strian had not been outworld in a year and the rising waterfire had leveled the landscape more than he had imagined, but the idea of fragile Faia dead and his brother sliding into the dark distracted him from thinking too much.

And when he arrived at the Podani Plains...the tumult had made his head ache. He had forgotten how busy, how loud, how *bright* outworld could be, and particularly the streets of Podani Town. But the hubbub was different now because Faia was dead and the world had gone to Dara Lal, the hells of the hyagoths.

The sight of the Palace draped in broad white streamers, the traditional Kuriti color of death and rebirth, stopped him cold as he and Son-Toruai made their way up the road. He remembered turning to Son-Toruai. After all, Faia had been Toruai's niece, and well-loved. Presumably.

"How could this be?" Strian asked in grief, his heart shredding. "They could have been happy forever and a day."

Toruai patted him on the back. "There is no why," he replied, and for a moment, despite all their other disagreements within Kama, Strian agreed with him.

That was also the next to last time they spoke.

Then they entered the Palace—and the sound of a child crying somewhere within was almost the end of him, the sobs fading away after a few moments. The servants, scurrying around preparing for the funeral procession, were the first to notice Strian and Son-Toruai. But Strian didn't see them. All he could see was the great hall, draped in white silk and lined with slender white tapers much like the outside of the Palace itself, being readied for the funerary procession.

The child's sobs began again. Strian broke away, running up to the bedchambers, afraid of what he would find. He ran down the broad flagstone corridors, past familiar faces twisted with sorrow, following the whimpers. He did not pause to greet them. That would come later.

He halted in front of the Court's chambers. The sobbing came from within. He pushed the door open.

Strian nearly gagged. The scent of burning wax inside the chamber was almost overpowering. Peering past the layer of smoke, he could see the large white candles marking a death clustered around the bed, smoking and burning bright.

Gilcris was huddled on the floor, looking like a marionette whose strings had snapped. The candles around him flickered when the door opened but he didn't look away from the bed, where the still form lay. The Swan Bed, where their son was born.

Strian stepped in and closed the door behind him, waving his hand to thin the haze a little. "Gilc," he said finally, coughing. "We came as soon as we heard."

There was no response from his brother. As Strian got closer, he could smell the distinctive snap of lene wine and he saw a bottle, empty from the looks of it, rolling in a nearby corner.

Strian tried again. "Gilc, what happened?"

That finally got a response. Gilcris raised his head. "She lost the child," he burst out. "The seers said it was a girl this time and she was so happy—"

He started to sob and it was more than Strian could stand. He knelt and grabbed his brother by his shoulder. "Gilc, I'm so sorry—"

"But she got weaker and the physicians said the baby was twisted somehow, and she started to bleed and bleed—"

"Gilc, don't." Strian's voice cracked. He wanted his brother not to break into pieces, not when there was so much to do—not when he would break too. "Gilc—"

And before he could stop, he started to cry too.

And the honorable uncle too, he thought. But as Gilcris and Strian wept, while the body of the Swan Queen was prepared for her final ceremony, Toruai had been making preparations for his own.

As his niece was readied for her final journey, her uncle had been, by all accounts, asking questions not out of the ordinary—then. Son-Toruai inquired about the funeral, about the plans for the procession, which route to the crematoria, how long it would be, and it was only then he had chosen to speak to Gilcris.

Strian couldn't remember what they had spoken about—and if he couldn't remember, certainly his brother would not.

"I am so sorry. I cannot tell you how sorry I am," Son-Toruai said soothingly.

"Thank you, honorable uncle," Gilcris had said after a moment, wiping his eyes. He stood, finally, to greet Toruai and took a deep breath. "I must tell you, her father's brother, of my sorrow for your loss as well."

"Of course," Toruai murmured. Then he glanced at the still form on the Swan Bed. "I remember her when she was but a girl. I cannot believe she is gone. And your son?"

A whimper interrupted them. Strian turned. Toward the head of the gigantic bed, almost hidden away, was a small, so-familiar form, trembling. Temer had almost been forgotten in the uproar.

Strian took a few steps and swooped to pick up the little boy, who snuffled into his shoulder. He was so small, his clothing askew and crumpled, his face stained with so many tears.

"My son is mourning as well. As much as he can understand," Gilcris added, with a touch of calm that alarmed his brother. "He knows his mother has gone to Hala. But after the procession —"

"Will he be in it? He is so little," Toruai interrupted.

And the Court made the decision that changed the course of two nations. "No, he is too young," Gilcris told his uncle by law. "He will remain here. After the procession he will be presented with the torc his mother wore, and then we will decide what to do about his education."

"Of course," Toruai murmured. "It is a difficult decision."

Strian remembered how Toruai's words made his skin crawl and at the time he could not understand why. He remembered thinking it might have been caused by his own memories of being educated on the Island Garde, where the imperial children were by tradition taught. But of course that was not the reason at all.

Finally, the procession was upon them, the rituals prepared, and Temer was readying himself to be as stalwart as a small child could be, when in truth the little prince could not understand what had happened to his mother, was taking the words and wisdom of his father as well as he could.

The honorable uncle seized his chance then. The procession was at the ready and there was a fury of activity, and the prince was the last thing on the minds of the Palace servants. Son-Toruai took that moment to pay his last respects to his niece or so he said, and he slipped into the Queen's bedchambers what must have been minutes before the coffinbearers arrived to take her away.

It would have been dark. The drapes were pulled closed in deference to the dark in the hearts of the Court and Kurit itself, with only a single candle burning at the foot of the Swan Bed. Toruai slipped the heavy golden torc from around his niece's neck and hid it on himself. And then he paid a visit to the little prince's chambers.

The death coach was ready, the horses draped in white, and the crowds had gathered along the procession route when Strian realized the little prince was not in his rooms.

"His nurse hasn't seen him in hours," Strian reported to his brother minutes later. "Not since Son-Toruai went to see him."

"I don't know what you're saying," Gilcris said dully, resplendent in formal mourning garb as he rocked back and forth in a tiny chair built for his son. He didn't look around — it seemed to be too much for him. "He must be somewhere. I need to see him before the procession starts. I must tell him to be strong."

"I know, brother," Strian said. He stopped. "Faia."

"What about her? Do you think he's there?" The Court looked around, his expression finally shifting from bleak indifference to anxiety. "He should not see her without me there. He would be frightened. I — "

Strian bolted out of the nursery, his brother following. Strian's heart pounded as they ran down the corridors — from the nursery to the imperial suites, the way he had run when he had been a child, running to his own parents.

Now, he was running as an adult, in search of his nephew, to the chambers of his late honorable sister.

It was dark, but it became darker when they realized the prince was not there; the candle illuminating the queen in her eternal repose until the procession had gutted and died. And when the candle was relit, what happened became clear.

The torc was gone.

The prince was gone.

The Palace exploded into a frenzy of activity. The servants searched the premises top to bottom for the prince and the torc, on the off chance either had been misplaced, unlikely though it was.

Within the hour, when it became obvious neither was on hand, a messenger appeared on the steps of the Palace with a sealed note from Son-Toruai.

That was how the war between Kurit and Faiora began anew and how Gilcris, though burning from time to time with determination, spiraled into the darkness he had been in since, now exacerbated by the report of the death of his son.

Now, Strian took a good look at his older brother. Gilcris had certainly lost weight since the death of Faia, and his demeanor made him look as though he had aged decades since his queen's death. Ending the war was his brother's sole purpose now. Gilcris had taken the oath of rule when he took the Phoenix Throne, and he would abide by it to his death.

"Can you vouch for her, this woman? Is she at least—" Gilcris paused. "Does she at least seem as though she could *not* be the uncle's spy?"

"Who, this creature who calls herself the Sleeper?"

"We gave her the nomen of Sleeper, brother, she did not name herself," Gilcris said with a sigh. "The time is right. She could be the Sleeper. Does she look as though she could be?"

Strian snorted. The past was beyond his control and the future unknown, but the present he could grasp. "She's sickly and she's mad as a loon, brother. If she's the Sleeper, we have been blessed with the runt of the litter."

Gilcris glanced at him and for a moment the overwhelming grief seemed to fade away. "Yes, but does she seem as though she could be who we think she is?"

Strian did not answer at once when, suddenly, words failed him. One way or another, his words could sway the battles ahead, decide their lives, and he knew he had to choose what he said carefully. "She is exceedingly odd, brother. She talks of a place that does not exist, she believes she has scars when she has none—"

"Scars? Why would she have scars?"

Strian shrugged. "She thought she had scars from when she was a child. She thought she was a cripple. And then she cried, Gilc. She cried when she saw her legs and saw there was not a scratch on them."

"She cried?" Gilcris asked, mystified. "She shed tears for scars she did not have?"

Strian shrugged. "She is odd, Gilc. But...fierce."

She was as determined as anyone he had ever met, and Strian could not understand how and why, but he found himself watching her. From the time he first saw her, weak and confused, he had been torn between disbelief and curiosity.

"She seemed to think I was someone else as well," Strian added. "I don't know who, but then she seemed to settle in, and she never spoke of it again."

"So she is odd and fierce and perhaps deluded, but is she our Sleeper?"

Strian paused. "I think she may be, brother."

Wearily, the Court glanced at him. "I need more. Would you give your word? Your word she could be the answer to our scriptures, and not a spy of the uncle?"

Strian thought of the face of the woman who could be the Sleeper. She was small and stubborn and as different as anyone he had ever met. She could be the Sleeper, and for all he knew, she could be the one who could save them.

He looked at his brother. "Yes."

Gilcris glanced at him one more time before he nodded and turned away. "Then I should go and meet her, brother. We're almost there, and I can see for myself."

Together, they mounted their respective steeds, signaling to be on their way again, leaving the flies to what should have been the Court's noonday meal.

The village S'nal came into sight soon enough. Sheltered on three sides by the rolling swells of the valleys of Kenai, on the smallest and oldest of the hills was Gates Mount whence the Sleepers had arrived. The Gates were in the shadow of the two hills on either side of Gates Mount, but in the dry lavender sunlight of the late morning, the Gates almost seemed to gleam.

Strian, for all the toughened warrior he was, shivered.

His brother noticed. "Is there anything wrong, Stri?"

"Gates Mount is a mystery in itself, yet I cannot help but think there is more to the story of the Sleepers," Strian said.

Gilcris in private was different from Gilcris the Court. If they had not been alone, Strian would have thought twice about making such a statement, but here in the daylight, surrounded by his retinue safely at a distance, Gilcris only laughed. "You think there is a mystery behind everything, brother. You were meant to join the Kamaites and look behind every rock and tree for those who would wish Kurit ill."

Strian shrugged, knowing he could not say what he wanted to, as his suspicions of Son-Toruai had been of note for some time before Faia's death. *And I have been right, haven't I?*

Reaching the peak of the last hill before descending into the center of S'nal, Strian saw the outskirts of the village. Even from a distance, he was pleased to see the village green had been prepared. The wooden platform at the heart of the green had been swept clean and painted, the damage from the most recent burst of waterfire quickly repaired. The roof protecting the platform was whole and polished, the edges of the copper shingles curving high and shining in the sun—whether it was newly cleaned or kept in good order, he couldn't say.

The platform was left over from the time of Strian and Gilcris' father, whose time away from the Podani had been spent in large part in the nearby Kenai valleys. The previous Court had rarely made a formal appearance in S'nal, preferring to spend his time simply. But the possibility he might choose to do so was always there, and the previous village elders, not wishing to be caught unawares, made sure a village platform was waiting, just in case.

Not unlike Gates Mount itself.

When they reached the edge of town, they were met with cheers as the townspeople recognized the crest on the shieldry and gathered alongside the road. Strian glanced at his brother, and was gratified to see him smile and even wave, nodding.

As they approached the village green, Strian gestured for the traveling party to stop, allowing Gilcris to continue alone. Strian watched, glancing left and right to make sure nothing was amiss, as Gilcris dismounted and walked to the path of red stone leading to the shallow steps of the platform. He started to climb the stairs.

More townspeople came running out, not having to be told who had just arrived. They too watched Gilcris, the Court of Kurit, the Emperor of the Winter Gardens and the Sea Cities of Dangurra, the Bearer of the Treasure of the Phoenix Throne, and the heir to the Silver Seas, ascend to the platform in the village green.

Strian simply watched, his eyes prickling with an unexpected emotion, as his brother walked to the slatted wooden chair in the middle of the platform. He could not get past the feeling that somehow this would be the last time his brother would be laying claim to his throne.

* * * * *

Strian glanced around as he took his own place next to his brother, a little behind him but close enough to have the same view. He glanced to his left when he heard a murmur from among the gathered townsfolk, and he knew without checking first who else had made an appearance.

He glanced toward the murmurs. As expected, first was the Elder, a distant cousin of his and the Court and a loyal supporter in these parlous times, logical and knowledgeable.

After her was her granddat, young enough to be impressed, but too old to show it. And after her—

He blinked. It was the Sleeper, looking like he had never imagined.

She made her way past the gathered villagers, following close behind the Elder. The Sleeper—what was her name, Cat? like the creature?—was dressed like a Kuriti villager, far more practical than the thin, exotic shift he had seen her in last. The faded colors of that shift had washed out her face. Now, the bright hues of the Kuriti tunic and skirt made her glow, her hair braided in Kuriti fashion.

At her hip was a slim leather sheath, and his sharp eye caught a glint of silver in it. She had had no sciarra when he had met her, so she must have acquired one during his absence.

Quick work, his suspicious mind said.

Then he focused on her face—and he took a deep breath. When he had first met her, she resembled a drowned rat. Afterward, of course, he had thought she was a lunatic.

But now—now she could not have looked less like a drenched vermin. She looked—and he found he had to look at her again in surprise—she looked *happy*.

The paradox struck him fresh. She was a Sleeper, in the middle of a place she was unfamiliar with, and she looked *happy*? He didn't know whether he should be suspicious or not.

Strian watched, alert for who knew what, as the Sleeper walked up the path. Ahead of her the Elder approached the platform, and when she arrived at its base she turned and waited for both her granddaughter and the Sleeper. Her weathered face held an encouraging smile, and as Cat caught her eye the older woman nodded. Some form of communication went between them without words, and he could only see the Sleeper's face light up and saw her nod back. Then the Elder turned and bowed to the Court, then stepped aside.

Strian watched as the Sleeper approached the foot of the platform. She looked up at the Court.

His brother. He quickly squelched his unease, instead looking around again, wary of anything and anyone out of the ordinary, like the Kamaite he had trained to be.

But his eyes kept going back to her. He tried to imagine what it was she was seeing as she looked at Gilcris. Could she understand, as she looked at him, why he would keep the loyalty of the various peoples who populated Kurit?

"Are you the Sleeper?" the Court said finally, breaking the silence between them but not the eye contact. His voice didn't carry as far as it should have, but at least the first few rows of villagers could hear. "If you are, I bid you greeting."

Strian watched her come out of her daze and blink, as if she realized she had been staring. But what she said next made him lean forward in confusion.

"Kevin?" she whispered.

Strian started. She called him by a strange name when they had first met, he remembered. He glanced around him, to see if anything or anyone had a reaction that did not fit. Nothing. Her question must have been too quiet to be overheard. Odder and odder yet, this would-be Sleeper.

His brother looked at her. "I am Gilcris, ruler of the Court of Kurit, the Emperor of the Winter Gardens and the Sea Cities of Dangurra, the Bearer of the Treasure of the Phoenix Throne, and heir to the Silver Seas. I open my hand in friendship. Do you?"

Carefully, as though she had been recently coached—as Strian knew she was—she bent her right arm so the tips of her fingers touched her left shoulder and then bowed from the waist—the Elder had taught her the non-native, neuter form of greeting, he noted—and then uncrossed her arms and raised her hands to show her weaponless state.

"I am called Catherine Deveney. I come from beyond the Gates," she said carefully. Strian felt a flash of pride, whether in her training on the part of his cousin the Elder or the Sleeper herself, he didn't know. "Beyond the seas, beyond the mountains. But I do not know why. Does the Court?"

She shivered as a light breeze swept through the village green, and Strian, trained to be ever-vigilant for waterfire, looked around quickly; but it was a brittling breeze, those icy winds that presage the coming winter, nothing more.

She was still as he, and the rest of the village assembled, waited for the Court's ritual reply. She could go find a fire to huddle beside as soon as the ceremony was over, but until then, she had to tolerate the chill, he thought.

It had become biting cold, but the Court did not seem to notice. He nodded. "I bid you greeting, Cadrine Debney," he said, the unfamiliar consonant combinations creating a new name, one easier for the Kuriti tongue. "Your coming was foretold to us through the generations. We have been waiting your arrival during this time of unrest."

The Sleeper gaped and slipped out of ceremony. "Well, I still d— I am a woman, of mortal birth," she said hastily. A glance at her expression made Strian search his memory, making him hazard a guess she skipped over a line or two from the ritual when the reference to her as Sleeper unnerved her. She was trying to find her way back to the ritual greeting. "I—I bring no magic, nor skill. I am a librarian. I deal with the written word of my land. I can't even *read* your language," she added, slipping out of the formal greeting again.

Over the murmurs of the village audience, "We were told three strangers would come through the First Gate, and they would put to rest the times of unrest," the Court explained. He slipped out of ritual for a moment and added, "There was more, but it was lost when the library of the Dangurra was burned."

It seemed to Strian she hesitated, and he knew she was on the verge of wandering off ceremony again. But she did not. "My sympathies are with you and your people," she said, her eyebrows together as she remembered the ritual, adding, "There is nothing more barbaric than the destruction of knowledge."

The Court's jaw tensed before he answered, and Strian knew what he was thinking. "Only the deliberate destruction of children, but that, too, has come to pass."

Before, the crowd had been whispering. After Gilcris' words, the villagers in the square hushed. It was clear they remembered this man, their ruler, their beacon of hope in these times of misery, had every reason to be dark.

Strian could see his brother take a deep breath and continue. "Who are you?"

The question came unbidden, becoming lonely in the breeze. Strian sympathized. The townspeople remained silent as they watched the drama unfold, a drama they thought they would never see, certainly not within their lifetimes — the appearance of the Sleepers and the meeting of a Sleeper and the Court in the shadow of Gates Mount.

"I am myself," she answered, more reflective than descriptive, Strian thought. "I awoke here. I am not of your land. Who I am is up to you."

He accepted her answer, and let it wither in the winds. "You came with the other Sleepers."

She nodded. "They remain asleep."

"Do you know our ways?"

"I know my ways," she answered. "I can learn yours."

"Do you want to? You ask for our help. We ask for yours. We must learn the ways of each."

Did she want to? Strian watched her, keeping a close eye.

He knew what she was thinking. She did not know how she had gotten to this land. She did not know how to return to her own land, let alone fulfill the Kuriti prophecy.

Did she want to?

Strian watched as she formed words without voice, almost as if she had to convince herself. *Take a risk, take a risk,* he read.

"Yes, I do," she burst out. "I want to."

Chapter Six

SO

Cat clenched her teeth, refusing to let them chatter. The ritual was almost over. She had recited the lines she had been instructed to, with only a few detours, and the king—the Court, she corrected herself—had said his part, and soon enough, they would be back inside and she could huddle next to the crackling fire and try to warm up, and then maybe they could be on their way tomorrow. Not today, because she was so tired.

She tugged at the heavy wool manteau wrapped around her shoulders, trying to coax more warmth out of it. She was running out of time, she could feel it. She was walking on two perfect legs now by some chance, but she still tired more easily than she should have, and the tumor that would ultimately end her days would be making its move soon enough. Quick, quick, she wanted to see this dream to its end before she met her own. She wanted to see if there was a happy ending somewhere, one where this sad man—she'd never seen such eyes of sorrow—smiled again and Strian stopped looking so angry.

She continued to watch the thin man on the throne—the Court, she reminded herself—who sat on the platform, trying to ignore the darker, intense man at his side. Why Strian kept watching her she didn't understand but she wasn't going to flatter herself. Perhaps it was because it would be too difficult to watch his brother in this ritual they were participating in.

She shivered again. "I can," she said in answer to a formal question. "I will."

And that was that. Behind her, the Elder took a deep breath as the Court turned to his brother, and the townsfolk finally stirred. "Now what?" Cat asked.

The older woman looked relieved. "Now we prepare you for your journey to the Podani Field." Then she broke into a smile. "You will get your answers one way or another now, Quer'Cadrine. The Court and the prince will help you do so."

Despite her exhaustion, Cat smiled too. She felt as relieved as the Elder looked. "When can we go?"

The Elder looked up, assessing. Cat followed suit. The mild lavender of the morning sky had given way to thin, wispy clouds.

"A needling rain tonight, late. Tomorrow," the Elder judged. "Morning. Best get you ready."

* * * * *

She had no idea how long she stood there on the balcony of the Elder's home, staring at the sky as the sun set and the twin moons rose. All she knew was by the time she felt someone behind her, those moons — both of them — had climbed into the evening sky, surrounded by galaxies of stars she knew she had never seen before.

A tap on her shoulder caught her attention.

Cat turned — and blinked. "Holy moly!"

He — she was pretty sure it *was* a he — was the shade of an olive, a color described as "seasick green" on a human — which this creature clearly was not. At least not where she came from. His hair was a deeper, emerald green. And it looked natural.

Then he bowed, swinging his arms to the sides. When he straightened, he proceeded to gabble, a series of clicks and glottal stops that made him sound like a feline with a hairball. Cat found out there was one telling difference between the

Kuriti she had met and this creature—now, she could not understand word one.

"Hold it, hold on!" she raised her hands. "I don't understand a word you're saying. Who are you?"

"Sleeper, have you met the jackoval?" she heard Q'Atha say.

Cat turned. The Elder's granddaughter stepped onto the balcony and beamed at them both.

"Not yet. Is that you?" Cat asked the green-skinned person.

He nodded and opened his mouth—and then, perhaps realizing doing so was no use, started to use his hands.

"The jackoval is the prince's manservant," the Elder's granddaughter informed Cat. "And he is a master cook," and here she leaned in and whispered, "much better than Poro, but I would not hurt her feelings for the world," and here she straightened again, "and no matter what exotic spice I give him, from wherever in the Seas or even Faiora, he can devise the most wonderful dish. He has been teaching me."

The young woman beamed again, and the jackoval—Cat didn't know if that was his name or his title and decided maybe it didn't matter—beamed back, his teeth bright white against his skin, and he gabbled something again.

Cat rubbed her neck. "You know, I have no clue what he's saying. Sorry, what you're saying," she said directly to him.

"It takes a while, Sleeper. You'll see."

The jackoval said something, and Q'Atha nodded. "That's right, we should pack, Sleeper. We will not have time later." The younger woman seized her hand and dragged her back inside, the jackoval waving—Cat understood that, at least.

If Cat thought the Elder's household was busy when Strian appeared, that was nothing compared to what had to be done now with the Court as a guest. It was like shopping on

Christmas Eve, except no one was trying to throttle anyone else.

But just in case, she sat near the fire and kept out of the way. No room was good enough, no hall grand enough, no fire hot enough for the Court. Cat could understand that. Back home, if the President had dropped by unexpectedly, the fever of activity would rival this. No matter how much the Court and his brother assured the Elder that their lodgings, a complex of tents erected directly outside the village, were adequate for their needs, that didn't stop the Elder from fussing.

Cat found herself sucked into the vortex of work. She packed one huge satchel—too much, she realized—and by the time she managed to tie the flap closed, she was exhausted.

She looked. Was that a cry?

Yes—and voices, loud and rapid, and the house began to tremble as the thunder of galloping horses filled the air. What the—

Cat grabbed onto a table to stay on her feet. "What the hell's *that*?"

"Quer'Cadrine! Come see!" she heard Q'Atha shout.

Grabbing her cloak, Cat slipped out the door and was nearly knocked down by the stream of people as they ran by. They all seemed to be looking at something in the distance, something she couldn't see over the crowd.

The jackoval ran past, nodding as he did, gesturing for her to follow. She lost sight of him almost within seconds. Next she tried to flag down someone who could tell her what was happening. She chose a matronly-looking woman. "Excuse me, what's—"

"The festival has begun," the woman said, a broad smile on her face, barely slowing to answer. "Toward the hills!"

Cat looked up, but from her vantage point, she could see nothing. "When in Rome," she muttered. She, too, began to run, feeling like a lemming.

She turned the corner and immediately saw Quer'Ali and Q'Atha ahead of her on the stone terrace that rose above the street and ran parallel to it, going from building to building. "Well, maybe they can tell me what's going on," she muttered. She ran up the shallow set of steps and joined them as they walked toward the hills.

"Sleeper! The firewarriors have come!" Q'Atha said, her eyes shining. "They've come out early for the festival because of the Court!"

"The what?" Cat asked as she held onto the railing, out of breath by now. The girl slowed to match her pace.

The Elder did the same but said nothing, instead watching the hills, finally visible above the villagers. She stopped. "Look!" she said with a smile. "They come!"

Cat looked and saw the looming darkness of the hills in front of them. During the day, the hills were just...there, evoking no emotion, certainly not for a Seattleite, accustomed to being surrounded by mountainous territory.

But here...the village was surrounded by hills close by, and somehow, they seemed menacing in the darkness. For whatever reason, it made her skin crawl. She shivered.

Q'Atha noticed. "Sleeper? Are you aright?"

Cat closed her eyes for a second. "I don't—" she stopped as, finally, she caught sight of what had the villagers in thrall.

From the top of the hill nearest Gates Mount came riders, perhaps a dozen, maybe more, dressed in black from head to toe. A bloodcurdling cry rippled from their throats and carried down to the village and it surrounded them, in front of them and above them and below them.

The keening cry cut through Cat's bones. Her heart pounding, she watched as hooded riders, whooping and waving wooden staffs with both ends ablaze, came thundering into the village. The fire on the staffs burned a vivid green, spitting and sparking, making the men and the horses seem to glow emerald.

"What *is* that?" Cat whispered. She rubbed her arms.

"Firewarriors. To signal the start of the Festival of the Firesleepers," Quer'Ali said, rapt.

"Firewarriors," Cat repeated as the crowds parted to let the men through. "What the hell is a firewarrior?"

It was a festival, she discovered. As soon as the horsemen vanished back into the darkness whence they had come, the entire village stirred with purpose. Within hours, the village was transformed, filled with streams of bright red and blue raffia hanging from home to home, music wailing from instruments Cat couldn't identify, on which were played melodies she had never heard. The streets filled with festival-goers in bright clothing, each celebrant with something that looked like a parchment flower in hand. Q'Atha slipped one into hers.

"What is it?" Cat asked. It looked like parchment, but it wasn't. Instead, it was a light, oiled paper, intricately twisted and folded to form a flower, looking like a cross between a dahlia and a star.

"It is a memory bloom, Sleeper," the girl told her as she picked up another scrap and deftly began to fold it. "*Huirin.*"

They were sitting on the steps of the Elder's house, and Q'Atha, clearly a veteran at folding the flowers even at her age, had a pile of the paper blooms already formed beside her, all in similar shapes. Nearby were Infa and her daughter, who were both industriously twisting paper.

"They're for the festival, Sleeper," explained Quer'Ali, who was sitting on a stool on the terrace behind them. Instead of twisting the paper, the way her granddaughter was, she had her sciarra in hand, cutting a flower. Considering the older woman had been in a frenzy of activity only an hour before, she seemed amazingly calm. "They're to guide the firesleepers."

"I see," said Cat politely, though she didn't.

She picked up a bloom the Elder had just finished and examined it. This one had been cut into a five-petal shape with small notches at the tips of the petals. It was dainty, smaller than the curved portion of her palm.

She looked down toward the village square, where there must have been nearly a dozen women and girls, all industriously producing flowers, by hand or by sciarra.

"The firesleepers were just here, weren't they? They wouldn't know their way back?"

The Elder smiled as she finished another parchment blossom. "We welcomed the firewarriors, Quer'Cadrine. The firewarriors protect the firesleepers."

Firewarriors, firesleepers. Right. Swiftly, Cat raced through few Kuriti terms she had gleaned thus far and came up empty. "I don't remember you having mentioned the firesleepers."

At that, the Elder put down her knife. "The firesleepers are the dead come back for the festival, Sleeper," she explained. "For most of our days, they are simply our dead, our ancestors gone home. But one night each year they come back to dance with us. And every festival we pray for our dead, killed from waterfire. This year," she added, a note of sorrow creeping into her voice, "we all pray for the little prince Temer. Perhaps his mother will show him the way here, for otherwise he's too young to know."

Not for the first time since she had heard the story of the abducted child, Cat winced. "Is that why I haven't seen the Court since the ceremony? I've seen most everyone else who came with him here, but I haven't seen him or his brother."

The flower-makers around her stirred uneasily. "The Court is preparing for the coming battle," the Elder said.

The more Cat heard about this coming battle, the less happy she was. She picked up a huirin bloom and examined it. "Is this something the Sleepers take part in?"

"Only in spirit," the Elder said. "The preparation is part fast, part prayer, part grooming." She paused. "You'll see."

A sudden cheer went up. Cat looked up at the hillside, not far from Gates Mount. She dropped the delicate bloom. "Oh, my God! *Fire!*"

Panicked, she looked around—but all she could see were happy faces, and worse, they were cheering. Was she the only one who saw the glow? "*Fire!*" she screamed. "The hillside's on fire!"

Cat felt the Elder's hand on her shoulder. "Calm, Sleeper. Watch," the older woman said, below the exultant cries of the crowd. "The firesleepers can find their way now."

As Cat watched, she realized the bursts of flame she could see in the hills surrounding Gates Mount were not outbreaks of wildfire. What she had thought was uncontrolled fire was, instead, individual lights—lanterns—that coalesced into patterns she could discern but couldn't fathom the meaning of.

"This is how we greet our dead, Sleeper," the Elder said. Cat glanced at her; the woman's face was bright. "This is how we greet our loved ones, gone from us. For me, it is my son, Q'Atha's padeh. And my lover, who is gone from me many years."

Startled, Cat said, "I'm sorry. I didn't know."

The Elder smiled. "They both died in a waterfire burst many years ago. But my son left me children to remember him by, though I miss him terribly everyday. And he comes home to me once a year as a firesleeper."

The points of fire up in the hills began to move toward town, and eventually Cat could see they were lanterns held by the hooded warriors. But the intricate patterns etched in the hillside remained, burning briskly. There were three distinct symbols, she saw. "Do the patterns up there mean anything?"

The Elder smiled again—or perhaps she had never stopped. "Kuriti symbols for life, death, and fire. That is how the firesleepers know to come home. And the lanterns we use to dance with the dead," she added. "You'll see."

Cat watched as the black-hooded horsemen rode back into town, lanterns high in their hands this time instead of flaming staffs.

It was surreal. The horsemen came galloping down the main street of the village, yelling...and one of them came to a hard stop in front of the Elder's home, kicking up the dust. He yanked off his stallion's black hood, only pulling off his own after he dismounted. Cat stood there, gaping, as Strian grinned at her, his face streaked with black soot. "Sleeper," he said. He laughed. "You look surprised."

The Elder didn't seem fazed at all. "It has been many years for you, has it not?" she asked.

His features were almost unrecognizable. He flashed a grin, his teeth bright against his smudged face. "More years than I care to count, cousin."

Amused, the Elder handed him a huirin bloom. She looked happier than when she was talking about the firesleepers, and for that Cat was glad. "You looked as if it was the first time you had ever played a firewarrior but I know it was not," the Elder exclaimed, reaching up to pinch his cheek.

Cat stared as Strian grinned and kissed the hand of his cousin.

"It has been years. Until now I have not participated in the fire festival since before I entered the Kama," he mused. "I think I was seventeen, but I cannot be sure."

"So young," the Elder said with a laugh. "Do I remember you being unseated by your fiery torch?"

"Has my cousin told you of the fire festival, Sleeper?" Strian asked, shifting his focus. The Elder cackled, but let the change in topic go.

"Only a little. Who rides? Only the men?" Cat asked, intrigued. "All the flower-makers seem to be women."

"It depends," Strian said as he accepted a wet cloth Q'Atha offered and wiped the soot off his face. "Closer to Faiora, men and women both make huirins. But mostly, the firewarriors are chosen by lots and the youngest men in the village are allowed to participate after they come of age. I lost the lottery my first year but I won in the second, and afterward, I went to Kama."

That explained his and his brother's familiarity with the region. "So you grew up here?"

"Here and the Podani, with our cousins. The children of the Court grow up everywhere," he told her. "We grow to know our country well, and that is how it should be. For our right to rule it, we must know it."

What had he looked like as a kid? In her mind's eye, Cat could see him as a boy, barely out of puberty, eagerly smearing the ash on his face and donning the black garb that marked the firewarriors. She could imagine him following the older, more confident firewarriors in their rides through town, the slower, more elaborate rides down the hills, arriving at the village green in triumph.

She could see Strian eagerly doing it all—but somehow, she couldn't see his brother doing any of it. "Not your brother? Not the Court?"

"The Court has other worries," Strian said, shaking his head. "Even as a child."

Gilcris had never been a child. She knew that much.

The Elder noticed. "Quer'Cadrine, are you aright?"

Cat shook her head, then nodded when she realized what the question was. She was getting tired, and it was starting to show. "I'm overwhelmed, Elder. I've never seen anything like this festival."

"Your world sounds like a sad one, Quer'Cadrine. Like a dark place filled with perils and ills you cannot control."

Cat looked at the older woman and then at Strian. "And you can control yours?"

Quer'Ali paused. "We cannot control our ultimate destinies, but we can control who and what is around us. Can you say the same?"

Cat was about to tell her yes—and then she remembered Mark, who looked so like Strian she had confused them, and how he was waiting for her to die.

After she thought about it, she shrugged. "I don't have an answer, Elder," she muttered. She rubbed the back of her neck.

"Come, Sleeper. Cousin," Strian said. He took one last swipe at his face, leaving it almost clean. "It is time to go to the river."

"Why?" Cat asked. The others around them seemed to know. They started walking in groups toward the water, arms full of the dainty folded-paper huirins. This time, they were in no hurry, almost sauntering. "Do the firewarriors put on a display there too?"

"Now it is our turn to put on the display. Do you have loved ones to remember, Sleeper?" the Elder asked as they joined others headed toward the river, their faces bright. Somewhere nearby, music Cat couldn't identify began to play, a lively tune, befitting a party. "Do you have someone, although I do not know if they can visit from where they are?"

Cat started to shake her head—but then stopped. "My mom and dad," she said finally. She hadn't thought of them except in passing for years. "They died when I was very young."

"Have you been alone all this time?"

Cat turned her head at the question. It came from Strian.

"It must have been hard for you growing up," he said.

She shrugged, reflecting on the question. "Hard or not, I grew up, Pir Strian," using his title for the first time. "We all do. It was one thing when I was too young to understand but not now. Life just is."

"Did you grow up with family at all?" Quer'Ali asked.

Cat didn't know how to answer that either. More than anything else, she wanted no pity. "I lived with an aunt for a while, but I found out I had an inheritance she was embezzling from me so I moved out and—anyway, I grew up. Case closed." She waved it off, hoping that would be that.

"It must have been hard to be alone," he persisted.

She sighed. "It was at first but then I figured out the only one I could depend on was me, and so I did. I went to school, I got scholarships, I graduated."

"No lover?"

That was it. Cat stopped and faced both the Elder and Strian. "He wanted my money too. I mourn my parents, and no one else."

She couldn't look at Strian. That was the part of her life she was glad to escape. She didn't need to be reminded of it by people in her dreams.

She didn't say anything else until they arrived at the riverfront.

Her dark disposition lifted a little when she looked around. The riverfront was illumined by a cluster of torches burning a vivid apple green, making the festival-goers look a little seasick. But the mood of everyone seemed too cheerful to be put off by the blazing, spitting glow. Not only that, if she thought the music was loud before, she was mistaken, because this was clearly where the heart of the festivities lay.

Cat recognized Boyo, the farmer's son, in the crowd. He was carrying a worn, lumpy leather folder, bound with strips of black leather. He saw her and waved, and as she watched, he turned to a gray-haired man who she guessed had to be his father, noting their resemblance. The man was wearing a heavy, sturdy leather belt around his waist, on which was fastened a series of what looked like miniature bongo drums of varying sizes with piping connecting each drum to the next.

She turned her attention back to Strian and the Elder. Strian apparently had not noticed her focus had wandered since he himself was looking away, at anything and anyone but her, Cat guessed. "I'm sorry to have caused you discomfort, Quer'Cadrine," he said. "I never suspected the Sleeper for our time of need would be so alone."

As she watched, the farmer's son and the farmer himself, musical instruments in hand, laughed at something. The farmer clapped his son on the shoulder, and together, they slipped into the crowd.

Envy, unusual and unwelcome, flooded Cat. With a bitter taste in her mouth, she answered, "What did you expect the Sleepers to be? We're here as sacrificial lambs, aren't we?"

"I expected them—you—to be Kuriti, Quer'Cadrine," Strian answered. "I expected them to know us and for them to be as familiar as ourselves." His mouth set.

"Surprise," she said, and she wasn't sure how she meant it.

"Well, you will know us soon enough," the Elder said.

The woman tried to sound cheerful. Cat had known her long enough to tell that and shrugged. She thought she had long accepted her life, but to her dismay she was wrong.

Cat was amazed at the crowds of villagers now clustered at the riverside. Where had they all come from? "What's going on here?" she asked, her dark mood lifting. "Is everyone in town here?"

It sure looked like it. She saw every single soul she had met in her stroll around town with the Elder's granddaughter. Further, they all looked bright-eyed and happy, as though they celebrated a reunion whenever they could. "This is basically Halloween, right? Elder, what *is* this?"

The older woman flashed a smile. "Soon," the Elder promised. She reached out and grabbed three huirin blooms from Q'Atha. "Take a flower, Sleeper," the older woman invited.

"Your granddaughter—granddat—already gave me one."

"Take another," the Elder persisted. "One for each hand."

Cat did. "Now hold it out," the Elder said, gesturing so the huirin was nestled in the palm of her hand.

"Now what?"

"Wait," Strian said, who had blooms of his own in hand.

The crowd around them hushed, waiting for something she didn't understand, when out of the darkness she heard...something.

In a matter of seconds a flurry of individual lights seemed to appear out of nowhere, drifting down like a cloud of cherry blossoms. "What is that?" Cat whispered.

"Look," Strian said, his voice low. "Wait."

Cat watched as the bright, tiny lights came closer and finally became identifiable as fireflies, brightening the riverside. Then one by one, they settled into the huirin blooms the festival-goers held.

Cat stared, barely breathing, and watched as a firefly hovered and burrowed into the bloom in her right hand. "What are they doing?" she whispered.

"Shh," Strian said, keeping his voice hushed. "Just watch."

The firefly burrowed and burrowed until all Cat could see of it was the glow of its light through the folded paper, dimming and growing in turns.

She glanced at the Elder and Strian, who were both staring at the huirin in their hands as they began to glow. Her hand began to feel warm.

"*Firri*, Sleeper," Strian whispered. "Firri will light the way for the firesleepers to return to us."

Cat stared as a firri sank into the waiting huirin in her other hand. The creature took shelter in the folds and — "Elder, are these bugs setting the blooms on fire? The palms of my hands are starting to feel…"

"Calm, Sleeper," the older woman soothed. "Watch."

Tiny fires were burning in the middle of both paper flowers, and as soon as the blooms started to burn brightly, the firri rose and went about their way.

Cat stared at the firri floating away. She didn't notice the quickly warming sensation on the skin of her palm until…

"Ahh! Fire!" she screamed. She started to drop the flowers.

Strian swooped and caught the blooms, deftly balancing them. "No, Sleeper. Wait and see," he said, handing them back to her.

"They're on *fire*! Why do I want to hold onto them?"

"The heat spreads but does not overwhelm," he told her. "Wait."

She looked at him. He was holding onto his blooms, and those firri had set his on fire too. The tiny blazes didn't seem to bother him at all.

In fact, Strian and the Elder were smiling. Confused, she examined her huirin. They *seemed* to be burning, but other than the initial warmth she felt on her hands, and the light at the heart of the bloom, the fire consumed no more of the folded paper. Her hands felt no hotter than they did when the firri had first landed. "What *is* this?"

"The huirin act like lanterns, Sleeper," the Elder explained. Smiling, she brought hers close to her face. "That is how our loved ones find their way back to us for the festival. Watch what we do. To the River Pon now."

They made their way to the riverfront, and Cat followed the lead of the Elder and Strian as, one by one, they gently placed the brightly burning blooms on the surface of the water and watched as the huirin, so many of them, drifted down the current. Dozens of burning flowers were bobbing on the river, Cat saw, all making their way to the beloved dead, until she couldn't tell anymore which ones were hers.

The tiny blazing blooms bobbing down the river drained her sour mood. "They're beautiful," she whispered. Her eyes started to water. She wasn't going to cry. She wasn't.

Would she be one of them, she wondered? The beloved dead?

She looked around and watched as the festival-goers clustered around to place their own huirin on the river current.

Cat recognized a tall, dark figure, odd in the crowd in that he had no huirin in hand…though he should have, she realized. "There's your brother. Isn't he going to do this thing?"

"The Court is here?"

Strian and the Elder whipped their heads around, searching. "I thought he should—" the Elder began, but Strian shook his head.

"Not here. My brother, I could have told you, Sleeper, was—preparing for his duties," he said. But his voice was strained. The Elder placed her hand on his shoulder.

Cat glanced at the two of them. They weren't saying something, but it was none of her business. She shrugged. "I just figured he would be out here with a couple of those flowers—"

"He has had too much to bear," Strian said, and his tone of desperation made Cat stare at him. "He shouldn't be here. He should be resting."

Well, whatever was going on, she wasn't going to find out right then. "How much can he relax when there's this much noise and music nearby? Must as well invite him, right?" Cat waved, trying to get the Court's attention.

She succeeded. One minute Gilcris, Ruler of the Silver Seas—or whatever, high muckety-muck—was an isolated individual in the midst of a crowd, but once he saw her wave, he became human again, connecting with those around him.

He didn't look particularly happy, Cat noted. Rather, he looked...resigned. He tried to smile as he approached them though. "Good festival to you," he said. The smile made him look as though he was in pain. "Have my brother and the Elder explained the festival to you, Sleeper?"

Cat shrugged. "They've tried, but I'm not sure I understand."

"Surely you have loved ones who have passed from your life in your Shiatta."

"My parents. But I don't think I'll see them tonight."

Gilcris smiled—or winced, it was hard to tell. "We do not see our loved ones, not unless we are very fortunate. We feel them."

Cat frowned. "How?"

That must have been a silly question, because Strian laughed. "We do things differently here in Kurit, I think."

It was hard to learn anything if no one explained the details! This was giving her the start of a headache, a little niggle between her eyes. "No shit, Sherlock. I still don't—"

"They're here!" she heard someone cry. She turned around.

An old woman Cat remembered seeing during her walk around the village, memorable for her long silver-white curly hair flowing past her shoulders, raised her hands. Something—something Cat didn't recognize, but could have sworn looked like a film of gossamer—floated down out of the sky and surrounded her. "My lover! My babies! My madeh and padeh! They're all here!" the woman cried. Tears started to pour down her creased, worn face.

Collective sighs went up around her as others began to search the sky for signs of their own. Cat continued to watch the old woman, whose face shone with ecstasy as she seemed to embrace her loved ones long gone. "Does she think she's seeing her family? Really?" Cat asked, hushed.

Her head started to hurt and she didn't know why.

"But she is," Gilcris said, with a confidence Cat would have thought he could not have felt. "Years ago, I saw my own madeh and padeh at festival when I needed them most. Why would you disbelieve what the old woman believes is true?"

Cat paused. "I don't know. Just because it's not our way."

"You must lead quiet and tragic lives if your loved ones cannot come to visit you on occasion."

His eyes were the most sorrowful she had ever seen. "You may be right," she said, for the first time in years yearning to see her parents again.

"Believe, Sleeper," the Court whispered, audible despite the crowd. He raised his face to the skies. "I wish I could see them again, but I know this year I will not."

He opened his hand, where he had his own huirin after all, burning bright. He made his way to the river, where he floated his single blossom, and they watched as his tiny blaze of light meandered down the river, soon lost in the cluster of bobbing blooms.

"Why not?" Cat asked, barely in a whisper. Her head was starting to ache from the incessant drumming and loud music, but she ignored it.

Gilcris watched until his light of huirin disappeared, swallowed by the darkness. "My children are too young to make the journey, and their mother would have to be with them," he said matter-of-factly, as though, indeed, his family had simply stayed home. "But I will see them soon. The war will be over, and I will see them again."

Behind her, she heard Strian catch his breath. "No, brother," she heard him say.

"It can't be helped, Stri," the Court said, and his voice grew unexpectedly strong. "I will do what I must do, then—"

"Brother, you have more years ahead of you than I can count. There will be better times—"

"No." Gilcris' voice sharpened. "My years are behind me. Understand me. But I will do what I must."

Cat glanced at them both. Whatever was going on...

All of a sudden the earth began to tremble, then quake, as though someone were knocking on a very large door. Cat looked up—and staggered. *The sky was swaying.* Then she heard a scream. Someone shouted, "Waterfire!"

Strian looked around. *"Where?"*

Where became clear. "Run!" screamed the elderly woman who had welcomed the ghosts of her family as she hurried past, back toward the village. "Waterfire, at river's edge!"

Cat pressed her hand against her temple. The pounding in her head was threatening to split it in two, but she wasn't going to let it. She willed herself not to black out, so she could see this thing that seemed to hold the country in thrall.

When she did, she was sorry.

At first glance it didn't look like anything more than a mist hovering near the river's edge, and as she watched it became more solid, sparkling. It changed form. Before, it resembled a spool not unlike a tornado, but then it twisted and reformed in the shape of a wave, not large yet but threatening to grow. The wave crystallized. It seemed to grow arms—it threatened to grab a child who wasn't moving fast enough, but Strian raced forward and shoved the little boy to safety, rolling himself away from the danger. The wave had voice—it roared and swallowed noise all around them, and it seemed to swallow light and everything concrete in front of its path.

"Run!" Gilcris yelled above the roar. "Run now and don't stop until you get to higher ground!"

He shoved Cat in the direction the other villagers had gone, and then he leaped to help his brother off the ground. "*Go!*"

Cat froze.

I know you.

She had never seen anything like it, but it had a beauty she never would have suspected. She closed her eyes, willing herself to remember it.

"Sleeper! *Go!*" she heard Strian yell.

Her eyes opened.

With a thunderous roar, the crystalline wave spread, stretching its arms into either direction, scattering the villagers moving too slowly. At another familiar voice, Cat turned and recognized Yosh the butcher. "Quickly," the Elder shouted. "Up to Gates Mount!"

The servants from the Elder's great hall bundled wailing children and began to run toward the Gates, near where Cat had seen the symbols of life and death and rebirth blaze in the darkness just a short while ago. "Why that way?"

"To safety, Sleeper," the Elder shouted. "The Gates will keep us safe! Come! Yosh, take the Sleeper and run as fast as you can!"

Yosh picked Cat up as though she were a child herself. "Welcome to the fire festival, Sleeper," he shouted above the roar of the crystalline wave. "The waterfire season has begun."

Chapter Seven

ॐ

The enormous butcher hoisted Cat like a sack over his burly shoulder and started to run, the Elder keeping up. "Let me down," Cat gasped, struggling. "I can run as well as the rest of you!"

Yosh paused, but with a glance at the Elder, he obliged.

"Go on, Yosh," the old woman ordered. Cat had to hand it to her, the Elder was remarkably spry, keeping up with those half her age. "We'll be right behind you."

Cat stumbled when her feet hit the ground. She wasn't used to running for anything, not in years. The Elder didn't slow down, however, simply grabbed her hand and pulled her along.

"Are we going straight up the hill?" Cat wheezed. Her head still hurt, but the pain was dissipating, at least. The path was steep up to the Gates, and she wasn't sure she could make it without at least a pause, with or without the Elder's help.

"The waterfire will not follow us uphill," the Elder said, her grip firm, not seeming out of breath at all. "We must climb the nearest hill and Gates Mount is closest. Now hurry!"

Cat looked around as she was pulled along. The once-festive atmosphere of the villagers, dressed in their finery and celebrating the return of their dead, had turned into a riot. If she were to pause or even slow down, she would be trampled, and she would have no one to blame but herself.

So she ran, stumbling on occasion but not stopping until she felt the ground beneath her feet curve upward. She slowed, straining to look around as much as she could.

Whereas the village itself felt unfamiliar to her, somehow new and unknown, this hillside felt...familiar.

Gates Mount. Gates Mount, where she and her two coworkers had been found.

"Sleeper, did you sense any waterfire?" the Elder asked, slowing to a quick walk, glancing behind her from time to time. Like the others moving up to Gates Mount, the older woman was watching the village down below.

Cat winced. "I had a headache," she confessed. "It didn't occur to me. I just thought I wasn't feeling well." She had forgotten. An emotion she didn't let herself feel very often, guilt, leaked into her consciousness. But this time she felt guilt with no resentment. This time no one like Mark was trying to manipulate her.

The Elder glanced at her as they arrived at Gates Mount. They were surrounded by the villagers, all waiting. "For you there seems to be no such thing as a simple headache, Sleeper. Please. When you feel it coming on, tell us."

"I will. I'm sorry," Cat said. She took a deep breath. The pain between her eyes was diminishing.

"The waterfire's died down," she heard someone shout. Instead of looking toward the village, as the others were doing, she took the opportunity to look up the slope of Gates Mount.

It was cool and green and peaceful. It was so green it looked unreal. As if AstroTurf had been improved to look more and feel more like the grass it was meant to replace. As some of the bolder villagers started to walk back toward the village, she looked around some more. Walking all the way up to the Gates, past the villagers who were starting back down, she knelt and felt the grass. It was dry, it was soft, it was clearly real, but unaccountably, it looked — artificial.

She straightened and looked around. Everything looked perfect. It was all organic, no plastic or steel, she had no doubt. But it was too perfect.

She shivered.

"Sleeper, we can go back to the village now. The waterfire has dissipated," she heard the Elder say.

Cat turned around. "So this is Gates Mount."

"Yes. This is where you were found."

It was only the two of them now, their voices muffled in the thick silence. Behind them were the Gates. Cat found herself alternately wanting to look at them, even examine them, but dreading the idea as well. "So we were found at the top?" she asked, her voice hushed.

The Elder nodded. She started to look around then stopped. Perhaps she wasn't comfortable there either. "We saw something glint at the top of Gates Mount. Boyo came running, all the way from his farm to tell us he saw something. And we came up here to find out what."

"Why would you bother? It could have been anything."

The Elder shook her head. And started to look around but stopped again. "Gates Mount is sacred, Sleeper. It also does not invite—the casual traveler. And the villagers stay away. Something up on Gates Mount was odd enough we had to see." She shifted from one foot to the other, looking like her age. "Shall we return?"

Cat glanced at her and realized the woman, who seemed to be the wisest person she had met, in Seattle or otherwise, was uneasy. She was nervous, like all the others who came up to Gates Mount.

And she herself felt comfortable.

She was truly an outsider.

* * * * *

The realization stayed with her as she accompanied the Elder back to S'nal. The waterfire outburst had been small and done comparatively little damage, but the Elder told Cat where the waterfire touched the river, fish of all kinds had exploded from within, raining fish on the docks.

"Like a tornado," Cat mused as she followed the Elder, holding her hand over her nose as they walked through the area, sidestepping the cleanup under way. The fish were starting to stink already.

The older woman glanced at her. "You have something like it?"

Cat shrugged. "We have something called tornadoes that can sort of have that effect. I don't know much about it, except they occur when the atmospheric conditions—" She stopped when she saw something shine on the ground. "I know that hair," she said, realization dawning. "I saw that hair before the waterfire…"

She stooped and gingerly picked up the lone curl of flowing silver-white hair, on the ground next to a pile of blackened ash. "Elder…"

The older woman touched Cat on her shoulder. "At least she is with her family," she reminded her softly.

Cat pressed her hand against her mouth. "I'm going to be sick now," she mumbled. The stench she had assumed came from just the fish had other sources.

"Sleeper, go back to the great hall, check on the other Sleepers," the Elder said. "I will follow, but for now I must see what has happened."

Cat did, hurrying away from the waterfront littered with spoiling fish guts and dust, hand still pressed against her mouth. First she checked the Elder's home. She was relieved to see it was more or less untouched, save a brand-new layer of dust. Then she checked on Kevin and Margot.

They slept on, the only things in the house untouched by either time or dust. Kevin was as smooth-chinned as he had been that morning in the university library, while Margot was no more and no less pregnant than she had been that morning as well—and by Cat's reckoning, it had been at least some days. It was as if they had remained in a place and time that needed no change.

Yet another oddity. Because they did look alike, she could understand why she would be reminded of Mark when she looked at Strian, even though they were so dissimilar in personality.

She could understand, even, why she would see in Gilcris' face some semblance of Kevin, because Kevin always treated her with respect the way Gilcris did. And if she looked hard enough, she could see pregnant Margot in the face of the Elder's granddaughter, Q'Atha, who looked the way Margot had when Cat first met her, when they were both college freshmen, fresh and optimistic about the world.

But why in the world would she dream Margot and Kevin would be untouched by dust when dust covered everything?

Cat bent down and touched Margot's face. "I don't know what's going on but whatever it is, I hope you're dreaming good dreams, Maggs," she whispered. "I wish I could promise to find out what was going on, but I don't think I'm going to have the time."

"It's good to say farewell to your friends, Sleeper."

Cat turned. It was Q'Atha, with an armful of woolens in her hands and a broom tucked into the crook of her arm. Cat guessed the young woman was sweeping away the dust the waterfire caused, taking the opportunity to pack yet another bag for her grandmother. "It's good to bid them away. You'll not be seeing them for some time at least."

"I still don't know why they shouldn't go with us," Cat said. "I think they should stay close to us. Me, at least."

The younger woman shook her head. "Grandme thought they should stay as close to Gates Mount as possible."

"Then why should I be going?"

"Because you woke up, Sleeper, and they did not."

Cat stared at Kevin and Margot again. "I don't know," she began uncertainly. "I'm not sure I want to leave them alone in a place we don't know —"

"But they are the Sleepers and no one would dare touch them, Sleeper," another voice said.

Cat turned to see the farmer's son trailing Q'Atha, holding another armful of linens. "Boyo. You were the one who saw us first up on Gates Mount."

Unaccountably, the girl beamed when the boy nodded. "I was out in the field with my brothers when I saw some sort of light up there, and I ran into town."

"But why would you do it? Run, tell people. The glint could have been anything."

"The scriptures, Sleeper," the young man said. "The sacred scrolls. We knew the Sleepers would be coming at our time of greatest need, and you came."

"Just like that? The light could have been anything up on the hill. A piece of glass."

Boyo shook his head. "Not up on Gates Mount. Nothing lives up on Gates Mount. And nothing else could have been up there."

He believed it. The trust in his voice was so pure, it made Cat's throat hurt. She didn't know what else to say. Finally she managed, "Thank you. I might have gotten sick, and my friends, if we had been up there soaked to the bone for very long."

The boy shook his head. "Nothing could have happened to you, Sleeper."

And he was going to stick to his guns, no matter what. Religion is the opiate for the masses, no matter where they were, she thought, and while she wished she could believe her own cynicism, she couldn't. "And that's why you don't think I should have any problem leaving my friends behind when I go to this ritual ceremony thing?"

"That's right," Q'Atha piped up.

Not unlike Boyo's, the girl's shining, peaceful expression made Cat envious. She couldn't remember a time when she had believed in anything with that much certainty. She chewed on her lip. "I wish I could be so sure."

"In any case they will be watched. One of my brothers has volunteered to be one of the guards," Boyo said. "We will protect them, no matter what."

"But not you?"

The young man shook his head. "I will be accompanying you, Sleeper."

"Boyo is going with his padeh, who is the ceremonial otho drummer," Atha said. She beamed. "Boyo plays the ranne now but he's been practicing the otho, and he's very good already. He could take over for his padeh if his padeh took sick."

That explained the flute-like instrument Cat remembered Boyo had during the festival. "What's an otho drum? I think I saw you with your father during the festival," she said. "It looked like a bunch of drums? He was wearing them on a belt? Was that your father?"

"That was him. And those are the drums for the waterfire ceremony," Q'Atha explained, her eyes shining as she glanced at the farmer's son. "There's an otho drummer, a lupe player and a bonoist, and they all take part. But the lupe player and the bonoist are coming from other villages, and they will meet us at the Podani."

The girl's enthusiasm was infectious, and despite her misgivings, Cat smiled. "I can't wait," she murmured, and she was more serious than not. A music specialist she wasn't. "Do you think you could let me hear you play? Your otho drum?"

Boyo shrugged modestly, though his grin was fit to burst. "There is not much to it. But I will play for you after supper on the journey because someone will find a lupe and start playing, and I'll join in. Or perhaps I'll play the ranne."

The mention of others on the journey reminded Cat. "Who else is going from the village? The Elder?"

"No, I am not," the familiar voice said.

Cat turned. The Elder had the shattered remains of a small stoppled bottle in one hand, a broom in the other. "The waterfire has taken its toll," she said dryly. "I am sending Q'Atha in my stead as S'nal's representative, since that will be her job before long, and I will stay and be part of the watchguard for the other Sleepers." She paused. "Say your farewells, Sleeper. You will not see them awhile."

The others left on their respective errands, leaving Cat alone with Kevin and Margot again.

In her heart of hearts she knew nothing would change, that they would be safe. And she would be doing all the traveling, all the experiencing, for the three of them.

She had better make it good.

Cat knelt between them. She tried to score the image of them in her mind to keep them with her. They had been her friends, Margot for many years and Kevin for only a few, but she could not have had better ones.

Her eyes were starting to prickle. She had to get out of there before she actually cried.

Cat swallowed hard and touched first Margot's hand—cool, moist, still—and then Kevin's. "Bye, guys," she whispered. "And with any luck, maybe I'll see you awake."

She reached into her pocket and touched her sheathed sciarra. Its hilt had her face carved into it, as well as those of Margot and Kevin, and she received it from a man who claimed to have known nothing about them when he had created it. What did *that* mean?

"How long is this trip? How long does it take to get there?" Cat asked when she caught up with the Elder and her granddaughter, Boyo nowhere to be seen for once.

"Five days' ride, Sleeper."

"So what happens when we get there?"

"The Court will be there, as will Pir Strian, for they have two of the Three Treasures of Kurit. The honorable uncle has the third. In the latest parley he agreed to participate in the ceremony, for it is nothing without the final Gem."

"What happens if he changes his mind?"

"Kurit and the outlying regions are consumed in a mass of waterfire, and all living things will die," the Elder said in an almost conversational tone. "That is when the largest burst of waterfire should be on the horizon according to our seers, and that is why the ceremony must take place then and there. With the ceremony, the worst of the waterfire that plagues us will be gone for another century, and we can rest easy again. Without..." Her tone was almost casual, as if this was something she spoke of every day. And perhaps it was.

"So there's no waterfire except every hundred years?"

"There are outbreaks every year, but the waterfire then are minor, easily avoided. The most those can do is to cause an unpleasant surprise."

"How much of a surprise?" Cat didn't like surprises, and she was finding all sorts of them here.

The Elder shrugged. "The fish you saw blown out of the water? Far less than that. Deadly nonetheless, if we are caught unawares and unable to get away."

Cat looked out the windows. Despite the late hour the townspeople were still cleaning up, as though it had been a particularly rowdy Mardi Gras celebration instead of a natural disaster. And maybe for them it was, although she could not fathom that either.

"Will there be any more waterfire occurrences between now and the ceremony?" she asked. She felt a pang of guilt for not having mentioned her headache, then scolded herself. These villagers had survived before her waterfire-predicting abilities, and they would survive after she was gone. But she liked the village and its inhabitants. She didn't want anything to happen to them.

This time, it was the granddaughter who shrugged. "Not likely, Sleeper. Those of us near it know to run when we see it. We learn when we are small, and we do not forget."

"Will you and the other townspeople be in danger from it?" Cat asked the Elder.

The older woman smiled faintly. "We will be wary, do not worry," she promised. "We have learned to be."

The old woman's eyes were still clear though more than a little worried. But it wasn't for herself, Cat guessed. The Elder was sending her grandchild on what was probably her first real journey. "Aren't you frightened? I mean, after what just happened—"

The Elder laughed. "Our time is short, Sleeper. It is something we always know. We do not invite its end, but we cannot deny it, either. We do what we can and we trust in those who can do more."

Cat smiled back. "The way you trust me to do what I can as your Sleeper to do whatever I must?" Was that clear?

It must have been, for the Elder nodded, choosing to say nothing more.

Cat sighed. She still had no clue what she was supposed to do, but she had others who were depending on her to figure it out. "I'll do what I can."

"We have faith in you. And we will help you in whatever you need, Sleeper," the Elder's granddaughter added.

"And Boyo too," the Elder added quickly, a twinkle in her eye. "Going along with his father. He'll be learning the otho for the ceremony, I hear. And keeping my Q'Atha company."

Her granddaughter blushed, and it became obvious what was going on there. Cat smiled wryly. "Should I be acting as chaperone?"

"No chaperone for my Q'Atha, Sleeper," the Elder told her. "Too young, as is Boyo."

The wise older woman did have a few blinders on. "Young is as young does," Cat said, before realizing that probably didn't mean anything to these people. "You'll have to explain things to me, Q'Atha."

The Elder's granddaughter had been beaming just a matter of minutes before. Now she was blushing, her gaze lowered. Cat smiled. So young. Had she been so young?

She was that young when she first met Margot. It had been sheer fortuity they had been assigned as freshman roommates at college. They hadn't gotten along at first. Margot was messy, Cat was neat. Cat had nothing else to do but study. Margot was from a large family, and this was her first opportunity to run free. They had learned to get along though—Margot had settled down eventually, and Cat learned to live it up a little. Margot had tutored her in calculus when Cat had been in danger of losing her scholarship, while Cat tutored her roommate through French.

She and Margot had gone through college together after that and they stayed on to graduate school, and when Margot decided to have a baby—tick tick tick, she said, *brrring*—Cat had been her Lamaze coach and certainly would have been there whenever she needed help raising the baby. Cat had provided the cynical eye for the most part while Margot had protected her from her own skepticism, reminding her there was a silver lining in a cloud once in a while.

Margot hadn't succeeded in making sure Cat was safe from the likes of Mark, though. From the beginning, he had proved to be less than wonderful. He cheated on her right from the start. When she had been diagnosed with her cancer, terminal, nothing to be done, he had stayed away for a month then come back—and started to pressure her to marry him, thanks to that insurance policy he knew she had.

Funny. Before, she had had Mark. Now, she had Strian, the likeness of Mark, but from what she could tell, nothing like him. And now she had Q'Atha, who reminded her of Margot.

"Will you be ready by dawn?"

Cat turned. It was Pir Strian, and he was dusty, too, as if he had joined in on the cleanup of the village.

"She will be ready, cousin," the Elder promised. "As will my granddat."

Strian nodded to Q'Atha. "And certainly, if all goes well, you will surely be welcome to explore the Podani."

Q'Atha's eyes lit up. She turned to the Elder. "Grandme! May I?"

"All *will* go well, cousin," the Elder emphasized to the prince. She and Strian exchanged glances. "If the Court and the prince welcome you, I have nothing to say nay to that, little one."

"I will make sure the Court welcomes you with open arms," Strian told her.

At that, Q'Atha squealed with delight—causing Cat to wonder once more, *Was I really so young?* —before she quieted down, grinning madly in some attempt at decorum. "I should finish the packing preparations now, Pir Strian," she said, her excitement bursting through as she began to gather the mounds of woolens she had dropped in her glee.

"The morrow, young cousin," Pir Strian said as Q'Atha skipped out of the room. They could hear the clack of her shoes against the floor as she started to run.

"You have made my granddat merrily glad, cousin," the Elder said, looking toward the doorway. "I have not seen her quite so happy in some time."

"She will be a good replacement for you when the time comes, cousin. Though that time, the hyagoths willing, will not be for many years yet."

"It comes when it comes," the Elder said. "It came, I am told, for Ginkgar of the guild of silverists, who was caught by the waterfire. He completed his last batch of sciarra only a fortnight ago. His grandson told me."

Cat looked up from the woolens she had been trying to fold. "Ginkgar? Oh, no."

The Elder and Strian looked at her. "He was the one you met on your walk around the village with Q'Atha, Sleeper?" the Elder asked.

"Yes. He told me this had been waiting for me." Cat drew the knife out of her pocket, untied the rawhide thongs and slipped out the sciarra from its sheath, its sleek lines glinting. "I certainly don't know what to do with it."

"Use it, no doubt. Keep you safe." The silver gleamed in the candlelight. Strian leaned forward, curious. "May I?"

Wordlessly Cat flipped it and offered him the hilt. Strian took it, and the Elder came closer to look as well.

"Your face is graven on the hilt, Sleeper," Strian observed. He turned it toward the light. Cat looked too, to see if she could figure out what other details they might be looking for, and she also wondered if they would recognize the other two faces on the hilt.

The Elder did. "The other two, they are of the other Sleepers, are they not, Quer'Cadrine?"

Cat nodded. "Ginkgar said he had been holding it for me and he'd made it weeks ago. It was—weird."

"Ginkgar knew," Quer'Ali said. "I will miss his wisdom, though his grandson's skills are excellent as a silverist."

Strian, meanwhile, was getting the feel of the knife. He hefted it, sliced through the air with it, let his wrists twist with it, as though, Cat thought, he imagined fighting with it. Well, better him than her. "Good weight," he said, approving. "Too light for me, but not for you."

"I thought it felt—warm," she said, remembering the meeting. "I wasn't expecting that. I thought it would be cold."

Strian frowned. "How do we know you didn't bring this with you?"

The Elder sighed. "Because I was there when the Sleepers were found, cousin, and we found nothing like this on her. We found things we had never seen and we would surely have recognized this, and how much it looked like Ginkgar's work, if we had found it with her. And remember, Q'Atha was there when the silverist presented it to her, and she too noted the images on the knife. That, too, was a sign. It is no trick."

Strian looked ashamed for a moment, as though the old woman must have scolded him on a long-ago occasion many years ago, and he had nothing else to say.

Sourly Cat said, "I can't tell you anything else." Though she felt a twinge of hurt for his disbelief, she had to approve. People here were too trusting by half. They had to distrust something, sometimes. "You don't have to trust me. I'm just telling you this. The knife—the sciarra—was given to me."

"If nothing else would satisfy, you could ask my granddat," the Elder pointed out. "And you know Q'Atha."

Strian turned away, rubbing his neck. "As you say. I do not understand this. This story of the Sleepers arriving, I did not think, would involve a woman who knows nothing about us."

"Perhaps you didn't expect to see Sleepers at all," Cat guessed. "Maybe you didn't expect to see anything helping you out. I know how it feels. I've had it plenty. You assumed you would do what you could and not depend on anything else."

Strian's irritated expression suddenly smoothed. "Perhaps you are right. I thought we would have to win the war and banish the waterfire on our own. I did not think we would need, or at least have, the prophecies to aid us."

"Sometimes you don't think God is going to help you at all?"

Strian frowned. "Our gods have been sleeping for lo these many years, Sleeper. I stopped believing they would awaken when my brother's queen died and took her stillborn daughter with her. Since then—I have thought we would have only ourselves in this. It is a private grief."

There was that pain in his eyes again, the one whenever he talked about his brother's late wife. "You must have been very fond of her," Cat guessed.

"She was sunlight itself. She laughed, and the world became a brighter place for a while. And then—"

She thought she knew. "Sometimes we all need help, Pir Strian," Cat said. Her voice got a little stronger. "You just didn't expect help to arrive in the form of *me*." She grinned, but it was a rueful grin. "And I have no idea how I am going to do it, so hang on. You may be right yet."

Strian laughed—actually laughed. Of course, Cat recognized, it was as much a laugh as her grin had been, but perhaps they were coming to a meeting of the skeptical minds after all. "The only thing we can do is find out what we have to do and whether we can."

He turned again to his cousin, who had been as still and quiet as a statue, or even the Gates up on the hill, during this exchange. "We ride at dawn," he said abruptly. "Will she be ready?"

The Elder met his gaze. "She will be ready if I must put her, trussed, on a horse myself, cousin."

"I'll be ready," Cat said.

Chapter Eight

ഋ

Cat helped in the preparations as best she could and before she knew it, she was huddled in the predawn chill, watching the last of the arrangements being made, waiting with the Elder.

"Waterfire appears mostly in the valleys, Sleeper." The Elder responded to Cat's muttered question. "From time to time during the season, but small. But the mother of waterfire…the burst of waterfire we cannot run from, the one that destroys everything it touches…every hundred years."

Cat had to marvel. Despite the hard chill of a winter daybreak, the older woman had not bothered with a cape, choosing to watch the activities in what amounted to shirtsleeves. "Waterfire is second nature to us," the Elder explained. "Most seasons, small bursts, we can avoid them. But every hundred years…the bursts of waterfire grow and grow, and there is nothing we can do…not until the Court summons the other holders of the Three Treasures to meet on the ceremonial grounds at the Podani. "

Cat shook her head as she huddled in her cape. "And you just accept it?"

"It defines us," the Elder said, her mouth drooping, and for a second, she looked tired. "Through the generations we have suffered for it, but we have always known the Sleepers will help us. Though it has been so long in the coming."

Cat shivered. The readying was almost finished. The Elder's granddaughter, perhaps gearing up for her eventual duties, supervised the final loading. She was barely visible in the heavy mist. Even the noise in the loading was dampened by the fog. "Pir Strian tells me your journey will be over higher ground, to avoid any unforeseen outbreaks," the Elder said.

"So it's safer in the higher elevations. I've been to Europe, and Russia, and even Asia, places thousands of miles away from Seattle, Elder, and I knew more what to expect in those places than I do here."

"Nor do we know," the older woman pointed out. "This journey will tell you what you need to know. Those journeys you must keep a clear mind for, Sleeper, as there is never any telling what to expect. All you can do is try. No one else can do that for you."

Her voice was calm and comforting, and a pang shot through Cat's heart. "I wish you were coming with us, Elder," she blurted out. "You've helped me so much since I've woken up here. I don't know what I'm going to do without you."

The Elder smiled. "I will always be with you, Sleeper. Think of me, and I will be there."

Cat's eyes teared up—and she was instantly embarrassed. "Thank you."

The Elder patted Cat on her cheek. "No thanks necessary. Do what you must," she said with a watery smile. "Poro, my cook, will be going along also, and she knows to do this, but please, look after my Q'Atha for me, that is all I ask."

The elderly woman brushed at her eyes. "Now, have you yet met your ride?" She took Cat by the hand and led her to a saddled gray mare. The horse, which was in the midst of feeding, stopped chewing for a moment and raised her head to stare at the two women. Cat had never seen a more dubious expression on an animal's face, not even on a cat. The horse snorted and shook her head as she took a step back.

The Elder stroked the nose of the mare and spoke softly. "This is Arriya," she said. "She is of good temperament and enjoys her apples, don't you, my dear? Come and say hello, Sleeper, for she will be your companion when others of your own kind cannot be."

Cat looked at the gray mare, which was bigger than she would have expected. If the horse were typical, it would also have teeth, which she knew by ugly past experience.

"Just reach out and stroke her nose, Sleeper," the Elder instructed. "It's all right. Just relax and open your thoughts."

Tentatively, Cat touched the bridge of the horse's nose. It was warm and the hide was smooth.

The mare snorted again and edged away, startling Cat, who hid behind the Elder. The mare whinnied and bucked and pawed at the ground before being stopped by Quer'Ali. "Calm, Arriya, calm," the Elder soothed as she grabbed the reins. "Sleeper, I don't know what's wrong. Arriya should have read you—"

"*Read* me? She's supposed to *read* me? What's that supposed to mean?" Cat cried as she inched back. "I don't think this is such a hot idea. I haven't been near a horse since I was a little kid and then—"

"Shh, shh, Arriya," the Elder soothed, stroking the horse. "Arriya should have read you, Quer'Cadrine, and introduced herself to you. She should have—"

"She didn't," Cat broke in, willing herself to stay put. After all, she was a human, a superior being, humans had domesticated horses for thousands of years— No. It didn't matter. The horse was bigger and a lot heavier. "Maybe she can't," Cat gabbled. "Maybe I'm not close enough to your kind and she can't read me. I don't think I can do this."

"Of course you can. Arriya, calm. The Sleeper is our ally," the Elder stage-whispered to the mare, keeping an eye on Cat. "She has come to help us. Please help her. She cannot read you, and you cannot read her. But she means well, and she is not used to your kind."

Perhaps it was the Elder's tone, or perhaps the mare did understand her, but Arriya did calm and stood still, breathing hard. But Cat noticed the mare didn't stop giving her a look of suspicion. No matter what anyone else said, Cat would have sworn that was the expression.

She was a human, Cat kept saying to herself. Superior being. *Homo sapiens* and all that. Heart pounding, she walked forward, one step at a time, until she was in front of Arriya again and the mare was staring at her, daring her.

Cat sighed. She didn't really need her fingers anyway. She touched the mare's nose again. "Hi, Arriya," she whispered. *Superior being, superior being,* she reminded herself.

Arriya didn't flinch, didn't buck, didn't bolt. She did, however, stare at Cat again before eventually going back to her feed.

The Elder stroked the horse one last time before she turned back to Cat. "So you heard nothing, felt nothing from Arriya?" she asked, a crease between her eyebrows. "That is most odd. Horse and rider always exchange pleasantries. It's the best way to ensure nothing happens to the rider if there is a mishap."

Cat exhaled and wiggled her fingers. She couldn't remember ever being so grateful she still had them. "Back where I come from, horses just do what humans tell them to and then once in a while there's an accident," she muttered. "They're beasts of burden."

The Elder glanced at her, as startled as Arriya's expression had been. "They are our allies. With an understanding forged between rider and horse, the journey fares much quicker and without incident."

Arriya snorted, but didn't stop eating. Cat glanced at the mare and could only guess what the horse was thinking—*I'm stuck with this one? I better eat while I can!*

"This is going to be so much fun," Cat muttered.

When the time came, the mare was patient when Cat had to mount. Arriya patiently waited as Cat tried not once, not twice, but three times to get up on the back of the horse.

Eilis Flynn

Cat finally managed to sit on Arriya and straightened—and realized she was much higher up than she was comfortable. She grabbed at the pommel of the saddle and held on tight, uncomfortably aware she was a single movement away from bad bruises and broken bones and even certain death.

The Elder caught her eye and smiled, patting the gray mare on the rump. "Arriya will take care of you if you take care of her, Sleeper," the older woman reassured her.

Cat looked at the horse. Flicking an ear, the horse chewed on an apple, seemingly oblivious. "I'll do my best," Cat told the Elder. Quickly, she patted Arriya, then went back to holding on for dear life.

Then the call went out—it was time. The collective horses pawed at the ground, restless to get on the way.

Cat took one look around. S'nal was a village, nothing more, a tiny settlement in a verdant valley surrounded by rolling hills and one distinctive one, Gates Mount, most people tried to avoid. The Elder was an old woman but clearly in charge, keeping in mind the best interests of her people. Surely there was nothing more.

But, Cat admitted, she would miss it all. She had gotten used to it, and it was something familiar—it was the only thing familiar—and the Elder was the calm voice of wisdom she always yearned for. It was too bad she had to find it all in her dreams.

"We will watch after your friends, Quer'Cadrine," the Elder said with a comforting smile. "No worries about that."

"Thank you for everything you've done," Cat said, her eyes welling again.

"Find what you need. Save us, Sleeper." The Elder patted Arriya again. With a toss of her head, the gray mare started off at a trot.

Cat bounced along with the horse, but that didn't stop her from looking back until she could no longer see the Elder. She

126

could remember doing just that her first day of kindergarten, turning around to check if her mother was still standing in the back. She never thought she would be doing so again.

Her journey had begun, but she wished she could feel more excited about it. If nothing else, she remembered quickly why she had never gotten back on a horse again.

She shifted around, trying to find a comfortable way to sit, only to discover there was none. Soon it became the proverbial vicious circle—beneath her, Arriya hesitated every time Cat shifted, and every time the mare hesitated, Cat had to shift.

"Have you ever ridden a horse before, Sleeper?" the Elder's granddaughter asked, coming up alongside her, riding easy on her own Depper. The morning fog was starting to lift; Cat could almost see in front of her.

"Not in a long time," Cat said shortly, shifting and doing her best to hang on. "Not since I was four. That was the last time. It was a country carnival and it was a pony, it bit me, and that was the last time."

"Ah," Q'Atha said, and nothing else for a while. Presently she said, "The journey would be weeks instead of one if we decided to walk, Sleeper," her upbringing with her grandmother evident in her calm voice.

But the soothing tone was easier to tolerate from an elderly woman.

Cat's lower back was starting to ache. Not to mention portions of her were going to be sore very, very soon. Not to mention she was starting to feel queasy. She decided to keep her focus on her pommel. The last thing she needed was to lose her breakfast. Fanadi, the mushy yellow stuff that seemed to be a great morning favorite among the villagers, did not sit well with her.

"Sleeper, Q'Atha, how goes it?" a familiar voice inquired.

Cat looked up warily. Strian looked comfortable astride, moving with enviable grace, in sync with his ride.

She really, really missed her car. She understood her car, broken taillight and all.

"Considering I haven't been on a horse in thirty years and I'm getting carsick, just fine, Pir Strian." She gulped air.

"You are not comfortable riding a horse, Sleeper?" he asked. "How do you travel? You do not travel long distances?"

Cat rolled her eyes. She shouldn't have mentioned it. "I have a twenty-mile commute on the monorail, over…never mind. I ride a carriage made of iron. That's our ride of choice." That was close enough without getting into specifics. "But yes, I travel distances when I have to."

But traveling in a convoy, surrounded by guards protecting the Court and his entire entourage and now even her, was nothing like a commute on the freeway. Instead of being trapped in a car, alone but for the sound of the radio or a CD, traveling on a horse meant she could speed up to speak to someone ahead or drop back to visit. Or at least Arriya did. The reality of dealing with horses—well, Cat could get used to it, but the smell of a horse was on a par with gasoline fumes.

There was one thing she couldn't get around. She was going to be stiff when she finally got off.

But no car could ever travel without her control. True, Arriya could no more read Cat's mind than she could the mare's, but clearly the horse knew the path and what to do so Cat didn't have to. That meant Cat could relax—or at least not worry about other drivers—and admire the countryside.

And there was so much to see! The evergreen of the rolling hills was like the better-kept parks she was used to, emerald and moist, and she recognized the ferns that crowded the side of the dusty road, similar to those she knew from home. But no concrete roads and no sidewalks.

Cat took a deep breath, smelling no more than fresh air—with only an occasional whiff of horse, but she was getting used to that. A glance at the sky indicated that smog was not yet a concern—perhaps never would be. She sought a phrase from her studies and found it. "Pre-industrial," she muttered aloud. Definitely before industrialization. Which had its pluses and minuses, but at the moment, she appreciated its lack thereof.

The valley was for the most part dense and green, but occasionally pitted with areas of blackened, desolate ground before the land smoothed out into a verdant field free of trees, covered with scarlet-bright flora she didn't recognize and irises and daffodils she did. Watching a row of fat rabbits hop across the edge of the field reminded Cat of something Quer'Ali mentioned. "I thought we were going to be traveling by the high road," she said.

"The road curves up once we pass through this one last valley, Sleeper," Q'Atha said, her tone absent, as though she were thinking. She shifted in her seat, and in response, Depper picked up speed. In fact, everyone around them did, including Arriya. "And we must pass through here quickly. We are not safe here."

Cat glanced around her. The broad field looked as though it had not been touched by human hands, at least in recent memory. At the far end of the field, Cat could see a grove of trees into which the road disappeared, to wind uphill, she guessed. Overall, it looked peaceful and like a place any urban Seattleite tired of the city would be glad to slip to, at least for the day. "Why? Are we in danger from the enemy? This field looks pretty, and it's empty enough we'd be able to tell if we were being attacked, right?"

"The honorable uncle's faction is not what we fear, Sleeper."

Cat saw Strian, who had pulled up alongside them again, the jackoval following. "Then what?" She touched her forehead. There was that vague throb behind her eyes again. Maybe the food was finally disagreeing with her. She certainly hoped so. She'd use any excuse not to eat any more fanadi.

But then she remembered she had felt the pain before. "Pir Strian—"

"Waterfire, Sleeper. We must hie across as fast as we can. Just ride, cousin," he said to Q'Atha. "Fast. The quicker we are, the quicker we're on safer—"

Cat pressed her hand against her forehead. That didn't help. "Pir Strian, my head hurts. It's the same pain I—"

"The same pain from before?" Strian tensed as he looked around. His eyes suddenly became wary.

Cat nodded and looked too, but saw nothing meriting sudden tension. Then—

"What's that noise?" she asked as the pain in her head sharpened. "Whatever it is, it's really annoying." It was a swirling sound, as if water had been placed inside a shell and agitated, magnified many times over. The noise filled the air and seemed to reflect the abrupt change in the skies, for the soft lavender hues of the overcast clouds were suddenly replaced with a flat, ominous gray.

Cat shivered. All of a sudden, the air cooled sharply too.

She looked around. The little animals, the rabbits and the deer, had disappeared. It was like the silence before a storm, except—except the sky looked as though it was trembling.

"Earthquake?" she whispered. *Please let it be just an earthquake*. But she knew it wasn't.

"Waterfire," Strian whispered, his face suddenly as leaden as the sky.

"This can't be," Q'Atha exclaimed, her voice ringing in the stillness before being swallowed whole in the hush. "It's too early in the season for a big burst."

"Then what did we see last night? Wellah!" Strian yelled to the horse wranglers and the guards of the Court. "To those caves across the field, *now*!"

The Elder's granddaughter pulled the reins and urged her mare forward. "How do we know the caves are safe?" Q'Atha yelled.

"We don't," Strian yelled back. "Now *ride,* little one!"

Clinging to the saddle, Cat shrieked as, under her, Arriya bolted toward the caves, following Q'Atha.

Cat yelped as the mare jumped over the shallow indentations and little mounds, gripping the saddle. "*Oh shit! I'm going to fall! I'm going to be trampled!*"

"No you're not!" Q'Atha yelled. "Hold on and Arriya will take care of you!"

Cat couldn't think, not as she held on for dear life, bouncing with no control as the mare under her thundered toward the caves. The pounding in her head didn't help, but it was a close race. "Won't the waterfire just go away sooner or later?" she called out, confused, barely hanging on as the wranglers around her exploded into action, steering the horses.

"Just head for the caves," he yelled. "Hurry!"

Cat scrambled off Arriya as soon as the mare came to a dead stop in front of the caves. "Take whatever you can and carry it into the caves!" she heard behind her.

She glanced up. The sky looked as though it was going to loose a downpour within seconds. But she got the feeling it wasn't rain they were guarding against.

She seized a nearby container of foodstuffs and dragged it into the closest cave. Behind her, she noted out of the corner of her eye, Arriya walked into the mouth of the next cave, again without prompting.

Cat shook her head in amazement, pressing her fingers against her temples. Her head was still pounding, but at least she could think this time. Maybe she was getting used to it. *It's a seeing-eye dog, not a horse. It knows where I'm supposed to go, it knows better what to do than I do.*

"Hyagoths save us," she heard someone cry out. "It's moving fast for this time of year!"

Waterfire moves? *What the hell was it?*

The cave she had run into was bigger inside than the small entrance would have suggested. She was one of the last in the cave; it already had most of the travelers in it, including the Court himself. Squeezing in last of all was Strian and the jackoval, who Cat gathered had supervised the last of the wranglers in the adjoining cave.

Cat peered out across the meadow, where the dust from the frantic dash into the caveside should have been settling — but wasn't.

Rain started to fall, making her smile. It looked like Seattle on an autumn day. But then it wasn't a gentle sprinkling anymore — the rainfall was erratic.

Pendulous, bulb-like drops splattered as they hit the ground, replaced by a fine mist almost at once, which in turn died out almost immediately.

The branches of the trees nearby started to tremble.

Cat noticed everyone else crowding away from the mouth of the cave. "Is this rain acid or something?" she asked. She touched her forehead again. Her head was clearing. "This doesn't look like the waterfire we had last night. That was almost crystalline."

Across the mouth of the cave, Strian snorted. "That was nothing, Sleeper. That burst was over the river, and waterfire of a different sort. You'll see. It should be coming right about — *now*!"

He flung himself backward, far away from the mouth and almost falling onto Cat, who tumbled out of the way. A great roar filled her ears and for a moment she could see nothing but a gray blur beyond the mouth of the cave. Then her eyes cleared and her ears adjusted.

She sat up. "What is that?" she whispered, but no one could hear her over the great sound that filled and bounced off the walls of the cave. Dimly, she could hear screams from what had to be the neighboring caves, and then the nervous whinnies of the horses that had been led to the back of this cave too. She strained to see outside, but she could not. Instead, she could feel the heat from the whirling grayness. And it drew her.

I know you. Don't you know me?

"No," she breathed. That couldn't be. She had to be imagining it. How could it...

She edged closer to the entrance, reaching out to it. It couldn't possibly be...

The closer she got to the mouth of the cave, the more she felt her face warm up. It had to be hot out there. "Hot rain?" she said aloud. Curious, she reached out toward it.

"You idiot, keep away from there!" she heard Strian say. She felt herself seized by her shoulders and pulled back, her heels dragging on the ground.

"Hey!" she cried out. She was down on the ground again. For a split second, she felt bereft, for reasons she couldn't fathom. Then, furious, she shoved at Strian. "What do you think you're doing?"

"I'm saving your life, Sleeper," he said, his teeth clenched. He grabbed a stick of firewood from one of the carts, a stick almost as long as his arm. "It doesn't occur to you why we're huddling here in the caves? Do you think we fear rain? Why we ran the way we did last night? Do you want to see what happens when you get too close to waterfire? Take a look."

He strode toward the cave entrance and when he got there, he extended his hand, with the stick held as far away from him as he could manage and dropped it, letting it roll to a stop on the ground just outside the cave. There he stood for a second.

Cat wasn't impressed. "So? I don't know whether it's—" She broke off. "What—"

The stick of firewood caught on fire. Her mouth open, she watched as the entire stick burst into flames and disintegrated.

"That could have been me," she whispered. She swallowed hard as she watched the remains of the stick being swallowed by the whirling gray mass. Cat had never seen anything consumed with such speed or ferocity. She didn't want to again.

Suddenly she remembered the curly silver white-haired woman, the night of the festival. How long it must have taken...

"What is it, some sort of wildfire?" She stumbled away from the entrance, eyes fixed on the howling mass.

Strian shook his head. "No, waterfire, Sleeper. You're doing a very good job of making me believe you're an outsider."

Cat stared at the gray mass. "If I knew what it was, do you think I would be stupid enough to get anywhere near it?" she said, her voice trembling despite her best attempts to keep it level. She shivered when she realized how close she had come to being a cinder. "I'm not crazy!"

Strian turned away. "My apologies, lady," he said after a while, and she could have sworn there was a tremor in his voice too. "Waterfire is the most frightening thing the first time you see it in full force. And only if you see what it can do." He looked toward the mouth of the cave. "It's too early in the season for this to go on too long. It should be over soon."

Sure enough, the swirling mass faltered within seconds. The howling lessened. The grayness was replaced by the fat, pendulous, trembling drops of water she had seen before the horror started, looking for all the world like simple, ordinary rain. Soon enough that, too, abated.

Within minutes the sun came back out. The birds were singing again. A fat brown hare hopped past the cave entrance.

Strian walked to the mouth of the cave and looked around. "It's safe," he called out over his shoulder.

Cat hesitated before she joined the others leaving the cave.

For a moment, she didn't recognize what had become of the pretty little meadow. Instead of the thick carpet of grass they had crossed, the irises and daffodils and scarlet flowers abloom and waving along the way, all she could see was endless black ash. The field they had crossed to get there had been densely covered with green. Now —

"What is that?" She pointed to twisted stark peaks in naked relief that suddenly loomed beyond the field of ash, no longer hidden by lush greenery. "I didn't see that before."

Strian looked up too. "Those peaks are the Forgotten Lovers, my lady. They are how we navigate in Kurit," he said. "They can be seen no matter where you are. And sadly, they are best seen when waterfire passes through."

"Hard to miss," she said as he made his way through the crowd readying themselves for the journey again. The distinctive shape of the formation looked exactly like a pair of lovers, entwined in a passionate embrace, their faces hidden and their limbs curved around each other.

Cat clapped her hand over her nose. "Oh, my God!" she gasped. "What *is* that?"

The stench of burnt flesh, the result of some creature who hadn't made it to shelter, made her gag. Nor was what she was seeing any better. Here and there she could see the remains of such creatures turned to black ash, frozen in place until the stiff wind that whipped up broke them into pieces.

A question came to mind, and she had to have an answer. She made her way past the horse wranglers, who were calming the beasts, readying them to continue the journey, past the cookingwomen, who were sorting what they still had in the way of foodstuffs. She made her way to Strian, who was rounding up his own men.

Cat had to know. "What would have happened if the caves hadn't been there?"

He looked at her, unsmiling. "We would be ash, my lady."

Chapter Nine

 හ

"Waterfire has a specific season, my lady," Strian explained as they rode, the horses picking their way out of the devastation of the meadow. "And we're only at the beginning of it, else we would never have chosen to pass through here."

"Those areas we passed—those were the way they are because of the waterfire?" Cat remembered the occasional areas she had glimpsed, barren and black. She had assumed the scarred land had been the result of fire, or even flood. Apparently not.

"Both water and fire feed the bursts. There is an island you can see from the sentry tower at the edge of the Podani ceremonial grounds—" He paused. She noticed his mouth turned white for a moment. "Across the channel. The island— it is called Feren—used to be a beautiful place, years ago, home to the most magnificent mar trees you could imagine," he went on. "Where my family, and Faia's, would vacation. Then my honorable sister's father decided to go exploring one day. Gilcris and I were there too. We were just children then, as was Faia. Her father did not know about waterfire, except by reputation. Waterfire is the bane of Kurit, and it has rarely, if ever, ventured into Faiora through the years. A tiny burst of waterfire broke out—no bigger than my fist—and he tried to put it out with a jug of water. He didn't know." He stopped. His knuckles were white as he gripped the reins. She opened her mouth to stop him from saying any more, but it was too late.

"He died almost instantly. He was gone within seconds." Unbidden, his stallion stopped and grazed at the tender green shoots on the outskirts of the field, taking the opportunity for a snack. Ahead of them was the thick, rich forest. Behind them was the devastation. Cat willed herself not to look back. "Nearly half the island was destroyed. Neither my brother nor I, nor Faia, have ever gone back."

He nicked softly, persuading Lol to start moving again. "I must have been all of seven years, my brother twelve. The honorable uncle, Faia's uncle, became regent then, and Gilcris married my honorable sister some years later, after Faia became of age and took the throne from her uncle. I remember now how Son-Toruai kept suggesting he should remain regent, keeping rule over Faiora. But Faia and my brother both thought Faiora should rejoin Kurit, so..."

"And so—all this," Cat said. "Is it worth it? You actually considered letting him still be regent, right? Maybe it would have been easier."

Strian glanced at her. "Has anyone mentioned about the three Treasures of Kurit, my lady? Why as the Court, my brother does not simply have all of them in his possession?"

Cat shrugged. "Your cousin—the Elder—started to mention something, but we got distracted. What some jewelry has to do with all this, I—"

"Waterfire can be controlled, lady," Strian interrupted. "You know that much. This land boasts any number of luxuries compared with the rest of the Silver Seas, but none of that would matter if waterfire burned freely. By tradition, the three first members of my family—the Court, the consort, the heir—hold one Treasure each. When the time comes we all must meet at the Podani, with each our Treasure, and perform the ceremony. When the honorable uncle—" He paused and made a face. Cat guessed the title, which she gathered was the Kuriti reference to an in-law, did not sit well with the prince."When Son-Toruai seized the torc from the body of his niece, he ensured he became part of the succession to the rule of not only Kurit, but Faiora. Without the torc, we are lost. Have you seen the earring my brother the Court sports in his ear?"

Dimly she recalled the day she had met Strian's brother. She remembered the simple, dangling earring swinging in the breeze, the vivid sapphire gemstone at the end as bright as the silver-violet iris in his eyes. She nodded. "But how —"

"When used together, the three Treasures of Kurit can control waterfire," Strian continued. "That earring has been worn by every ruler of Kurit for more than four hundred years, and it must be used with the Sword Gem, the one in the heartsword —"

"The one you wear?" She gestured at the ornate weapon he wore strapped across his chest.

"Yes. And the Torc Gem, which my honorable sister wore, is the third piece. Which my honorable uncle now has, claiming his right with the death of the little prince. If we guessed his ambitions were for Faiora, my brother would have gladly let him rule for the rest of his days. But then his ambitions grew…and now, we only have two gems."

"Two of the gems won't do," she said slowly, realizing what the problem was. "It has to be all three. It makes a difference? Really?" All the bits and pieces of the chaotic activity she had been witnessing started to make sense.

"At the start of waterfire season, there is one burst, the mother burst of waterfire, that rises from the depth of the sea and heads toward land to lay waste on all it touches," he continued. "Every hundred years, the ceremony at Podani and all three gems ensures the waterfire is driven into submission. But without the ritual —" He stopped.

Her lips dried. "What happens?"

"The last time the ceremony did not occur, waterfire raged through the farmlands and there was starvation for two winters." His voice dropped. "Those who survived died horribly, eating waterfire ash, and even each other."

Cat winced. "How many days do we have again?"

"Five days. We meet my honorable uncle and his overgrown rats for good or ill and use the Gems for what they were meant. Otherwise—" He stopped, gripping the reins. Lol noticed and flicked an ear, but didn't stop.

"There's nothing," she finished. Her stomach roiled.

They continued in silence, until he spoke up. "You may wonder what role in all this the Sleepers play."

"The thought did cross my mind."

"I do not know. No one does. The sleeping Sleepers," Strian mused. "Perhaps we should ask the Nurui if it is significant you awoke and they did not."

"I thought you didn't want to associate with these people. Now you sound downright chummy."

"'Chummy'?" He frowned. "I do not trust the Nurui. But they have their uses. But certainly, I would not ask them for advice or offer my soul to them. They are too likely to take it."

"Isn't that the kind of thing people like you do?"

"Who, the Kuriti?"

"You priests."

He turned to stare at her. "Why would that be?"

"The Elder told me the Kama was a monastery. Where I'm from, monks and priests spend time…" she floundered. What did they do? She had no idea. She had been to a Catholic church perhaps once.

Strian didn't notice her discomfort. "Priests here contemplate existence, lady," he said. He rubbed his chin. "And the warrior priests of Kama mediate quarrels, take up arms to defend the ruling family, track those who would threaten Kurit. That is our calling."

Cat gestured to the Sword Gem of Kurit strapped across his chest. "Where I come from, priests don't take up arms."

"They do here. An entire regiment of Kama priests will take up arms and preside during the ceremony with us and my honorable uncle."

"What if the Kama priests decide your honorable uncle is in the right?"

He shrugged. "Then as brother to the Court and not as fellow Kamaite, I must take up arms against them." He suddenly looked tired. "Afterward, I would leave the order. And it is possible, your question. The head of the order, the Eid, has been known to consort with my honorable uncle, who was also a Kamaite. But I choose to believe the Eid has honor until I know otherwise. My honorable uncle, I know he has none."

Strian stopped and looked around and so did Cat. The forest was thick around them, the meadows long behind them. The trees masked the fact they were winding uphill. "We are near dusk. We will rest here for the night," he decided. "I beg your leave, Sleeper." He swerved, nudging Lol into a trot, the conversation at an end.

Cat watched him leave. Not talkative, although once she'd gotten him going he'd been helpful enough.

But the more she heard, the more she felt uneasy. Why was she here? Who or what were the Nurui, who might have a clue?

Cat sought the womenfolk and found them clustered, already starting the evening meal. She looked around until she spied Q'Atha, who was tending a fledgling fire with the Elder's cook.

"Who are the Nurui?" Cat asked.

The young woman looked faintly alarmed, though she kept poking at the flames. "Nurui are seers, Quer'Cadrine, not far from here. You'll see."

Ordinarily so ebullient, Q'Atha seemed subdued. But that wasn't going to distract Cat. "I'd like to know why I'm getting mixed signals from you and Pir Strian about the Nurui."

"The Nurui are themselves," Q'Atha said, shrugging. "I could not even imagine where to begin to describe them."

"There must be some way of explaining to me what I'm going to be facing," Cat persisted. Looking around for something to do, something to help, she dug into the burlap sack sitting next to Q'Atha. Carrots. She could help with the meal while she tried to get an answer.

She dug into her pocket and brought out her new knife. She unsheathed it, letting the daylight catch the gleam. Was she allowed to use it to peel vegetables? Well, she sure wasn't going to stab anyone with it.

She began to peel the carrot, slowly and carefully — considering the kitchen was not her normal territory, being careful not to cut herself. The color of the freshly exposed bright golden meat under the top layer almost hurt her eyes.

"I would think you will know when it is time for you to know," Q'Atha said as she picked up the sack. She stopped. "Sleeper?"

"Yes?" Cat peeled another strip off the carrot, admiring how long and thin she had managed to cut it. She hefted the knife. It felt good, even natural in her hand. The silverist had done a good job.

"Sleeper, what are you doing?"

Cat looked down. Admittedly, she was no carrot-peeling expert, but— "I'm peeling this carrot."

"Why?"

"Why not?"

Both Q'Atha and Poro were staring at her. The Elder's cook in particular looked bewildered.

"We don't eat those, let alone peel them," Q'Atha told Cat. "We feed them to the fire. What do you do with them in Shiatta?"

Cat looked at her, then at the carrot in her hand. "This is *kindling*?"

Q'Atha stared at her. "What else would you have us do with it, Sleeper?"

"Well, eat them," Cat said. She rubbed the tip and despite Q'Atha's cry of alarm, stuck it into her mouth.

That was a mistake. It tasted like nothing that would ever be mistaken for food. Cat spat it out. She wiped at her mouth and tongue frantically and spat again. "That's not a carrot!" she finally babbled, then spat again. "What *is* it?"

Poro's eyes were wide as she tried not to smile while Q'Atha was less than successful in maintaining a solemn face. "I told you, Quer'Cadrine. It is kindling. It is rich kindling and we do not eat it. We can start a good cooking fire almost instantly with a single stick." The girl paused, then continued, choosing her words carefully. "Is this what you eat in Shiatta, Sleeper?"

Cat stared at the stick in her hand. She rubbed at it, bent it a little. It looked like a carrot. It even smelled like a carrot. It sure didn't taste like one. "We eat something that looks just like this," she muttered. She wiped at her mouth again. "We eat them raw, we steam them, we eat them with peanut butter. What do you call this stuff?"

Q'Atha shrugged. "Mecklewood. The trees are not easily found, which is why we treasure what we find and carry them with us when we travel. Let us take care of that, Sleeper," she said tactfully, taking the stick and slipping it back into the sack.

"Then what should I be doing?" Cat said, exasperated. "Neither one of you will tell me what I should expect."

Q'Atha winked. "Think about your role as Sleeper." With that, she stood up and, taking the sack of mecklewood with her, joined the cooks.

Even Cat could take that hint. Out of sorts, she wandered away, so she was not present when the pigeon flew into the clearing.

At first, she paid no attention to it, assuming it was yet another example of the scourge of the city…but there wasn't a city anywhere in sight. "Sleeper? Where are you? Come see!" she heard.

"I saw," Cat said. "It's a pigeon. What about it?"

"It's from home!" Q'Atha cried, delighted. She clapped her hands as Boyo reached for the bird. "No, don't scare it!" she scolded as those standing by cheered him on. "It has news from home!"

Cat brightened when she realized there was a tiny scroll of paper fastened to the bird's leg. "It's a carrier pigeon? You guys use carrier pigeons? You guys still *have* carrier pigeons?"

Boyo caught the pigeon. "Calm now," he soothed the fluttering bird. He gingerly untied the scroll from its leg. "It has the mark," he declared with a grin, showing the maroon seal on the tiny scrap. For a moment he stood, uncertain. Cat guessed he wasn't sure of the protocol. Holding both the pigeon and the scroll, he started in the direction of the tent of the Court.

The guard standing outside hesitated, then shook his head. "His Imperial Majesty the Court is asleep," he announced in a stage whisper.

"Let me," Strian said, putting down the brush with which he was caring for Lol and coming forward.

His eyes wide, Boyo bowed and handed Strian the scroll.

"Is it the Elder?" Cat asked eagerly. "She promised to keep in touch."

Strian raised a finger and broke the delicate little seal. He unwrapped the missive and started to read from it. "She sends greetings to all," he said, raising his voice to be heard. "She writes the village surrounds are being swept still after the burst of waterfire. Q'Atha, your grandmeren bids you a good time when we reach the Podani and reminds you of your pledge to guide the Sleeper. And Sleeper—"

Cat tensed. "Yes?" The Elder had promised to let her know about Kevin and Margot and whether they remained asleep.

Strian looked at her. "No change, my cousin says."

Cat slumped, releasing a breath she hadn't realized she was holding. They had all ducked under the table at the same time, back at the library, her and Kevin and Maggs. So why was it she ended up awake and they had not?

"Thanks. I think I'll look around now," she muttered.

She slipped away from the crowd intent on a couple minutes of solitude, when she felt a tap on her shoulder. "Sleeper, you should not go alone," a familiar voice said.

Boyo stood behind her, his eyes concerned. "You should have someone with you."

Cat snorted. The last thing she needed was a chaperone. "I wasn't going far, kiddo. Just going for some peace and quiet. Do you mind?"

The farmer's son hesitated—and Cat realized that despite his name, he was a boy no longer. He would be taking part of whatever rituals S'nal required for its young men soon—but he went on. "I will not say anything. I just want to make sure you are protected. These woods are not your Shiatta."

Someone—Q'Atha, most likely—must have persuaded him to stay close. "I don't need a nursemaid," Cat said. "I don't think I'm going to be eaten by a bear. Geez."

"If you want to explore I can take you, Sleeper," Boyo persisted. "I know there is a creek nearby—that is one of the reasons we stopped. It feeds to the River Pon. It is a pretty spot. Would you like to see it?"

"Oh, to hell with it. Sure," she said, giving up her plans for alone time. "Should you get a leash for me or something?"

"Oh, I do not think so," Boyo said seriously. "If you choose to wander off, I believe I could bring you back."

145

Cat stifled a smile. "Gee, thanks." She paused. "I'm being sarcastic."

The boy's face didn't change, his gaze not wavering. "I see."

"Do you know what that is?"

"No," he replied amiably.

"Do you care?" Not waiting for an answer, she started off. She bet she could ditch him in five minutes flat and get some quiet time to boot. She wanted to think. She *needed* to think.

"If it's important to you, yes, Sleeper," he answered, following tight at her heels. "Otherwise I see it as an honor to accompany you on your walk."

Cat stopped and turned around. His eyes were clear, and there was not a speck of a twinkle in them. She thought she could lose him, even if this was his territory and not hers.

Oh hell. She couldn't do it. She probably couldn't shake him, either—she never even wandered off the sidewalks in the parks in Seattle.

"Okay," she said with a sigh. "I just wanted some peace and quiet."

"I will not say a word," he promised. He followed, whistling under his breath.

Almost within seconds, the hubbub of the group behind her died away, swallowed by the greenery, until finally, all Cat could hear was the sound of her own breathing—and Boyo's whistling through his teeth.

"Listen," she whispered, her words unnaturally loud, yet swallowed into the stillness. "I haven't heard that in years."

"What, Sleeper?" Boyo said. His voice, though soft, seemed to fill the space. But she didn't have to reply, because the answer was all around them.

Nothing.

She'd been city-bound all her life. Noise was a part of her life. Even in the depths of the quietest of parks, there had been noise.

Nothing.

Suddenly greedy for more of it, she looked around. To her surprise, a path had been worn through the woods, not wide or trodden bare, but a path nonetheless. Intrigued, she followed it, the soft steps of her companion echoing hers.

The woods were dark but there were flashes of daylight from above. She followed the path, Boyo behind her, until she came to a clearing, the remains of a fallen log in the middle. True to Boyo's word she could hear the burbling of a creek nearby.

Cat sat down on the log and gestured for Boyo to do the same as she looked up. The sky was a smooth lilac as the sun faded. Somewhere she knew the sunset was beginning, but not right then and there.

Little by little she felt the tension that had plagued her ever since they had started on this journey, the worries haunting her since she had first opened her eyes in the Elder's home, melt away.

"Back home finding a place this quiet is impossible," she said aloud, surprising herself with how loud her voice sounded. "Something's always in the background—a dog barking, a kid yelling, a car honking—something."

"Does your Shiatta have so many people, Sleeper?" Boyo asked, his voice as hushed as hers. He looked around the clearing.

"Not as many as others," she said, considering raising her voice, but not succeeding. Too loud. In normal tones she sounded as though she were shouting, and there was no reason to do that here. "Boyo, you can't imagine how you miss quiet until you don't have it. It's like the stars. There's so much light pollution in the city I haven't seen the stars in years, either."

"Must you live there?" the young man asked. "Out on the farm, we have both. I do not know what it would be like to live without the stars. Although there is a legend about the waterfire—sometimes, when the waterfire is at the worst, the stars disappear for seasons on end, as does the sun."

Waterfire again. "Pir Strian was telling me about what happens if the waterfire isn't contained," Cat said slowly. "People starve. People eat—" she stopped. *Cannibalism* wasn't a word she was going to bring up.

Neither was Boyo, for he shuddered, and said nothing else.

She looked at the sky again, then at the trees around them. "How far are we from the Nurui settlement?"

"Another full day's ride," the youth said promptly. "If they have not been moved."

"'Been' moved?"

He shrugged, twisting his lips. She took a guess. "Does a move like that involve threats and torches?"

"I do not know, Sleeper," and with that, Boyo sounded like a boy again. "I think so. I know there are whispers but no one seems to say anything out loud. I imagine I will find out soon."

"Shades of Frankenstein," she muttered.

"Sleeper?"

"Never mind," she said quickly. She closed her eyes and took a deep breath, enjoying the tranquility. The bubbling of the water seemed to accentuate the peace.

Come to think of it, she had never thought to spend time out of doors in the evening since she had woken up here, save the night of the festival in S'nal. "I think I'm going to look for the stars tonight," she said after a while.

"Of course, Sleeper," Boyo said agreeably.

The sound of the running water was too much for her. She decided to try to find it. "Boyo, where's the creek?"

"This way, Sleeper," he said, leading the way into the trees.

The creek was only a few feet away, it turned out, beyond a little grove of tall, heavily leafed trees. She thought she might have been able to find it alone—but maybe not.

So quiet.

She took a deep breath. The water smelled good; she knew no other way to describe it. It ran over small rocks of bright jeweled colors, and the dimming light peeking through the thick branches made the running water sparkle.

"Would you like a drink, Sleeper?"

"What, drink from it?" she said, startled. "Is that sanitary?"

Boyo looked confused before he answered, "It is running water, clear, and we have drunk from it for many years. We none of us have ever sickened from it. This is toward the beginning of the Pon. It is as sweet as we could ever want."

Cat stared at the creek dubiously. "I dunno, kiddo. I'm used to treated water."

"Yes, in your Shiatta. We are in Kurit."

She couldn't deny that. She took a step closer, and stood staring at the water.

"If it makes you feel any safer, let me," the young man offered. He knelt at the water's edge, and without hesitation, he dipped his hand in and drank.

Her throat was dry, Cat realized. She needed to drink.

Oh, to heck with it. She knelt, and touched the water. It was ice-cold. She cupped her hand in the water and brought it up to her lips.

So *good*! She almost purred with satisfaction. The water was cold and fresh and sweet. "This is wonderful!" she exclaimed after her third handful. She splashed some on her face, and almost immediately she felt better.

"The creek is known for its good water," Boyo offered with a grin. "I am glad it is to your liking."

She took another handful and wiped her face again, the clean chill of the water invigorating her. Afterward she sat and closed her eyes and listened again.

Finally the silence was enough for her to remember, to commit to memory. No matter where she went after this, no matter how quiet it would be, there would be sound. At least she could remember that once, she had true quiet.

She exhaled and opened her eyes. "Ready?" she asked Boyo. She stood.

* * * * *

"The Nurui near here are not as—accommodating as those in other settlements," Q'Atha said after a pause, when Cat asked her again about the Nurui. "We will find another camp."

"Accommodating? How accommodating do fortune-tellers have to be?" Cat asked. She remembered the conversation she had had with Boyo, and it chilled her. "I need to know what I'm doing here. I need to know how I'm going to do what I'm going to be doing when we get to the ceremony."

Cat hadn't seen the girl look that way since she had first opened her eyes there. "I know, Sleeper," Q'Atha said, her eyebrows furrowing. "But I'm not sure how to explain the Nurui and the dangers to you." Her silver hair, bound in its usual crown of braids, glinted in the sunlight.

"Fine, I'll ask Strian," Cat muttered as she turned away. Had she been roped into this trip under false pretenses? She didn't want to believe it. They seemed to be so open and honest and forthcoming. She didn't want to believe she'd been duped.

Strian was equally unforthcoming about when they, or at least she, would approach the Nurui. Any Nurui.

He had stepped out of the tent holding the Court and his advisors when Cat had nabbed him. "I don't have the time to talk to you about them right now, Sleeper," he snapped. "And not that settlement. There is another farther on. Did you ask my cousin?"

"Q'Atha said we couldn't go to those Nurui, but she didn't explain why," Cat snapped back. "I came on this journey to talk to the Nurui. Why can't I?"

Strian glanced at the tent behind him. "Sleeper, there are settlements of Nurui...and there are settlements of Nurui. And these Nurui are not those you wish to speak to. After what happened to my little cousin, we will find others."

"I wish someone could tell me what's going on, instead of talking in circles!"

"If we tell you now, you would not believe me, Sleeper."

"How do you know?"

"Did anything anyone said about waterfire prepare you for it?"

The memory of the swirling netherness sent a chill down her spine. She shook her head. "But—"

The waterfire had been both more and less than she had expected. She knew what the syndrome was. It was like the descriptions of war and participating in war. And she knew one could never adequately describe the other, no matter how many games of chance or strategy or video games anyone ever played.

She had to know. She was running out of time.

"Fine," she muttered, turning away. "I'll wait."

"It's better we do, Sleeper," Strian called out after her. "I will explain as soon as we are away from here."

The questions gnawed at her for the rest of the evening, even as she stared at the stars and after the traveling party got under way the next morning. She waited—and waited and as the first settlement of Nurui slipped away—at least she

151

assumed it was a settlement of Nurui, considering the way they hurried past it—she saw her chance at understanding what she had to do slip away.

"There is another settlement of Nurui not far from here," Boyo said, looking troubled. He chewed on his lip.

Cat brightened. "Are we going to stop there?"

The youth shrugged, looking around nervously. "If the grand prince deems it time. Sleeper—you know the settlement we passed, that was the one Q'Atha went to."

She shook her head. "Shouldn't we have gone to that one, then?"

"No." Boyo looked around again and leaned forward. "The prince threatened to burn down that settlement."

"He did *what*?"

"Pir Strian threatened to burn down the settlement if they got near any of him and his again, so we will have to go to the next Nurui settlement," he said matter-of-factly.

Cat stared at him. "What *happened*?"

"Q'Atha went to the Nurui. She was younger, and she went with her friends, and they went to have their fates told. Her two friends died, and Q'Atha—it took her a long time to recover."

"If they're so dangerous, why did they suggest I go see them?"

"Sleeper, you wanted answers, and the Nurui are the closest thing to answers we have." Boyo scratched his head. "But you should know it is dangerous, and you must ask yourself if you are prepared for the risk. Your answer will be a riddle—will you be satisfied with that?"

The youth excused himself, dropping behind to ride alongside his father. Or so he said. Cat guessed her questions might have been too much for the farmer's son.

She was prepared for the risk. She had to be, whether or not those around her thought so. And she had to take her chance. Heart in her mouth, she slipped out as preparations were being made for the noon meal, and she backtracked to the Nurui settlement.

Cat was glad all she had to do was follow the road back, because she didn't know if she could control Arriya. The mare was obedient enough but this was the first time the two of them had been alone together, and the way the horse kept looking over its shoulder at her made Cat think the mare didn't think much of her. But she kept to the road, didn't try to turn around or pause for a snack at any handy vegetation and kept up the pace until the Nurui settlement was in view.

It wasn't what Cat expected. She expected the settlement to look pretty much what a fortune-teller's booth would look like at a country carnival back home. She expected it to look sleazy and sad, with torn fabric and faded paint, and the fortune-teller in question to look equally tired and faded.

Far from it. The Nurui settlement was resplendent in gilt and silver, gleaming so much it hurt Cat's eyes just looking around. Instead of tired-looking tents doing service for telling flimsy fortunes, one large structure squatted in the middle of the settlement, surrounded by smaller tents just as shiny. The big one looked like an oversized gazebo that by all rights should have sat in someone's backyard in the wealthier suburbs of Seattle.

Above the structure's entryway was some writing Cat instinctively knew said something she should know—but she couldn't read it. She was illiterate in whatever the language was. She couldn't even tell if it was Kuriti.

A shiver coursed down her spine, warning of her subconscious unease. But she had to know.

As Cat approached, she knew she should have pressed for more details from Boyo or Q'Atha or even Strian. As it was, she was walking in knowing nothing. She didn't even know what it would cost. She still had some local coins in her reticule, the result of her afternoon of bartering back in S'nal. She just hoped it was the currency they would ask for.

A riddle. How was a riddle the answer to what she needed?

A small child — at least she assumed it was a small child — was sitting on a stool outside. It didn't budge or even acknowledge she was there. Taking a deep breath, she entered.

It was dim inside, but she expected as much. It was cool, almost damp. She could see little around her save a large fireplace, which stood empty and cold, and in the corner, a little shrunken person sat in the shadows, in front of a large glistening copper bowl on a low platform, sitting — and waiting.

Cat took a deep breath. "I want my fortune told," she announced, looking at the person. She couldn't see him or her clearly. All she could see was an approximate shape, huddled on the large, ornately carved wooden chair dwarfing it. "Who do I go to?"

She must have said the right combination of words, for she got an answer. "Welcome to the Nurui. We can give guidance," the shrunken creature answered. Now that he had stirred, Cat noticed he had long, twisted fingers clutching the arms of the chair. "Approach."

Cat nervously approached him, her hands open. She tried to breathe evenly, and she tried to ignore the hammering pulse in her throat. "W-what do I do?" She tried not to flinch when she got another step closer. She guessed the Nurui did not bathe.

"Sit and we may speak. You are not of Kurit," the creature intoned. Those long fingers gestured to an armchair nearby.

Cat sat. Now that she was close enough, the Nurui was perhaps the ugliest creature she had ever encountered, except maybe the worst of the grunge rockers in Seattle. The Nurui was swathed in colorful woolens, piled high and deep, so all Cat could see clearly were his hands, large and bony and almost green, with those long fingernails she realized were sharpened to a point, all tipped in gilt.

Her stomach churned. She shouldn't have come.

"We see into bowl," the Nurui said, again gesturing. Those nails looked like lethal weapons. Cat had to stop herself from shrinking away.

The copper bowl seemed to glow when the Nurui looked into it. Out of the corner of her eye, Cat felt, more than saw, another Nurui come in and start a fire in the gigantic fireplace. It was a small fire; it barely seemed to make a spark in the vastness of the hearth.

Why were they starting a fire? She didn't get it. It wasn't cold. She started to ask but realized it had gotten chilly all of a sudden. That explained why the Nurui in front of her was swathed in woolens. Perhaps the gigantic structure had an insulation problem. Or maybe the Nurui felt the cool keenly.

Cat shivered but for a different reason this time. She wished she had remembered to come in her own warm cape, but when she had slipped away from the traveling party, the sun had been high in the sky and it had been warm enough. She had a feeling that was no longer the case.

She was vaguely aware of a tiny puff of air she exhaled as she watched the Nurui stroke the rim of the bowl. "No, I am not of Kurit," Cat said finally.

"And you want to know why you are here. That is question?" the Nurui whispered. His thin, reedy voice dipped until it was almost inaudible, and there was almost a hiss to it. The Nurui raised a long-nailed finger and drew a pattern in the air above the bowl.

"Yes," Cat answered, trembling. She swallowed.

"Serious question," the Nurui whispered, his voice echoing. "Hard question to think about. Maybe no reason at all? Maybe not necessary to answer? You think?"

He was fishing. The Nurui was fishing for information. Cat could have laughed, except she was starting to lose feeling in the tips of her toes. She tried to will herself to relax. It didn't work. "No. I think there is a reason," she said, out of breath. She wrapped her arms around herself. There was a definite chill in the structure, and it didn't matter the blaze in the fireplace seemed to be growing, since none of the heat was reaching her. "I want to know why, and I think you can tell me."

The Nurui glanced at her. "This Seeing Bowl. How Nurui see past, future, maybe even present. You travel with Kuriti Court, no?"

"Yes," Cat said. She started to rub her hands together. She was starting to lose sensation in them too. It shouldn't have been so cold.

"You go to ceremony with Court, with Court's brother, with others. Yes? Waterfire scary?"

"Yes. *Yes.*"

"Maybe you go home when ceremony over," the Nurui said. "See you leave. Not know why. You know why?"

"No," Cat said. "That's why I'm here, remember?"

The Nurui must have thought that was amusing, for he started to cackle. "True. Many forget Nurui tell things. Don't answer all questions, don't tell all things. Not know enough to tell. Leg hurt now?"

Cat bit her lip. She had forgotten about her leg—not that she could feel it at the moment anyway. "No. Not since I've gotten to Kurit."

"Not hurt as long as in Kurit. Kurit magic for you," the Nurui said with a smile. His teeth gleamed green. Cat felt queasy.

The blaze in the fireplace started to roar, reaching toward the ceiling, but Cat couldn't feel the warmth at all.

"Maybe go home after ceremony," the Nurui continued. "See leave. Not want to leave. You want to leave?"

Cat tried to take a deep breath and found she couldn't. Shallow breaths were all she could manage. "I want to go home," she said, gasping. "I don't belong here."

"Cat not think about these things. Maybe Cat do," the Nurui said.

"Do you know why I'm here?" Cat persisted. Dimly in the back of her mind she wondered how the Nurui knew her name, but that was the least of her worries now. Breathing took precedence and she was having a hard time doing it.

"Maybe here because of split in Treasures," the Nurui said and he smiled again, droplets of spittle at the edge of his mouth. Cat wanted to vomit. "Need to bring Treasures back together. Know Treasures?"

"I know the Treasures," Cat said, her teeth starting to chatter even as she was willing her stomach to settle. "I know about the Treasures. I've seen two of the three. What about it?"

"You see all three, very close, very good."

"I guess that means the ceremony is going to go off as planned," Cat mused. "Since it's not in the hands of Pir Strian or the Court right now." She shifted in the chair. There was no way it could have gotten this cold this quickly. Maybe her blood sugar was dropping. Maybe she shouldn't have skipped lunch to sneak off here.

"Maybe. Not see. See you go home, see you with third Treasure."

"So what does that mean for me? What should I be doing to get home?"

"Not see that. See you smile but cry too. Not know why."

"Do you know why about anything?" Cat said irritably. She couldn't feel any of the heat from the roaring fire, even though it should have been blistering in its intensity. Did she have the flu? Could she get the flu here?

"Know many things. Don't know many things. Need to know to live and die," he said and smiled a smile that was irritating her more and more.

"What does that mean?" Cat inhaled and exhaled. She could see the breath come out of her mouth, not little puffs any more. "Could we get closer to the fire?"

"Can't tell anything closer to fire," the Nurui said. "Not help, at least. Scared?"

"A little," Cat said. She closed her eyes for a moment. "More than a little. You're making me nervous."

"Nervous good. Still alive," the Nurui said cryptically. "Dead, no feel nervous. Yes?"

"That's true," Cat said, distracted. "But I still don't know why I'm here, and I'm still hoping you'll tell me."

"I tell you why you here. The way to know why you here? Why you here clear when you die. That all. Don't know more."

Cat stared at the Nurui in horror. "What?" Her palms started to sweat despite her profound chill. "You said I'd go home as soon as the ceremony was over. You said I was probably here because of the split in the Treasures. What do you mean you don't know? How am I going to get home?"

The Nurui tilted his chin, looking her in the eye. His eyes, Cat realized, were blood red, reflecting in the flickering candlelight.

She wrinkled her nose when the smell of something rancid wafted by. She should have known better than to come alone. She didn't know the rules. She didn't know the culture. Worst of all, she didn't know how to deal with the Nurui.

But they knew all about how to deal with her, she realized with horrifying clarity. "I say not know," the Nurui repeated softly, a smile twitching around its lips. "Not say no idea." He pointed to his bowl, where the water covering the bottom seemed to be rippling—but Cat could have sworn there hadn't been any water there before.

The Nurui put his hands around the bowl and stroked the uneven curves, lifting the bowl up by the little curly toed feet on the bottom. "See many things," he continued, glancing at Cat from time to time. "Many puzzle things. Maybe Sleeper's world, not here. Mostly see prince, without sword, taking off shiny necklace. Give to you. No why."

Cat recognized the Nurui's description as the Kamaite emblem Strian wore. "Why would he give me his medallion?" Cat asked out loud, then mentally kicked herself. Asking a question of this Nurui was at best fruitless and at worst exasperating, that much she *had* learned.

"Not see why, not know why," he murmured, tapping the rim of the bowl. Cat could see tiny grooves in the top, where the Nurui must have tapped a long, curved fingernail many, many times in his vision quest. "Ask prince why no sword, why no medallion. Tired," he announced abruptly, pushing away the bowl, a gleam in his eyes. "Very tired. Payment now."

Cat was both glad and dismayed—but she found she couldn't move anyway. "Ssssure," she slurred. Payment. She had brought coins. She couldn't reach for her reticule. She was so sleepy, as though she couldn't feel or think anymore…

Just then Cat felt an icy cold flow of air from behind her. "Sleeper, why are you here?" an irritated voice asked.

Chapter Ten

Ꮹ

The flash of light when the door was flung open made Cat's eyes water.

Despite her extreme fatigue and cold, Cat knew the voice. And immediately she got irritated. "What are you doing here?" she snapped at Strian, who stood in the doorway, sword—and medallion—very much present. He had one hand at his knife's sheath, while in his other he held her cape. He handed it to the safekeeping of the little Nurui child who was sitting guard outside the structure. Peering around Strian, the child peeked within, its eyes like saucers.

Strian didn't notice. "Never mind, *Sleeper*," he said cuttingly. "How much does she owe you?" he asked the Nurui.

The seer Nurui grinned. "Pir Strian. Surprise to see you. No torch this time?"

Strian bared his teeth. "Do not tempt me," he snarled. "Considering the Sleeper here chose to seek you out instead of choosing to heed those who know better, I can only call this a truce before I take her away. Or did you have other plans?"

The seer didn't seem particularly worried. He grinned even broader. His teeth, glinting lime green in the light of the flickering candles and roaring fire, were streaked yellow in daylight. "A mystery, a sight," he answered. He shrugged elaborately. "How much worth to prince?"

Strian's jaw set and his fist relaxed. Cat saw the glint of gold and silver coins in his palm, and she realized his other hand was guarding his money bag, not touching his sword hilt. Whatever the Nurui's motives, then, they were monetary, not violent.

"Here," the prince snarled, tossing what was in his hand onto the ground. One of the coins rolled, tilting crazily, and hit the side of the bowl. The soft metal of the coin clinked against the copper of the vessel. "Don't come near here again," he said to Cat. "I mean it. If you don't even have enough sense to keep a companion with you —"

He grabbed Cat's hand and tugged her to her feet. She went, shivering. "I can t-take c-care of myself, thank you very much," she said, stumbling over her words.

Maybe not. She swayed as she tried to stand up. The sunlight she saw through the slit in the entrance curtains hurt her eyes.

The sun was also much lower in the sky than it should have been. How long had she been there?

"I don't understand this," she said, her face strangely stiff, as though it were midwinter and she had been exposed to the elements. "It wasn't this cold when I went in. How can the temperature drop so quickly?"

Strian looked at her sharply. "Sleeper, your lips are blue."

"C-considering how c-cold I am, I'm n-not surprised." She blinked, but her eyelids wouldn't move as fast as she wanted them to. She couldn't feel her feet anymore.

He seemed to understand, because his tone gentled. "Let us go, Sleeper." He looked over to the Nurui, who was huddled closer to the roaring fire. "You knew and you accepted her question without thought of the consequences. You knew she had no idea what she was doing. I do not think any of ours should meet with any of yours again."

"You be back, sooner or later, Court," the Nurui said with a cackle. "Not any time soon, though. Go."

Cat felt Strian lead her out of the structure. It was getting dark much earlier than she thought, and it was also much colder.

She started to shiver. "W-why is it so cold? It-it hasn't been this cold the ent- the entire time I've been here. D-does winter set in this f-fast here?" She couldn't get *warm*.

Somehow calmer now, Strian draped her cape around her shoulders, but it seemed to protect her against the bitter cold no better than a layer of gauze would have. "When did you decide to do this, Sleeper?"

His voice was lower. Torches illuminated the Nurui settlement around them. Dreamily, she fantasized about bathing in fire, so warm—"I d-don't remember," she murmured, shaking her head. "It was about noon and we stopped for lunch, and I knew the Nurui camp wasn't far behind us and I n-needed to know." She folded the cape around her and tucked her stiffened fingers in the folds of the cape. Nothing. She couldn't feel it.

He looked up. She looked too. The stars were coming out. Had they come out this early before? "How long do you think you were there, Sleeper?"

She shrugged then huddled in the cape. She had to warm up soon. "Fifteen, twenty minutes," she guessed. "It can't have been long."

Strian shook his head. "You have been in the Nurui tent for what must have been nearly five *hours*, Sleeper. No one warned you about time and the Nurui?"

Her eyes widened. "No. How could it have been that long? I went in, sat down and the Nurui looked into the bowl. We talked for a few minutes. You came in." She shivered. Why couldn't she get *warm*?

He looked at her again, and his expression gentled. He reached out and carefully fastened her cape's ties. With a hand on her shoulder he began to lead her. "You will be colder yet tonight and tomorrow, Sleeper," he told her. "Next town, we will find you some gloves. Your hands will be cold for years before they feel warm again. We will wrap you in blankets. You will not feel well at all, not for a while."

Cat shivered again. "I don't know why I'm so cold. I wasn't cold when I was in the tent. I was sitting next to the fire. This is how I felt when I had pneumonia."

"The fire was false fire, Sleeper."

"It wasn't *real*? What was it, a special effect?"

"It is real. If you pass a hand through it, your flesh will burn. But everyone who comes out of a Nurui camp feels cold. The Nurui steal our warmth as we sit there asking our questions and waiting for our answers." He turned away. "Q'Atha!"

"She came with you?" Cat mumbled. She wanted to be louder, but her throat was too cold to give her more sound. "That's good. You know, I'm not feeling so hot." The Elder's granddaughter must have guessed where she had gone.

"The Nurui are masters of heat-theft, Sleeper. Q'Atha! The Sleeper needs you! My pardon, lady," he said to Cat, bowing. "I have things to attend to."

Cat watched as the Elder's granddaughter dismounted from her Depper and came hurrying over. "Sleeper! This was not the best choice for you to have made," she exclaimed.

A worried expression on her face, the girl kept glancing at the Nurui structure Cat had just come out of. As they walked away, she looked over her shoulder. "Quickly, Sleeper," Q'Atha whispered. "Let us away while we can."

"'While we can'? What are you talking about?" Cat tried to ask, but her words were cut short with a fit of coughing. She felt Q'Atha's hands around her shoulders, keeping her on her feet. The flurry of tears from the coughing blinded her for a minute and by the time she could see again, they were on the outskirts of the Nurui settlement.

"Just in case something happens," Q'Atha said with no further explanation. She quickly swaddled Cat into a fur cape over her woolen one and helped her onto Arriya. Wasting no time, the girl climbed onto her own mare and softly nicked. "Come, Sleeper," she said, her mouth set. "It is best for all concerned if the Nurui are behind us." And just to make sure, it seemed, she looked behind her one more time before they were off.

It seemed to Cat they made good time in getting back to their camp—a camp, she realized blearily, they should have struck and gone on their way hours ago, and instead, where they would stay another night because of her.

The camp was quiet—not only the noon meal but the evening meal had been partaken, by the looks of it. "How long was I there?" Cat whispered.

Q'Atha glanced at the sky. "About six hours in all," she said, leading Cat over to the nearest campfire. "Sit down, Sleeper." She thrust a mug of hot *oja* into Cat's hands. "You will need this. And in great quantity."

Cat wrapped her hands about the cup. She knew, rather than felt, the scorching hot metal was against her skin, but she couldn't feel it. Her teeth chattered. "Oh, great," she muttered. "Of all the times to get sick. I have the flu."

She couldn't stop shivering. She looked at the palms of her hands, expecting to see them as pale as the rest of her, but they were beet-red. Yet she couldn't feel the heat. Her hands were developing chilblains. *How?*

Q'Atha saw them too. She grabbed the cup and exposed Cat's palms in dismay. "Oh, Sleeper," she exclaimed. "Oh, this will not be good."

The fire was starting to spin in front of Cat's eyes. She put down her drink and closed her eyes. "I don't feel so good," she said faintly, her breathing getting more and more labored. "It didn't feel like more than a few minutes."

"It never does," Q'Atha said in a soothing voice. "You should rest, Sleeper. You will need it."

Cat nodded, her eyelids drooping. "I think so, too."

She put her head down. Vaguely, she was aware of a sudden burst of activity around her, of being led to a tent and covered with blanket after blanket, but she didn't care. The very core of her body felt as though there was a stick of eternal ice thrust through her, one nothing could melt.

"I don't feel so good," she whispered. She burrowed her head under the covers and tried to breathe in warm air and perhaps she did, but she didn't know anything else for quite a while.

* * * * *

The dreams swirled around her and past her as though they were water, threatening to wash her away. But these dreams held no fear for her. They were disturbing in their imagery and their portent, but oddly the portent did not scare her.

She dreamt of crystalline caves warm to the touch but soft. Her hands seemed to drift among the shards of crystal, not cutting her skin but muzzling them with layers of comfortable heat instead. She dreamt of water that could kill, turning life into ash, and she dreamt of fire that could bury her and drown her in a single caress. She dreamt of a man in the distance as she explored the mysteries of a contradictory universe.

And though the perverse forces of nature did not fill her with fear, this man did—yet she found herself taking a step toward him each time she saw him. She knew she should not, but in the same vein she knew she would not regret it if she reached him.

And the skies seemed to fill with stillness, to be replaced with a thunder that seemed to reverberate. And she saw, once again, life turned to ash with a rain.

I can't, she whispered aloud. *I can't do this. I have to go home. I don't belong here.*

But you can, it whispered. It was a voice without body, firm but gentle. *And you must. You can go home when you are finished, and not before.*

How will I know when I'm finished? Cat asked.

A cold and chilling gray mist surrounded her. Beyond the mist was something that could hurt her yet heal her, and it was calling for her. She trembled as the mist swirled around her shoulders much the way the rolling dreams had, but the mist was not threatening to take away all she knew the way the river of her dreams had.

The moment will be inescapable, It told her. *Nothing will make as much sense, and the answers to your questions will be presented to you. It will be a sacrifice you will* want.

The skies shivered for a coming terror, and it seemed to Cat such an occurrence was not new. In the distance, beyond the mist, she could see the vague outlines of a mountain range, sharp, jagged, proud, hidden behind clouds. One peak caught her attention. It seemed to twist coyly around itself, partly hidden by vegetation. It almost looked like a human form but it seemed odd. It looked familiar but she didn't know why.

Then she saw in the distance something amorphous but the size of a small house. The mist itself seemed to cringe, shying away from it. All life seemed to twist away from it. She had never seen anything like it.

Finally she was afraid.

But three steady lights in the distance gave her a hope. They were almost pinpoints of light but grew with each passing second. They seemed to be moving in the direction of the gray mass, which in turn retreated from the light.

The retreat of the mass filled her with hope. Then in the distance, she saw the amorphous burst of gray that was the destroyer fold upon itself, until finally it disappeared in a *pop!*

She slumped. She was so tired, and so cold.

The mist enveloped her again, and she could no longer recognize anything around her. The jagged peaks in the distance that had piqued her curiosity were obscured again.

The ground on which she was standing shifted, becoming flat and sandy, soaked with blood. But at least she could hear water nearby, the ebb and flow of the tide comforting her as nothing else could.

She was so tired. She had never been so tired in her life and the ache in her head that had receded for a time was back in full vengeance. Was it her time? No, not yet. Not waterfire, either.

So tired. Cat decided she would feel better if she closed her eyes, and so—

* * * * *

The clanks and dull thuds awakened her. It took her a split second to identify the sounds of pots and pans the traveling party used. *Food*, she thought, and dimly she knew her lack of enthusiasm about the topic was not a good sign.

Her eyelids seemed sealed shut, and they seemed determined to remain so. Slowly she fought to open her eyes, and when she finally succeeded, she had the sensation of being very, very tired, as though she had not had any sleep at all.

She was too tired to move her head, so she contented herself with whatever she could see. The cracks of light peering through the closed tent flaps were gray, which meant it had to be dawn. Then she smelled fanadi, that bland traditional breakfast food of the Kuriti, and she knew without a doubt it was dawn.

Cat grimaced. *Dawn*. She must have slept through the entire night. And though she couldn't feel it, she knew she was starved.

A snort startled her. Gingerly, she turned her head. She saw Q'Atha, fast asleep. The girl was dozing in a propped-up position, huddled in a pile of blankets and capes and a jug of what was most likely cooled *oja* beside her.

That was odd. Why hadn't Q'Atha gone to sleep?

Fumbling into a sitting position, Cat grabbed her cape, which was sitting on top of the pile of blankets on the cot, and then pulled on her soft boots. She flinched at the cool air when her toes came out from under the pile of covers. Her feet had been cold even under the pile of blankets, but the touch of night air made them colder. This was one hell of a flu, she mused.

Her fingers were stiff from cold, though they too had been firmly tucked under the covers. She found her sciarra under the covers, right where her fingers had been.

Her struggles to slip the knife into sheathed position at the top of her boot as the Elder had taught her finally awoke Q'Atha, who twitched and snorted as her eyes opened. "Sleeper! You're awake! How do you feel?"

Cat shrugged and blew on her fingers. That didn't help. Her breath was cold too. "Sluggish and stiff, but otherwise, fine. How long was I asleep?"

"Two nights and a day, Sleeper," Q'Atha said, her eyes wide. "Pir Strian was frantic with worry."

Cat shook her head. She couldn't have heard right, or maybe she had. "Two nights and a *day*? Some flu!"

"Mostlike not, Sleeper. If you had been in with the Nurui much longer, you would be dead."

Cat stared at her. "How?" For such a dangerous people, she could have sworn the Nurui were at most unprepossessing—red eyes and green teeth were too weird—but not dangerous. "If they're so harmful, why doesn't everyone avoid them like the plague?"

"Everyone avoids the plague, Sleeper, but everyone also knows the Nurui can be useful in measured amounts," the girl said matter-of-factly. "We did tell you to keep away from them, and we would take you at the right time."

"Yes, but no one ever told me *why* they were dangerous!" Cat said, exasperated. She rubbed her eyes. Now that she was awake, she was tired, she was cranky, and most of all, she was frightened. "Are there any lasting effects?"

Q'Atha shook her head. "You'll be tired today and tomorrow and you'll be starving for most of it, no matter how much you eat. But you're awake." She touched her silver braids and added, "When I was a child, years ago, on a dare I went to see the Nurui. When I came out, I fell into a trance and did not wake for days. When I did, my hair had turned as silver as my grandme's."

Cat tried to stand up but promptly sat back down on the cot when the tent spun around her. "Am I supposed to be dizzy?" she asked, her eyes shut. She was hungry but she was also nauseated. "I don't feel so good." She opened her eyes again, but she couldn't quite focus. "And I had the strangest dream."

"Sleeper, stay down," she heard Q'Atha say. She heard the girl scramble to her feet. "It will be some time before you feel better."

Q'Atha was right. Taking off her boots again, Cat curled back up under the blankets and stayed there.

By the time Q'Atha came back with a tray of food and *oja*, Cat was flat on her back again, propping herself up only to eat what she could. The cold roast geene from the night before was tasty, but she could only keep down a few bites. The pickled radishes that were a staple of Kuriti travelers made her want to heave, the fanadi was warm and filling but completely uninteresting. Mostly, she had cup after cup of *oja*.

It was like a flu, but not. Her soul had caught a chill, and it would not be dislodged.

But at least she was awake. She was stuck for two more days—two days they should have been on the road—in bed, unable to get up long enough to leave the tent, and visited by every Tom, Dick, and Harry Kuriti in the traveling party.

Except Strian.

She was dozing when a soft clapping of hands made her open her eyes. Strian's jackoval stood at the entrance, garbed in his usual distinctive gray and violet and fuchsia manteau. He bowed and tilted his head.

Cat knew what that meant. "Please come in," she croaked, waving him in. She cleared her throat. "What can I do for you?" she asked, not expecting an answer, at least not in words.

The jackoval stepped in and in his elegant way bowed again. He produced from the depths of his manteau a small, silk-wrapped package. He drew a circle in the air and then, using both hands, offered the package to her.

She thought she knew the symbol he had drawn. "From Pir Strian?" she guessed. The jackoval didn't, couldn't, speak in a way she could understand, but he made himself understood.

The jackoval bowed again, and this time he came forward and knelt in front of her, offering the package.

"Thank you," Cat said, nodding, and accepted the package.

The wrap, a simple white square of silk, had been folded and knotted cleverly, negating the need of ribbon or fastener. It took her a minute to undo the knots but when she did, she smiled. "Thank the prince for me," she told the jackoval.

Nestled inside was a pair of gloves, soft cream-colored leather, close to elbow length. Fur lined, she saw with pleasure. Vaguely, she remembered her hands feeling so icy after leaving the Nurui camp they could have flash-frozen a waterfall, and she remembered the prince mentioning gloves.

Q'Atha came in, a jug of *oja* in hand. "Sleeper? Oh, the prince gave you gloves," the young woman exclaimed once she caught sight of the jackoval, who in turn bowed to her, sweeping out his arm. "Greetings, oh jackoval. Pir Strian said he would. You will need them, Sleeper, for your hands will be cold for a long, long time." She put down her burden and raised her hands, showing off a pair of well-worn leather gloves of faded teal.

Cat stared at Q'Atha's hands. She realized she had never seen the young woman without them. "How long ago—"

Q'Atha shrugged. Clearly, it had been long enough the subject was no longer uncomfortable. "Seven years, Sleeper. My hands are still cold in the spring, but not the summers now. And Grandme told me by the time I marry, my hands will be warm again. Would you like something to eat? Some nice, hot fanadi?"

Cat shook her head, shuddering. "Not fanadi. Not on an empty stomach. But what you said...you're planning on getting married? Aren't you a little young?"

Q'Atha dimpled, and all of a sudden Cat could see she was not as young as she had assumed. "But not for much longer, Sleeper, and Boyo too. Most who choose to see the Nurui end with gloves," she added. "To end with hair like mine," She touched her silver braids tipped with dark. "Happens seldom." She started to roll the blankets stashed in the corner. "I will make sure you have the warmest blankets, but the lightest, so our traveling is as quick as possible."

Cat sighed, and felt tired all over again. "We're behind schedule."

"You are," the younger woman said matter-of-factly. "But the Court and his party left two days ago after you sickened, and Pir Strian promised you would meet him there at the right time. I am here to nurse you and after you are better, I will set out."

"You're not going with me?"

Q'Atha half-smiled. "The prince promised the Court you would be at the Podani in time for the ceremony. He and his jackoval will accompany you, taking the road over the passes. I am hoping to do so too."

Something niggled Cat's memory. "Isn't that the dangerous road?"

The younger woman shrugged. She sat on the mound of satchels, bouncing a little. "I should have done this before," she said with a grin. "It is a fine surface. In answer to your question, Sleeper, the low roads are not quick but they are safe, but not in waterfire season. The high roads are less than safe, as robbers have frequented it during times of war. But the overpass is most feared at least these days...it used to be the protected highway, sacred to the imperial family, under the guardianship of the Court, before the wars. Now it is also the most dangerous as Son-Toruai claims it as his own, and without an armed guard...even royal messengers have disappeared while traveling on it."

Great. They were going to be traveling in Kurit's version of a cross between the Bermuda Triangle and the South Bronx. Cat took a deep breath. "We'd better go. Can't get there if we don't get going." She felt so weak. "Do we still have a riding carriage, or did those go with Gilcris?"

Q'Atha shook her head. "I am sorry, Sleeper. You must ride."

On a horse that didn't like her, as far as she could tell. Great. "I can do it," she whispered, for her own benefit as much as Q'Atha's. She had to go if she ever wanted a chance to go home, she knew that now. What she could remember of the bizarre dream told her that much. "I'm going crazy anyway," she said a little louder. "If I were back in Seattle, at least there'd be something on TV."

Q'Atha smiled sympathetically—at least Cat assumed it was sympathetic. "Some cold roast geene and pickled turnips would put you back on your feet, Sleeper. Perhaps you will be strong enough to ride tomorrow."

She was going to be strong enough, whether or not she could sit on the damned horse. "Sure, fine, whatever. But no fanadi." Cat shuddered. So she ate the geene.

Her eyes closed eventually but she couldn't recall when. It was the third day by the time she woke again. This time she sat up and began to dress, careful not to wake Q'Atha, who was snoring blissfully in the corner on the mound of satchels.

The sciarra seemed to stick a little as Cat slid it into place in her boot. The woolen cape was light and insubstantial in comparison to the layers upon layers of blankets she had been under. Only her new gloves felt right.

Cat stepped outside for the first time in days.

The stars were still shining in the darkness before the dawn but even this early, there was activity in the camp.

What was left of the camp. The sprawling compound had dwindled to her tent and one other, no more. And in front of the other, the jackoval tended a fire beneath a caldron.

Then she saw Strian sitting outside the other tent, his head against the external support of the structure. His eyes were closed. He was dressed for the chill in the night, bundled in a cape that looked worse for wear, his boots muddy and his headcover resting to one side. A bowl of fanadi rested in his hand, uneaten.

The bowl was going drop out of his hand in a minute. As quietly as she could, Cat walked over and slipped the bowl out of his hand, placing it on the bench beside him.

Strian opened his eyes. He hadn't been asleep after all.

"You're awake." He yawned. "I was wondering if your Sleeper self was different from ours, in how much sleep you needed."

"Not much, I think." She sat down next to him, the bowl of fanadi between them. She gestured toward it. "Shouldn't you eat? I'm sure your jackoval will fuss unless you do."

"I'm not hungry. Take it."

She looked at him. His eyes were smeared with bruises of sleeplessness, and his mouth was pinched. "If you're not going to sleep, you should eat. How long have you been awake?"

He considered it. "A day and a night. I decided to make use of our delay to see what was in front of us."

Which meant he rode ahead and rode back. If her butt ached with a half-day's ride, he had to be virtually paralyzed. "What did you find?"

He shrugged, then closed his eyes. "No sign of anything that will slow our progress."

She looked at her gloves. Her soft, warm gloves, which she had accepted without a thought. He had said he would find her gloves in the next town they came to. He must have ridden on ahead and sent them back for her. "Thank you for these," she said, raising a covered hand. "They're the only things that felt normal when I finally got dressed this morning."

He glanced at her hands, at rest on her lap, and smiled. "I remember my hands being icy when I was sick with Nurui cold."

"Is going in to see the Nurui something everyone does when they're young?"

Strian laughed. "Only when they're young and foolish, Sleeper. Some, like Q'Atha, have more consequence than others. I was cold and tired for a week after I took that dare, but poor Q'Atha was on her sickbed for a month, and her grandme frantic with worry and her friends died."

Cat looked at her gloved hand. Her gaze drifted over to the fanadi, now rapidly cooling and congealing with a pasty-colored skin on top. She was hungry again but even if Strian wasn't, he had to eat. "I'll split the fanadi with you," she said. "If we're going to ride for the entire day, you have to eat something. Falling off your horse isn't going to do you any good. Besides, you have to pick me up when I fall off," she added, aiming for light and not entirely succeeding.

But Strian didn't seem to care, for he shrugged and picked up the bowl. "Lol is used to keeping me astride." He selected a fat, still-warm chunk. "Open your mouth."

"You're not going to feed me."

"I may be bone-tired but you have days of recovery ahead of you, Sleeper. Now open."

"No."

"Yes. Open now," he said, waving the chunk in front of her.

She picked up a chunk and positioned it in front of his mouth. "If I eat, you have to too. Open."

He smiled. The shadows in his face lightened up for a moment. "If I must." He opened his mouth and she placed the chunk between his teeth. He took it, biting down. "Delicious," he said, chewing. "The jackoval is a genius. Your turn now."

He gently pressed the chunk of fanadi between her lips, and she started to nibble on it reluctantly. Her eyes popped open. It was tasty. The usually bland food was actually tasty!

"This is *good*! Does he carry his own spices?" Strian's jackoval had added a touch of something like oregano. "The Elder's cook is very good, but her fanadi..." Eagerly, she picked up another chunk and carefully lobbed it into Strian's mouth.

He caught it adeptly. "As far as I know," he said, munching. "Open." He gently tossed another morsel into her open mouth.

"Is this part of your training exercises?" she asked, chewing and swallowing. "Improving your eye-hand coordination?"

"I think my coordination suffers not at all, thank you, Sleeper." Instead of tossing, however, the next piece of fanadi he placed at the edge of her lip.

He looked so tired. More than food, what he truly needed was sleep, which Cat knew he would not permit himself, not yet.

"I sent my brother the Court ahead to the Podani. We may not be able to stop tonight to make the ceremony in time," he warned. "The trip from here gets perilous with our new route."

She nodded. "I know. I'll keep up."

"I understand you've no seat for a horse."

Well, she couldn't deny it. "In my own defense, I've never seated myself on a horse but once before this, Pir Strian."

"How is it you have never had to be on a horse? Have you stayed in one town all your life and had no need?"

She shook her head. "I've lived in half a dozen places, but we don't travel by horse. We have a—" She stopped. How was she going to describe a car? "Many of us have boxes made of iron that move faster than horses," she devised. That much was true. "I have one. I learned how to drive one when I was sixteen."

"Magic boxes," he mused. "This Shiatta sounds like a wondrous place."

She shrugged. "Those boxes—they're called *cars*—are commonplace. I think I saw a real, live horse maybe a dozen times before I woke up here."

"Well, you'll be well-acquainted with Arriya before long. You'll be sore for days on end."

"I already am," she said, shifting. But she wasn't as sore as she thought she would be. But then, she had been flat on her back for the better part of three days.

"If Arriya decides not to throw you," he added. She hoped that was a twinkle in his eye. "If you do not have that instinctive bridge with your ride, there's no telling what she'll do."

"You make it sound so appealing, Pir Strian."

"I can think of no other way to make it sound, Sleeper." But he said it with a smile.

After that, the conversation died, but not uncomfortably. They each took a chunk of fanadi from time to time as they watched the stars move and the sky lighten toward dawn.

Cat had no idea how long they had been sitting there, the last of the stars fading away, when she heard shouts. "Sleeper! My prince!"

Q'Atha? Cat turned as Strian stood. The young woman was running toward them. Behind her was Strian's jackoval, and behind them both was a dark-caped young man wearing a badge on his hat.

The badge. It was Gilcris' emblem. It had to be a message.

Strian saw it too. He jumped up, the bowl, half-full by then, clattering to the ground. He started to run toward them, and Cat followed—except she reached down and grabbed the fanadi.

The messenger skidded to a stop. "By your leave, sire," he panted when he could, bowing quickly and nearly falling. Undaunted, he reached into his cape, fumbling in its pockets, before producing a slightly crumpled scroll, hastily sealed with the distinctive maroon wax and smeared seal of office. He kneeled and offered it to Strian.

"Enough," Strian said, reaching for the scroll and with his other hand laying a hand on the boy's shoulder. "Eat while you can. I may need you to ride back with an answer."

He broke the seal and unrolled the scroll, scanning the lines. The messenger bowed to Cat and Q'Atha and accepted what was left of the fanadi, proceeding to chew as fast as he could.

"Quer'Cadrine—"

Cat looked at Strian, surprised. It was rare he acknowledged she had a name. "Yes?"

He was paler than he had been. If she didn't know better she would have sworn he was coming down with something. "What is it?" she asked in alarm. "Strian, what's the matter?"

"The other Sleepers have disappeared."

Chapter Eleven

ഇ

"Kevin and Margot *disappeared*?"

Blank-faced, Strian handed her the note. "It says nothing else. How came you here?" he asked the messenger.

"When it happened, the Elder bade me to find the Sleeper—" at which the young man bowed to Cat—"to tell her. I took the road leading to the passes, met the Court on his journey, and I was directed back here."

"What happened?" Cat demanded. She grabbed the piece of paper from him—only to remember she couldn't read it. "Tell me what it says exactly," she ordered.

Strian glanced at her, a flicker of something in his eyes. "It must have been written quickly, Sleeper, but in full. Quer'Ali says,

"*Hail to thee, cousin. I hope the journey finds you well, but I regret to tell you one day after I wrote to you previously, the other Sleepers vanished from sight this morrow, bright and early after the break of dawn, in front of two guards and the town's councilmen, when they floated into the air and disappeared. Else naught was disturbed, and naught was left to mark they had ever been there, save the furs on which they slept. Tell Quer'Cadrine this is a mystery, but not one for which she should return for the moment, and tell her it is her destiny, I feel, to continue the journey with you to the ceremony and perhaps there discover the fates of the other Sleepers.*"

Strian looked up at Cat. "And then signed is her name."

"Wait a minute. They *floated* and they vanished?"

"Sleeper, do you trust my cousin?"

"Yes. She may be the only one I trust." A touch of bitterness crept into her voice.

Strian didn't say anything for a minute. "I'm sorry for you. That you feel so. We are honorable people...for the most part. In any case, I trust what she says," he added, turning away. "Perhaps you will know later why your fellow Sleepers disappeared but in the meanwhile, we must be on our way to the ceremony."

The waterfire. Her stomach, which had been insisting on more fanadi, twisted. She felt nauseated for a moment.

"Are you ready for a long ride?"

Cat took a deep breath. She'd eaten enough. "Sure."

"If the prospect of riding long with Arriya is not to your liking, you can ride with me, Sleeper," Q'Atha offered. "You'll be safe enough, I think."

"No, cousin, you are going home," Strian said. He rolled up the scroll and handed it to his jackoval, into whose voluminous manteau it disappeared. "The journey from here will be too perilous on the overland pass and your grandmeren would never forgive me if something happened to you."

"Oh, cousin," Q'Atha exclaimed, her bottom lip quivering and making her look as young as she sounded. "I was so looking forward to the ceremony. And seeing the Podani."

"We are going on the passes, cousin, and that's no place for you. And that is the only way we will get there in time with an inexperienced rider."

"Oh, please," Q'Atha cried, dismayed. "I'm a good rider. You know this."

"She can come with me, sire," the messenger offered. "I have a message for the Court. She will be safe."

Strian gave the messenger a hard look. "What road?"

"The high road. I travel with protection," the courier said, gesturing behind him. Cat glanced over his shoulder. She realized a good dozen horseback riders waited in the shadows on the edges of the clearing. "She will be safe, I swear, my prince. We will not have time to stop, and that will be in our favor."

"Are *you* ready for hard riding?" Strian asked his young cousin.

"Yes please," Q'Atha said, her eyes shining as she clapped her hands. She didn't look like a young woman who would be married soon enough, not right then. "I'll be good. And I can ride."

"I know you can. Well, Sleeper, we ride—you, the jackoval, and me," Strian said. "You will ride with me, and that way, you can doze and Arriya will carry our provisions and my jackoval. Are you ready?"

For a moment, Cat was taken aback. She hadn't considered this alternative. "I guess."

It was like being on the back of a motorcycle, and you've done that, she reminded herself.

But a motorcycle couldn't bite, she shot back.

"I promise you will not fall if you ride with me."

Immediately she was embarrassed. For the first time in years, she was nervous being that close to another human being. If he was human, of course.

"Cousin, finish packing. The messenger cannot dally long. As it is, the Sleeper and I will be arriving at the Podani hard on the ceremony."

Q'Atha squealed and ran to pack. Cat watched her go. "Ingrate," she muttered. "She kept saying how I needed someone to help me. All she wanted to see was the gay lights of Paree."

"I beg pardon, Sleeper?" Strian said, frowning.

Cat shook her head. "Never mind. When do we get going?"

Strian looked at the sky, squinting. The edges of dawn were breaking over the horizon. "Once I talk to my jackoval, we pack," he told her. He turned to the messenger, who had been waiting, scraping the sides of the bowl for the last of the fanadi he had divided amid his fellow riders. "I have another message for you to deliver," he said. "Sit while I compose it."

Cat gave the messenger—no older than Boyo, she figured—another bowl of cooling fanadi as the jackoval prepared him a packet of food to take. The messenger dove into the second bowl eagerly, startling Cat. He must have ridden nonstop to get here in time. But he shared this one with the others in his company too.

Before he was done, Q'Atha appeared again, carrying two large satchels. She dropped one bag and then offered Cat the other.

Cat recognized it. "You packed for me? That fast?"

The Elder said her granddaughter was quick when motivated, and she was right. "I thought I could spare you the task, Sleeper," Q'Atha said cheerily. Cat took the bag, and when she did, Q'Atha skipped over and gave her a hug. "Good journey, Sleeper," the young woman whispered. "I'll see you at the other end of the journey, at the Podani."

By the time the sun finally peered over the horizon, camp was broken, with little trace it had been there at all. "Stay safe," Strian instructed his young cousin. "Move quickly, tell the Court what happened to the Sleeper. Traveling in strength, with no incident and without stopping, you should be there in a hard day's ride."

The messenger touched his finger to his cap. "We'll keep to the overland and keep the young lady safe, my prince." And then he and Q'Atha left, already at a gallop.

Cat watched them leave, envious they could move that quickly on horseback without discomfort. As for herself— "I will lift you onto Lol and then you can hold onto his mane as I mount behind you," Strian said.

She flushed. "I'll skootch forward so you can get on," she muttered.

"No need," he said. He did exactly what he said he would do, expending less effort to get on the horse than Cat did to eat.

She tried to feel uncomfortable, she tried to feel tense. Instead, she sat still for a minute...and had to admit sitting on a horse with Strian felt...right. Which was ridiculous. It was idiotic! He looked like Mark, but he didn't feel like Mark, he didn't smell like Mark. He felt...good.

Face flushing, she looked up, around, anywhere than to feel him behind her. "Which way?" she queried, more for conversation than anything else.

"Up," Strian told her, his single word causing a breeze that tickled her ear. She burrowed into her cape. Her fingers were tingling. She tucked her hands close to her body.

"Ready? Which way?" he asked his jackoval, who mounted Arriya as easily as Strian had. The jackoval started to wave, his hands making concentric circles. None of it made any sense to Cat, but she felt Strian nod.

"Well, it's up," he told her, speaking into her ear again.

Cat closed her eyes. "I'll take your word for it," she said, fighting the urge to turn her head.

"My jackoval is expert in reading landscape, Sleeper. I know you do not understand him; it takes a while. Our only problem," he added, "is that Son-Toruai has pockets of supporters through the hills. My jackoval knows where many of them are, but not all."

Get ready to rumble, Cat guessed. "We're going to be packing heat, aren't we?"

"We will be armed, if that's what you mean, Quer'Cadrine."

She stopped herself from whipping her head around in surprise. Somewhere along the way she had stopped being "Sleeper".

* * * * *

"What happened?"

Behind her, Strian turned his head as he looked around. "What is it?" he asked, perplexed. "This is the way this terrain has always looked."

"It looks so different from everything else I've seen. It looks…exotic." Her voice trailed off.

The lush greenery that characterized the verdant farmlands Cat had become accustomed to had fallen away little by little as they climbed to reach the passes. The higher elevations made for fewer conifers, thinner air, Cat realized as she started to breathe deeper, striving for more oxygen. The air was a touch more rarefied, the light a bit sharper, the game scarce—the abundant shy deer and the confident fat rabbits littering the landscape down below were little in evidence.

Too, the distinctive rock formations that marked Kurit were more evident the higher they climbed. Cat could feel Lol's steps under her become more careful as they climbed, with only a stumble from time to time. She took a deep breath, then exhaled. Her fingers were chilly but she gripped the pommel anyway, not willing to let go when Lol swayed. The hillsides were nearly impassable in some areas, manageable but only just in others, she guessed.

But at least there was no waterfire this far up.

But it was getting harder and harder for her to take a breath. "How far do we climb?" Was that her voice? It was so little. When did that happen?

She had to keep a grip, but that was getting harder and harder to do.

Just when she should have been feeling better after waking up from Nurui sleep, she felt lousy again. At least the migraines hadn't come back—but at this point, she wouldn't have been surprised if one bloomed hard, just for icing on the cake. She had to breathe deeper, make more of every breath, but to be free of those headaches was worth every bit of it.

"Sleeper? Are you aright?"

Strian, asking after her health again. And she was "Sleeper" again.

Right now, she didn't care. She tried to take a breath, let it out, but the best she could do was a rasp. "I c—" *Can't breathe,* she tried to say, but all she could manage was a gagging noise.

"Quer'Cadrine? Can you hear me? Cadrine?"

She could hear Strian's voice, sharper with worry. Not again, she thought, despair and guilt cutting through the fog. She'd already cost them three days. She fought, gasping, and coughed. "I'm okay. Just have to adjust to the thin air," she whispered. She swallowed once.

Cat tried her best, but as they ascended, the higher they went, the harder it was to breathe. She tried to keep quiet, for she knew if she said too much, Strian would surely be forced to stop, and they had no time for anything beyond a few minutes here and there. But when she nearly slipped off Lol, only to be seized by Strian and kept astride, did she realize they had no choice—falling could mean off a cliffside, and not only her but Strian and Lol as well.

"I'm sorry," she gasped as Strian jumped off the horse first and then lifted her off. "I can't breathe."

He looked at her carefully. "Your color is poor, Sleeper," he said. She was Sleeper again, not "Quer'Cadrine". She wondered why, but only vaguely. She was having a hard time keeping her eyes open. She had to be suffering still from the Nurui chill.

Strian gently pressed two fingers against the side of her jaw, and she could feel her own pulse then—a little thready, a little fast. Not good. "We stop for the night," he said. "That is all we can do for the moment."

"Okay. I think I'll sit down now," she said faintly and sat hard on the ground. Her eyes closed.

The next time she decided to open her eyes, she realized she could smell baking fanadi—how? How would Strian's jackoval manage to cook fanadi in the middle of nowhere without utensils? And second, she realized she was very, very—

"Oh my God, I'm on fire!" she cried out in alarm, rolling over and scrambling into an upright position.

She heard laughter from two sources, one loud and hearty, and the other higher-pitched and flute-like. She blinked, letting her eyes adjust so the campfire was clear in front of her, and she could finally see. Strian and his jackoval were settled on the other side of the campfire, a small iron pan holding the nearly cooked fanadi she had been smelling.

Both Strian and the jackoval looked relaxed and rested. It was nice they'd both relaxed while she was out cold, she thought disagreeably. She shook her head. She hated waking up.

"Are you awake at last, Sleeper? You are truly called."

She also hated jokes about her sleeping. "I was tired," she muttered. "And I'm not used to the altitude." She edged a little closer to the fire, now that she knew she wasn't actually burning. "I have never felt so cold as I have in the past few days. People must die of frostbite feeling like that."

"How do you feel now?"

"Warm. And a few minutes ago, way too warm."

"You were very close to the fire, Sleeper," Strian told her. "You kept edging toward it as though you were a moth to the flame. But we watched to make sure you got no closer."

The jackoval gabbled something, and Strian nodded. "That you were too warm for comfort means you are on your way to recovering from your Nurui chill, Sleeper. Congratulations," he said. "You have done something Kuriti have died doing."

She sidled as close as she could to the crackling blaze without actually settling on it. "What I don't understand is why Kuriti would know about the dangers of the Nurui and still go see them."

"Knowing one's future is a very attractive thing."

Cat shrugged. "But if someone had told me I would get terminal cancer and find myself in a place I can't tell if it's a dream, I would have laughed and thrown them out. I mean, why bother? What could I have changed?"

It was Strian's turn to shrug. He reached out with his sciarra to poke at the fanadi, browning quickly now. "It is mainly youth, Sleeper. The older do not want to know, because they know they will see what awaits them soon enough. And even the young who have seen war and terror have no desire to see what awaits them."

Cat nodded, letting her eyes close against the blaze in front of her. "The young soldiers know how precious their time is. How much they waste…" She gasped.

Both Strian and the jackoval glanced at her, startled. "What's wrong, Sleeper?" the prince asked, lines of concern distorting his face in the firelight.

She scrambled, folding the blanket in front of her. "We have to get going!" she cried, looking around for her belongings. "We have to get to the Podani! Didn't you say we don't have much time?" She started to get to her feet, wavering a little. She stood still for a second trying to get her balance. "I'm sorry I was so tired, but I'm better now, so we should get going. We—"

"Quer'Cadrine."

She sat back down, feeling drained and sitting still for a moment. "Why aren't you moving?" she demanded, but without much emotion. She was too tired to go nuts.

Strian looked around. The jackoval reached over and poked and turned the fanadi, just about ready now. "Because we are stopped for a few hours. Only a fool rides over the passes at night without the benefit of the full moons."

She looked up. The night was clear, the sky full of stars, but the large double moons dominating the evening sky in Kurit looked as though they were merged into one.

"Like being in the wrong part of the Bronx at the wrong time."

Perhaps Strian was getting used to the non sequiturs, for all he said was, "As you say, Sleeper. But we are here for some hours, so you should rest as much as you can. Fanadi?" He reached into the iron pan with his sciarra and brought out a chunk, still-steaming, lightly toasted, offering it to her.

Funny how she had nearly vomited the first time she tasted fanadi, but now she sort of didn't hate it. The jackoval was a whiz with the stuff. "Yes, thank you. And thank you," she said to the jackoval, nodding as she bit in. He'd done his magic again—a little nutty, a little sweet, the flavor popped in her mouth. "I didn't think you could cook this without more equipment."

The jackoval smelled like cinnamon, which was good, because apparently that was the native scent of his people in a good mood, Q'Atha told her. The jackoval beamed and gestured, gabbling something she could make out one word out of five. "He says he'll make fanadi for you anytime," Strian translated. "You're lucky. If jackoval likes you, you'll get fed well."

It was a never-ending source of amusement for her that "jackoval" was apparently his name as well as his title. He never volunteered another and from what she gathered Strian had, through the years, never asked again, respecting his wishes. "It's delicious," she told him. "Is it native to your country?"

And then they talked—as much as they could, with Strian translating when the jackoval's gestures became incomprehensible. The jackoval told her about his native land, outside the Sea of Circles, which had been devastated by wars that had managed to destroy most of the mercantile centers of the region. Where once the country had been bustling with trade, after the war was said and done, all that was left was rubble—and in some towns, such as the one in which the jackoval had grown up, nothing at all, with every home, every building, destroyed so not even rubble was left to name it. That was when the jackoval had chosen to make his way to the Circles, before ending up at this campfire.

Cat squinted at Strian, assessing. "Is he really saying all that, or are you embellishing?"

The prince raised his hands. "This is not my story, Sleeper. This is the jackoval's, roughly translated."

"Is his language only by hand?"

Strian paused. "No." He glanced at the jackoval, who shrugged. "His language is rich and varied, and even uses hand gestures, but the jackoval's tongue was cut during his travels."

The jackoval shrugged again and gestured, from what she could make out—*A long time ago. How jackoval met Pir Strian.*

The jackoval's devotion to Strian was a curious thing, he began, his hands waving with an occasional click. The world was a bigger place than he had imagined, he explained, so much so he could not tell her all about his travels, but at one point he found himself in a tavern far from the Podani, far from the border, many years ago, when the Court was still being schooled at the Island Garde by the Skyriders. The jackoval was recognized as one of his kind, renown for their talents, not often seen in the Circles.

"What talents?"

Strian stepped in. "They are known to be cooks beyond compare, able to make the least of ingredients into a feast. But

I had no idea of that when I wandered into that tavern, having escaped from the clutches of my tutor in the crowd of the market."

The jackoval grinned. *Pir Strian boy,* he informed Cat. *Skinny, curious. Good fighter.*

The prince arrived at the tavern but he did not know he should not be there not because of his tender age but because of the place it was, the jackoval explained. At least that was how Cat translated it. Nor did the jackoval know. It was a tavern frequented by slavers, and the prince came upon the slavers already having cut out the jackoval's tongue and on the verge of cutting his hamstrings.

Though young, Strian turned out to be a surprisingly good fighter, good enough—with a little help from a pain-crazed jackoval—to run off the slavers. The prince made sure the jackoval had medical care and, after he recovered, placed him on Strian's personal staff. Barely out of his own adolescence and already preparing to join the brethren of the Kama, Strian gained a manservant he hadn't counted on.

After all these years the jackoval was Strian's right-hand man still, cooking for him and tending to the details of his life. When his master joined the contemplation of the Kama the jackoval had followed him, his cooking making him the favorite of the priests, his varied scents of cinnamon usually and coriander when he was upset quickly becoming a standard of those halls.

Cat took a bite of the piping hot fanadi and sighed. "I never thought I would like fanadi, but this is absolutely delicious," she told the jackoval.

The jackoval beamed, though he tried to look modest. And with that, he began to clean and straighten up, leaving Strian and Cat at the campfire.

"Do you think he misses his home?" Cat asked wistfully after the jackoval took the pan and dishes away to scrape them clean, far enough away to avoid attracting wild beasts. Her eyelids drooped. She was finally almost warm and filled with tasty fanadi, and she was ready to sleep again.

"No doubt. But I think he misses what was his home before the war more than what it is now, Sleeper," Strian said, reflecting. "I miss the Podani as it was when I was a child, and not as it is now — empty, dust-ridden, Gilcris walking alone through its halls, wondering what happened to his life."

Cat positioned her blanket around her shoulders. "And still he fights."

"For Kurit," he added. "And for our way. The uncle is a cousin and while he is family, his way is not ours."

"And now, all your brother has left is to fight a war?"

"That, and on occasion, a thirst for revenge. But that fire burns out quickly, and then he is simply tired."

"How does he fight a war if he's falling apart?"

"Not well. That was when he called for me."

They sat for a while, staring into the fire.

"It's good you did," she said. "Come to help, against your principles and everything."

"The Kamaites were formed to protect the Court and the imperial family, and I am a Kamaite priest as well as his brother. My duties were clear — to protect."

"A priest," she said curiously. She knew that word, but she didn't know if it meant the same thing. "Do you have nuns?"

"The convents of Laoni train our healers, but they are cloistered."

"How do they heal if they are cloistered?"

"We bring the long-term wounded there, and it is there they recover."

"How far is it?"

"A week and five days."

"So if they're healthy enough to last that long a journey, they get to go somewhere where they're going to be healed? What if you're not healthy enough to get there?"

He looked at her for a moment. "I have often wondered myself."

"Never mind. It must be one of those Kuriti things I don't understand."

"Quer'Cadrine, I agree with you," he confessed. "It struck me long ago if the Kamaites were to leave the monastery and fight for the Court, surely the Laoni should come out to tend to the wounded. But the Laoni do not."

She shrugged. "That's what traditions are. They may not make sense, but they've been around for a long time."

"And they may have made sense long ago, but no more. A memory of sorts," he suggested. "Nothing anyone could remember having any basis for, but something you know from your heart."

"Like that," Cat whispered.

She stole a glance at the prince. He was staring into the fire, but for once his face was relaxed.

"I don't remember my mother and father," she said, and hesitated. "But I remember how they felt. Warm, and as though they were all around me. I haven't felt like that since."

"One's lovers should do that, Sleeper."

"Mine never did."

He stared at her. "Why not?"

She thought about it. "Maybe because I never thought they would and so they didn't. If I didn't expect it, I wouldn't be disappointed."

He shook his head and then, all of a sudden, he raised his arm. "You win."

"What?"

"In miseries. That must be the saddest story I have ever heard, and I have heard plenty."

Cat shook her head. "It's the truth. I can die knowing that what's behind wasn't what I wanted, but if I can do something at the ceremony, maybe it will have been all worthwhile."

"We should all have a goal, Quer'Cadrine," Strian said, hoisting his cup in salute. "We all should."

"What is yours?"

"Mine, like my brother's, is to see the end of this war and the end of my honorable uncle," he said, his voice deceptively soft as he said the harsh words. "For he killed my brother's son just as surely as if he had stabbed the boy until he was dead. For his own ambition. War for war's sake as a warrior I can understand, but to cause the death of a child for the sake of ambition is intolerable, and he will pay for it. By the hyagoths, I swear."

Cat stared into the fire, willing her eyes not to well with tears. "You win," she whispered. She closed her eyes, trying not to think about a little boy and how he died.

"Is this your Sleeper then, Pir Strian?" an amused voice asked, cutting through the darkness. "Odd. She doesn't look like someone who would bring in a new era of peace for Kurit."

Cat's eyes popped open.

Chapter Twelve

❧

"Are you sure you didn't pay coin for her someplace outside the Seas?"

There was a crackle and a hiss. The fire, which had been burning only a few minutes before, was out, the result of a douse of water. The second before the water hit the flames she caught sight of a man's face, a neatly trimmed beard framing his jaw, and she had a suspicion he did not stand there alone.

Part of the water splashed on her. "Hey!" She started to stand up, only to tumble back when a hand shoved her back down.

Just to make sure, she stayed down, rubbing her elbows. She could dimly see Strian across the remnants of the fire, sitting still but his eyes darting around. She peered a little more and she could see the tip of a sword gleam as it pressed against the bottom of Strian's throat.

"What do you want?" he said. His eyes stopped moving at a spot above and beyond her. From the look on Strian's face she could guess who it was.

"I was passing by and had to have my say," Cat heard. She didn't recognize the voice. "I think the queen's uncle would be just as suited to ushering in a new era for Kurit as this—"

Strian moved his head sharply at that. Cat was horrified to see a trickle of blood course down his neck. "Careful with your speech," he warned. She had to hand it to him. If she couldn't see the blood on his neck, she would have thought he only had a fly bother him instead of ignoring the flash of pain that prick of the sword must have caused. "Unless, of course,

Beven, your estimable master has now chosen to insult women and children as well as killing them."

Beven. Who was Beven? Getting bold—as far as she knew, there wasn't a weapon being pressed against her—Cat looked up at the man who had spoken.

She couldn't see any details in the dark but from what was left of the glowing ash of the fire, she could see his face, twisted in a smile, his long, narrow face rodent-like as she looked at it upside down.

"Your traveling companion seems curious about me. We should shed some light so we may be introduced, Pir Strian." He nodded to someone behind her and all of a sudden, a torch was thrust in front of her.

She blinked, letting her eyes adjust. This place obviously had a fixation with gloves. Beven's hands were sheathed in unexpectedly sleek, oiled black leather gloves at odds with the shabby, patched cape. The gloves were edged with tiny glittering silver balls. Then he shifted and she caught a glimpse of the gold medallion on his chest, like the one Strian wore. He had to be another Kamaite.

Strian, meanwhile, was ensuring his fellow Kamaite was distracted. "Or is killing women and children part of what you do these days for Son-Toruai?" he snarled, his eyes fixed on the other man.

Kamaite or no, Beven did not take well to the comment. His eyes narrowed into slits. "Brave talk from someone on the down side of a battle," he said with a spat. "Will you be retiring up to Kama after the battle, Brother Strian, or will you join your brother in eternity with the hyagoths?"

The trickle of blood made its way down the cord of Strian's neck, disappearing into the darkness of his collar. "I would sooner join you in Dara Lal, Brother Beven," he said, teeth clenched. "Was it your idea to imprison Temer in the pit, or was it my honorable uncle's? Did you think you would

195

curry favor with anyone by killing my nephew, an innocent child?"

Cat tensed as she watched them. This man had to be part of the faction of the Kamaites that had rallied behind the late Queen's uncle. How many of them were here?

Beven stared at him, his hands twitching. "I am surprised at you, Brother Strian. It was a merciful death, certainly," he hissed. "As you would realize if you were to think of it. The child would have had to be either exiled or executed after his father was put down, and by then he would have been old enough to realize what would happen to him. The way he died was best for all concerned."

Cat interrupted with a snort. "You call that a merciful death? From what I hear, a kid what, three, four years old? Dies of pneumonia because you put him in a pit, and you claim it was *better* that way? Mister, are you crazy?"

Beven raised a hand and snapped his fingers. A larger, burly man stepped forward, his hand raised. Cat backed away. "You better not!" she warned.

The other Kamaite stared at her, musing. "No, we should not touch the Sleeper, should we? The hyagoths protect you, and we would regret it. No, the prince," he said, his eyes lighting up. "I think the prince should be the one to get a taste of it."

What happened next occurred so fast Cat barely had time to react. The burly man stepped forward and struck Strian across his face with a pair of gloves. Cat cried out. After the man stepped back, she realized the gloves were, like Beven's, edged with tiny decorations, but instead of little silver balls, these decorations had been sharpened to a point. The pinprick of blood on Strian's neck was joined by a profusion of tiny bloody welts across his jaw.

"Strian!" she cried. Ignoring the thugs surrounding them, she scrambled over to Strian and touched his face. He flinched and moved away, but not before her hand came away with a smear of blood.

"You can't even do your own dirty work? Strian, are you all right?" She yanked out her relatively clean kerchief and pressed it against his jaw, and watched in fright as the light-colored fabric turned dark and damp, the scent of iron in the air. "Some priest you are!" she accused Beven over her shoulder.

Beven shifted his gaze toward her. Now that she sat across from him, she could see his face—thin, lined, his eyes hunted. He looked more like prey than predator, but the twist of his mouth belied that impression, as did his words. "Careful what you say, *Sleeper*," he sneered. "An eternal sleep may be your destiny otherwise."

"It will be anyway, you asshole," she shouted, furious. "That's true for everyone, you flipping psycho. Strian, are you all right?"

Strian was staring at her.

"What?" she said. "Are you okay?"

He gently wrested her kerchief from her and continued to press it against his jaw. "I am aright, Sleeper," he said, and it looked like he almost smiled. "As for you, Beven—an eternal sleep is the destiny of all of us. But you and your master seem to run toward it."

The other Kamaite scoffed. "Some of us are destined for better things before we sleep, Pir Strian. But for you, I believe your options have dwindled. Now get up, both of you."

Cat looked around. Sure enough, there were only the two of them—Strian and her. The jackoval was nowhere to be seen.

But if he...

Beven mistook her movement. "There's no easy way to escape, my lady. And if you are who they say you are, you would not be familiar with the territory. You should be just fine for the pit."

He was right, she didn't know the lay of the land. Neither did the jackoval, but he would surely follow them.

But if the three of them had anything to say about it, she decided, none of them were going.

So she and Strian got up and she carefully brushed off her clothing, first making sure the blood flow from Strian's jaw was stanched for the moment. Out of the corner of her eye, she could see Strian doing much the same, smoothly grabbing both his and the jackoval's belongings with the same economy of movement to make it look as though he had brought it all. "Are you okay, Strian?" she said as loudly as she could without calling attention to herself. "Should we put a bandage on or something?"

There were four of them. Beven and three thugs, and from the way they were standing looking into the fire instead of out into the darkness, they had no clue the party of two they had stepped into was a party of three. There was the big one behind her, who had been willing to hit her—scum—and then there were two more, who weren't as large but both looked fast. But they clearly took orders, they didn't give them.

Strian looked at her before he answered. "The flow should stop soon, Sleeper. My thanks." He kept his gaze on her a second longer, and she knew what he was trying to tell her—*Keep an eye out.*

"Good," she answered in as normal a voice as possible, grabbing her satchel. She kept a wary eye on the thugs in front of them. "I wouldn't want to have all that blood slowing us down."

Beven laughed, his giggle grating on her ears. "Your Sleeper's an odd one, Brother Strian. Are all of them like this one?"

Strian shrugged. "I'm only familiar with this one, Brother Beven. And I have learned to accept her foibles, much the way you accepted mine when I joined the order of the Kamaites."

Beven's lips thinned but he had no rejoinder. Strian added, "I of course learned to move whenever you came by, just in case your boot would once more miss its target of the ground and kick me instead." He nodded, glancing at Cat. She blinked once and drew a breath.

Beven laughed out loud. "You're in a happy mood, for someone whose life has just come to an end."

Strian shrugged again, his eyes shifting away from the ledge of rock above Beven and his thugs. She watched Beven intently as she gripped the strap to her satchel, tense and alert. "You have the better of me, Brother," Strian answered. "You have me surrounded with your men, your weapons are drawn and my brother's cause is about to be devastated. As possibly, your own — *now!*"

Cat bolted to one side as the slide of rocks struck Beven and his men from above. Some of the larger stones struck the two smaller men squarely and they stumbled. But Beven and the large one was only showered with a river of pebbles and they only staggered. From above the jackoval leaped on the big, burly one, his knife drawn, slitting his throat with an economy of motion.

Strian didn't waste any time. He kicked Beven square in the chest, knocking him down, but Beven tripped him and he fell, cushioned by the satchels he had thrown down when the rockslide began. Strian unsheathed his sciarra from the top of his boot and sprang at Beven, who neatly sidestepped him.

Cat clambered to her feet and swung her satchel as hard as she could, knocking one of the shorter, shiftier guys down again, and she swung it again when he tried to get up once more, hitting him hard. After that, he didn't get up again. She turned and saw Strian lost his balance over the fallen rocks while Beven was ready to leap on him, his own knife in hand.

"Strian!" she screamed, running toward him. "Look out!"

Two more, the big one and a smaller one. The jackoval. Where was he? Had he gotten the larger one? She couldn't see him or the burly one, so she promptly attacked Beven, leaping on his back and holding on for dear life, knowing she was doing no more than slowing him down. "Strian! Get up!"

Strian rolled over and got up, yelling, "Jump off, Cadrine!"

She did, hitting the ground with more emphasis than she would have liked. She was going to be bruised later but it didn't matter right then. She rolled and then scrambled up again.

By this time, the jackoval was down on the ground, his knife drawn and slashing at the other, smaller stooge. Cat ran toward them, grabbing hold of her own sciarra, ready to use it.

She brought it up, intending to stab anything that was not one of her own—and stood in astonishment. The jackoval had both of the henchmen who were left by their throats, one in each hand, dangling high in the air. "I guess you don't need my help," she said.

The jackoval smiled and bowed slightly—but not too much, because after all, he did have to maintain his own balance. "*Jackoval have fun*," he gabbled, as far as Cat could decipher. "*Jackoval take care.*" Effortlessly, he knocked the heads of two men together—Cat never knew that could ever happen outside of a movie—and dropped them.

She stared again as the jackoval next picked up Beven off of Strian with ease and threw him aside. The other Kamaite hit the ground, where he stayed, groaning.

"You should have killed him," Strian said, panting. He rubbed at his jaw. "I was going to."

"Brother Beven die, no tell where Brother Son-Toruai," the jackoval reminded him.

Strian waved. "I know. This is the problem with the overland passes, Sleeper," he said finally to Cat. "Once, when this was the protected highway, neither side could touch the other. Now—"

"I can see why you would want to avoid it." Cat took a deep breath.

Strian looked up. "We'd best be going now. That way, we can at least have some distance on them. As for Beven—" He looked at his fellow Kamaite, unconscious in a pile of thugs. The jackoval was, if nothing else, neat in his cleanup. Strian shook his head. "I doubt he was told anything but to find us."

They spent no more time in talking after that. They packed and were on their way within minutes, kicking what was left of the fire dead. "What was that about?" Cat said after they left the campsite, stepping over the unconscious bodies, the body of the biggest one lying where he had dropped. This time, Strian nearly threw her on Lol and hopped on after her, and together with the jackoval galloped away as fast as they could to get some distance. "Did they want to capture us, bring us to your uncle?"

He shifted his grasp so one hand was around her waist and one on the reins. Cat was helping—she was gripping the pommel, which she was starting to regard as her favorite thing to grip. "Not my uncle, my honorable uncle," Strian was quick to correct. "He is no uncle of mine. He is my brother's wife's uncle." They slowed down, letting the horses slow to a trot.

Cat rolled her eyes. He didn't answer her question, but she wasn't going to push it, not at that moment.

Time passed—she had no idea how long—but long enough her heart slowed to normal. "Did they want to take you prisoner?"

"No, lady," Strian said as he nudged his Lol back up to a trot. "I would guess he wants *you*."

"What the hell *for*?"

"You are the Sleeper, Cadey," he told her, his words in her ear. "The linchpin for our plans. If he were to kill you, the legend of the Sleepers would be no more, and he would have control again."

Her mouth was dry but not because she was thirsty. Despite, or perhaps because of, their recent brush with disaster and danger, she was starting to feel his proximity, his presence. She could smell the scent of his blood, now drying on his skin and in the wool of his clothing. As horrifying the confrontation had been, it had awakened her senses in a way. "Well, how rude," Cat said after a moment, feeling safe. Strian would make sure nothing happened to her. "I've never even met the man, and he wants to kill me?"

"Temer never did anything to him, and the child died of exposure."

She shook her head. "I still can't…"

"If he were to kill me, that would be a boon for him as well. Then Gilcris would have no plausible heir but the honorable uncle—the other cousins, one and all, are more distant. But to kill me *and* you—Son-Toruai would have what he wants in the palm of his hand, and there would be no stopping him."

Cat shivered. "Don't worry, Sleeper," he whispered in her ear, and his grasp tightened. "I'll keep you safe."

She smiled a little. "But you need to be at the ceremony. Will I be able to keep you safe, my prince?" She glanced over at Arriya, where the jackoval had fallen sleep, out of long experience able to let the horse have her lead.

"I don't know. Let us keep each other safe," he said, and she knew he would try. She could ask nothing more.

She didn't know how long they rode. The moons in the sky had faded and the dawn set, and the birds were singing again by the time she raised her head after an eternity of dozing and riding horseback. Strian's hands were both firmly around her waist by then, holding the reins with the tips of his fingers.

"Are you awake, Sleeper? You do sleep a great deal," she heard Strian say, barely audible above Lol's steady plodding pace.

Cat stretched as best she could. "Maybe it's your conversational skills, Pir Strian," she answered with a laugh. "Geez, my back is sore."

"And more, I suspect. Or if not now, soon. And you may wish never to see Lol again. But you'll learn."

She looked around some more. The protected highway looked as barren in daylight as it had in the dusk. It was rocky and it was uneven with a sharp ledge to one side, and if she looked down a little more, she knew she would be able to see a deep, dark drop where if she were to fall, they would never find her body.

She shivered at that, and Strian seemed to know why. "Son-Toruai will not get his hands on you if I have anything to say about it," he whispered. "I will keep you safe. This I pledge."

Finally, when the dusk had come again, Lol stopped. Cat jerked out of her fitful doze when she tilted forward, crying out when her body barely responded. She grabbed onto the pommel as Strian dismounted. Then he reached up for her too. "Sleeper, you win. Time to rest on the ground," he whispered.

"I'm sorry," she muttered back, not sure whether she was hearing the real thing or not. She had spent the past few hours in a daze. In fact, she couldn't tell whether she was awake.

"We'll hie off the path for a time. Would you like some more fanadi?"

"No. I'd just like to sleep on something that doesn't move," she muttered, dizzy. She didn't remember much after that. She felt his arms around her, as though they were still on Lol together, and she pressed her nose into his chest and breathed deep. He smelled of smoke and sweat, and he was sublimely comfortable. "Sleep, Cadrine," she heard him whisper.

Cat smiled, and then — nothing.

The sound of thundering hooves jarred her awake. She froze, waiting as the dust, the noise and roar of the horses died away. Then she opened her eyes.

She was alone, surrounded by her satchel and Strian's and the jackoval's. But it was just her, not even Lol or Arriya.

Where *was* she? She looked around again. Strian and the jackoval had managed to secret her in what was essentially an indentation in the harsh wall of stone that characterized much of the road but this indentation actually had a bend to it, one affording them a little privacy and protection.

A familiar nicker caught her attention, and she glanced around the corner to see Lol and Arriya, both waiting patiently. Now they were both looking at her.

"I don't know," she whispered, guessing they were wondering what was going on about as much as she was. "But I'll see if they're around. I'll be right back."

She edged around the corner from her safe place, looking cautiously at either direction. Nothing and no one was in sight, and she was glad. She had some time to get her bearings.

What had happened? Cat remembered falling asleep and—*ow*. She tried to straighten and couldn't. She had been sore and then she hadn't been able to move any more, and then she remembered Strian had decided they would stop for a while.

She ventured out onto open road. It was as barren a patch as the rest of the pass had been, and she wasn't sure which way was which. She chose a direction, figuring it wouldn't matter much.

It did! She lost her balance when she slipped on a few pebbles too close to the edge of the path, and she scrambled to hold on to the sheer face of stone, clinging.

"Geez Louise," she muttered. The road was a little tricky. Especially when the road narrowed treacherously only feet away from where Strian had tucked her in to let her sleep. And the horses didn't have a problem with this? Amazing.

So where was he?

She stepped back to the wider part of the road, taking care not to misstep this time. She couldn't figure out where in the world those horses would have gone because—

Hm. Cat looked around the corner again, this time not looking down at the chasm but at a tunnel cut out of the sheer rock wall farther down the path.

That was where they had to have gone. All of them, Strian, the jackoval and whoever had been on horseback that had awoken her.

Was that it? Had Strian and the jackoval realized they would be discovered too easily and so decided to lead Beven and his men on a chase away from her?

If that were the case, she had no choice but to wait. She wasn't going to try this road without knowing it, not knowing which way to go. Not having to lead two horses, neither of whom, she suspected, would allow her to have any say in what they did or where they went.

Cat sighed. Damned if she did and damned if she didn't. She went back to the hidey-hole, where she found Lol and Arriya starting to forage for their own food, pushing at the satchels. "Not the fanadi!" she cried. "Hey, here's where the jackoval keeps the oats. Have some of that and don't touch the fanadi." She unhooked the feedbag from Arriya's saddle and opened it for Lol and Arriya, letting them both feed.

She continued to talk to them as they chomped on their makeshift meal, getting the courage to actually stroke Lol, who eyed her warily for a second before going back to his oats.

"I don't know how long we're going to be here, but I'm sure it won't be long," she said, feeling vaguely foolish but knowing these horses understood more than she realized.

The minutes ticked by, and the horses seemed to slow in their eating, so she coaxed the feedbags away. She didn't know what else to do so she petted them both again—almost as if they were very large, equine dogs or cats—and tried to figure out her next movement.

She glanced at the sky. It had to be late in the afternoon and she must have been asleep for two hours, no more. She started back toward the cave again—and felt something under her boot.

Cat looked down.

It was a frayed piece of rawhide, cut stringlike. Like a lace.

She picked it up. Hadn't the jackoval had been wearing boots with rawhide laces?

Nearby, she spotted the ground scuffed, the dirt turned. She looked a little closer— Were those prints?

They were. And they led into that tunnel.

She packed up the horses the way she had seen Strian and the jackoval do, and she led them both to the mouth of the tunnel—and paused.

No. Waiting was no longer an option. Cat took a deep breath and entered the tunnel, the two horses following.

It was black inside, and it was damp. But it wasn't totally dark. Someone, somewhere had recently left torches burning at intervals along the way, but the dark seemed to swallow most of the light.

She felt cocooned, and it reminded her of her dream, when she had dreamed of crystal that was soft. All sound within the tunnel seemed to be sapped away, draining somewhere, and it left a silence at once profound and profane.

The horses waited patiently behind her and she knew they would get nervous if they sensed she was—that much she knew. So she started to walk into the tunnel, going toward the next blazing torch.

Step by step, soon she walked so far into the cave the entrance had long since disappeared behind her, and all she had was darkness to the back of her and darkness to the front of her. All she had to guide her were the intermittent torches and the presence of the horses to accompany her.

But then the torches were spaced farther and farther apart, and the tunnel was starting to twist and turn, making each turn an iffy proposition. Cat had to walk to the edge of each twist and feel her way and then, when she felt no barrier, no drop, she would lead the horses around, little by little.

The distance between the torches became farther and farther still until, finally, the last burning torch. Nothing was beyond it except the vast darkness — and it was all-consuming. She never knew darkness could be so absorbing.

Then she heard something, not a product of her imagination. A hand clamped down over her mouth and dragged her back.

No!

That had to have been Beven and his minions who had passed her as she dozed. She wasn't going to let Beven get her, not now!

Furious, she started to hit at her unknown assailant as hard as she could, though she was smaller than her attacker and outmatched in the strength department. What made her even madder was the ease with which she was being dragged back.

You'll regret this, you son of a bitch, she fumed as she was dragged a few more feet — and then, much to her surprise, set upright again.

Then she heard a familiar voice in her ear, soft and clear. "Don't scream. Are the horses with you?"

His hand slackened from her mouth. She breathed through her nose, and then she realized Strian was breathing the same way. She nodded then said, "Yes," almost without voice. "I guess that's why they didn't seem to react to you at all."

"I heard them," he murmured in her ear. "Was there anyone behind you?"

She felt his hands near her hair, so she shook her head and waited. Then he whispered, "The jackoval and I followed just the three then."

"Where are they?" she asked, her lips barely moving.

"They're gone. There's an exit from the tunnel around the corner here. I was hoping you would wake up and find your way."

Purely accidental, she wanted to tell him. "I didn't know what else to do."

"Good. Now let's get the horses and we can feel our way out."

They did. Cat made her way back to the horses and felt for their reins, and started to lead them. Then she returned to where she could hear Strian breathing and gave him Lol's lead, keeping Arriya's for herself. "Where's the jackoval?" she asked, a little louder, but not by much.

"He's on the other side of the tunnel mouth," Strian said, his voice echoing in the dark. "He was the lookout, in case they came back."

Cat felt his hand on her shoulder, raised hers to clasp his. In the infinite dark around them she could hear the trickle of water running down the walls and smell the acrid scent of the pitch burning in the torches, and the warmth of his hand made her grateful that here, at least, was something she could hold onto.

They made their way out, step by cautious step. She felt him, smelled him on one side of her, and heard and smelled the comfortingly sour smell of the horses on the other. She stumbled a little but managed to stay upright.

"And it should be right around the corner h—" she heard him start to say—then stop.

Cat turned the corner after him. She was nearly blinded in the mild daylight after the utter black of the tunnel behind them. She squeezed her eyes shut. Then when she thought her eyes had adjusted, she knew why Strian had stopped.

The jackoval was sprawled on the ground and standing above him was Beven, his knife touching the jackoval's throat.

"No sudden movements, my prince," the Kamaite said, "or you'll have to find yourself a new jackoval."

Chapter Thirteen

ഇ

Cat gritted her teeth. The jackoval looked dazed, as if he had been knocked on the head. Behind Beven stood two of his goons, their swords drawn, looking as though they would need no encouragement.

Come to think of it, they wouldn't.

"Where's your third man, the big one?" Cat asked, looking around. Then she remembered, with a flash of the burly man falling after the jackoval...

Beven's face shifted. "He was of no further use to me, so I left him there," he sneered. "He will find his own way to the hyagoths. All I want is the Sleeper, and you and your jackoval can be on your way, my prince."

"I'm sorry, we're on our way somewhere," Cat interjected.

"The life of your jackoval for the safety of the Sleeper," Beven said, ignoring her.

"We need to be on our way to the ceremonial grounds," Strian said, staring at his fellow Kamaite. Cat watched him out of the corner of her eye. His hands were twitching. He had long since dropped the reins to Lol.

Behind them, the horses were restless. They had sensed the unease. Cat couldn't blame them.

"Why do you need to take her now?"

"Because your honorable uncle has requested her presence in the pits and I am not one to countermand Brother Son-Toruai's request. And neither should you, my prince — if not as your honorable uncle, but as your fellow priest."

Strian snorted. Cat saw his hands still, and she realized he was staying clear of his knife and sword. "Son-Toruai left on his accord to start this war, Beven. He is no fellow of mine. Nor should he be of you."

"But he has as much right to be the head of our combined countries as Gilcris does, if not more," Beven retorted. "His side of the family line is older."

"But we are not speaking of Faiora. We are speaking of Kurit."

"But they were one, not so many generations ago. If Brother Son-Toruai were to join the two countries together, think of the increased power in the Seas," Beven said silkily. "Think of the presence at the accords. Think of the fear we could inspire!"

He was practically salivating. Cat couldn't stand it anymore. "What kind of priest are you you're drooling at the prospect of scaring people?"

"My prince, you didn't mention the Sleeper could talk," Beven said in mock surprise.

"I don't bother until I hear something to comment about," she shot back.

"What a surprise," Beven said. His vulpine face twisted. "Too bad she doesn't seem to be terribly bright."

"Screw you," Cat muttered. "You and the horse you rode in on. No, that's not fair to the horse."

Beside her, she felt Strian tense. He leaned in.

"You want the Sleeper? You can have her," he snarled, seizing Cat by her arm and shoving her in Beven's direction. "She may be the answer to the legends, but all I've seen is a sick mewling woman who's been in the way since she's come out of the Gates!"

For a moment, Cat felt a flash of hurt before she knew what Strian meant her to do. She purposely stumbled as Strian shoved her and she fell forward into the arms of the bigger minion, who grabbed her. Then she let herself go limp, throwing the thug off-balance.

Strian seized his chance. Unsheathing his sword, he slashed at Beven, who stumbled back, startled. The jackoval shoved the knife away from his throat and rolled away, springing up almost instantly and knocking down the second minion in an effortless motion before he went after the first one.

Meanwhile the first minion dropped Cat like a stone, and she hastily crawled out of reach. She watched near the horses, her hand at her own sciarra, as Strian and Beven drew their swords.

"You drew on a brother monk, my prince. Do you remember the punishment?" Beven shouted. The grin on his face made Cat want to punch him. His movements and countermovements as he swung his sword were forced, as though he had to remember every step, but the smile surely meant he had planned this, meant for this to happen, and he could not contain his triumph for it having finally occurred.

Strian bared his teeth. "I remember, damn you, Beven. Expulsion from the order. And I will see you in Dara Lal for it!" He lunged, slashing at Beven's heavy woolen tunic, drawing enough blood to soak into the fabric. But Strian had not thrust through Beven, even though he could have. Even Cat, who knew nothing about swordsmanship, could tell that.

Cat stood up, catching hold of Lol's reins. The horse was pawing at the ground, restless. "Stay still," she whispered, her blood racing. "Calm, boy. Down. Or something."

Beven backed away, screaming in pain. "I will see you drawn and quartered for that!"

Cat turned and saw his minions battling the jackoval, who was fighting them both. The jackoval was brandishing a sword in one hand—Cat looked a little closer and realized he must have taken the sword from one of his opponents—and his knife in the other. And he looked calm and serene as he was doing it.

"Forget the jackoval, you idiots!" Beven shouted.

The bigger one looked as if he had woken up from a dream. He took one more ineffectual slash with his sword and then lunged for Cat, who couldn't scramble away fast enough. He grabbed her and thrust his own sciarra against her throat.

"My prince, it's up to you," Beven shouted, grinning.

Strian stopped dead still. He paid no attention to his opponent. Instead, he stared at Cat, his sword not yet lowered.

"If the Sleeper does not come with us, she will not go with you either. It is your choice," Beven said, his voice conversational again. One of his hands rubbed at the long slash across his chest, his hand stained with blood. "It is of no consequence to me. I am willing to tell your honorable uncle she was killed in a battle. He still has his advantage, and once I have killed you, your brother will have none at all."

He gestured at his minion, who started to press the sharp edge of his sciarra into Cat's throat. She gasped and winced at the motion.

"Fine," Strian said. His voice crackled with tension. "The Sleeper will go with you."

Beven smirked. "Thank you, my prince." He snapped his fingers. His second thug immediately stepped forward and slit the throat of the jackoval, then kicked him aside before the blood began to spill.

"I gave you what you wanted, you son of a cur!" Strian shouted, finally sheathing his sword before running to the side of his jackoval. "Why?"

This time, Beven laughed. "You scratch me, I scratch you." He snapped his fingers again. "And your jackoval for my man. Perhaps they'll meet in Dara Lal. In the meantime, I will have the Sleeper."

"Strian," Cat said. Her breathing was shallow, Strian saw, to avoid the sciarra's blade. But she didn't seem to be paying any attention. Instead, she was watching him.

There was no fear on her face. There was no despair. Determination, yes.

"Cadrine," he answered…and words failed him.

By the hyagoths. He had failed her.

And they were gone.

Strian touched his fingers to the pulse of his jackoval, but it was too late. The jackoval's eyes were glazing over, his body relaxing. "Wake up, don't fall asleep," Strian said frantically.

"*Jackoval sleep*," his manservant said laconically, his words slurred. "*Jackoval watch.*"

The jackoval's breathing slackened and slurred, and then it ceased. Strian stared at the calm face of the servant who had served him for so long, who had connected with him when they had both been so young, serving together in war and peace.

Strian's vision blurred. He wiped his eyes. "Bid you safe journey," he whispered. "You were the best companion I could have had, and I will avenge your passing."

He sat for a while, his tears falling onto the still face of the jackoval. He would have sat longer in mourning, but he had a task. He had to track down the Sleeper and get her back, no matter what else.

He rubbed his jaw, and he realized the leaded gloves Beven's man had hit him with had left him with scratches that had finally dried. He had slashed at Beven and Beven had slashed at him. The jackoval had defended him in an ambush and lost his life for it.

Strian didn't understand why war was so attractive. As children, he and Gilcris had played in mock battles, carefully supervised by their tutors, critiquing their style, making sure they knew what had to be done, to thrust, to parry. And when he was slightly older, a young man before going to the Kama, the idea of war had still been attractive, filling his head with thoughts of glory.

But no more. He knew how Gilcris felt.

With his own hands he buried the jackoval in the traditions of his people, his head pointing to the sunrise, his arms crossed, fingers curled around his sciarra. On the burial mound, Strian left the ornate stone necklace marking the jackoval as a servant of the imperial family, making sure most of it was buried, with only a little showing.

It was time.

He stood up, his legs stiff. He checked his own sciarra, his long sword and he checked even the Gem of Kurit embedded in the hilt of his heartsword.

He frowned. The Treasure. Why did he still have the Gem of Compliance?

Surely Beven should have asked after the Treasure of Kurit. Surely the "honorable" uncle could have done more with two of the Treasures of Kurit than just one. But Beven hadn't. Instead, he had only wanted — and gotten — the Sleeper.

Why?

Strian shook his head, puzzled, as he coaxed the two horses back out of the tunnel. He petted Arriya, who had been the jackoval's ride, telling her soothingly, "Your master has gone to his home beyond. We will find your mistress, I promise," he added, thinking of Cadrine.

What did Son-Toruai want with her? What in the legend of the Sleepers would make Beven forgo the enticement of another Treasure in favor of the Sleeper? He knew the Book of Gates as well as the next Kuriti child, and it wasn't even clear anywhere in the scriptures what role the Sleepers had in quenching the waterfire.

Granted, he still had his doubts about the Sleeper, about Cadrine herself...but there was nothing in the scrolls that would say, one way or another, if the battle would be lost without her. *What was Toruai up to?*

He had to find her. And now, he would have to do it alone.

He took one last look at the resting place of his jackoval, whose true name in his native speech he had never known and now he never would.

"Your place is assured in the annals, old friend," Strian said aloud in the quiet, his words swallowed by the breeze.

And with that he was on his way.

* * * * *

At least he could track their path.

The warrior priests of Kama, among their other traditional duties of protecting the Court and family, boasted the ability, hard-earned, to track virtually anything. Virtually anything, simply because they could not track wind or the sun or the rain—but they would and could track anything else, even, sometimes, waterfire.

It didn't matter the ground was hard, the result of months without rain up in the overland passes, and there were no tracks to speak of. After years of practice, he had achieved a certain amount of skill in the science of tracking—a simple touch, a glance at a rock or a branch, and he could deduce where and when someone, something, had gone by, and how long ago. It was not something inborn among those entering the priesthood of Kama. It was, however, drilled into them from the moment they stepped into the great stone halls of Kama and the study never ceased until they stepped out of those halls again.

And the grand prince of Kurit was no exception. Strian had been earmarked from his earliest days to enter those halls and he had looked forward to it, with the exception of the few years he had considered other venues. But those other venues always paled in comparison to the elite of the Kama. Kamaites were men of peace, they were warriors, they could settle a war even without raising a sword, and in times past they had even begun them, but mainly these days, they were feared and appreciated for their skills and abilities. One of which was tracking.

After he touched the stone wall outside the tunnel and determined which way Beven and Cadrine had gone, Strian mounted Lol. Due east, toward the setting sun and, as it so happened, toward the mountains of Kama — not far, staying on the overland pass.

Would Beven dare? Would he dare to take the Sleeper there?

Why not? He had just slain the jackoval in cold blood, he had goaded Strian into drawing his sword, he had thrown in his support with a traitor to Kurit — there was no doubt in Strian's mind his honorable uncle was a traitor. No, there was nothing in the other priest's behavior that would prevent him from taking the Sleeper to the monastery, where no woman had set foot in a hundred years.

Strian got off Lol and touched the ground again, his eyes stinging with tears. Suddenly he missed his jackoval, who had known all his secrets and more besides. He missed the Court, for him his brother before his liege, who drifted far from him in his grief. And most of all he missed Faia, his brother's wife, who had been his keeper of secrets when they were children long before his jackoval.

He shook his head. No. He had too much to do to wallow in self-pity. He had a job to do and not much time left. He had no choice, and he would succeed.

A breeze picked up again. He raised his head. Was there waterfire brewing somewhere? He didn't have time to worry about that now. There was a scent in the air, too, something he recognized.

The lady Cadrine. Quer'Cadrine. It was the perfume of her hair. He knew it intimately after all those hours of having her ride in front of him, nestled against him, sometimes sleeping, sometimes talking to his jackoval, sometimes talking to him.

Was she a spy? He had been almost certain in the beginning, but now, he was almost certain not. He had learned his scriptures and the scrolls and the legends as well as anyone, and of course, during his training at Kama, he had learned more, but something about the legends had never set well with him.

Of course, his mother and father had always called him "the suspicious one", the one who always thought there *was* something behind what everyone said and did. He had been a suspicious child, but once he had gained entrance into Kama, everything he learned only proved to him he had been right all along. There was something behind everything everyone said and did. But he also learned that much of the time it didn't matter—sometimes it did, sometimes it didn't and the trick was to know which was which.

He'd never learned. Perhaps if he hadn't left the Kama, he would have learned it eventually, but he doubted it. Trust was something inborn in his heart and without it, knowing the trick seemed to be impossible.

That was why, when the story of the Sleepers had come to his attention, he had been immediately doubtful. Why would the Sleepers come now? Why to Gates Mount, when the Gates had been silent and unseeing for all these generations? Why had only one of the Sleepers awakened?

He took a deep breath. The Sleeper was, like Faia had been, small and fragile. But Quer'Cadrine, unlike Faia, was bright-haired and loud and—surprisingly—tough. For someone who claimed to be mortally ill, she was determined. Faia had been the ultimate princess—she had been fair and fragile, too fragile in the long run.

But even Strian, with his suspicions, had never dreamed Son-Toruai would have seized the torc from around Faia's neck as her body lay in state. The thought made him shiver. The idea a loving uncle could have done that while supposedly in mourning made him want to retch.

Strian came around a curve in the road and spied a shred of something on a sharp-edged rock. He prodded at it with his sciarra. It was a bit of fabric and it looked remarkably like the heavy wool from S'nal making up Cadrine's skirts. There were several, as if a struggle had occurred.

Gingerly, he unhooked the shreds and stared at them.

Strian tucked the shreds into his reticule, safe next to his spare sciarra and the locket from his mother. He wished he could have had time to teach the Sleeper—Quer'Cadrine—how to fight; she would have taken to it quickly. Even in the two skirmishes they had had with Beven, she had been quick to know what she could do. She even understood his signals, even if he had not given her any. She had just guessed. A fighter. He respected that.

He mounted Lol and started on the road again. Closer to the Kama there were more signs this was indeed the way they had come, as if she managed to struggle more as the road had grown wider and wider as the overland passes began their slight descent into the flatlands before leading up to the Kama.

Strian stopped at a step of the stone-edged road, staring at the ground. The hard dust had been disturbed. Deep heel marks gouged the ground in an irregular pattern, as though there had been another struggle of some kind. Small mounds of dust edged the impressions of those marks, to be filled back in only when the rains began—if they ever did.

He peered at a jagged edge of rock. A dot of blood. Hers? Or one of theirs? Against a small, weak woman?

In a strange place, without anything to give her ground or even hope, she struggled.

He stopped grinning. Beven would not have liked that, and he would still have been smarting from the slash across the chest. Strian should have killed him outright, not given him a chance.

That reminded Strian once more of his manservant. The jackoval had been a good judge of character, with a life worn smooth from war and hostilities. He had liked Quer'Cadrine. She had been as curious about his origins as she was about everything else, still murmuring to herself on occasion that the dream she thought she was dreaming was as bright and vivid as anything she had ever had.

No dream. But Strian knew from his studies the scriptures and the legends meant a time of change was coming, and it would be a time of consequence.

Strian continued down the road, this time walking the horses instead of riding Lol. He stopped again. This time, what he saw was far less subtle. He took a closer look.

It was the heavy outer-tunic Cadrine had worn, the one she needed to keep her warm. Since she had wakened from her Sleep, she was cold—understandable, considering Shiatta, wherever that was, seemed to be a place of different climate, and then she had arrived wet in addition—in any case, she was cold all the time. The meet with the Nurui surely hadn't helped.

He picked up the tunic and pressed his nose into the fabric. It was hers, again no doubt. The scent was hers. And it was torn, which did not bode well.

He looked around. Deep heel marks again, gouged into the hard-packed ground. Another drop of blood, and this time more of it. A strand of hair was nestled next to it.

Using the tips of two fingernails, he picked it up. Tight-curled dark hair. It looked as though it belonged to the larger of Beven's minions, the one who had killed the jackoval.

Strian smiled grimly. There had been another altercation of sorts. "Good for you, my lady," he said aloud.

A larger mark, more shallow this time, disturbed the dirt. Farther on, crushed bushes hugged the stone walls as though there had been a more intense struggle than before. He knelt next to it, this time leaning in.

She must have woken up or become more active, struggled — perhaps screamed — and then in retaliation Beven must have threatened her. The scuff marks on the ground might have been Cadrine lashing out, and then she might have scored a hit. He must have pushed her down, landing her in the bushes.

Then — marks on the ground in front, softly erased with someone, Cadrine, kneeling there —

He saw a glint of metal, almost hidden in the bushes.

He swallowed. He pushed the bushes aside to take a look.

It was Quer'Cadrine's gloves, rumpled and tossed aside, and her sciarra, the intricately carved hilt unmistakable. The tip of the blade was slightly blunted, as though she had tried to strike something stronger than flesh — had she tried to stab one of the lurkers, and had instead met up with his soft armor?

Strian picked it up and examined it. She tried to stab the minion — probably the minion, not Beven. The scuffs were heavier, and Beven was slight — and found, to her dismay, her sciarra was no good against chain mail. The minion had at that point twisted the knife away from her and thrown it aside, and then in anger thrown her into the bushes.

She must have gained more energy as they got closer to the Kama and started to struggle. At that point, Beven — the marks looked like the soles of Beven's boots, soft and created specially for him by Kamaite craftsmen — ordered her to be tied more tightly and gagged to boot, he guessed.

Despite it all, Strian smiled as he stood up. Good for her.

Strian tucked Quer'Cadrine's knife into his own reticule and her gloves and torn tunic into his satchel, and then looked at the landscape. The Kama was in front of him, only an hour's ride. Beven was going home, to Kama. Then so was Strian.

He was as careful as he could be, considering the sun would be setting soon. When he arrived at the fork in the road, there was not even a question of which way he would go since it was clear no one had gone on the other path for some time — not even if Beven and his two lurkers wanted to fool him. Beven hadn't been any good at the tracking science, and he had certainly not been any good at disguising his own tracks.

The easiest way to answer the question of whether Beven had taken the Sleeper there, of course, would be to ask. The warrior priests of Kama would always answer the question posed of them from another priest of Kama. It was tradition.

Of course, that tradition did not take into account one of those monks drawing sword against another. But these were tumultuous days. Few things remained the same.

Strian began to climb the road to Kama. By now, he knew, the sentries posted to watch the roads would have seen him and sounded the call. The horses once he arrived there would be handed to the stablehands and once he was there in front of the massive doors, he would knock. And the door would open as it always had.

He gave the reins for Lol and Arriya to the stablehands who came out when he rang the small copper bell off the stables. The stablehands took them, nodding at him in recognition. They were mute, of course, as tradition dictated, but one of them looked back over his shoulder as they took away the horses, making Strian wonder.

Had Beven already said something?

Strian went to the doors and knocked. Then he beat the gong sitting to one side exactly once — the formal request to enter the monastery.

The bell vibrated, spreading through his bones, his head, and even through the gigantic, ancient mar trees shading the entrance of the monastery, the branches shivering, the leaves rustling and whispering. Legend had it the trees were planted a thousand years ago, when the Kama had first been established, but nothing in the official history indicated whether that was true.

There was no answer, even after the vibrations died away and the stiff breeze the only answer to his request for entrance. That too was not unusual. Gaining entry to the monastery was not necessarily a simple task.

Once more, Strian swung with as much power as he could, hitting the ancient brass gong again. Once more, the gong burst forth with sound, not only through his body and his teeth but echoing through the courtyard. A branch fell off one of those venerable mar trees and in the stable, Strian could hear the irritated protest of the horses that had been in the middle of a cleaning and a feeding as the noise buffeted them too.

It took a while but at long last, he could hear the ancient iron locks of the doors being worked, before finally the doors creaked open.

Despite his worries, Strian broke out into a happy smile. The ancient face peering out was familiar. Brother Wayas was a particular favorite, having been Strian's instructor in the art of tracking. Wayas was the best example Strian could think of that age was a deterrent to nothing. Wayas had been a child during the last rise of mother waterfire, a century before, and told stories about it. And here he was, ready to tell stories about the current rise.

"I ask for entry into Kama, Brother Wayas," Strian said formally.

The ancient face wrinkled into a smile. "Brother Strian! I knew you would be here. I gave you entry into Kama when you were but a lad, and now I welcome you back into our fold."

The elderly man stepped aside. Strian walked in, looking around with longing.

It looked the same. The hallway had been ancient when he was a priest here. The torches burning for light in the dim, dark place smelled of honey's-foot oil and milk, the way it always had.

"I did not see your jackoval, Brother Strian," the elderly man said as he struggled to close the doors and lock the many and sundry locks. "Did he not travel with you?"

He's dead, Strian almost said. But he didn't. First things first. "I need information, Brother Wayas," he asked quickly. "I am in pursuit of Brother Beven, who would have come here with two men and a woman. I need to find them."

Wayas shook his head. "I cannot."

Strian stared at him. Had he been mistaken? Could Beven have taken the other fork and not come to Kama after all?

But…

"I am a fool, Brother Wayas," Strian said, shaking his head. "After all you taught me of tracking, I could have sworn upon my life they came here."

"That they did, Brother Strian," Wayas answered. "But I cannot tell you how to find them."

Chapter Fourteen

ഇ

Cat screamed until her voice was gone, sheer fury of sound swallowed in the confines of the dank cell. She beat her fists against the heavy wooden door, scratching at it until her cramped, frozen fingers ached, slick with blood. She hurt.

She shivered. Even with her heavy tunic she always felt cool, and in the evenings she had been cold most of the time. And that was before the incident with the Nurui.

So *cold*. She shouldn't have mouthed off, but it had been inevitable. After they had trussed her and tossed her onto one of their horses, she had screamed and threatened and struggled until one of the thugs, the smaller one, gagged her. But the binding had been too tight and she choked and almost blacked out, and Beven had ordered him to take it off. The smaller thug had but reluctantly.

Being slung like a slab of meat hadn't been comfortable, but at least she had stayed on. When she realized how rocky the road became, she learned to stay as still as possible. She had got a very good view of the chasm she could have fallen into had the horse misstepped because she struggled. And she didn't like heights to start with.

Before too long she had found herself in this cell in the utter blackness of this place, her hands and mouth freed and her eyes unblindfolded—but it didn't matter, because there was no light to see with.

And it was ice-cold. The stone walls—at least they felt like stone—were cold and the moss on the walls made them feel even cooler. And the surfaces were moist. She had to be below ground from the feel of the damp and the cold.

She shivered. At least she tried, because if she shivered she could try to regulate her body temperature. She remembered reading that from her undergraduate days about the Australian aborigine.

But shivering wasn't working. She was too tired to shiver for one. And she was starting to feel numb.

Footsteps.

Footsteps outside the door. She held her breath.

Cat heard fumbling at the door's rusty locks and before she knew it, the door swung open, the light pouring in blinding her.

"Sleeper, how good to finally meet you," she heard a mellifluous voice coming from the silhouetted figure. "Let us bring you out so we may speak in comfort."

She felt a large burly arm—it had to be that big thug again—fumble for her arm and yank at it, and before she could resist, she was dragged out again—she was getting tired of being manhandled—and pushed along a passageway she couldn't see, still blinded. Then she felt herself being pushed down into a chair and her hands bound again.

"Would you like some hot *oja*, Sleeper?" the same smooth voice said again. "I'm sure you're well chilled right now."

She blinked hard once, twice, and then squinted so she could see who she was talking to. It didn't work at first, but shapes started to coalesce little by little.

When she could finally see, whoever he was, was remarkably—unremarkable. "Can you see now, Sleeper?"

It was coming out of a short, skinny man with a sparse ring of hair left around his head and the largest, gaudiest rings on his fingers she had ever seen. That was in direct contrast to the heavy golden collar sitting loosely around his neck, which had in its middle a clear, brilliant sapphire-blue gem in the middle of it. After the black of the cell, the way the jewel gleamed was enough to blind her. Not only that, that gem looked familiar.

Finally, she remembered. She had seen something like it in the Court's earring. She had seen something exactly like it in the hilt of the short sword that Strian wore —

Cat stared at the collar. It was a torc.

It had to be. She knew who this man was.

"You must be the honorable uncle. You've got to be Son-Toruai."

The skinny little man smiled an almost toothless smile and nodded. "My reputation precedes me."

She stared at him. He didn't look evil, just creepy. "You," she breathed. "I would have thought you would be bigger. I thought you would be more menacing. You would be —"

"Bigger," Son-Toruai said, nodding, although there had been a momentary flash of something in his expression as she spoke. "I am more a man of the mind than the flesh. Which is just as well, for I have been finding being a man of the flesh is a bother." He gestured to his rings. "After all these years of dreaming of such gawds, I am finding these to be cumbersome. I have always wanted these, and now I find I do not want them at all."

"Then why don't you give up this insane quest you're on?"

The nearly toothless man gaped a grin at her again. "Because I am a man of the mind and I know the one thing I have always wanted is to rule both Kurit and Faiora as a united country. And that is something I can do without being a man of the flesh."

"Even if it means killing people to do it? And the little kid," she said, remembering the fate of the prince. "Temer. Was any of it worth it considering you killed your own grandnephew?"

The gaping smile vanished in a second. "That was an accident," he snapped. He grimaced for a moment. "That was through no fault of my own. I simply wanted to keep him safe, and what happened was—"

"How can it *not* be your fault? He wouldn't have been there if you hadn't kidnapped him!"

The attempt at sociability disappeared. "Sleeper, you do not understand how our world works. Do me the honor of being quiet so I may explain what I want."

"I *know* what you want," Cat shot back. "For some reason, you think destroying everything in front of you is going to make you a king. And that's in addition to the waterfire ceremony, right? You have how many days left before it has to go off? Two? And threatening to get rid of everything and killing off everyone you can is going to do the trick?"

He slapped her. The skin of her face felt as though it exploded with the blast of pain. At least it heated up her skin. Tears sprang to her eyes, but she wasn't going to keep quiet.

"That's not going to shut me up," she choked out.

The honorable uncle's thin lips tightened before he smiled again—and it was an alarming sight. "Untie her. It will be impossible for us to have a real conversation while she is bound like an animal and she is cold and wet and shivering like a prisoner."

"I *am* a prisoner," she added, but she sighed and slumped as she felt the bindings on her hands loosen.

"You are only a prisoner if you want to be, Sleeper. Have some hot *oja* to warm yourself," he invited. "I know those cells are freezing. I was in one myself when I was a young man, as was the prince himself, as was every priest here in Kama."

"What is it, some sort of initiation prank?" She rubbed her hands and wrists to get some circulation back into them. She had bruises and cuts, she noted, from how tight the ropes had been tied.

"Every monk in Kama spends time in the cells, Sleeper. That is how we learn not to fear the dark. It is not a kind lesson, and it is brutal for some, but afterward we know the dark."

"Only those who have something to be afraid of should be afraid of the dark," Cat answered, her lip curling a little. She wasn't going to shiver, she told herself. She tried to curl her hands into fists, but she couldn't feel them enough yet.

Just then, a handleless mug filled with a steaming liquid came sliding down the table, the scent of piping hot *oja* drifting from it. She gripped the chair she was sitting on to avoid grabbing it.

"Go ahead, Sleeper. It will warm your bones," Toruai invited.

She stared at the renegade monk, doing her best to ignore the steaming mug. "How do I know it's not poisoned?"

"I need your help, Sleeper. I would not poison you."

Yet. "Then why were your goons threatening to kill me half the time on the way here?" she demanded, still ignoring the mug. She started to rub her arms rather than reach for the *oja*. She refused to give him the satisfaction. "Not only that, they cut off my clothes and told me I could freeze to death. If you need my help, that wouldn't be the way to do it."

Son-Toruai's gaze slid away. "They were only doing that to frighten you."

"I don't think so. That Beven is a menace to society." She went back to staring at the cup. She breathed deeply, hoping perhaps the steam would be drawn toward her. Whatever she did, she wasn't going to give him the advantage of going for the *oja*.

"'That Beven', as you refer to him, will be the head of the order of Kama next month, Sleeper. He is hardly a menace."

"He's psychotic! He killed Strian's jackoval!" She remembered, and not for the first time, she never knew the jackoval's name. He died in battle. She bit her lip. She didn't know if his people had a heaven, but if they did, surely he was there, like Valhalla.

"I'm sure there was just cause, Sleeper."

"Is that what you're telling yourself? You've probably noticed he's got these tendencies, and you're telling yourself everything he does has just cause. Right? A little kid died and there was just cause. All those soldiers dying don't count because it's a war. And the war is justified because it means you can get something you want. Aren't I right?"

The *oja* was cool enough to drink. But she still wasn't going for it.

"Sleeper," and here Son-Toruai's voice began to sound clipped, "I suggest you guard what you say."

"You don't like the truth? Well, guess what? You wouldn't recognize the truth if it hit you in the balls. You wouldn't know the truth if it handed you a card and introduced itself!"

The skinny little man raised his hands and turned away. "Tie her hands and force the *oja* down her throat," Son-Toruai said to his henchmen. "I want no accusations she did not at least have a cup after a session in the cells."

Cat choked as the *oja*, now lukewarm, was poured down her throat, but it was the most warmth she had felt in what seemed like eternity. She began to sputter, her chest racked with coughs, as her hands were tied behind her once again.

Once her coughing spasm passed and her nose stopped running, she could breathe again. And Son-Toruai sat patiently in front of her, his hands steepled, his expression blank. "Are you feeling better, Sleeper?" he asked. "I know how the cold and the damp can drive you out of your mind in the cells before it kills you. I wanted to make sure you had something warm to drink so you can stop shivering for a while."

"Why, thank you," Cat said, venom in her voice, her teeth clenched. "Good to know you have my best welfare in mind."

"Now about why I've asked you to come here—"

"You have trouble with words, don't you? I wasn't *asked* to come here. I wasn't *asked* to speak with you. I wasn't asked to do *anything*. And I certainly wasn't asked to drink the *oja* you just forced down my throat. Was it poisoned, incidentally? Will I be convulsing anytime soon?"

Son-Toruai was having a hard time controlling his emotions, Cat could tell. He clenched his fists. "I wanted to speak to you because of certain concerns I had," he said, ignoring her outburst. "I understand you are one of the three Sleepers mentioned in the legends. Am I correct?"

She rolled her eyes. "*I don't know.* I'll tell you what I told everyone else. I woke up in the village near Gates Mount. My two coworkers were with me. They were still asleep. After I started on this trip to the Podani, I got word my two coworkers, who unlike me never woke up, disappeared. Then you kidnapped me. Am I a Sleeper? Your guess is as good as mine. I don't even know why I'm here. I tried asking the Nurui, and they gave me squat."

Son-Toruai stared at her, a finger tapping on his cheek. "You asked the Nurui, and they gave you no hope on the matter?"

"Nothing useful."

"I went to the Nurui when I was young," the wizened man said thoughtfully. "Many years ago. I asked what my future was. They told me my meaning in life would be found in dying."

She stared at him. "They're full of crap," she exclaimed. "They told *me* I would find meaning in life by dying."

Son-Toruai stared at her, his mouth ajar. "They gave us the same prediction? How unusual. At the time, of course, I was infuriated. That prediction was of no use to me."

She wouldn't have believed it, but they actually had something in common. "Pretty much the same," she agreed reluctantly. "How horrible. What'd you do, kill them, or did you start doing that later on?"

"That must be the only time the Nurui have given identical predictions," Son-Toruai mused, once more ignoring her outburst. "I asked, of course, because at the time, I was the youngest in my family, and I was keenly aware all the choice positions of responsibility had been taken by my elder siblings. I would be left with nothing more than to serve in Kama, which I had no desire to do. But I did so after the trip to the Nurui, for I was without choice by then. If the Nurui had given me a forecast with which I could have negotiated, I could have had my choice of fates—but I did not."

Cat snorted. "You make your own fate," she reminded him. "You make your own memories. You make yourself into what you will. There's no honor in destroying things, you moron. There's honor in building things."

"Why would you care, Sleeper?"

"Because I don't have any time left," she admitted. She didn't know how much, but she had to guess her cancer was well on its way. It was hard to tell. "I don't have any time left and I'm not even sure I'm not in a dream."

"So you think you're in a dream, Sleeper?"

She shrugged, which was tricky to do with her hands tied behind her back. "I used to. But more and more I think I must be awake. I must be, because I don't have enough of an imagination to make all this up."

"And what do you think your place here means?"

Cat thought about it. "I think my *title*, the thing you use instead of my *name*," she emphasized, "must mean something. That's why I think I must be the Sleeper, and that's why I have to be at the ceremony the day after tomorrow. If I'm not there," and she paused, "I think the consequences are beyond what you or I want to imagine. I think I'm a sacrificial lamb."

"Which is?"

"I think I'm here to live or die so others may live. Surprisingly I'm cool with that."

"I think you are cool because of the chill in the cells," Son-Toruai said, misunderstanding. "Give her more *oja*."

After some more of the warm liquid had been forced down her throat—and this time she was ready for it, so she didn't choke—Son-Toruai asked, "And what do you think my role in this is?"

She shrugged. "Maybe you're a sacrificial lamb too."

"Why would it matter to me if others live or die?"

"If you want to rule over them, you should *care* whether they live or die! You should care what happens to them, whether they're happy or even if their crops come in, you asshole!"

Toruai didn't realize he had just been insulted. Cat realized with some shock he was too self-centered to even think of it, whether or not he understood the words.

Not for the first time, she wondered what "asshole" meant in Kuriti.

"In view of the people, they must learn to obey me when I give a command," he decided, slapping the table in front of him, as though he were giving a command in preparation for his coronation. "It is not any concern of mine whether they are happy about it."

"'Do what I say, or you're going to regret it'?"

"Something along those lines. How astute of you, Sleeper."

She groaned. "You're never going to understand anything I say, are you? Aren't you afraid of—" she tried to remember what it was Q'Atha had talked about, once—"nightmares of the hyagoths haunting you?"

He waved his hand. "The hyagoths have never bothered me. And it is of no concern to me what you think of me, Sleeper. In fact, it is time for you to go back to your cell. I have decided," and he said it with a glint in his eye she didn't like at all, "I will not allow you to go to the ceremony after all. It is clear to me if you are not present at the ceremony, my fate as well as yours may be changed. I think there will be more harm in your attending than good."

She glowered at him and at that point she had had enough. "Screw you," she said, and she spat at him.

That he understood. After he had wiped off his face, he looked at her coldly. "You will stay in the cell until you die, and I will make sure your body disappears into the chasms. Thank you for your company, Sleeper."

And he had her shoved back into the cold, dank little cell, making sure she was gagged. As an afterthought, he made sure she had one more thing with her, should any of the elder monks take a stroll down in the cells—a monk's habit pulled over her, so at first glance, she would look like a novitiate priest in training—until a second look, complete with the gag, would prove she was not.

She found herself in the darkness again, curled up, slowly freezing to death.

Chapter Fifteen

ɞ

Strian fought the urge to grab the elderly monk by his robe. Instead he limited himself to, "What do you mean you can't tell me? Brother Wayas, why not?"

The elderly man looked distressed. "You know we must be neutral on this, Brother Strian."

"But Kamaites are the protectors of the Court! Brother Beven has allied himself with Brother Son-Toruai, who killed the heir and now plots to blackmail the Court into giving up the throne! Not only that, Beven slit my jackoval's throat! My jackoval, who never did a day of harm!"

The monk's mouth dropped open. "My condolences, Brother Strian! Your jackoval—I am so sorry. He was the gentlest of souls and the most faithful of retainers."

"What I found," and here Strian had to think, choosing his words most carefully, "most disturbing to the way of the Kama is my jackoval was a tool between Beven and me. Beven went against his word and killed him. My jackoval, who had done nothing but protect me against attackers."

He was sorry he had to place this on the elderly monk's shoulders, but he wanted to say it once, no more, as long as he was here. He wanted it clear there was more than reason enough he would ask and do what he had to.

"Pir Strian—" Wayas began then stopped. Strian knew that he too had to choose his words carefully. "Brother, my heart grieves with yours, but this is a dispute between two Kamaites and so we may not interfere. I am so sorry."

Strian stared at the elderly monk. The little man looked pinched and Strian was sorry he had to press, for he and the monk got along very well. "I assumed treachery to the Court would be enough, Brother Wayas."

"I would have thought as well, but," and here Wayas leaned in and whispered, "Beven has of late gotten the ear of the Eid, and I have heard he will be appointed his successor a month hence."

Strian stared at him in horror. The Eid was the high priest, who had the ability to countermand any decision of the Kama council. "I have been gone for a short while, and this is what happened? Has the Council gone mad?"

His words echoed through the halls of stone, and came back to Strian angrily. All he could hear was his last words about the Council, and even so, he could not fault himself for them. He had left the Kama reluctantly. The Kama, to him, had been a haven, a place of peace, of meditation, a place of true purpose.

Now it was a distortion of what it had been. Beven the high monk of Kama? The Council in assent? The Council, it seemed, was ready to turn its back on the Kama's origins as protector and guard for the Court?

The Council had gone mad. The world had gone mad.

But he would not.

"Beven is holding the Sleeper," Strian said, his voice back to normal. He kept his voice even, because he knew, as well as any Kamaite, that raising it did no good. "On orders from Brother Son-Toruai. Those plans may call for killing her in order to prevent the prophecies from coming to pass. I must find her."

The elderly little monk's face distorted in horror. "Surely not. How could that be?"

"Brother Wayas, listen," Strian said urgently. "Did you open the door to Beven?"

The rule to neutrality between Kamaites was clear—those questioned could answer questions, but they could volunteer no new information.

"Yes," the elderly man said, with a hesitation.

Strian hated to bring Wayas, who had never done anyone any harm, into this, but he had no choice. "Was a woman with him?"

"No." This time, the rule on neutrality firmly in his mind, Wayas' voice was stronger.

Strian thought about it. "Was Beven accompanied by two men?"

Wayas nodded. "Brother Bur and Brother Merta. Oh!" he cried. "I should not have said that."

"Did they have a," and here Strian took a leap of logic, "a large, bulky package with them?"

Wayas nodded, sure of himself now.

"Did they say where they needed to put this large package of theirs?"

Again the little monk nodded.

"Was the package by any chance wiggling?"

The little monk nodded vigorously.

Strian paused and scratched his chin. Where in the vast monastery would they have gone? Where would afford them the most privacy, the most likely to be away from prying eyes?

"Did they go out to the boathouses?" The monastery was built on a cliff and a dozen boathouses, perhaps more, could be found at the bottom, whence the Kamaites kept seafaring vessels.

No.

"Did they go out to the armory?"

No.

Strian thought some more. They had not gone to the farthest outpost, which would have been the boathouses. They had not gone to the armory, which would have afforded them weapons—but they would have been unable to gain entry anyway for the entrance was closely guarded, more than they could have managed without previous work.

"Did they say they would be going to the guard posts?"

No.

The guard posts were the highest points of the monastery, isolated simply by height and distance, where centuries before the Kamaites had placed their own on sentry duty on the lookout for invaders from beyond the Seas.

Then he had it.

"Did Beven ask about the cells?"

Bull's-eye. Wayas' eyes widened and he nodded vigorously.

"Did he say he required privacy and asked whether there were any novitiates undergoing training down there?"

Yes.

Strian was close, he knew it. He had to think of how to phrase his next question. "Did they inquire whether the keys were still kept in the same place they had been?"

Yes.

Strian had what he needed. He touched his sword at his hip before he looked around, taking a deep breath. "In that case, Brother Wayas," and here Strian leaned down and whispered, "will I be able to find them there, complete with a wriggling package?"

Wayas looked confused for a second before Strian remembered the strictures and rephrased. "Will I be able to find them there?"

Wayas broke into a big smile. "Yes. Good luck, Brother Strian. I will tell the Council you are here. Perhaps you will be able to join us later to celebrate Patima."

Strian glanced up at the leaded-glass windows at the top of the great hall. "I may be able to, Brother Wayas," he said, judging the time and how long he thought his search would take. "I hope so. And I hope to present to you the Sleeper, of whom you may have heard."

"It will be an honor, Brother Strian," the little man said, beaming.

And Strian bowed and took his leave, starting to run only seconds after he bid farewell to the monk.

He had forgotten how large the monastery was, vast and ancient. It had been built on the site of the oldest stone structures that existed when Kurit had been formed, centuries before. When the earliest Marini travelers from beyond the Seas had come to this bit of land, they had decided to stay, victims of persecution evicted from their homes. According to legend, they had come upon the soaring structures of stone that stood mutely, already worn smooth through the generations, and they realized right there and then something else had been previously at this place, something else of which there was no longer any sign, but nonetheless something called to them to be recognized.

The earliest Marini had settled there and called themselves *Kuriti*, meaning "the end of travails". With that they had started to explore the great stone structures of these mountains, which they called "Kama", after their old home. Eventually, the settlers had gone to greener pastures, to explore more fertile plains that would support farming and hunting and abandoned the great stone structures.

But they did not forget them.

After a great time, after the inevitable wars man wages, the warriors who fought them decided to withdraw from the affairs of everyday men. A group of those, who now knew themselves as Kuriti, being Marini no more, rediscovered the great stone structures—and so the monastery of Kama had been born.

In front of Strian, the stone steps, wide and broad, began to narrow and tilt as he pressed his memory, remembering how the halls were constructed. That had been part of the Kamaite learning — how the earliest builders had constructed the halls, the many smaller monasteries making up the Kama, as a result making them almost unnavigable to outsiders.

The halls narrowed from five abreast to three abreast to finally one. The halls as they dipped down narrowed to allow only one monk through at a time. There was never any need for more than one at a time to come through that section.

And finally — finally Strian reached the final set of stone steps, the ones leading to the deepest part of the Kama, down to the cells that played a part in the training of the priests.

He had not been there in years, not since his first year in Kama — that was all the time most novitiates spent willingly in the cells and for good reason. It was dark and it was damp and it was unpleasant. But it was a good lesson. He recalled vividly when it was his turn for a stay in the cells of infinite black.

Strian had been grateful for light, any light since then. He had also never been frightened of the dark afterward.

Cadrine had to have been put into one of the cells. It would be the safest place, the most secure place to keep her while Beven and his lurkers planned.

He stopped.

The one question he should have asked of Wayas, the one question he had not. And he had no time to go back and ask him.

He had not asked whether Son-Toruai was here.

Why else would Beven bring the Sleeper here? He could think of no other reason, considering the ceremony was — and had to be — in two days' time to confront the waterfire.

He started to move again down the halls. He had no time to consider what the ramifications were. He had to find Cadrine.

When had he stopped referring to her as "Sleeper", except on occasion? It was a title, and a formal one. She was the least formal person he had ever met.

Strian looked around, gauging his whereabouts. He was coming up to the cells.

The narrowed passageway stopped at a heavy wooden door, dented and scarred, above which burned a torch. He pounded at the door.

"Who wants entry?"

"Brother Strian, late of the Kama." He was still entitled to the moniker.

"Why do you want entry?"

"I seek information."

"Can this knowledge be gained elsewhere?"

"Not easily."

"Do you know the history of the cells?"

"I do," Strian said. Anyone who had been in those cells knew the history of those cells. Certainly anyone who survived the ordeal did.

The door opened slowly, pulled by a tall young priest, pale and ashen and sloop-shouldered. "Brother Strian," he said. He smiled, and his teeth fair gleamed in the light of the burning torch. "I have not seen you since you left for Podani."

"Brother Dai," Strian said, smiling with a nod. "It is good to see you again. You have cell duty?"

The pale young man nodded. "This month. I have forgotten how one yearns for light after only a few days, but at least I have light in the form of candles and torches."

Strian nodded. This was duty the younger monks took after their turns in the cells. The advantage, he knew, was it allowed the sentry monk to study in peace for his exams without interruption.

But it was lonely duty, which was why, Strian suspected, the young monk seemed willing to converse. "I suspect you are here for another reason other than to talk to me," Dai said.

Strian nodded. "I met Wayas, and he answered some of those questions. Is Son-Toruai here?"

Dai nodded, his eyes watching Strian's. "Yes."

"Is he with Beven?"

Yes.

"Is there someone or something being kept in one of the cells?"

Yes.

"Are you or they making sure the someone or something is fed?"

No. Dai's eyebrows furrowed but Strian knew he could not ask any questions, and unlike Brother Wayas, the young priest was unlikely to let additional information slip.

"Yes, I think it is someone who is kept that way deliberately," Strian said, guessing what Dai's unspoken question. There was nothing in the strictures forbidding him from guessing the questions. "Is that something or someone a Kamaite?"

No.

Strian glanced up and down the passageways where the torches burned, but so dim they were practically not lit at all. They were just enough to light the way.

"Is that someone or something in a cell this way?"

Yes.

"Is there anyone else I should know about?" Now there was a broad question, and if Dai looked confused, he could blame only himself. But Strian was fortunate, for Dai's answer was a shake of his head.

"Are Son-Toruai and Beven in the windowed rooms beyond?" Strian asked. The rooms were where the sentry monks took residence during their time here.

The young monk nodded. "If Son-Toruai and Beven are using the windowed rooms, where are you staying, pray tell?"

Dai rolled his eyes. This question he could answer with words. "I am staying in a cell."

"Surely you are not happy about *that*."

"I will tell you, I am not. Beven has changed," Dai exclaimed. "He has become arrogant and I am not so sure he is not questioning his Kamaite beliefs."

Strian snorted. "I am sure of the answer," he said dryly. "I have one more question. Can you show me which cell the someone or something is in?"

Dai grinned and nodded. "This way, Brother," he said, picking up a torch and leading the way. "I am not so sure Son-Toruai or Beven will like this but I am sure this is the way to truth. I have been uneasy about how things have been going here, Brother Strian. I am glad you are here."

"I am glad I am still welcome here, considering Beven's turn of allegiance," Strian said. He still had friends here after all, allies. There was a chance the Kama had not been corrupted after all. He had to make sure it remained so.

Dai stopped in front of a cell, and from his pocket he produced a ring of keys. He looked expectantly at Strian.

"I—" Strian stopped. He had forgotten. Dai could not identify the key.

"The hyagoths help me," he muttered, but without heat. It was the last hurdle, and he had to be patient. "Is this the key?"

No.

"This one?"

No.

"This one?"

Yes.

Strian grabbed the large, iron key from Dai and thrust it into the lock. It wouldn't turn.

"Are you sure it is this key?"

"I am very sure, Brother Strian," Dai said. "I have been using it to slip the something or someone hot food whenever I think Beven is nowhere near. Let me."

He took the key out and then jammed it back in, using both hands to turn it. The lock screeched in protest, but finally he heard a click. He pushed the door open.

The door creaked a high screech before Strian shoved it open some more.

"Quer'Cadrine?" he said softly into the black.

No answer. He paused to listen. Nothing.

"Cadrine? Are you here?"

He took a deep breath. "Cadrine? Sleeper?"

He grabbed the torch from Dai and thrust it into the cell, where there had been no light for years.

All he could see in the glare of the torch was the sheen of white lichen clinging to the walls, damp and moist and cold. Very, very cold.

There was nothing else.

Strian turned to Dai. "Where else could she be? Could they have moved her for some reason?"

Dai was staring into the cell. "No, I would have known it," he said frantically. "She has to be here somewhere in the cells—I know. They have been taking—her?"

"Quer'Cadrine. The Sleeper of legend," Strian said, gritting his teeth.

Dai rolled his eyes. "The hyagoths help us. They have been taking her once in a while, I think. She may be there now. But this is the only cell they have asked the key for, and I would know otherwise."

"Show me the way to the windowed rooms," Strian said grimly. "Perhaps it is time I confront my honorable uncle."

Chapter Sixteen

❧

Brother Dai led Strian once again, this time through the narrow passageways and up. The incline was gradual and would not have been noticeable to any but those who spent time down there, but it was and had been the savior of many a foundering novitiate, who took heart in getting out of the dank cells once more. To go up meant to go toward the sunlight, and the light was what every single novitiate aimed for after time in the cells.

Strian remembered the first time he had made the trip up, after his own four days in the cells. He had staggered, like all his fellow novitiates had, because after the first day none of them had been able to stand. All of them had squinted, because even the dimmest of lights were too bright after time in the cells.

And after they stepped into the windowed rooms, they all rubbed at their necks, feeling a rash of heat, because after days in the cells, everything felt too warm.

As Dai led him up to the rooms, Strian could almost hear the keening. Was it the wind, the crackle from the ever-roaring fire, or was it something else?

He had no time to think about it now. He had to find Cadrine, make sure she was unharmed, that Toruai and his kind had not touched her.

He wouldn't. At least Strian hoped. Not even someone who would kill his own grandnephew, a small child, would plot to kill a defenseless woman. A defenseless, ill woman. A defenseless, ill woman who didn't even belong there.

But with a great chill in his heart, he knew Son-Toruai would kill her, given the convenient rationale. It had always been rationale with him.

And now — now, with his alliance with someone who had the ear of the Eid, it bode no good at all.

The incline was steeper now. Both Strian and Dai were climbing a little slower, and if the two of them in the prime of their lives were panting from exertion, he did not want to imagine how a delicate thing like Cadrine would react. With an ache he should not have allowed himself, he wondered how many times Son-Toruai had dragged her up the incline to sit her down —

He doubled his speed, almost outstripping Dai with his burst of energy. He would not think of it. He was going to do what he had to, and the hyagoths help him if someone tried to stop him.

Finally. The last landing before the windowed rooms. Another burst of speed, and he was there. He, and a few seconds later Dai, stood in front of the heavy copper-edged wooden doors that marked the complex of windowed rooms beyond. He could hear the winds whistling. He shivered, thinking of the constant chill.

He gritted his teeth, thinking about Cadrine. Weak, but she had a heart as large as the Gates themselves.

"Is the door open?" Strian asked, gripping the handle of one of the doors but not attempting to open it yet.

Dai nodded, gesturing with his keys. "They asked only the cell be kept locked, not the windowed rooms. Will you require my help?"

"Only if there are more than four of them in there," Strian said. "Are there?"

Dai shook his head. "I would have known if anyone else had been allowed down here, and there have only been Son-Toruai, Beven, and his two lurkers, Merta and Bur."

"Be ready to call down the guards, for they will not be willing in their departure."

"What reason should I give?" Dai asked eagerly, and Strian guessed the four had been giving the young monk reason to wish them out of his life.

"The truth," Strian answered cryptically. And with that, he pulled open the door.

The foyer was as it had always been, low-ceilinged and intimate, torches burning on the walls that had been burnished for centuries with honey's-foot oil. Strian breathed in the unmistakable scent. His youth came back to him in a powerful wave, the memories of his novitiate days spent in waxing on yet another layer of the oil to protect the walls. The floors had been laid of the same wood, from a season-resistant timber not seen in Kurit for more than a thousand years. He stroked the wall, indulging in a moment of reminiscence.

He heard the murmur of voices from one end of the hall, from the rooms closest to the water. He turned on his heel and started down that passageway.

He sidled up to the door. The voices were male, and it sounded as if they were conversing with each other, no one else.

Where else could she be?

He looked up and down the passageways. Where would they put someone they were keeping in the cells most of the time if they wanted to keep that sensation of being isolated? There was a good reason this complex was referred to as "the windowed rooms". There was little space here that didn't involve windows somehow.

The safety room.

That was the room used if the seas were pounding against the side of the cliffs, threatening to break the heavy leaded glass. It was small, and a place those with a fear of closed spaces avoided. At least it had light, and it was warm.

Which way was it? Strian walked, then started to run, down the hall, sure now where Cadrine would be. The safety room was warmer than the cells, less damp of wall.

She had to be there. She had to be.

He approached the last door. This must be it.

Strian pressed his ear against the door. He heard nothing, but that did not surprise him. She was probably tired and dazed, and no doubt all she wanted to do was to curl up in the corner.

Strian waited a few minutes more, then took a chance. He pressed the latch and eased the door open.

A candle burned but he judged nothing else was there. If there was a candle there had to be someone. Was she—?

That was when he heard it.

Someone was breathing. It was a purposeful breathing, indicating that whoever it was in the room was awake and wary.

Whoever was waiting for him.

He tensed, his fingers still on the latch. It could have been one of the youngest novitiates, or someone brought in from the outside, also something he should have thought to ask of either Wayas or Dai. But he had not, and so he had to take the risk. He had been trained for the possibility.

One. Two. Three. Then abruptly he shoved the door open.

He heard a muffled cry and then the door stopped on something solid.

Something occurred to him, something that made his stomach sink. He leaped inside the room and glanced around. It was empty save for a table and two chairs, and a candle was indeed burning in the middle of the table, almost gutted.

He looked around the door.

Quer'Cadrine was slumped on the floor where he had knocked her down, and she was murmuring fretfully. "Cadrine!" he said in a horrified whisper.

He knelt and pressed two fingers against her throat. The beat was strong, and even after being struck with the door, she was trying to rise. Impulsively, he began to pick her up but before he could, she began to struggle, pushing him away. "No," he heard her say. "Let go of me!"

Even now she fought. "Quer'Cadrine," he said urgently, ignoring her struggles, "open your eyes. You have light."

She froze. He lifted her close to his face. Her eyes fluttered once, twice and then slowly, they opened.

"Strian?" she muttered. "Is that you?"

Her voice was hoarse, and she looked—and most likely was—exhausted beyond measure. He glanced at her hands. Her fingernails were broken and the tips bloody, probably from scratching at the cell door. She was as pale as the moons, and at the moment, she looked as though she were closer to death than he had ever seen her.

The thought frightened him more than anything else could have. He checked her pulse again. Strong.

"It is," he said softly. "I've come for you. Can you walk?"

"I don't know," she said, faint. "I haven't in years."

Time in the cells did that to the inhabitant every time. The days she spent in Kurit since being discovered had slipped away temporarily. "You've been down in the cells for a day, Sleeper." He tempered his voice for her agitated state. He helped her up, keeping a firm grip on her as she gingerly stood.

He noticed she kept her eyes closed after opening them initially. "Are your eyes still sensitive, Quer'Cadrine?"

She nodded. "They feel like they're going to explode."

"Just slit them open for a few minutes," he said gently. "They will adjust."

"You're so nice and warm and solid."

He stifled a smile. "So I'm a bed, am I?"

"Just a pillow," she murmured, sounding dazed. "A big pillow."

"Can you walk?" he repeated. He looked around. "I do not know what Beven and Toruai plan for you so we must get you out of here as soon as possible, to the open presence of the Kamaites. In public they will not lay a hand on you."

At the mention of Son-Toruai and Beven, she slit open her eyes. "Let's go," she croaked.

Still willing. He looked at her, smiling. His heart tilted. If he could protect her from all the ills of the world, he would. "Tell me if you can walk."

"I can walk. I'm not letting them near me again. I'll kill them before I let it happen."

"You sound firm on that," he told her as they began to walk, his arm around her shoulders. He looked out the door, both left and right, before they slipped out. Her breathing picked up but she did not hesitate, and he could do no more than keep a protective hand on her until they came to the door leading away from the complex of windowed rooms.

He inched it open cautiously until he caught the attentive gaze of Dai, who gestured for him to come out. Strian nodded and did, holding Cadrine close to him.

"This is the Sleeper of legend, Brother Dai," Strian said, keeping his arm around her. "She is who Son-Toruai and Brother Beven have been holding in the cells. Quer'Cadrine, this is Brother Dai. He helped me find you."

Dai's eyes widened. "It is an honor to meet you, Sleeper," he said, his voice cracking.

She dipped her head a little. "It's an honor to meet someone who's been helping the prince." She tried to smile.

"You will feel better soon. It is almost time for Patima," Dai said to Strian.

"I know," Strian said grimly.

"You know the way. If Son-Toruai and Beven discover her absence, I will tell them she is not here."

Strian snorted. "That is a statement no one will be able to deny. My thanks, Brother."

"Thank you, Brother. Good luck."

Strian kept his hand around her waist to steady her as they made their way through the corridors, twisting and turning and then doubling back. Only one who spent years as a novitiate could remember the way. It was something once learned could not be forgotten, because getting out became the top priority by the time they spent any time there at all.

Her skin began to feel warmer too as he held on to her. She was getting stronger—her steps began to take on speed, even though they were heading up the steps and inclines by then, and they needed to be out, quickly!

He responded to her need and held on a little more tightly, making sure her steps did not falter. It was a grip that also reassured he was there with her, worse for wear, but with her nonetheless.

Finally, the passageways broadened. The torches on the walls began to glow brighter and the acrid scent of the sea began to dissipate. Finally, they slowed when Strian recognized the set of doors leading to the main halls of Kama. Beyond the door, he could hear the start of the Patima as thousands of steps shuffled by, getting into position for the evening ritual of prayer, in time for the setting of the sun.

He should have had regrets, but he found he could not. Previously, when he thought of the Patima, he always had a sharp pang of regret about having to leave; now he felt only eagerness. It had been so long and not just for prayer—he wanted the companionship, the communion the prayer symbolized. But it was more a memory than the desire to return. Too much had happened.

"It's time for the evening ritual," Strian told Cat. "We can hide in the open. You have never seen the Patima, have you?"

"I don't even know what the Patima is," she answered, her voice stronger than it had been. She was more alert too. She looked around curiously, and once in a while, looked up at him.

He liked that. He felt as if he were a young boy again, showing off for Faia, who had been his confidante, older-sister substitute. Except this time, he could show the joys of a new world to someone who was as innocent as a child about his world.

"It is wonderful and you will enjoy it, Quer'Cadrine."

She tried to laugh but ended up with a cough. "Lead on, my prince," Cat said, clearing her throat. "I can't wait."

The voices of the Kamaites swelled, blending together in song just as Strian opened the doors to the great halls. *Patima nay*, thousands of voices greeted the setting sun. *Patima nay*.

* * * * *

The stone structures were larger than anything Cat had seen in Kurit. Manmade but not machine-built, the surfaces were worn smooth on the sides facing the rain and the wind, but inside, nestled within the niche of the chiseled stone and soaring to the heavens, was still rough and almost sharp.

She and Strian blended into the crowd of Kamaites, settling toward the back. She still had on the monk's habit Son-Toruai and Beven had given her, but she knew anyone looking too closely would know she didn't belong.

The song of opening prayer swelled and faded, leaving only an echo in the golden glow of the setting sun, floating to a ceiling so high she could barely see where it ended.

Then there was a silence. During it, Cat enjoyed the warmth of the golden sunlight coming through the intricate, colorful leaded glass; the look of the windows themselves seemed to give off heat. After the relentless pitch-black of the cells, the warmth was particularly welcome. She was captivated by the way the colors danced in the brilliance of the setting sun.

"How long has it been?" she overheard someone to her side say.

She glanced over. It was a pair of monks, young, but not in the flush of extreme youth, like Dai.

"A good ten years," the other one replied. "The ceremony of the waterfire does not require it. It must be Beven who is causing it."

"Well, we do not know," the other replied, obviously someone who spent a great deal of time smoothing ruffled feathers. "And his priests seem to say nothing."

"What of the Council?" the other persisted. "How often do you see them out of the hills of Kama?"

"Not often, for certain."

"*Patima nay*," a soft chorus sang. The rustling, the whispering, the conversation around her ceased. She looked up and abruptly, without warning, found herself enveloped in a cushion of warm sound and gentle light. The harmony swelled to fill the space.

"*Patima nay*," another chorus answered.

There were at least a dozen Kamaites, all black-robed instead of the robes of tawny brown, near a peak toward the top of the stone structure. At least a dozen more Kamaites stood in the hollow of the monolith to the side of them to the right, and another dozen to the left.

But unlike those at the tallest stone structure, the ones to the left and right were not in black. They wore instead bright yellow robes, and instead of the round medallions around their necks the Kamaites in black wore, their medallions were diamond-shaped. Novices, she guessed. They looked even younger than those in tawny brown—some of them looked as if shaving would be something they would look forward to in the near future.

But young and old, seasoned priest and novice, at this moment their voices all blended and soared in harmony as they greeted the end of the day. Each of the yellow-robed priests held a small lantern, the flames within each wrapped in an opaque glass. The light glowed and lit up the layers and smoothed surfaces of the stones. Until they did, she could have sworn the rocks were a dulled gray, but the flickering flames brought out the subtle shades of pinks and corals and faded reds of the stones.

"*Corolo ma nay, dera lay ma nay, tenele ma nay,*" a chorus behind Cat answered. She looked behind her. Another group, this one in white, stood on the projections of the stones behind them, a little recessed, in the hollowed-out caverns.

"Let us rejoice, this day of lights," a deeper, flat voice chanted. A hush came over the singers, and Cat watched as one of the black-robed Kamaites, this one taller and heavier than most of the others with an elaborate mantle of gold brocaded silk, stepped forward from the chorus. Then in a voice calculated to project across the small canyon, he said, "Let us pray."

The warm lights surrounding them abruptly vanished as the priests extinguished their lanterns, leaving them in semi-darkness. As Cat's eyes adjusted, she could see the white-robed Kamaites climb down from their eyrie and walk among the monks, their only sound the rustling of their robes and the faint creaking of the lantern handles.

One of the white-robed Kamaites passed behind her. She felt a hand on her shoulder, and then a familiar voice in her ear. "At least try to fit in, Sleeper," Strian mocked gently. "Even if you don't close your eyes, at least cast them down. See the Kamaite in black? He is the Eid, the head of the council that oversees us. And a friend of Son-Toruai, more's the pity."

Cat hadn't even noticed he was no longer beside her. She guessed she was the only one with opened eyes, but that didn't surprise her. The black-garbed Kamaite had instructed the audience—the congregation, rather—to pray, but she didn't even know who, or what, they were praying to. "I shouldn't be here," she muttered, that sensation of being other overwhelming her.

This place was higher than any enclosed stadium she had ever been in, but it was broader. It seemed to be as vast as the Grand Canyon, but it was for lack of a better term cozier. She had never seen anything like it in her life.

The stone structure that was the linchpin of the hall was a prayer wheel, she recognized, with the spokes and the center of the wheel where the thousands of Kamaites stood and sang for the setting sun. It was a prayer wheel larger than a football stadium, as high as the Space Needle, as distinctive and as ancient as Stonehenge. How it had come to be there she didn't know. All anyone had to know was it was here and here it would stay.

Without being told, Cat knew the Kama prayer wheel had been here as long as anyone could remember, and it was without beginning and without end. "This is wonderful," she whispered without thinking, and then she realized Strian was next to her again and would have heard her.

He nodded, and she glimpsed a smile as he did. "This is why the Kamaites exist. We were told the prayer wheel had come into existence for the Kuriti, and we were to protect it and the Court. And so we have, until now."

The monks chanted again, and she had no idea what they were saying, but that didn't matter. It was beautiful, and the peace and the love that flowed out of the singing was enough to make Cat's eyes sting with tears.

Then she forgot about it when she saw a familiar face. It was a face she would never forget. "Strian," she hissed, pulling on his sleeve. "We have to go. Now!"

He looked up and she knew he must have seen what she had — Beven and next to him, Son-Toruai, who had just come into the hall of the prayer wheel. They were accompanied by the two lurkers, and it was clear they had seen Cat and Strian as well.

"Let's go," Cat said, and she knew she sounded as if she were pleading. She just wanted to be far away from them. She had never felt as—abused—as she had in those cells.

"It's all right, Quer'Cadrine," Strian said, staring hard at the other men across the prayer wheel. "You're safe. You will not be touched by them. I swear it."

She wasn't buying it. "What's to stop them from just coming over and getting us again?" She backed up, getting dangerously close to the edge of the stone projection on which they stood.

"They won't," Strian said again. "Just enjoy our prayers, Cadrine."

But she couldn't, not anymore. As she watched, holding onto Strian, first the lurkers, then Beven, then finally Son-Toruai slipped into the vast sea of worshipping Kamaites, making their way closer to them.

But Strian didn't move. In fact, he started to sing with the rest of the Kamaites, only occasionally glancing over at the men who were gradually gaining ground, coming toward them. She tried to edge away, but Strian held her fast. He kept her in his grasp, his arm around her waist.

"What are you doing?" she muttered. She began to tremble as they got closer and closer. *Let me go*! she wanted to shout. She wanted to run, she wanted to hide, she wanted to fight—but all she could do was stand there.

Finally, they were near enough she could hear their breathing under the harmony of the priests. Beven made a quick gesture to his lurkers, who unsheathed their swords. "A betrayal of the Kama," Cat heard Strian murmur, almost as though he didn't care. "Swords drawn at Patima? For shame."

Suddenly, the music died and one of the lurkers—fellow monks—yelled as one of the other Kamaites near him grabbed his arm, twisting it just enough. The sword that had been in his hand clattered down the edge of the spoke of the prayer wheel he was on. The other lurker's weapon met the same fate.

As Cat watched in disbelief, the Kamaites who only seconds previously had been singing in perfect harmony had quickly and unobtrusively surrounded Beven and Son-Toruai, hands on the shoulders of each.

The tense silence of the hall sharpened as the swords Beven and Toruai had each drawn clattered under foot of praying monks. Cat watched in disbelief as the faces of Beven's minions turned pale. But the faces of the praying Kamaites never shifted. One of those who had taken hold of Beven's minions was a small, elderly man. Clearly, with more muscle than she would have imagined.

"Kamaites are warriors, Sleeper," Strian murmured in her ear.

"Then why aren't they attacking them, instead of just holding them?" she asked, still shrinking away from the men.

"Neutrality in a quarrel between two Kamaites, Quer'Cadrine. Neutrality and they cannot interfere," Strian explained. "But no sword can be drawn here in the great hall, and no one, not them, no one, can touch you. That's why you are safe here."

"So what do we do, just stand here until someone decides to do something?" she whispered, trying not to tremble. She tried to relax, but found she couldn't. She tried not to tense up, but she found she couldn't do that either.

"We walk out. We will walk out and they will not be able to touch us. They will not be allowed to touch us for some time."

"How do you figure?" she asked, her shivering diminishing.

"For drawing their swords in the great hall, Beven, as the only one I believe still a Kamaite, must go to the cells for a night."

She swallowed. "The cells?"

"The cells. Let's go, my lady."

And with that, he turned and walked out, still holding Cat's hand. Smiling for what felt like the first time in days, she looked back as they made their way. The two lurker monks, Beven, and Son-Toruai were surrounded by monks keeping a firm hand on each of them.

Into the cells. "Go to hell," she muttered.

Once they were out of the prayer hall, Strian grabbed her hand and together they ran until they got to the largest set of wooden doors she had ever seen. She knew that had to be the way she had come here. He jerked a door open. "Now, my lady, let's get out of here. Let's go!"

Chapter Seventeen

ॐ

They rode hard. They were on the once-protected highway again before long, this time not stopping for high water or the gates of hell. There was no question of them riding apart, not now. They rode together, his arm wrapped around her waist, Lol eating the miles beneath them, Arriya following close with what was left of their supplies.

She ached and she was cold, this chill the result of her stay in the frigid cells and the persistent questionings in the breezy window rooms. She hadn't eaten in well over a day, but it didn't matter—she was too tired, numb and aching. There would be time enough to eat and sleep later. Just not now.

The overland pass gradually broadened, the road beginning to resemble a boulevard of pebble and smoothed rock. Together they descended to the flatlands as the sere environs of the once-protected highway ended, to become the lush, verdant surroundings of the lowlands once more. She had never seen such quick changes in climate as she had here.

Cat looked around, trying to get her mind off her mortality. "I keep seeing them," she said, pointing into the distance. The Forgotten Lovers were sharp in the lowering light, a mist obscuring what would be their faces.

Just for a second he tightened his arm around her. "We can see them from anywhere in Kurit," he reminded her. "The Lovers are in sharp relief when the season is dry and the vegetation dies away, but hidden when the season is wet and the grass is thick. When the waterfire season is upon us, the Lovers themselves are coy but the plains are green. But one way or another, we can always find our way home by looking up.

"The Lovers are, in fact, where we are headed, just for a while, before we head for the Podani. With a hard ride, we will be in time for the ceremony."

Cat tipped her head and rested it on his chest. "Sounds good. That sounds like a good place to be for a while."

Her eyes popped open when she remembered something. "Are we going to see Son-Toruai at the ceremony? If he's in the cells—"

"The Kamaites will not keep them for long," he told her, his voice muffled. "As much as I would wish it, it is not the Kamaites' way, and we have need of at least Son-Toruai and what he holds. Beven will stay in the cells overnight, but Son-Toruai, since he is no longer a professing Kamaite, will be there a shorter time. The Council will detain them long enough for us to be on our way."

"As long as we don't have to see them before the Podani. If there's even the tiniest chance they catch up with us I'm going to get a big stick and I'm going to use it on them, I swear."

Cat felt him chuckle. "Of that I have no doubt, Cadrine."

A flush of pleasure came over her again. When had she become Cadrine? Did it matter?

Live for the moment, Cat told herself. *Enjoy the time you have left.* "I never thought I would see anything this pretty again," she said aloud, looking at the exotic flowers blooming around them, scarlet and purple and gold.

The Forgotten Lovers grew closer, and as Cat watched, she could see the distinctive features of the sharp-edged mountain take shape as the mists parted. She could discern the arms of the lovers curving around each other, their bodies seeming to tilt back, their faces obscured by a passionate embrace.

Something else caught her attention. "What's that sound?"

Before he could answer, she recognized it—the sound of voluptuous, bubbling water, gurgling. Then she could smell it, to her surprise—slightly floral, slightly spicy.

She smiled. Just the sound was enough for her to luxuriate in fantasies of water, warm and comforting. She couldn't remember the last time she had taken a bubble bath.

Cat felt Strian against her take a deep breath. "Those are the waterfalls. You will see them soon," he assured her. "They are beautiful too."

Tears prickled against her eyelids, but she willed them away. "So many things about Kurit are beautiful. So many things, and I didn't see most of them."

"We will. I promise."

She smiled, though her lips trembled. His words were nice, but she couldn't believe them.

The Forgotten Lovers was almost directly above them now, and the bubbling sound of the pool was all around them. The soothing sensation of the waterborne breeze caressed her skin.

"We're here," Strian said in her ear, and it seemed to her his voice changed. It was richer, and deeper, and she felt as though she could reach into it like honey and stroke it over her body, feeling the texture surround her.

She smiled, and that was good. Strian got off Lol, then helped her down. Reluctantly she let go of him once her feet touched the ground. He held her hand until she was there.

He wasn't like Mark at all. No, that was wrong. He was…in that they were both male.

"Why are we here?" she asked after a moment. She touched his shoulder, brushing at nothingness. Enjoy, she told herself.

"You'll see," he said, smiling at her. She smiled back, and they both seemed to be ready for something they weren't willing to admit to yet.

She was flirting with someone who was a figment of her imagination, she realized. And she was going to enjoy it. Whatever happened, she was going to enjoy the time she had left.

Still smiling, Cat looked straight up the side of the mountain. The twists of the Lovers differed from this angle. From where she stood, she could see small openings for caves up high, marking the surfaces of the mountain, some obscured, some almost hidden by thick vegetation. The gaping mouths of the caves became smaller and less accessible closer to the base of the mountain until the caves themselves disappeared into…a waterfall. The one she had heard.

"This is beautiful," she said, her words softening into a murmur, transfixed by the sight.

"It is the pride and joy of Kurit." She heard him take a breath, as if to add something, but he didn't.

"I can see why," she said softly, still staring.

In a land made of wonders, this had to be one of the most wondrous. The violet sky…the double moons…waterfire, and the firewarriors, not to mention the Nurui. They were exotic enough.

But the waterfall! She had never seen a waterfall made up of colors. Never like this with a rainbow beginning and ending at the pool of churning waters, foaming and bubbling. "Strian, this is unbelievable." She laughed with delight. "It's…wonderful!"

"It is," he said. As Cat watched, he walked to the edge of the bubbling pool and, sitting on the edge, slipped off his boots and waded into the rainbow pool. Well before he was at its center, he stopped and looked up at the waterfall, facing away from her.

"I am Strian of Kurit and I am afraid!" he shouted.

At least Cat thought he shouted. His words seemed to get swallowed, and it took her a moment to realize the sound was muffled into the falling water. What was he doing?

"I hate what has become of my country during my time in Kama!" he shouted.

Once more, his words were muffled into nothingness by the bubbling water. She frowned.

"I hate what's become of my brother in the tragedy he has had to face! I am afraid of what he might do at the Great Ceremony with his grief if it comes to a battle!

"I am afraid of what may become of me and the Sleeper…" and here his voice softened. "For I have grown to love her, more than I ever thought I could, though both our days may be numbered."

Cat stared at Strian's back, straight and now, waiting. She saw him take a deep breath. He turned his head a little.

"Strian…" she said, her voice small.

"I should have told you," she heard him say, his words muffled but still clear. "Rainbow Falls is where Kuriti come to proclaim their inner truths before riding into battle. It is a tradition."

"Oh, Strian," she said, tears in her voice. Her heart twisted. She slipped off her boots and waded in after him, tucking her skirts in her waistband. The water wasn't cold and even if it had been, she wouldn't have cared. "Please…" She touched his shoulder.

He turned to face her, and she touched his cheek. "Thank you," she whispered, and though her words shouldn't have been audible, they were. The colors of the rainbow drifted past Cat and Strian, the tiny, fiery droplets settling briefly on their shoulders before they floated away, absorbed back into the pool of water.

Emboldened, Cat stroked his cheek, but that almost felt too much. Contentment washed over her, every nerve on fire, rainbows adrift in the breeze, kissing every inch of her skin.

Strian smoothed her hair, sending an avalanche of tiny rainbows cascading. In turn, she stroked his lips, tracing them, chasing the bubbles away. One of them floated up and unexpectedly burst near his nostrils; he sneezed and they laughed.

Nor were the colors like anything she had ever seen, not simple reds or blues or yellows, but gradations deeper than the sea. It was as if she could touch and taste and feel the colors of the rainbow. It was the most beautiful thing she had ever seen.

Hot tears prickled beneath her eyelids, but she refused to let them fall.

"Quer'Cadrine, why the grim look?" Strian whispered. He was warm and his breath was warm, and it was all she could do not to shake from the contrast of his heat and the water's cool.

She swallowed. "The rainbow's making me cry," she said after a moment and to her horror, her voice quavered. "I'm never going to see anything so beautiful again."

The tears cascading down her cheeks were hot as she stopped trying to stop them. She had gone through too much—the abduction and imprisonment in the cells of Kama broke the camel's back—and she couldn't hold back anymore. "Too much," she sobbed, and she pressed her forehead against his shoulder. "Why did I have to discover this now when I don't have any time left?"

After a moment he wrapped his arms around her. "Shh, Cadey," he soothed. "Hush."

"But there isn't anything I can do," she said desperately. He still wore the monk's robe, and it was scratchy against her face. "All I can do is cause more trouble, no matter what I do or say."

"You may not have to worry about it," he whispered in her ear and she could have sworn there was a suggestion of a smile in his voice. "Who knows? The waterfire may destroy us all, and you and I along with it."

Her eyes popped open. She pushed away from him—or at least she tried. "How could you?" she said indignantly, struggling to step away from him and not succeeding. "How dare you make light of a situation like this?"

She looked up at him, and her heart clenched again as she looked into his eyes. The violet hues she saw there reflected all the colors of the rainbow falls, warm as the sun. The colors in his eyes made up all the colors of his world.

And he was trying to distract her, she realized. She tried to smile when Strian tucked a strand of her hair behind her ear. "If we do not laugh, we cry, and there's no point in crying, Cadrine." His eyes seemed to track each line, every curve of her face. He wiped away an errant tear. The rough pad of his thumb scraped her skin. "Kuriti have cried too much in the past years. We can only do so much," he reminded her. "One way or another, we must see to it they can laugh again."

"With the ceremony."

"Yes."

"Is it dangerous? The ceremony?"

The muscle in his jaw twitched. "Only to those who do not understand what is at stake." She felt him relax as he stroked her hair again. "Danger comes to those who do not heed its power."

"What happens if it doesn't work?"

He caressed her cheek. "Then it's out of our hands, my lady," he whispered. "We must do our part, but beyond that, we can do nothing else."

And then he kissed her.

Once more, her eyes stung with tears. She had been expecting it, wanting it, but when it finally happened, it was more than she could ever have expected.

The way she could with the rainbow mists around her, she tasted and felt and smelled the pure male perfume Strian exuded. The strong, steady beat of his heart surrounded them. She could have sworn she heard the roaring of his pulse, even over the thundering of the waterfall around them. And the taste. He tasted like vanilla and cinnamon, the pure ice water of the River Pon, as smooth and rich as fresh cream, and for the first time in a long while she knew real hunger and how to slake it.

His muscles tightened and relaxed, the heat of his body warmed her, the touch of his skin against hers awakened her. She knew at once this was what she had been waiting for her entire life.

Through it all, she could feel him tremble, though it was almost imperceptible. She felt the moisture on her cheeks and did not know whether the tears were her own or the mist from the waterfall. She felt him take a deep breath and felt his lips leave hers.

She closed her eyes as he kissed her mouth and nose and cheeks. "You are eternity," he whispered. He kissed her throat.

She stilled, her fingers frozen in their path through his hair. She could feel his warm lips against her cool skin. "Strian?" she breathed after a moment.

"You are my heart and I am yours, and I will forsake all others for you," he said as he straightened, tilting her face up to meet his gaze. In the light of the waterfall, his eyes were the color of the sapphire embedded in his heartsword, reflecting in the multicolored, shifting patterns of the water, and his lips were trying to curve into a smile. She reached out and touched them.

"Do you mean it?" she whispered. His eyes were as warm as his lips and after a moment, so was the smile that broke out on his face.

He laughed a bit, and his eyes shone. "Yes, Sleeper," he said. "My love for you will glow like a diamond in the sun, as long as the sun shines upon Kurit and the Circle of Seas."

She couldn't breathe. Her heart hammered and every vein in her body threatened to explode. "Strian," she began. She couldn't meet his eyes—they glowed too much, almost blinding. "Strian," she began again. She closed her eyes and bit her lip.

"Cadrine?" she heard him say. She felt him duck to meet her eyes, but resolutely she kept her eyes closed. "Quer'Cadrine?" For the first time, she heard uncertainty in his voice, and her heart filled with remorse. "Are you aright?"

She shook her head. She sniffed and squinched her eyes tighter but kept a firm grip on him. "No, I'm not," she managed to say, and she hated how her voice quavered.

"Why not? Life is short, my lady," he whispered, and his voice kissed her much as the rainbow bubbles had. She knew whatever she thought, this was as real as her life had ever been, and this man was as real as any she ever met.

She touched his lips and tried to commit to memory their texture beyond her own lifetime, so she would have one thing to cherish when her eyelids finally closed. She tried to keep firm in her mind the fire in his eyes hid a gentle touch, a steel that was softened by the iris of his gaze.

How could she give any of this up?

"Lady, my life span is as short as yours," he said, his voice low. "If the ceremony does not do what we mean it to do, we will meet oblivion together."

"You will succeed," she insisted. "I don't know why I'm here, but you— We will succeed at it. I know it."

"Nonetheless, we do not *know*. We are of a pair, my lady," he told her with a faint grin. "Our lives are short, and we should do what we were meant to do now."

He paused, as though this was difficult for him. She reached out and touched his arm. "Then what is our fate?"

Strian caught her hand and pressed it against his cheek, tracing the lines of worry and exhaustion on his face until they softened away.

"First of all, I must apologize."

"For what?"

"I was suspicious of you when we first met and it was something for which I had no cause. All I knew was this war had gone on too long and my honorable sister, Gilcris' queen, was dead and so was their son, and here, all of a sudden, the answer to a legend had come into my life, and I could not believe it to be true."

She traced the lines around his eyes. Some were lines of fear and despair, but some had to be of joy. She had to hope. "I wouldn't have blamed you. I would have been suspicious if someone like you had walked into my life back in Seattle. I would have turned you over to the police."

"My suspicions were born of my own fears. You could have been my warrant of trust long before, and we could have pledged ourselves long before now."

"But we wouldn't have been ready. Things happen when they happen because that is the time for them to happen."

He stared at her for a second—his brow furrowed. "I think you are right, my lady. But still I must apologize. Because my feelings for you go beyond the promise I made to Gilcris to protect you."

"When was that clear to you?" she asked, smiling. She brushed his hair from his face.

"I knew myself beyond my own heart when Beven took you, and I was torn between losing you to that vermin and losing the jackoval."

"I'm so sorry," Cat said, something she had not had an opportunity to tell him before. The jackoval had been his shadow for so long. She touched his arm. "I know you two had been together for years."

"The pain was great," he admitted. "I knew you were my lifemate come to me at last, and then you were gone. And my friend, who had been with me beyond all these trials, was gone too, dying in my arms."

"I'm here now," she reminded him. She caressed his cheek. "And I'm not going to let you go as long as I can."

"I am glad," he said. "So very glad."

He knelt before her finally. "The Rainbow Falls are also famous for having seen the troth of lovers about to go to war, my lady. More children have been conceived here, I think, than anywhere else in the country."

For once, she didn't know what to say.

"Well?" he persisted. "Have you any reaction? I love you, Cadrine. My strange, sweet lady, filled with a life I know nothing about, who came to me when I gave up on so many things. And, it seems, who must return to her own home soon, leaving me bereft once more."

Life is short. Do what you must.

Take a chance.

"You are what I have been waiting for all my life," she whispered. "Through the times that were bad, through the times that got worse, through the lovers who didn't care—"

"And how they could not care, my lady, I cannot even begin to imagine—"

"Because they weren't you," she said finally with a watery laugh. "I've been waiting for you all this time. Where have you been?"

"I've been here, waiting for you to come through the Gates."

"I want to be everything to you." She bit her lip. "But all I can do is be myself, which I don't think is good enough for you."

"You are more than anyone or anything I have ever seen."

Cat whispered, "I would, if I could, give you everything you've lost—your family, your ambitions, children of your own."

"What would your dreams be, Sleeper?"

The rainbow mist kissed her skin. It left a faint moisture on his face, much as it did on hers. "I would explore Kurit with you, let you tell me about all its joys and sorrows and yours as well, and make love to you in the light of the full moons until the song of the morning glory wakes us from our sleep."

"Life is short, my lady," he said. He bent down and kissed her again. "Let us take advantage of what time we do have."

It was everything and it was nothing. From the moment his lips touched hers, she forgot what it was like to be alone and to have a void staring her in the face. This was what she had been waiting for, without reservation, without despair.

All she had to do was dream about it.

She didn't remember how they had managed to undress without letting go of each other. Their lips broke apart only once, to pull Cat's tunic over her head. They drank from each other with an eagerness that bordered on revelation. It was the most wonderful thing Cat had ever tasted because, finally, she knew she loved and was loved.

They touched each other on the heart and beyond the borders of anything either had ever experienced.

And when they had both drifted back to reality, like the rainbow mist around them, they touched and kissed each other and felt the loving warmth that came from having their hearts entwined.

Chapter Eighteen

෨

The Podani was a broad plateau easing down to the equally broad beaches, surrounded by sheer cliffs that abutted the Circle of Seas, Strian explained as he and Cat approached. The ceremonial grounds were on an isolated beach set apart from the Podani Plains themselves, almost as broad as the Kama great hall, but the sharp incline up to the cliffs gave it a feeling of being surrounded. Only one clear break in the cliffs allowed easy entrance to the rest of the Podani.

The rules of engagement had been set for the ritual of the waterfire. While the Court's army had thus far protected the Podani from the honorable uncle's forces, for this occasion and this occasion alone the uncle's army were allowed clear passage through the Podani, to surround half the ceremonial field, facing the Court's army. Under the watchful eye of the imperial forces and the uncle's men would the waterfire be brought under control.

Cat was only half-listening as she rode nestled in Strian's arms, her hands clasped to his arms, her stomach twisting in anticipation. She burrowed into his shoulder, and on occasion she could feel him give her head a kiss. It didn't help.

"The outbreaks of waterfire become more frequent on the plains and at the water's edge as the time of the ceremony grows near," Strian explained. She inhaled sharply, remembering the crystalline haze that cut the fire festival short. "Cadrine?"

"I'm fine," she said immediately and steeled herself so she didn't shake. She wasn't going to let him get nervous for her sake. He had enough to worry about.

"Are you certain? After your time in the cells—"

"I'm here with you," she replied, her words muffled in the creases of his manteau. She closed her eyes for a second, reveling in the feel of the heavy silken fabric. *Enjoy the moment,* she told herself.

The ceremony was going to mean the death of someone, she knew that. She didn't know whose. She didn't know how. She just knew. She just didn't want it to be Strian's.

She held on to him, scorching the feel of him into memory, knowing one way or another she would lose it.

If he knew her concerns he didn't let on. Instead she could feel him solid against her, reassuring in his presence.

She rubbed his forearm. It was real; he was solid. He was as real as her own life had ever been, and that was what counted.

"The ceremony," she said, trying to get her mind back on track. "What is it and what can I do?"

She felt him tense, and she regretted it. "All three of the Gems of Kurit must be brought together at the right time. You know this."

"Yes. That much I know."

"The ceremony must be timed when the largest burst of waterfire appears at a distance over the horizon of the sea and the winds are blowing straight toward land."

"Do you know when that happens?"

"A little. We can time it according to the seventh full half-moon of the season of the brittling winds," he explained. She guessed that was now. "At dusk, an hour before the sun sets, we know the larger moon will be eclipsed by the largest burst of waterfire, the one that eclipsed the sun and the skies and destroyed all life in Kurit for a generation. We know this from our Book of Gates, which tells of this in past waterfire risings."

She swallowed. "What happens if the ceremony doesn't take place? What if Son-Toruai doesn't show?"

He sighed. "That too we know. The First Abbess of the Laoni, she who called herself Mawg, wrote that on that occasion she witnessed, when the three Gems were not brought together, all known Kurit was destroyed and a generation later, after the land started to return, those who still called themselves Kuriti began to come back from Faiora to settle our land again. Another source calls those settlers the descendants of the Abbess, in that she called for it to happen."

"Is that why the two countries are so close?"

"Yes. That is why we count them our cousins, for our blood has mingled since then. All three of the Gems must be brought together. You know what they are."

"The jewel in your sword, the earring Gilcris bears, the torc that — that Son-Toruai now wears around his neck. Each of those three have the gems of Kurit in them. Right?"

"Yes. We bring them together in a pattern that brings the light of the jewels together to vanquish the waterfire. That is what we have been told, but I do not know how, nor have I ever seen it."

He shifted his hold around her. She stroked his arm, trying her best to reassure him. "Over the years, we have learned certain things," Strian explained. "This is not the only time we have had to wage civil war for this cause."

That figured. "Don't people learn?"

Cat felt his chest move, and she guessed he laughed. Good. She was glad he could still do that. "I can tell you, we learn well enough to do a few things. Going to the Rainbow Falls is one when faced with our mortality. Time was, when the crowds there were thick."

"If we were back in Seattle we'd call that Lovers' Lane," she mused, smiling a little.

"I could not forget your touch, my lady," he whispered. She could feel him smile back. "I will remember it in battle."

Just don't let it distract you, she wanted to cry out, but she didn't. "Be careful, Strian." It didn't matter to her at the moment how she felt. She just needed him to be safe.

"I will do my best, Quer'Cadrine."

"Tell me more about the ceremony," she suggested, searching for a way to calm him. "Tell me everything I should know."

"Of course. By now you know of the Kamaites."

"I am. I've been there," she added, with a touch of dry levity. Not that she would have thought she would ever have had the pleasure of being held captive in a monastery.

"You have seen more of the Kama's great halls than most Kuriti born and bred see in a lifetime."

"Most Kuriti born and bred aren't kidnapped by monks either."

"True. The warrior priests of the Kama are the traditional protectors of the Court and his family, remember," he told her. "They also have their own role in the waterfire ceremony."

"They'll be coming right after us," she exclaimed. Her stomach jumped before she quashed her unease. She was safe. And Strian would keep her safe. She knew that.

"They will."

"What do they do?"

"The Kamaites are not only protectors of the Court, they are also protectors of the ceremony."

She frowned. "Why would the ceremony need protecting?"

"Think," he said simply. "Son-Toruai."

Cat tried to think why the renegade monk would be involved in preventing the ceremony. Then, "You mean blackmail? What kind of thinking is *that*?"

"Desperation."

"How can you take advantage if you're going to die along with everyone else if the ceremony doesn't go the way it's supposed to?"

"I do not know, my lady," he said. "I have read Kuriti history and I have never found anything to indicate why this would happen. And yet it does."

She shook her head. "Human connivance is the same as it is in Seattle. And I was hoping it was different here."

"Men and women do not change, Cadrine."

She bit her lip. "I'm scared, Strian."

"I know, Cadey," he said, and she could feel him kiss her hair again. "But whatever happens, you are mine and I am yours, for now and all eternity."

She gripped his arm. "I'll hold you to that."

They rode after that in silence.

"I should be there with you."

"I think not, Sleeper."

Cat would have smiled if she weren't determined about this. "My destiny lies with yours, my prince."

"Your destiny does not involve being down on Podani Beach when a battle is brewing, my lady."

"My destiny has something to do with the waterfire ceremony, and I certainly won't be able to face it unless I'm down there with you."

"Cadrine. No."

"Strian. Yes."

"Not by the moons, lady."

"You know I'll be there, Strian."

"Cadey—" He sounded tired.

She didn't like to do that to him, but she had to. "Stri," she said, teasing, mimicking him. They were at an impasse, and he knew it.

"Cadey—at least stay back until you cannot avoid it. A deadly battle will be fought on Podani Beach this time, and there will be real casualties. Both the Court's men and the honorable uncle's men in presence guarantee it."

"Then I have to make sure you're not one of the casualties."

He sighed impatiently.

"Our first argument," she remarked.

"Not our last."

"Not by a long shot."

Why had she ever thought he was anything like Mark? Because she had been groggy, fresh out of a comalike sleep, that was why. In any case, she had found him, and a burst of exultation swept over her. But it was better to have found him now than to go to her death not having known.

"The Podani begins over the bluff there," he said, taking his arm from around her waist to point to the horizon. "Can you hear it? The forces are gathering."

Despite herself, her blood quickened. She sat up, eagerly awaiting her first glimpse of the Podani of which she had heard so much. This was Strian's home, and she was curious to see the place that held so many fond memories for him.

"I wish I could have met Faia."

"She was fragile but with a spine of iron, Cadey. But she did not have a fraction of the strength I sense in you."

"Thank you," she said, her voice trembling, "but I wasn't fishing for compliments. I was hoping meeting her could have explained more about you and Gilcris."

"What can I tell you about Faia? She was frail and she was optimistic. She believed there was good in her uncle no one else could see."

"What's done is done and cannot be undone," Cat said, uneasily aware she sounded very Kuriti. "What else?"

"She loved Gilcris. She loved her son. She loved me as a younger brother," he added wistfully. "She was the best friend I had outside of Gilcris and one who knew I was not meant for the priesthood, though that was what I had planned for most of my life."

"Then why did you join?"

"I loved the study. I grew to love the camaraderie. And I thought I could protect Gilcris and Faia, though in the end I protected neither."

"Let it go," she advised. "Do a Zen thing."

"A what? I will never get used to the way you speak, Cadey."

"I will teach you the mysterious ways of my speech if you show me yours."

"I will hold you to that. There it is," he said, his voice rising. "The Podani awaits you, Cadey." He gestured.

At first, she was surprised—and not a little disappointed. The Podani was plain and plateau both, cliffs and hills and beach as far as her eye could see, and in the distance, a walled city that had to be Podani Town itself, abutting an open sea of a vivid and restless muddy blue, choppy and swirling, with that disarming violet sky above.

Then she looked toward the broad, flat beach, protected by sheer cliffs on three sides. There were clusters of people down on the beach, keeping close to the relative protection of the cliffs, and there seemed to be a lot of them.

The ceremony. Cat's stomach roiled.

"That is the ceremonial ground," Strian said, as if he were reading her mind. "And that is the beginning and the end of our journey."

"Are all those people there for the ceremony?"

There had to be a thousand down on the sands. And more beyond the beach, she could tell. There must have been another thousand on the cliffs that surrounded the beach.

Strian pointed to a group down on the beach, dressed in monks' robes. "The first Kamaites are already here, waiting to move into formation for the ceremony. The others down there are soldiers from both the Kuriti army and Son-Toruai's army."

"So you have three armies waiting for this? *Three*? Isn't that overkill—so to speak?"

"I told you, the Kamaites are there to prevent either party from dishonoring themselves on this occasion."

"And the Kuriti army and the honorable uncle's army are there to kill each other if the waterfire doesn't?"

Her indignant tone must have amused him for he began, "Quer'Cadrine—" then broke off. He shook his head. "Yes. Now that you put it in such terms, that is exactly what it is. Thank you for explaining it all to me."

She laughed a little with him, because it was better than yelling. Not now, so close to the inevitable.

"Now do you understand why you should not be down there? The ceremony is attended by a thousand soldiers, and if nothing else, I do not want you caught in the crossfire of battle."

Cat started to look around. "I'll stay with Q'Atha. She should be here somewhere, shouldn't she?"

"She should be," Strian muttered. "Hang on, Cadey. We will find her."

With a shift and a nick, he urged Lol away from the broad path leading down to the beach instead following the one that led to the settlements she saw established on the cliffs. "Most likely she will be among those," he explained.

"How do you know?"

"Because that's where Boyo will be, and she would not leave him."

Cat smiled. She wondered if her own happiness glowed, the way Q'Atha's affection for Boyo did. Of course, there was a world — even a dimension — of difference between them, but as Strian pointed out, there wasn't much difference between men and women of Seattle and Kurit after all.

She looked at the cliffs. As they got closer, she could identify small groups, tents dotting the plain. There were food-sellers, she could tell, children running and playing, and there was even a village green of sorts. It looked like a three-ring circus.

One of those tents at the cliff edge looked familiar. "Those look like the Elder's colors," Cat said, pointing.

"Then that will be where we'll find Q'Atha." He nicked softly. "By and away, Lol."

As she and Strian got closer, she began to identify familiar faces. The noise she heard became more and more familiar as well as she heard the soft, rhythmic beats of the otho drums. Cat spotted Q'Atha, who was talking to someone in her energetic way, her hands in motion, so different from the shy, demure girl Cat had first met. And there was Poro the Elder's cook, who of course must have been in the middle of preparing the midday meal, for she was stirring a giant caldron with an equally enormous ladle, wiping her hands once in a while on her apron that looked as though it had the splattered makings of an entire meal on it.

On the edges of that settlement Cat recognized Boyo, who had his otho drum clasped around his shoulders, the mouthpiece daggling from his lips as he concentrated on the proper cadence, overseen by his father, who had his own drum.

With them were others she recognized from S'nal, and they too had objects she assumed were musical instruments, or at least from them were emanating the sounds of things that seemed as though they would be pleasant and distinctive once played with some form of melody.

"I thought it was just the otho drum at the ceremony," Cat said after she pointed out the familiar faces. "There's more?"

"The ceremony is the biggest ceremony Kurit has, for all that it comes about every hundred years and all that people may die."

"They could all die, so they all come to *watch*?"

"No one said we were of sound mind, my lady," Strian told her with a rueful smile.

She straightened, shaking her head. "It's like a really big train wreck, but everyone's on it," she muttered. "Or the Indianapolis 500."

"As many Kuriti as are able to travel gather on this occasion," he explained. "And from the time the ceremony did not happen and those who survived were forced to flee to Faiora, those who are here tend to be of the mind they would prefer to perish quickly in the onslaught of waterfire than see loved ones die a horrible death. And so they come."

"Does life stop for a while every century until this is taken care of?"

Strian didn't say anything for a moment. Cat couldn't blame him. "The farms pause in their production, the towns and villages stop in their trade—my grandfather told stories of what his father told him, when they would all wait and see if the next thing they heard was a roar that overwhelmed them all and the screams of those caught in the path of the waterfire."

Cat shivered. "How can you be so calm?"

He stroked her head. "Because for Kuriti this is life. And I know what I can do to stop it. What I cannot know is whether others will do their part."

She said nothing else, just squeezed his hand, letting him know whatever else, she was there for him. "Strian—please be careful—"

Strian brought Lol to a stop. "I know, my heart. Before the ceremony, I would like a few minutes alone with you." He smiled as he helped her down.

Despite her fears, she had to smile back. "I would like that."

He took both her hands and held them. "It cannot be for long but a few minutes, so I can remind you you are my lifemate, and whatever happens —"

"You are mine," she finished. She squeezed his hands. "I love you, Strian."

He smiled, but there was almost pain in it. "And I you. Let us take you over to my cousin, and let me be on my way. I have matters to settle before we begin."

She let him lead her over to Q'Atha, and when the girl saw them, she let out an undignified whoop and came running over.

Cat was taken aback when the younger woman hugged her. "I had begun to worry about you! Is your jackoval behind you, cousin?" Q'Atha burbled. "I have this wonderful spice I bargained from —"

Strian put up a hand to stop her. "The jackoval is dead, cousin. Toruai's men slit his throat."

His cousin froze, her eyes welling up. "Oh, cousin," she said, her lips trembling. "I am so sorry."

Strian sighed. "I promised him he would be with me at the ceremony, and all I can do now is keep his memory with me."

"He knows, cousin," the young woman cried. "And he knows you'll avenge his death."

Strian could say nothing more. Cat watched his face with the certain knowledge that love brings. He wished he could comfort his young cousin by agreeing, but he couldn't.

"Your Highness! Sleeper! You're finally here!"

Cat turned at the other familiar voice, strange in its new, lower timbre. Boyo staggered over to greet them, nearly overwhelmed by the complex cacophony of shiny metal and wooden tubes that made up the otho drum in full. He could barely walk, but clearly he was proud of his burden.

"Boyo!" Cat said, smiling. The otho drum was nearly his size. "Is that what you'll be playing?"

"Yes, this is the otho drum. It's been in my family for seven generations! My father's been teaching me how to play the waterfire ritual. Would you like to hear?"

"Not now," Cat said hastily, having seen Strian's face tense. "I think the prince has to go now."

"Good luck, Your Highness. We'll be here for you!" Boyo said exuberantly.

"Thank you," Strian said. "Cadrine—"

"Where should I meet you?" she said immediately.

"Down by the lowest cliff landing. In about an hour. Don't be late," he said, with a ghost of a smile.

As much as she wanted to, she couldn't return it. "I won't," she answered, setting her jaw.

She watched him leave on Lol, making his way down to the edge of the beach, where he dismounted and disappeared into the swirl of activity. She recognized the Kamaites, so recently having been surrounded by them. She recognized the Kuriti soldiers' colors, and since she did not recognize the third, she assumed those had to be Toruai's army.

Cat looked up at the open sea, as still as death and ominous. The skies were clear, but the waterfire was coming. Starting at the back of her head was the faintest suggestion of a headache. Nothing else was on the horizon…yet. But soon, she knew.

Until they could see the burst of waterfire out on the water, all any of them could do was steel themselves to meet the greatest fear any Kuriti had.

Q'Atha touched Cat's shoulder. "Sleeper? What happened? To the jackoval, I mean?"

The young woman's voice was tight with anxiety. Too late Cat remembered the jackoval and the Elder's granddaughter had shared a bond.

Cat didn't want to tell her the details. Later, if she had a later. "It feels like an eternity ago," she confessed.

"How did you meet up with the honorable uncle? How did he kill the jackoval?"

So Cat told her, explaining a little of what had happened since last they had seen each other, but without a mention of the stop at Rainbow Falls. But Q'Atha guessed. "So you and the prince—have—grown close?" she asked, her pained eyes brightening a little.

Cat looked away. "We have," she muttered but admitted to no more than that. It still didn't feel real.

"I'm glad. The prince has seemed so alone, Kamaite or not. And Quer'Cadrine—" her voice lowered. "Boyo and I have as well. And I am so happy."

Cat had to smile. If she had been back in Seattle, Q'Atha would have been jumping up and down, flashing a brand-new diamond ring on her left hand. "Congratulations. Are you of age, Q'Atha?"

"I am. Although Grandme would prefer I was not. She still thinks I am too young to be affianced, but I think I am old enow."

"And what about Boyo?"

"He is as old as I am, and his prospects of working his family's farm are good," the young woman said optimistically, her eyes shining.

"So your grandmother's not aware?" Cat smiled. "When would you tell the Elder?"

"When we return to S'nal. And Sleeper..." Here Q'Atha's voice dipped even lower. "I think I am with child already. I am so happy I could burst."

Cat's eyes widened. "You work fast, kiddo. But if you're happy, I'm happy for you. Hey, Boyo?" she called over to where the young man was fiddling with the heavy otho drum.

Still struggling with the instrument, he lumbered over, a broad smile threatening to split his face. Clearly, the drum was his pride and joy...after Q'Atha, fingers crossed. "Sleeper?"

"Q'Atha just told me. You'll treat her well, won't you? The prince will not let you live otherwise," Cat said, not joking.

Boyo's eyes grew round. "Sleeper, she is the light of my life, and has been for years," he exclaimed, beaming. "But I have been waiting until I reach my ascendancy as otho drummer, and I finally have." His eyes shone as brightly as Q'Atha's.

Despite herself, it was hard for Cat to be cynical. "Then congratulations, and be careful," she told them. Her heart ached a little at how happy the two seemed. "Though I most likely will not be here with you, be happy with each other. And keep each other safe."

"I will, Sleeper. We will," they said.

"Good." She smiled at them both, feeling old. Then she winced, knowing what was coming. The twinge in the back of her throat wriggled north, and before she knew it, the familiar, searing pain spread throughout her head.

Waterfire!

"It's coming," she said, groaning, dropping to her knees. This was the worst yet, and that was no surprise. From what Strian said, this was no ordinary blast of waterfire.

But he had said the plain was safe. *It shouldn't be, it shouldn't be*, she chanted within her mind. They were on the plains. *It was supposed to be* safe *here!*

Then she heard the scream. *"Waterfire!* Run!"

Cat rose to her feet, fighting the pain. She watched in horror as a burst of waterfire seared a tent in two before consuming it with a roar. *"Run!"* she screamed, her head feeling as torn asunder as the tent.

Run. But where? Strian had told her the plain was safe, that the beach was the center of the mighty mother-burst of waterfire when it arrived. He had said nothing about a smaller, secondary burst.

Cat looked around. Most of the Kuriti at the settlement were running all about, seeking shelter, but most were running toward the beach. She turned and saw Boyo struggling with the cumbersome otho drum, not willing to abandon it.

"Atha! Go with the Sleeper!" he shouted.

But the Elder's granddaughter stood on the path down to the beach. "Not without you!" Q'Atha screamed.

"I must save the drum! Move!"

Q'Atha stood for a second longer before Cat grabbed her hand and started to pull her down the rocky path. "Q'Atha! Get going!" Cat shouted.

"But Boyo!"

"Boyo will be right behind us! *Go!"*

With a grunt and a shove, Cat coaxed the younger woman into movement. The movement seemed to split her skull and she was feeling weaker and weaker, the pain even traveling down to her fingers, but she managed to move, though she was slower than she would have been only hours before.

Cat could hear the screams around her as she tried to push Q'Atha to safety, but she couldn't stop. She couldn't even turn around to see what was happening. They had to keep going. *Now!*

She could nearly feel the waterfire behind her, almost hot, almost wet, yet neither, reaching for them. Her head was pounding, but she knew what she had to do. "Q'Atha! Down the path!"

But Q'Atha paid her no heed. *"Boyo!"*

"Q'Atha!" Cat tried again, but the younger, stronger woman resisted, refusing to move. "Run! Veer to the right, sharp!"

"Boyo! Where are you? *Boyo!*"

With a moan, Cat finally dared to look behind her. The burst of waterfire was hot on her heels, so close she could almost touch it. Gritting her teeth, she—

"Now!" Cat shoved her into movement. The girl stumbled but finally moved.

Cat recoiled as she saw the burst consume an elderly man, wincing at his agonized scream. Her stomach roiling, she stood her ground and faced the waterfire.

It wasn't as large as the one that had destroyed the proceedings of the fire festival back at the village. But it still made her want to vomit, knowing it was only the beginning. "Go ahead," she whispered, her fists clenched. "*I know you.* I am your destiny, as much as I am Strian's, but I don't fear you. *Come get me.*"

It was a whirling mass of gray, but she could see something sparkling within. Something there called to her.

Not yet.

For a moment, Cat stood staring at it. She could have sworn it was staring back.

In what she sensed was a moment of recognition the waterfire exploded in fury, and in the next second it was ash, no more, glowing on the ground.

Cat stood staring at its remains as it cooled, becoming less and less like the threat it had been, only seconds before. "That was waterfire," she whispered, her heart pounding. "That was waterfire and I met it."

She didn't know what was coming next for her, but she had just faced down the fear of the country. And she wasn't afraid of it anymore.

Then she remembered. "Q'Atha? Are you okay?" she called out, looking around finally. "Q'Atha?"

"Boyo? Where are you? Boyo?" Cat heard Q'Atha.

"Boyo? Where is he? Are you all right?" Cat asked, running over to Q'Atha.

"I don't know! Where is he?" the younger woman asked, her eyes wild.

Cat glanced to the last spot she had seen the farmer's youngest—and she winced. "B—oh, Q'Atha. Oh, Q'Atha, I'm so sorry."

Cat turned the young woman around and wouldn't let her look. "It looks like he managed to save the drum, but he couldn't get out of the way in time. Don't look. Oh, Q'Atha, I'm so sorry."

"No, it can't be. Where is he? Boyo? Boyo!" Q'Atha screamed.

Cat kept her grip on Q'Atha, leading her away. "I'm sorry, Q'Atha, I'm so sorry," she whispered. She knew what was behind her, because she had seen it too often during the short time she had been in Kurit. A pile of ash lay where Boyo had been, vaguely in the shape of a person, only feet from where the otho drum, the pride of seven generations of a Kuriti family, lay on the ground, scored by the waterfire but otherwise none worse for wear.

The otho drum. Who would take it over now?

"I'm sorry, Q'Atha, I'm so sorry," Cat soothed, willing away the sight of the ashes, determined not to turn again. "I'm so sorry."

"Oh, Sleeper," Q'Atha said, sobbing. "Oh, Sleeper. I don't know what to do."

"Go on, Q'Atha," Cat told her, holding her. "That's what Boyo would have wanted you to do. Go on and remember him."

The girl started to cry in earnest, her heart broken in pieces, until finally, she was silenced by sheer exhaustion. Cat could do nothing but sit by her.

Cat knew how she felt. She would have felt the same, now.

The sun had shifted by the time she looked up. "Q'Atha, stay here." She stood up, squeezing the younger woman's arm. "It's almost time."

Cat didn't want to, but she left her there. She looked back one last time, and knew she would never see the girl again. "Q'Atha, remember — no matter what happens, Boyo would want you to survive. And your cousin is down there to make sure you do."

"I know. Oh, Boyo!" she screamed.

Cat left her alone with her grief, knowing the worst was yet to come.

Chapter Nineteen

ຂໆ

Cat stumbled to the tip of the Podani cliffs, doing her best not to look at the sad sight of shattered dreams behind her. Her eyes started to water as she squinted against the brittling winds started to rise. That tiny burst of waterfire was only the beginning.

She shivered. *Brittling winds*. When did she start using their phrases? When did Kurit start feeling more like home than home ever did?

At the horizon the sky was an ominous gray. Directly above her, despite the angry blast of waterfire that had just cut through the settlement, it was mild and fluffy-white-cloud violet, cool and breezy. Across the beach she could see Gilcris and the honorable uncle—she could never think of him any other way now—face each other, neither looking at the burst of waterfire building in the waters in the distance.

Her first instinct was to run as far as she could into the first deep cave she could find, far away from the beach. Instead she stood there, holding her breath. She was shivering.

She felt a touch on her shoulder and looked up. It was Strian, dressed the way she first met him, in black leather and wool and silver so distinctive of the Kamaites, having divested himself of the monk's robe. The sword of Kurit was strapped across his chest, the intense sapphire gem nearly vibrating in the uncertain atmosphere, and around his waist he wore the belt and scabbard of the warrior priests, his knife's hilt polished to a gleam.

She pressed her forehead against his chest. "You're ready," she said, her voice muffled. "I was wondering."

291

He slipped an arm around her shoulder. "Are you aright, Cadrine?"

"As much as I'll ever be." She gave him a perfunctory squeeze and looked up at him. He looked tired—and who could blame him, considering he had had a journey for nearly a week with little or no sleep—but his eyes were clear and peaceful.

Going to the Rainbow Falls did that for him. If only it could have done that for her.

"I heard about the burst," he said. "After this, I will give my condolences to my little cousin."

"He was so young," she whispered. "And he had so much to do with his life. And just like that—"

"The time he had was filled with what he wanted, dear heart," he reminded her. "He had his music from what I understand. He had his family. And he had his own Cadrine." He paused. "I will speak to the Elder when I can."

If he could. Always unspoken, always understood.

Cat squeezed him again. "Not much longer, is it?"

"No. You know where to run if the waterfire gets past the beach."

She took a sharp breath. If the ritual didn't work. "I don't *want* to run away if you're down there."

"I know. But I would rather do battle knowing you are safe than do battle not knowing where you are. I would be torn, and that would not be wise for either of us."

The otho drum started up just then, the steady beat and the softer brush of the lesser, more subtle snare drum beneath almost hypnotic. Boyo's father. She wanted to close her eyes and let her body respond to the rhythm, become involved. And forget, if only for a moment.

"Is the otho drummer going to be playing all through the—" Cat stopped. She didn't know exactly what to call what was going to happen.

"It is a ritual, and it is a battle. Yes, he is. It is an inherited position," he added. "His grandpe beat the otho drum during the ceremony, and his grandpe's mother before that."

But the drummer's son would not be beating the otho in the next generation's ceremonies. "What happens after Boyo's father dies?"

"If there is no family willing, the position will be available for purchase, my lady," Strian said. "But enough of that." His arms around her tightened. "Remember to run," he whispered.

"I will." She bit her lip. "Strian—"

"Yes?"

"You be careful," she whispered. She squeezed her eyes shut for a moment. She had another headache tickling the back of her head, but that was to be expected, considering the waterfire waiting out at sea.

"To come back to you."

"Come back to me," she confirmed. If he could. If she was there to come back to.

She could feel him smile against her hair. "I would come back to you after death if I could, lady. Beyond time and beyond the seas. I would even go to that place you keep talking about, that Shiatta, to find you."

"Seattle. It's a big place," she warned him, her voice trembling. She didn't look up. Her eyes were brimming with tears, and she didn't want him to see. "And you'll look mighty strange asking for directions, in a language no one seems able to figure out, for someone who may not even be there."

"I will find you," he whispered. "You know I will."

"I know." She looked down at the beach, her eyes watery, still avoiding Strian's gaze. The two armies, Gilcris' and the honorable uncle's, seemed to be angling into position. Cat glanced at the horizon, where she fancied the waterfire was getting into position as well. As she watched, the waterfire seemed to cluster tighter, changing from the gray of just moments ago to a threatening jet-black. The sky would start to shake soon.

Strian saw it too. "Lady, I have to go," he said finally, slowly unwrapping his arms from around her. "My destiny awaits me down below, and yours up here."

Reluctantly, Cat wiped her eyes and looked up at his face. He was as beautiful as the night she had first seen him, garbed in silver and black.

"Strian," she whispered again, letting the name flow past her in the breeze.

In the distance, she could see the tremendous, amorphous waterfire start to swirl, slowly forming the shape of the destructive force. Soon, it would start to move toward land.

In a few minutes the confrontation would begin.

"What is it?" Strian said, breaking into her thoughts. He cleared a strand of hair off her face.

There was nothing more she could say to him, not then. She couldn't even say if she would be there to greet him afterward. All she could hope was he would walk away intact.

"Remember," she whispered.

They stared at each other for a moment, mindful of the breeze. Then he bent and touched his lips to hers, cool and gossamer light. He squeezed her hands one last time, and then, without saying another word, he turned and made his way down the steep path.

She watched him go. The glint of his battle finery, so bright only a few minutes ago, dimmed as the waterfire began to make its way toward the land. She could see spectators catch sight of the ominous mass on the horizon start to move, and they ran as fast as they could toward the sheltering caves. Even the opposing forces on the beach began to shift nervously, some looking at the waterfire gathering strength on the horizon and others looking longingly toward the caves.

But the Court and Son-Toruai, facing each other, didn't move. Cat saw Strian join his brother, drawing his heartsword with one hand and keeping the other hand on the hilt of his dagger.

She watched as he slipped his sword into the waiting hand of his brother. The Gem in Gilcris' earring sparkled and echoed the glint of the Gem in the hilt of the sword. Gilcris held the heartsword up in front of him, letting the Gem in the hilt catch the quickly dimming sunlight.

Then it happened.

The glint in the sword's hilt and the sparkle in Gilcris' earring caught the last ray of sunshine before the blackened clouds obliterated the sunlight. First, the light played against each Gem, almost as if it were tossing the last spark of sun from one surface to the next. Then the light—by now no longer sunlight but something else, not as simple to identify— stopped in the air, pausing in between the two Gems, and slowly began to rotate.

It looked alive.

Unnerved, she glanced away but found she had to watch. The light, by now darkened to a deep, opaque sapphire, began to grow more and more intense as it began to revolve faster and faster. Then she saw the waterfire on the horizon had formed into the amorphous shape she recognized, that indicated it was at the beginning of its most destructive phase, the one she had seen before it began to destroy. It, too, was beginning to twist.

The wind whipped up again just then, no longer a pleasant breeze, but icy cold and threatening. Cat looked down at the beach again. She could see Strian shout something, but she couldn't hear it; then she saw Gilcris' lips move. Son-Toruai—the honorable uncle stood still, his jaw clenched. Even from her distance she could see the whites of his eyes.

The ritual began.

The intense blue light continued to build, balanced between the Gem of the earring and the one in the hilt of the sword. As she watched, the spinning light began to rise until it was above their heads. Yet Son-Toruai continued to stand still.

The gigantic burst of waterfire gained speed and size as it approached, solidifying the closer it came to land, the sky and the ground shaking now. Cat, holding onto the rock near her, looked up. Sure enough, the sky was black. Predictably, her head was starting to pound, but that didn't matter anymore.

Cat's throat was dry. Since she'd woken up in this world, she'd seen waterfire more often than she could bear to remember, but in her mind, her first experience was still as clear as Kuriti crystal. As she watched the inexorable expanse lumber toward land, growing in size, darkening in mass, shaking the sky, she started to tremble too.

At the confrontation, both sides fanned out. She could see Strian, still close to his brother, shouting his part of the ritual against the rising wind.

Son-Toruai finally moved. His eyes wild, he drew his sciarra and pointed it at Strian, wavering for a moment before he pointed it at Gilcris. The attendant Kamaites who had been keeping their distance watching the ceremony moved in, spreading out to form a half-circle, at the ready to protect the Court.

Out of nowhere the Kamaites seemed to multiply until the beach was thick with them. Dimly she recalled Strian saying the order, down from the monastery, was there in an official capacity to oversee the confrontation and to make the final decision if necessary. They watched the honorable uncle, then Strian, then finally, Gilcris.

But some of them were also glancing nervously toward the horizon, watching the waterfire gather. If the ritual joining of the Gems didn't do the job it was supposed to, they were all going to be ash within a half hour. Cat could almost see the thought running through their minds—*Run or stay?* Would they run for shelter, or would they stay to the bitter end, the way they had been trained?

Cat wondered who Kamaites prayed to when their time came—she had never thought to ask. She knew who Strian prayed to. But as it was, she didn't know who her own prayers would be addressed to.

Whoever any of them prayed to, she wanted Strian to be safe. Whether she found herself back in Seattle or in place here, she wanted him to be safe.

The floating, revolving ball of light seemed to dim. Through the winds whipping up, she saw Strian shout something. Son-Toruai reacted by raising his knife. Strian stepped back, suddenly wary.

Her lips were dry. "Strian," Cat whispered again. Unwelcome, unheeded, the headache she had been doing her best to ignore crept past her defenses and shot through her temples. The pain was breaking off, branching into other parts of her brain, as if slivers of glass were slicing through her cerebrum and medulla oblongata. In a few minutes, one way or another, no matter what happened down on the battlefield, she knew she was going to curl up from the pain, thanks to the mother waterfire making its way closer and closer.

No, she said to herself desperately. *I can't. Not without making sure Strian's going to be all right.*

Step by step, she crept down the steep terrain, grabbing at the vegetation that edged the stone steps for balance as she watched the confrontation. Through the splashes of pain cutting through her vision she saw Gilcris shout at his honorable uncle again. In response, Son-Toruai clutched at the ornate golden torc unsteadily perched around his neck and shrank away, killing any chance the floating light would have had to catch the sparkle of the third gem in its fire and complete the triangle of Gems.

No!

Quickly, the Kamaites reacted. The Eid of the Kamaites, the head monk—Cat remembered him from when Strian had pointed him out at the Patima—recoiled, stepping away from the honorable uncle. Son-Toruai didn't notice. He went back to staring at the disk of light even as it began to fade, his hands not leaving the golden collar around his neck.

The attendant priests drew their short swords and surrounded him, one of them touching the bottom of his chin with the tip of his weapon, encouraging him to complete his part of the ritual. Meanwhile the waterfire edged closer and closer, and the trembling sky turned jet-black as the winds began their song of lament. The Kamaites who encircled the honorable uncle looked up, distracted by the howling.

But Son-Toruai's indecision was a ruse. The honorable uncle took advantage of the priests' diverted attention and ran, unwilling to let go of the torc, away from the dimming light.

Strian shouted and began to run after Son-Toruai, drawing his own sword. Gilcris shouted after him. Strian stopped and turned back toward his brother. Gilcris unsheathed the heartsword and threw it toward him. Deftly Strian caught it and kept running without breaking stride.

The honorable uncle must have planned ahead. He ran straight toward the sheltering caves, but before he reached them, he swerved and headed toward the cluster of giant stones lining that edge of the beach. Strian followed him, accompanied by a phalanx of the Kamaites not guarding their head monk and a good number of the Kuriti army.

Son-Toruai slipped between two jutting stones and disappeared. Strian started after him, but one of the Kamaites stopped him and followed the honorable uncle instead.

Cat looked up. The waterfire was gaining speed. As she watched, it approached the tiny island off the beach she guessed was the island Feren, where the queen's father was killed. The winds were howling, drowning most every other sound. If Strian—

Above the wind, Cat heard a bloodcurdling cry from beyond the projection of rocks and saw the last Kuriti soldier who had gone past the stones come running back, shouting. His robe was torn and blood flowed freely from his shoulder, and he staggered to his knees.

Her heart stopped. *Ambush!* The honorable uncle had set up an ambush! As if unchecked waterfire weren't enough. Scattered Kamaites and Kuriti soldiers came scrambling back, but not many. Either the others were prisoner or already down, beyond the stones. And then...

Through the break in the stones poured a new army of combatants, ones who had not been involved before — Benihe mercenaries, Cat guessed, remembering Strian's earlier offhand comment, led by the honorable uncle.

Though startled, the Kamaites on the beach reacted the way they had been trained. Within an instant half of those who were left surrounded to protect both the Court and Strian, swords and knives both drawn and ready. Where the ceremony should have been taking place, the other priests of Kuril confronted the honorable uncle and the Eid, he who had been their master, but clearly was no longer.

The priests made quick work of the new combatants — though the Benihe were good soldiers, quick and efficient, Cat recalled Strian saying, they were still no match for the Kamaites — and grabbing the honorable uncle, shoved him in the direction of Gilcris and Strian.

Strian grabbed him and tucked his sciarra under Son-Toruai's chin, with a grip so tight Cat could see his knuckles whiten, even yards away. The honorable uncle shoved the point of the knife away, jabbering something as he did so; he gestured at the torc he still wore.

Above the keening wind, Cat heard a shout from one of the sentries nearest the water's edge. Gilcris and Strian turned. Taking advantage, Son-Toruai knocked the knife out of Strian's hand, grabbing the heartsword at the same time. He ran—but not toward the caves, nor toward the edge of the pitched battle between the mercenaries of Benihe and the Kamaites.

Cat sat down on the end of the path, unable to move, the pain searing through her temples. Son-Toruai was crazed, he had to be. He was running straight toward the waterfire, and in his hands he held two of the three Treasures of Kurit.

The waterfire, meanwhile, hung at the edge of the sentry island. If its howling could be heard as loudly from where she stood, surely it was deafening where Strian and Gilcris were.

She looked up at the sky again. The blackening clouds were shaking so hard they were blurring. And the grinding pain in her head told her the waterfire would hit the beach soon.

The hovering ball of light, coaxed into existence by the meeting of two of the Gems, had almost faded away by then, almost touching the ground. Son-Toruai stopped at the edge of the beach, the waves lapping at his boots. He turned to face Strian and Gilcris.

The honorable uncle unclasped the torc from around his neck and raised it in one hand and the heartsword in the other, and shouted at Strian and Gilcris. They stopped short. Then Strian sheathed his sciarra and stood with his hands to his sides, not taking his eyes off the approaching waterfire.

Slowly, Gilcris reached up and, hook by hook, unlatched the earring that had been placed in his ear since his coronation. Cat winced. That was the first time it had left his ear since then, she knew. Finally it was dangling from his fingers, the Gem glinting in what little light was left, and then he too looked up to watch the advancing burst of waterfire.

The sky was black and shaking. Under her feet, Cat could feel the ground start to roll.

It wouldn't be long now.

Agonizingly slowly, Gilcris extended his hand, the earring swinging in the winds. He stared at the honorable uncle, fury stiffening his features. That look of absent grief Cat had associated with him since she met him was gone as he faced the man who had caused much of the misery in his life.

By that time Cat was on the beach. Shakily, she stood, leaning for a moment against the boulders. The Kamaites and the Benihe, those who were left standing, caught sight of the waterfire. The Benihe took off in a dead run, past the projection of stones where they had ambushed the priests, abandoning their cohorts both dead and dying. Perhaps their cowardice would haunt them later, but for now, they had their own necks to save. They were mercenaries, Cat thought. Their loyalties were only to themselves.

The Kamaites, both rebel and nonpartisan, were left on the beach. Some, seeing the waterfire nearly on the beach, started to pull their wounded toward the shelter of the caves until it became obvious the waterfire was coming too quickly. Then they were caught in a dilemma—guard the Court, guard the confrontation, run for cover?

Strian made the decision for them, motioning the remaining priests toward the caves. The Kamaites didn't need to be told twice. They ran for cover.

The winds were roaring now, getting ready for the final burst of waterfire that would be touching land within minutes. Cat had never seen such a burst of destructive fury. Where the waterfire touched the already-turbulent waters, she could see strands of seaweed and fish being sucked into the vortex and devoured in a flash. Then it hit Feren and touched the promontory, and instantly sucked in the gigantic mar tree that marked the highest point on the island in a single gulp.

Her headache was cutting her apart now. She wouldn't have believed—wouldn't have wanted to believe—anything could have that much power. And the pain was getting stronger as the waterfire approached the beach.

Cat's instincts rebelled. She didn't want to do it, every bone in her body and every synapse in her brain screamed at the idea, then whimpered at the pain she would be in for, but there was no other way.

Perhaps this was what she was destined for. Perhaps this was why she had awakened from the sleep of no end. It would mean her death, surely, but if the headaches didn't diminish, her death would be inevitable. Kevin and Margot's disappearance — well, she didn't know what to do about that, but perhaps their part would be revealed if she did this.

And if it didn't, at least she wouldn't have to worry anymore.

Heart in her mouth and too weak to stand, she crept across the sands, toward the confrontation, closer to the nearing waterfire. Son-Toruai, Strian and Gilcris were locked in a battle of chicken — did they want to stop the waterfire more than they wanted to fight over the right to rule? At the moment, it looked as though all three would be meeting their ends, and then the right to rule would definitely be in question. Perhaps there were cousins somewhere.

From where he stood, Strian couldn't see her at the edge of the beach, but Gilcris could. His eyes flickered in Cat's direction for just a second, but he said nothing. Son-Toruai caught sight of her, but he said nothing as well. But their shared silence about her presence was driven by different motives. Son-Toruai didn't think her presence was worth mentioning, but Cat guessed Strian's concentration would be shot if he knew she was there, and Gilcris knew that.

The waterfire was almost at the waves breaking at the beach. The howling winds made any conversation, shouts or whispers, impossible. Cat had never been so close to waterfire, and she was shocked at the tears that sprang to her eyes. It was *beautiful*! How had she never seen it before? Through the haze of her pain, she could see the minute particles that made it up, sparkling, all the bits of sunlight and life it sucked in churning with a new life of its own, searching for something.

The tears ran down her face, stinging her skin. Maybe she could live there.

She reached out for it. As if it sensed her willing, even eager presence, it shied away from the confrontation and veered toward her. The closer the waterfire came, the more her head hurt, threatening to shatter it into a thousand pieces, but the closer it came, the more she was certain this was what she had been born for, woken for, and would die for. "Oh, come to me," she whispered, though not even she could hear herself. "Come to me and let it all be over with."

She knew without a doubt now. Her headaches would stop, the waterfire itself would end, and perhaps even Kevin and Margot would appear again. All it took was a simple sacrifice.

She stretched out her arms, welcoming it with a lover's embrace. A sudden movement out of the corner of her eye caught her attention. It was Strian, who had finally turned around and noticed her presence. He lunged toward her, but Gilcris sprang to his side and held him back, and even Son-Toruai did, the battle for the Jewels of Kurit temporarily forgotten.

Strian was screaming something at her, but she couldn't hear. But she had to try to make him understand. "This is the only way!" she shouted, her words swallowed by the screaming winds. "Stay back!"

The sparkling gray mass that made up the waterfire was almost within touching distance now. It wasn't gray at all, Cat discovered. It was silver, all the colors of moonlight gossamer and the sea at night, and she realized it was almost a mirror, it was so slick and smooth. She could see her reflection in its surface.

Strian was being held back, but he won the battle. At one point, he broke free and ran toward her, only to be forced to the ground by his brother.

The tears were pouring down her face, and she was only sorry he was close enough to see it. He was frantic.

Cat shook her head. "Don't," she whispered, knowing there was no way he could hear her. "It's for the best."

She stretched out her arms a little more. Just a little more and it would all be over with.

Suddenly, she felt herself shoved aside. *Strian?*

"No!" she screamed as she tried to get up, but her balance was off and her sight affected by the sharpening pain. She shook her head to clear it, and when she could see, for a second she felt a flood of relief. It was Gilcris who had knocked her down, not Strian. The Court of Kurit stood where she had been and he was reaching for the waterfire, the way she had been. "No, Gilcris!"

Gilcris turned to her, his face contorted and unrecognizable with fury. "What have I left, you fool? There's nothing left for me. *Nothing*. Let me do this!"

The Court had pain too. Cat had seen it all the while, from the day she had met him, and it was not something that would go away. His wife was dead, his children were dead, and provided he came out of this with his rule intact, he would spend the rest of his life on a throne that was his by right but no longer by inclination. The want of a throne had destroyed his family. He didn't want it without them.

In a flash, she knew he was more determined than she was to be rid of his pain. His hurt more than hers did. But there was nothing to say his sacrifice was going to mean more than hers.

She put out her hand to stop him, but it was too late. Gilcris shouted, "Take care of him," and then leaped into the swirling streams of silver.

With a blinding *pop!* and a gulping swallow, Gilcris, the Court of Kurit, the Emperor of the Winter Gardens and the Sea Cities of Dangurra, the Bearer of the Treasure of the Phoenix Throne and the heir to the Silver Seas Beyond, was swallowed by the juggernaut of nature that both cursed and defined his land.

And for nothing. The waterfire didn't stop. It didn't even slow down. It still moved relentlessly, heading toward her.

Cat looked at Strian, who was on the ground now, tears streaming down his face; then she looked at the honorable uncle, who had dropped the two Gems of Kurit that had been in his grasp, who was now grimacing, but what that meant she couldn't say.

She took a step toward the waterfire, to see if she could see Gilcris in its silver spinning, but she could see nothing there except her own impending sacrifice. She glanced at Strian, whose eyes were wild with grief now, and he was screaming something, but she couldn't hear him. Too late, she wanted to tell him. "I love you," she whispered, but whether he could read her lips, she couldn't say.

Dimly, Cat heard another scream, but it wasn't from Strian. She turned to see the honorable uncle, Son-Toruai, come running toward her, the Gems of Kurit abandoned in the sand behind him. "No!" he screamed when he was close enough for her to hear. "No, no! Not like this! I didn't want it like this!"

"A little late, isn't it?" she shouted, but her words were lost in the howling.

And it became abundantly clear what the honorable uncle was going to do to make amends. With a screech, Son-Toruai ran straight into the swirling silver vortex—and without a sound, the honorable uncle became a footnote in Kuriti history.

By now Strian was standing, staring at the waterfire into which his brother and his foe had both disappeared. Fighting the winds, he started to stagger toward the vortex, but he stopped when he saw Cat.

She knew what she had to do. Despite the sacrifices of Gilcris and Son-Toruai, she knew this was the reason she was awoken, the reason she had come this far. And Strian?

The tears were stinging under her eyelids, but she didn't bother to blink them away. "Good luck," she whispered.

She looked around to keep the memory of Kurit in her mind as long as she could. She wanted to remember the wide, graceful reaches of the plains; she wanted to remember the mystery of the Gates. Most of all, she wanted to remember the good. She looked past the plateau, past the ashes of the bodies littering the beach, toward the distant formation of the Forgotten Lovers.

She had never gotten to the peak. The view had to be spectacular.

"Goodbye," she whispered. She reached out to the waterfire, and it was done.

Chapter Twenty

ဢ

The heart of waterfire truly was crystalline. Cat was amazed—she never would have suspected. The sparkling she had seen was the dense clusters of crystals lining the inner walls.

The heart of waterfire was still and quiet, as quiet as the spot near the creek. She looked around. She was in a chamber made of crystal. The ground beneath her was sharp, with the edges of the crystals broken but not dulled, as they would have been if they had been worn by the elements. She could feel the jagged points through her boots. She still had boots. Did the dead wear shoes?

In the distance, she could hear the howling of the winds outside. But it was dulled, as though there were layer upon layer of soundproofing.

She reached out to touch the walls, but shied back when her fingertips brushed against the surface. The crystalline surface was almost slick. Her fingers felt moist from the contact.

Was she dead? She should have been. Everything she had ever seen touch waterfire had burst into flames and turn into instant ash, but here she was, clearly not carbon. Or was she and she didn't know it?

"Hello?" she called out. The word was muffled, as though insulated. Or was it her hearing? "Am I dreaming? Can anybody hear me?"

Then she heard it—a voice it took her a moment to identify. It felt like decades since she had heard it last.

Did she say something?

I don't know — It sounded like —

It sounded like "hello." We can hear you, Cathy honey, can you hear us?

Mark. Dear God, it sounded like Mark. It was Mark's voice too, not Strian's. In the heart of waterfire?

"What are you doing here?" Cat called out. Where was he?

What was that?

I don't know — Something about us waking up —

Can you open your eyes, Cathy honey?

"Don't call me that," she said irritably. "That's not my name. And what are you doing here? I told you to go."

I'm right here, don't worry.

"I'm not worried," she muttered. "I'm confused." She looked around at the crystal walls and tried to figure out how she had gotten in there, and how she was going to get out. Alive or dead, she wasn't going to stay in this crystalline incubator.

"Cadey?"

She stopped. She knew that voice. It was a voice she loved, a voice she would have known anywhere, even here in the middle of a capsule of crystal. "Strian? Is that you? Are you with Mark?"

"No, I'm not, my heart."

She looked around. She didn't see him. But his voice was closer than Mark was, she could tell that much.

"Strian, I don't know where I am," she called out. "Am I in waterfire? Is this what the heart of waterfire is like? It's beautiful but it's cold, Strian. But Gilcris—" She stopped. His brother had been turned to ashes in front of her, in front of him. "Gilcris isn't here," she said, faltering. "I'm sorry, I'm so sorry, Stri—"

"I know he is not, sweet. Stay still," he said soothingly.

"I can't see you. Can you see me?"

"I can see you. I have you in my arms, Cadrine. Please, wake up, my heart. Don't go away. I need you."

She's fading out! Get the nurse! Come back, Cathy! Don't do this!

"Why, so I can die?" she snapped at Mark's voice. "So you can string me along and I can be paralyzed for the rest of my life, what there is left of it? So you can make sure you get my insurance? Go away, Mark."

"Shhh, keep calm, Cadrine," Strian said soothingly.

Then she realized.

Her headache was gone.

She was in the middle of waterfire—and her headache was gone. For the first time in what felt like weeks, months, years, she didn't have a headache.

"My headache's gone," she announced to anyone who would listen. "Strian, my headache's gone. Where are you?"

"Then come back to me," she heard him say warmly. "Come back to me and we can go up to the peak at Forgotten Lovers. I love you, Cadey."

All of a sudden, she could feel Strian's hand on hers, although it was nowhere to be seen. She closed her eyes to feel it. He was warm and firm and she could even smell him. She covered his hand with hers. She could feel the tiny tremors in his body. In her mind's eye she could see him, battle-worn and weary, but smiling a smile that could have lit the heavens without the aid of the hyagoths of light. The hyagoths. That's what he would pray to. She finally remembered. "Could we go up there?" she whispered. "I wish I could see you."

A sharp, insistent noise sliced her concentration. She couldn't figure out what it was at first. The sound had the whining, piercing characteristics of an electronic device—and then she knew what it was.

No, she heard. *Come back.*

It's too late. Let her go, she heard. *Time of death —*

Stay? Or go?

Right at that moment, she knew she had a choice. Stay in Kurit, where she was in essence an alien, or go back? Go back to Seattle, where she was real, as far as she knew, where she theoretically belonged?

But she didn't belong there. She may have been an alien in Kurit, but for the first time in her life, she was happy.

Stay? Or go?

"Cadey? Cadrine? Can you hear me?"

She had her answer.

"Strian? Can you help me? I want to come to you, but I don't know how," she said. She gripped his hand, still unseen, as her crystalline cave began to shimmer. In the shards of crystal around her, suddenly, she could see reflections of her life in the only existence she had thought possible. She saw herself as a sad child, a sadder adult, the people around her, and she saw it all as though it belonged to someone else.

She saw Mark and Kevin and Margot, and then the backroom at the library collapsing. And then she saw reflections of the life she had just led in Kurit, with its cool sunshine and brilliant light in the wake of waterfire. She saw a life she had grown to love. She saw Gilcris, as sorrowful in Kurit as she had been in the otherplace. And she saw Strian, as vivid as the stars themselves, holding out his hand to her, and her taking it.

Then his hand began to fade and grow insubstantial, and a pain that was all too familiar shot through her as the crystal cave crumbled around her. She screamed. The noise was buried by the shattering of the crystals, and she tried to protect herself from the falling shards.

She closed her eyes when a rumble shot through the space, and she knew without having to look that a chunk of the crystalline cocoon was falling—and she had nowhere to hide. Something hit her, and the light around her was blacked out.

* * * * *

Of the last two times she found herself coming to in this way, the first time had been in Pacific Medical Center in Seattle, surrounded by muffled sounds and little beeps and boops and soft footsteps as people hurried around her. And the smell. Who really gets used to the smell of a hospital? Especially when you know each time you wake up to that smell it brings you closer to your eventual end.

The second time she had woken up had been in the Elder's great hall, which had smelled unlike any hospital, in that there was no antiseptic scent, no beeps or boops, no soft steps. The Elder's home had smelled like the previous night's dinner, a stew, she remembered, and fresh-baked bread, and the steps she heard were wooden clogs, from the Elder's granddaughter. Q'Atha. Oh, Q'Atha.

This time was different. Instead of the hushed sounds of a hospital, there was the sound of the sea, the tide coming in and going out, regular and steady, washing away sins and mistakes and battles of yesterday. The salt in the air cut through her memories of the antiseptic, and she could feel the sand shifting beneath her. She stirred as she felt a pebble press uncomfortably against her shoulder blades. She opened her mouth but found her throat was dry. Which was odd, because she was once more soaking wet.

"Cadey? Cadrine? Can you hear me?"

Strian. Her eyes popped open.

She was on the beach again. Strian looked like hell. His tunic was in shreds, and there were minute scratches on his hands, as if he had thrust his hands naked into a tangle of thorns. He was dusty and grimy, and there were tracks down his cheeks, forging little rivulets of clear skin.

She reached up and touched them. "You were crying," she said wonderingly. "Why?"

His eyes still looked wet. She smiled, and when she did, he smiled back. "I thought you would never wake up. You were so far away, dear heart."

His hair was a muddy, tangled mess. She reached and smoothed a few strands away from his face. "What happened?" she asked after a few seconds. "I jumped into the waterfire after Gilcris— Oh, Strian, I'm so sorry—" She took a sharp breath as she remembered Gilcris' sacrifice, pointless as it had been.

"He did what he thought was right. And he welcomed it, Quer'Cadrine," Strian said, trying to calm her. He slipped his arm under her. "Can you sit up?"

She felt a little woozy as together they managed to sit her up. She wanted to shake her head, but knew if she did, she would regret it; she was already on the verge of nausea.

Cat looked out at the sea. Her mouth dropped open. Then she looked up at Strian, a little too fast. He had to steady her for a few seconds until the vertigo subsided. "The sea—I've never seen it that color here," she said in wonder.

The water looked as if it had been color-corrected. It was the purest, brightest blue she had ever seen, because the sky was so clear. "The sky!" she cried when she realized what was so different. "Strian, it's blue! It's not violet anymore! It's *bright*!" Then she remembered what Q'Atha had told her, about the waterfire having something to do with the off-shade of violet the sky had been. But now—

Even in the clearest days, back in Seattle, the sky and sound had been off-color, the result of a century or more of urban living. But these colors were as pure as she had ever seen.

She blinked when he laughed. She could feel his laughter reverberate through her, and it was a comforting sensation. He tightened his arms around her. "The waterfire is gone. We are safe again."

"What happened?" she asked finally, when she could.

She felt him take a deep breath. Out of the corner of her eye, she saw the assorted Kamaites who were left after the bloody battle. Some of them were looking out at the sea, too.

"After Gilcris leaped into the waterfire, after you—" He paused, then continued, "After Gilcris, after Son-Toruai, the skies broke open. I don't know how else to describe it, Cadrine. The Earth shook, the rains and the winds came down in a crash, and we were trapped out in the open."

"But it wasn't like waterfire." She tightened her hold on his arms.

"No. It was as though a dam had burst, and all the elements were escaping while they could. But it wasn't waterfire."

"Did it swallow the waterfire?"

He shook his head. "No. The waterfire started to dissipate as soon as you— The freeing of the elements lasted all of a minute, and then—nothing."

Cat remembered. "He dropped the Gems of Kurit. Son-Toruai."

"I have them," Strian assured her. "I have all three now."

"That was his sacrifice." She hugged him. "To purify his soul. To rectify his wrongs. The meaning of his life was in the leaving of it."

"To sleep easy until he wakes again."

She remembered the stories of Kurit he had told her after she was getting over the Nurui touch. "Not to be tormented by nightmares of the hyagoths," Cat agreed. That one selfless action in his life had given the honorable uncle some comfort.

"After you disappeared, the waterfire vanished. The winds stopped, the rains stopped, and the mists blew out to sea, clearing the sky. After all that, I looked around—and I saw you. You were standing on the shore, as if you had just washed up there, even though we had all just seen you vanish into the waterfire only moments before. And then you collapsed onto the ground." He stopped. "We tried to wake you, but you would not be wakened. I thought I had lost you, too."

She closed her eyes. "I'm here now." She held onto his arms and squeezed. "And I'm here to stay."

* * * * *

After a minute more and feeling stronger, she stood up, leaning against Strian. It was almost a summery day, just as it had been in her dreams in the crystalline place. She could hear birds twittering in the distance, and on the sands, the phalanx of the Kamaites tended to the wounds of both their own and their enemy. The Eid, the head monk, had disappeared sometime during the fracas and Cat knew, without asking, if he ever appeared within the limits of Kurit again, that would be the end of him. He had disgraced himself and the order of the Kama, and while the honorable uncle had taken the easy way out—if throwing yourself into the heart of waterfire could be called "easy"—the monk had shown he was guilty of the supreme cowardice.

But as Strian gave orders for the Kamaites, she realized what it all meant. "How long until you take the throne?" she asked him. He was the sole survivor of the proud family of the Kuriti imperial family, and he was now the Court, in charge of the destiny of the country.

He glanced at her and it seemed to her he hesitated. "The ceremony is in the next full moon," he said matter-of-factly. "But first there are many things to be taken care of, my lady."

Cat nodded. She was "my lady" again. He was feeling formal again, and she guessed the reality of the losses he had suffered had hit him. He had lost a brother, a sister-in-law, a nephew and a niece, even an uncle-in-law—the entirety of his family, all in a short while. He was, in all but coronation, the Court, but it was not a position he had ever aspired to. Yet he had to pick himself up and rebuild a country after civil war. Alone.

"If there's anything I can do, Pir Strian," she answered, as formally as she could, because she was disoriented still and she had no idea how else to say it, "all you have to do is ask."

She was surprised to see the glint in his eyes. He placed his hands on either side of her cheeks and framed her face. He said nothing more for a second before he finally whispered, "Stay with me, Cadey. Don't leave me now."

In answer, Cat wrapped her arms around him and hugged him as hard as she could. She had turned her back on the only existence she had known because of him. But it was the right thing to do. She could do nothing else. "Yes," she said and she laughed as she sniffled, because her eyes were tearing up too. "I will stay with you forever and a day."

She turned and looked at the Kamaites, the fallen soldiers, the Benihe, and up on the bluffs, the Kuriti, speaking among themselves about the waterfire they had seen and the changing of the rule and Kurit had nearly been destroyed but for a final sacrifice, and she knew they would tell their children and their children's children, until the stories became legend itself.

"Can you walk? Lol and Arriya are both at the bottom of the path — we can take you back to Podani Town and have a physic see to you," Strian said.

Cat looked across the beach at the horses. "Yes," she began, and then Arriya lifted her head and looked straight at her.

Will you ride me again? Cat heard.

She blinked, and out of nowhere, she knew. "I can ride Arriya now." She knew she would be able to communicate with the horse as she never could before.

She turned to him and looked at the intricately designed medallion he wore on his chest, and realized the markings she had been unable to read before were letters and they formed words. She couldn't read it before; it hadn't been her language. But now —

"I'm home." The tears that fell now were of happiness. "Strian, I'm finally home. And I love you."

Also by Eilis Flynn

ഉ

Echoes of Passion

Festival of Stars

Introducing Sonika

About the Author

ഉ

Eilis Flynn has spent a large share of her life working on Wall Street or in a Wall Street-related firm, so why should she write fiction that's any less based in our world? She spends her days aware that there is a reality beyond what we can see - and tells stories about it for Cerridwen Press. Published in other genres, she lives in verdant Washington state with her equally fantastical husband and spoiled rotten cats.

Eilis welcomes comments from readers. You can find her website and email address on her author bio page at www.cerridwenpress.com.

Tell Us What You Think

We appreciate hearing reader opinions about our books. You can email us at Comments@EllorasCave.com.

Why an electronic book?

We live in the Information Age — an exciting time in the history of human civilization, in which technology rules supreme and continues to progress in leaps and bounds every minute of every day. For a multitude of reasons, more and more avid literary fans are opting to purchase e-books instead of paper books. The question from those not yet initiated into the world of electronic reading is simply: *Why?*

1. ***Price.*** An electronic title at Ellora's Cave Publishing and Cerridwen Press runs anywhere from 40% to 75% less than the cover price of the exact same title in paperback format. Why? Basic mathematics and cost. It is less expensive to publish an e-book (no paper and printing, no warehousing and shipping) than it is to publish a paperback, so the savings are passed along to the consumer.

2. ***Space.*** Running out of room in your house for your books? That is one worry you will never have with electronic books. For a low one-time cost, you can purchase a handheld device specifically designed for e-reading. Many e-readers have large, convenient screens for viewing. Better yet, hundreds of titles can be stored within your new library — on a single microchip. There are a variety of e-readers from different manufacturers. You can also read e-books on your PC or laptop computer. (Please note that

Ellora's Cave does not endorse any specific brands. You can check our websites at www.ellorascave.com or www.cerridwenpress.com for information we make available to new consumers.)

3. *Mobility.* Because your new e-library consists of only a microchip within a small, easily transportable e-reader, your entire cache of books can be taken with you wherever you go.

4. *Personal Viewing Preferences.* Are the words you are currently reading too small? Too large? Too... ANNOYING? Paperback books cannot be modified according to personal preferences, but e-books can.

5. *Instant Gratification.* Is it the middle of the night and all the bookstores near you are closed? Are you tired of waiting days, sometimes weeks, for bookstores to ship the novels you bought? Ellora's Cave Publishing sells instantaneous downloads twenty-four hours a day, seven days a week, every day of the year. Our webstore is never closed. Our e-book delivery system is 100% automated, meaning your order is filled as soon as you pay for it.

Those are a few of the top reasons why electronic books are replacing paperbacks for many avid readers.

As always, Ellora's Cave and Cerridwen Press welcome your questions and comments. We invite you to email us at Comments@ellorascave.com or write to us directly at Ellora's Cave Publishing Inc., 1056 Home Avenue, Akron, OH 44310-3502.

Cerridwen Press

Cerridwen, the Celtic goddess of
wisdom, was the muse who brought
inspiration to storytellers and those
in the creative arts.

Cerridwen Press encompasses the
best and most innovative stories in
all genres of today's fiction.

Visit our website and discover the
newest titles by talented authors who
still get inspired — much like the
ancient storytellers did…

once upon a time.

www.cerridwenpress.com